The Raid
More Than A Body Ought To Bear

Robert J. Rosenbaum

OcotilloPress®

The Raid
More Than a Body Ought to Bear
By
Robert J. Rosenbaum

For information address:
Ocotillo Press
8812 Mosquero Circle
Austin, Texas 78748
ocotillopress@yahoo.com

Any resemblance to actual people, events and places is purely
coincidental.
This is a work of fiction.

Cover Design and Art: triuneimage.com
Typesetting: Bruce Bryson

For orders other than by individual buyers, Ocotillo Press grants a
discount on the purchase of 10 or more copies, single titles, for special
markets or premium use. For details write Ocotillo Press, 8812
Mosquero Circle, Austin, Texas 78748. Attn: Premiums. Or email:
ocotillopress@yahoo.com

For orders by individual consumers, write or email Ocotillo Press, Attn:
Sales, 8812 Mosquero Circle, Austin, Texas 78748
Or email: ocotillopress@yahoo.com

ISBN: 978-0-9823182-2-5
Printed in the United States of America

For Jim and Laura Louise

"They say the Lord won't pile on more troubles than a body can bear. I sure hope He didn't miscalculate in Jake's case."

Billy Stanton

This is a work of fiction. However, the raid in the opening chapter is similar to one that actually to place.

1

AUGUST 21 — Early Morning

Jake Grummond was lying half awake fighting his bladder's increasingly insistent demand to leave the snuggling comfort of Mary Margaret's still firm forty-four-year-old bottom when headlights flashed across the wide pine boards of the bedroom ceiling. A flash, no more.

The hand-wound alarm clock on the nightstand glowed 1:30 — two full hours before the start of milking. With the economy of movement learned through twenty-two years of married mornings, he eased his legs out of the brass bed that had belonged to Mary Margaret's grandparents and padded barefoot to the window.

Dark shapes, visible in the moonless night only to eyes that knew what should be there, lined the road to the cattle guard at the end of his driveway a quarter of a mile of hard-baked adobe ruts away.

The shapes began to move. A dozen. Maybe more. The flash on the ceiling must have come when the lead driver made the turn before killing his lights.

Stomach knotting in fear and anger, he pulled on pants, stuffed feet into unlaced boots and was at the kitchen closet where he kept his hunting rifle when high beams and searchlights flooded the yard. Half-running steps echoed on the sun-cracked boards of the porch, followed by pounding at the door.

"DEA. Come out with your hands up."

Jake could hear the same order being shouted at the small frame houses and house trailers across the barnyard where his men and their families lived. He opened the door to six foot plus of agent, bulky as a defensive tackle three years out of training, who wore a dark blue jacket like the kind sports stars advertised on television. His left fist was raised to pound the door again and he held an automatic pistol at shoulder height in his right hand, pointed up. Behind him stood Cecil (C. W.) Blakenship, Sheriff of Sapinero County.

Jake looked over the agent's shoulder to the sheriff. "Thought they said DEA, Cecil."

"Just helping out, Jacob." Blakenship had maintained a civil coolness toward Jake after Jake had backed his opponent in the last Republican primary and in any event he couldn't abide being called by his Christian name any more than Jake could.

"What's this about?"

"DEA usually means drugs."

"Drugs? Me?"

"Ain't nobody said anything about you. Not that I heard. Word is that some of your meskins are smuggling when they go back and forth to see their kinfolk."

"Bullshit. My people have been with me for years."

Blakenship shrugged. "Ain't my call."

"No fraternization, Sheriff." The voice, a high-pitched rasp, came from a man of middle height, lean-built with a face like a knife blade. His hair was black except for gray at the temples and a streak of pure white along the part that gave him the look of a comic book villain. "Kiernan. Get him off the porch and into the light. And everybody else in the house."

"It's just my wife and she's ..."

"I don't care if it's your dying grandmother. I want everybody out."

Jake turned to Blakenship as Kiernan, the agent who'd been at the door, prodded him toward the harsh white light in the center of the yard. "Let me get her, C. W. Getting startled awake ain't good for her. Not since Paul's ..." Jake stopped in mid-sentence at the memory of their only child killed two years ago.

"I'm sorry." The sheriff sounded like he truly was.

"Get those beaneaters out here. Now." The thin agent had walked to the edge of the lighted circle. "Move, goddammit. Don't give those fucking wetbacks a chance to get rid of anything."

Startled Spanish and children's shrieks mingled in the soft night air with the law's orders and curses while some four hundred and fifty Holsteins in the pens near the milking barn began to mill, mooing in uncertain counterpoint to the human uproar.

"Production better not be one ounce short because of this shit. You hear me, Cecil?" Jake turned from trying to make out what was going on with the herd to see Kiernan bring Mary Margaret onto the porch, guiding her by the shoulder with a hand big enough to palm a medicine ball. Her eyes fought through sleep, trying to make sense of the confusion. When she saw Jake, she pulled away in a swirl of ankle length nightgown.

"That man said he was DEA." She rubbed her eyes. "That can't be."

"He is, all right. According to Cecil, our hands are bringing drugs in from Mexico."

"C. W. knows better than that."

"I got no idea what Cecil thinks he knows. We know our people ain't involved." He took a deep breath. "But that don't mean the uncles and brothers and *primos* who they can't say no to when they visit aren't. If we got a drug problem here let's get it straightened out." Another deep breath. "As long as they don't screw up the milking."

The circle of light began to fill with men and women and children and agents and deputies. The shrieks had died down to occasional sobs and most of the noise was coming from the law.

Eusebio Guerrero, a weathered man of indeterminable age who had worked at the dairy for more than two decades, walked across the floodlit dust toward Jake and Mary Margaret, dignity intact despite wearing only a sleeveless undershirt and a pair of boxer shorts decorated with faded valentine hearts. Fists clenched at his sides and a jerking of the corded muscles of his forearms were the only signs of anger. "Jake. *Senora.* What is …"?

"They think there's drugs here." Jake walked toward the DEA agent with the funny hair who was watching the last of the hands and their families being herded into the light. "How much longer's this going to take? Milking's got to start in," Jake squinted at his watch, "in less than an hour."

8

"We'll take as long as we need to."

"Do you know what happens if you're late with milking? Do you ..."

"*Chinga.*"

Jake and the agent turned in unison to watch one of the deputies with a shoulder patch from a neighboring county pistol whip Luis Montoya to the ground at the feet of his very pregnant wife. With a scream that pulled all eyes her way, the wife went for the deputy's eyes with her fingernails. The deputy knocked her to the ground with a backhanded blow and kicked at her stomach.

"Bastard." Mary Margaret ran between the two and knelt over the woman, catching the full brunt of the second kick on her tailbone.

Jake beat the agent across the yard by three full steps and tackled the deputy, driving him to the ground with the full force of two hundred pounds hardened by a lifetime of sixteen-hour days. He had the deputy by the throat with his left hand and the index finger of his right pointed straight at the deputy's left eye from one inch away and never wavered. "Believe this. If you ever ..."

He felt the gun barrel at his temple before he heard the voice. "Let go and get up. Very slowly. With your hands in the air." It was the big agent. "I appreciate why you did what you did, Mr. Grummond. But we can't have that."

"Put that man in handcuffs." It was the agent in charge.

"I don't think that will be necessary, sir."

"You heard me. Handcuff all the men. We're not going to have a single American hurt under my command."

"Sorry about this," Kiernan whispered as he fitted one loop of a plastic restraint to Jake's left wrist and the other to the porch rail. "Just take it easy, Mr. Grummond. I'll bring your wife over here and see how the woman is doing."

"C. W. You call EMS right now." Mary Margaret's voice cut across the yard. "Cecil Blakenship, do you hear me? The baby ..."

"Kiernan, Put her under restraint." The agent swung toward the sheriff. "Blakenship …"

"Cecil." Mary Margaret's voice was quiet, but the sheriff could hear every word. "Call. If you don't, you'll regret it the rest of your life."

"Blakenship …"

"I'm calling, Buchanan. Making sure the woman's not bad hurt ain't going to slow you up any." To Mary Margaret. "Are you O. K.?"

"I've been hurt worse." Erect and shoulders square, she walked with careful steps toward her house, Kiernan's hand a faint presence on her arm. When she reached Jake he wrapped his free arm around her waist and the couple stood in their yard watching the law handcuff the men with plastic manacles so frail-looking they seemed almost an insult and wincing in unison at the sounds of furniture and dishes breaking in the homes beyond the circle of light.

***

It took the best part of two hours for the law to be satisfied there was no marijuana, no cocaine or crack, no illegal substances of any kind in any of the houses and trailers that sheltered the ten families and four bachelors who worked and lived on the Grummond Dairy.

Still handcuffed to the porch rail, Jake was watching Mary Margaret supervise the Mountain View EMS team's treatment of Della and Luis Montoya when Buchanan approached, frustration cracking his voice. "Who tipped you off?"

"Make sure they check your back," he yelled to his wife. "What do you mean?"

"Somebody must have warned you."

"Didn't find anything, did you? Turn me loose then. We're already more'n hour late."

"Not yet. They look like illegal aliens. Need to check their documents. All of them."

"Jesus Christ. All of them have been with me for years. None less than two and some more than twenty."

"They're Mexicans and we have to check."

10

"Well, let them loose so they can get their papers."

"No way. They could escape. We'll hold them while documentation is verified."

"Women and children, too?"

"Every single one of those chili peppers."

"What about the milking?"

"That's not my problem." Buchanan swung on his heel.

"Goddammit. Do you ..."

Buchanan paid no attention and began giving orders. Blakenship was talking to him when a Ford 250 pickup with a rifle racked above the seat boiled through the parked vehicles and slid to a stop less than a yard from the agent and the sheriff. Jake's father, Joseph Grummond, called Grandpa by one and all because of a legendary bender in celebration of the birth of what proved to be his only grandchild, vaulted from the cab, moving his two hundred and thirty pounds on a six-foot two-inch frame with an agility that gave the lie to his seventy-two years.

He waved the four foot length of lead pipe that he called a cane but which had been used more than once to make a point on an unreasonable kneecap at Blakenship. "C. W. what in the absolute godfuckingdamn hell is going on? If they don't get to milking soon, Jake's going to lose half the herd."

"Take it easy Mr. Grummond. Having a little problem with papers is all."

"Papers my ass. I've known you since you were a snot-nosed puke running around in shitty diapers and your daddy before you and not once in all that time did I ever have trouble with the papers of any of my hands. And Jake's the same and you know it."

"Shut up." Buchanan pushed in front of Blakenship. "Shut up or I'll arrest you for obstructing officers of the law in the performance of their duty."

Grandpa Grummond looked him up and down and addressed the sheriff. "Who's the mouthy little shit?"

"Special Agent Buchanan of the United States Drug Enforcement Agency."

"Drugs? What the fuck are you talking about?"

11

"Kiernan, put this, ... put him under restraint."

Grandpa Grummond saw Jake cuffed to the porch and strode across the yard with Kiernan in his wake. "You O. K., son?"

"Been better. They knocked Luis and Della around pretty good." He waved at the ambulance with his free hand. "And Mary Margaret."

"Which ones?"

"Just one. Fat sonofabitch from Otero County. Breath would knock a buzzard off a shit wagon. But the main problem right now is they're not letting our people into their houses to get their documents. Going to take them to town. What I need for you to do is call Billy and Frog Bottom and anyone else you can think of on East Mesa who halfway knows how to milk."

Buchanan with Blakenship close behind came over as his father disappeared inside the house. Behind them, the families were being loaded into the bland sedans of the DEA and the Broncos and Cherokees favored by sheriff departments in the mountain counties.

"Where's he going?"

"To try and round up some help for the milking."

"Get him out here."

"Buchanan. Follow me." The sheriff led the agent to the edge of the light. "I've pretty much let you run this operation, but let me tell you something. Those cows you hear, they put down about thirty to thirty-five pounds of milk for every milking — some a whole lot more. Thirty-five pounds pushing down on their tits. If they don't get milked on schedule, serious problems can result. And missing a milking can cause very serious problems. Now, Jake's milking better than four hundred head. At fifteen to eighteen hundred bucks apiece that runs into a pretty fair piece of change. If he's lucky, he's only going to be two and half, three hours behind. But if you hold him up any more, he stands to lose a lot of cows — and that's pushing a million dollars not counting the lost milk. You haven't found any drugs ..."

"The search has not been completed."

12

"Save that for the civilians. You haven't found any drugs. You're going through with this foolishness about documents and I can tell you right now everyone of Jake's people has documents — unless your men fucked them up. If you compound things by not letting Grandpa Grummond get help, you're going to end up in so much shit the only way you'll see our nation's capital again will be as a tourist at cherry blossom time."

"Don't threaten me."

"No threat. Just letting you know how it'll be if you destroy a multi-million-dollar operation along with not finding any drugs or illegals. I'm just trying to help you cover your ass."

"You've got an ass, too."

"There is that."

***

Buchanan watched a full DEA sedan following an Otero County Bronco turn on the county road. "O. K. Grummond. I'll give you until five to bring in your wetbacks' documents. After that, the INS."

Grandpa Grummond clomped onto the porch, thumping the boards with his lead pipe at every other stride. "Froggie says he'll be here in twenty minutes with one of his boys. Marcy'll be along after breakfast to help hunt for papers. Billy says he can't make it this morning but he'll be glad to help after work." A car door slammed and he paused to watch Buchanan start down the driveway. "Show me where the sick milkers are and we can get started." He pulled out his pocket watch. "Shit. It's pushing six o'clock."

"They're in the small pen next to the calves. I'll be along in a minute."

In the house, Jake tried to lead Mary Margaret to the bedroom but she turned resolutely to the kitchen and began making coffee.

"How's your back?"

"Been hurt worse."

13

"When?"

"When I tried to jump a bar ditch on my bike. Went behind over teakettle and landed on my tailbone. Couldn't walk for a week."

"When did you do that?"

"See. You don't know everything about me. I'm still a woman with a past." She gave a sly grin and turned on the coffee maker. "Fourth grade. Compared to that, this is nothing."

"Why don't you take a hot bath, at least? Soak your back. The …" He caught "cocksucker" before it left his mouth.

She smiled tight-lipped as she began rummaging for mixing bowls. "Don't worry about me. Go help your father."

At the sound of the door's closing she put her head in her hands on the counter and sobbed without sound for a long minute, then started making biscuits.

***

Grandpa Grummond had milking machines on eight cows and was washing the teats and udder of another.

"How's it going?"

"Can't tell yet. But three hours late ain't doing any good. You have any idea of the usual order?"

"Not near as good as Eusebio."

The rumble of a pickup with a muffler on its last legs announced the arrival of George "Frog Bottom" Potts and one of the teenage two of his four sons. Potts owned a small sawmill which he and his oldest two boys ran with help from the younger ones when school year and sports schedules permitted.

By eight, they had settled into a rhythm with Grandpa Grummond leaving Jake free, free to run the International M with the front-end loader to deliver corn silage and haylage and oatlage and grain to the hungry cattle so they could make more milk.

***

It was 2:30 on the hottest afternoon of the year before Jake bounced the two-year-old Dodge Ram pickup over the cattle

14

guard and swung left in a spray of gravel that left a rising plume of gray dust.

With the help of Marcy Potts, Mary Margaret had found the papers for five families. Grandpa Grummond and the Pottses, father and son, had stayed hard at it, finishing an hour and a half before the afternoon milking was scheduled to start.

What with checking periodically on Mary Margaret's progress and being pulled off the tractor to answer questions in the barn, Jake had gotten minimal fodder and grain out. He'd have preferred to wait until he had all the papers together for everyone, but the need for hands who knew their way around the dairy was growing desperate.

It was one of those rare days in the high valley with no hint of a breeze and heat waves distorting the snow-capped peaks on 320 degrees of the horizon. Sweat glued his shirt to the seat back long before he covered the three miles to the intersection with Route 71, fifteen miles from the Sapinero County seat.

In town, he nosed into a space under a tall cottonwood across from the courthouse and unstuck his shirt, spat the exhausted dip of Copenhagen at the curb, gathered his papers and crossed the street, reloading his lip as he walked.

The blast from the window air conditioner sent a shiver across his back. Blakenship's drawl with its undertone of mocking amusement drifted from the glass-partitioned office at the back of the room. Nodding to the blonde at the front desk, who started to speak and then thought better of it, Jake walked to where the sheriff sat, phone to ear and booted feet on desktop.

"Got papers for five. Five complete families. Rest will be here as soon as Mary Margaret can find them in the mess your goons made."

Blakenship covered the mouthpiece with his hand. "Ain't my goons."

"You was there." Jake spat at the wastebasket. "But I ain't got time to argue. Just tell me what I got to do so I can carry my people home."

The sheriff spoke briefly into the receiver then hung up the phone. "They're over at the high school gym. In pretty good shape, considering. Been able to use the showers. Been fed breakfast and lunch. Rolled out some wrestling mats so they could lay down."

"Who's guarding them? Your folks or the DEA?"

"Little of both."

"Who've I got to deal with to get them out?"

"Not exactly sure about that."

"What are you sure of?"

"I know you're pissed off and you're trying to control it. And I can't blame you even a little bit for being put out. But don't take it out on me ..."

"Like I said, you was there."

Blakenship lit a Rum Crook with a kitchen match and studied Jake over the flame. "There's things you don't understand." He blew out the match with the first drag from the cigar. "Don't take it out on me and don't take it out on anybody else. And for crissake, keep your father under control. Last thing I need is an epidemic of busted kneecaps."

"What I need is some men who know what they're doing."

The sheriff sighed a stream of blue smoke while he watched the play of shoulder and back muscles under Jake's shirt as he walked stiff-legged to the front door. The whole deal hadn't felt right from the beginning. He checked the clock. Quarter to four. Another hour before he could plausibly get a drink at the Stockman.

***

The trace of shade had given way to the slanting afternoon sun and, even though both windows had been left open, the seat of the pickup burned his back and legs. Ignoring the heat, Jake started the truck and pointed it toward the high school.

It was dim inside and as cool as the sheriff's office but without the roar of the window unit. A pair of Sapinero County deputies blocked the double doors to the gymnasium. In their

16

early twenties, both looked familiar and he was willing to bet he'd gone to school with their fathers.

"Sorry, Mr. Grummond. You can't go in there."

"I've got papers for five of my families. I've got to get them out."

"You'll have to see Agent Buchanan for that."

"Where's he?"

"I believe he's at the command room. It's at the Alta," he added before Jake could ask.

Fifteen minutes later, Jake was knocking on the door of room 115 of the Alta Vista Lodge, three sprawling structures of logs and stone chimneys. Built in the twenties, the North Fork of the Flint River ran across the back acreage giving guests a chance to fish without leaving the premises. Owned by the son and daughter of the man who'd built it, the only concessions made to changing times were metal roofs and cable TV.

The big agent, Kiernan, opened the door. Behind him, five agents sat at a table littered with coffee cups and overflowing ashtrays. "Come in, Mr. Grummond." Kiernan turned sideways and gestured Jake into the room.

The men at the table were all armed, some wearing shoulder holsters, others with pistols high on their hips or centered in the small of their backs. To a man, they studied Jake with the impersonal calculation of a rattlesnake taking the measure of an unsuspecting mouse.

"I've got papers for five of my men. And their families."

"Beaneaters all ought to be deported." The speaker sat sideways at the table, belly straining the buttons of his wrinkled white shirt, his hand resting on his thigh in front of the automatic poking into the roll of fat above his belt. Jake wondered how he could tolerate the constant irritation of the gun butt.

"Never mind, Eaton." Kiernan's voice carried weary authority. The fat man shrugged and turned his back with a smirk to the others at the table.

"Grummond." Buchanan came through the door at the rear of the room, looping his tie under the collar of a clean, starched

17

white shirt. Fresh from a shower, his hair was wet and lined with comb tracks. "You have papers?" He leafed through the folder Jake handed him. "Just five families?"

"My wife's still looking for the rest. You tore things up pretty good."

"When will you have them all?"

"Don't know. Might have them by now."

"Why didn't you wait?"

"Because I've got milking to do and I need hands who know how to do it."

Buchanan looked through the folder again. "They look all right. But I'm not an expert. I'm going to have the INS perform the examination. They'll be here tomorrow."

"Tomorrow? That's not what you said this morning."

"Looks like I changed my mind, doesn't it?"

"Look. We're behind from the morning and we're already into the afternoon. You didn't find a single fucking thing and you're going to keep them another day?"

"Grummond, I could just have the INS cart them all to Phoenix or LA, so don't push your luck. Get the rest of the documents — if you can — and be at the high school tomorrow. At nine sharp."

"That puts me behind three milkings. Do you have any idea of what that means?

Buchanan took two steps to narrow the distance between them and all but screamed. "I don't give a rat's ass about your milking. I don't give a rat's ass about your Mexicans. I don't give a rat's ass about you. And don't threaten me with your congressman. No real American gives a shit about your aliens. Or you, either."

The pressure of Kiernan's hand on his shoulder stopped Jake's swing before it started. He looked at Buchanan, then at each of the agents around the table in turn. Finally he said, "Tomorrow at nine. Sharp."

2
AUGUST 21 — Early Evening

Two different young deputies were on duty at the high school, one of whom Jake thought had played football or ridden bulls with Paul. He wrote a note to Eusebio and handed it to the familiar one without comment. On the drive home, he gripped the steering wheel so hard his hands and forearms cramped and he had to pull over by the gurgle of an irrigation ditch to massage the pain away.

***

By the time Jake made the turn into the dairy, Blakenship had swallowed his third shot of Canadian Club and was resting his head against the tall back of his regular booth at the Stockman Bar and Grill. The timeworn essence of stale beer, fresh cigarette smoke and hot grease enveloped the ritual arguments at the bar and he relaxed for the first time that day.

From the jukebox, Lefty Frizzell's unmistakable tenor floated the "Mama and Papa Waltz" over the happy hour babble. Lefty had been his father's favorite. The sheriff closed his eyes and beat a soft one, two, three with the beer bottle snuggled between his hands, the left one of which was missing the first two joints of the index finger courtesy of a logging accident in the summer of his fourteenth year.

Lefty or no, the irritation from the raid wouldn't go away.

Not that he'd voiced concern. He hadn't thought there'd be any drugs and he'd figured after a quick look-see that would be obvious and no harm done except a little lost sleep — which would bother him and his men a lot more than the folks at the dairy.

His unease had begun when Buchanan called in help from neighboring counties and he'd been put out by the way the DEA man had ignored his suggestions. Discomfort had grown as events unfolded. And rounding up Jake's people — that was an

9

undigested lump in the pit of his stomach the whiskey hadn't softened.

Not that he cared about the dairy, particularly. He and Jake were within a couple of years of each other and they had never gotten along. Blakenship couldn't say why but somehow they ended up crosswise more often than not. Take the primary. No reason for Jake to back his opponent. Carried all the northern precincts, too, making it the closest race of the five Blakenship had won.

In fairness, he had to admit that Davis was from that end of the county and maybe that's all there was to it. Maybe it wasn't a matter of working against him so much as helping a neighbor. Still and all, an elected official lived and died by votes and the fact remained that with Jake's support, Davis had come perilously close to depriving him of his living — a prospect a man on the downward slide toward fifty didn't contemplate with enthusiasm.

On the other side of the coin, if Jake's problems weren't put to rest quickly, the resentment on East Mesa might spread countywide. He could lose the next primary. Or the general election. Eyes still closed, he sighed and took a full swallow of beer.

"Another CC, honey?"

He looked up into the face of Jessie Parsons, black hair in a single braid that reached her waist, dark eyes glinting affection above cheeks the color of an old saddle. A face that said waitressing was relatively new in a work history that had mostly been spent in the sun. A face that hinted at Ute ancestors in her not-so-distant past. A face that spoke of hard times and a weary tolerance for the vagaries of human kind.

"Thanks, but I've got a few more stops to make before bed."

"Speaking of, should I come by later?"

"After last night, I'll just be a snoring lump in your way."

"I don't mind."

"I appreciate that. But let's wait until I can do more than take up space."

Jessie pecked his lips good-bye and turned to her other tables. Blakenship tilted up the last of his beer and levered himself erect. He stretched, arms above head, to his full six foot two of fleshy height and settled his gun belt on his hip so the Smith and Wesson .357 Magnum rode low enough for comfort — after twenty-five years in law enforcement, he couldn't bring himself to swap his revolver for a 9mm automatic.

The sky over the Sublette Plateau was clear. It would cool as soon as the sun went down. A good night for sleeping — if he ever got home. First stop, the high school. See how many Jake took home.

***

"None? He came by my office hours ago with papers for five families."

"All I know is we sent him up to the Alta, then he came back and a wrote a note to one of his men. Jason delivered it."

"To who?"

The deputy, Carver by name, looked at his fresh-faced partner.

"I can point him out."

"Do that, son. Do that."

Blakenship followed the eager-to-please young man into the gym where mats were spread out in what looked to be family groups — mothers tending infants, older brothers kicking a basketball in an impromptu soccer game while sisters watched and giggled. The men sat in one large circle, talking and smoking and flicking ashes into Styrofoam cups half-filled with water.

The talk stopped at his approach and fourteen pairs of eyes regarded the lawman with the wary impassivity that he'd seen all his working life when dealing with Mexicans or Indians. They must learn it at birth.

"Him," pointed the deputy.

"Your boss gave you a note?"

21

Eusebio, still in the sleeveless undershirt but with the valentine boxers covered by green jailhouse trousers, rose to his feet. "*Si.* "

"What'd it say?"

"Why do you wish to know?"

"Because I want to know what's going on. Why are you still here?"

"You do not know?"

"No. I do not."

"According to Jake, the DEA is not able to read our documents and so we must wait until tomorrow for the immigration."

"Tomorrow?" Blakenship exploded. "The INS? What about milking?"

"That concerns Jake very much. As it concerns us."

Blakenship looked around the room. "When did you last eat?"

"Food was brought in at noon. But nothing tonight."

It was pushing eight. "Carver. Carver, goddammit, get your butt in here." The deputy came through the double doors on the run. "Carver, why haven't these people been fed?"

"Nobody told me anything about food."

"Well I'm telling you now."

"Where the hell am I supposed to get it?"

"Go to the fried chicken joint. Get a bunch of family dinners and charge it to the county. If they have any problem with that, tell them to call me. And get a move on. I want everyone in here to have supper in front of them by 8:30." Blakenship moved toward the double doors. "And, Carver. Take good care of the receipt. The DEA is going to pay when it's all said and done."

Outside, the sun was a bright ball just above the horizon. Blakenship sat behind the steering wheel, fatigue mingling with the three Canadian Clubs and two beers he'd had on an empty stomach. Bed was what he needed and bed he would have. But first Buchanan.

***

The DEA agent was enjoying dessert and coffee at a table for two in the Alta's dining room.

"Coffee?" Buchanan started to signal the waitress.

"No. I'm going to sleep tonight." Blakenship pulled the other chair away from the table, turned it around and sat with his arms resting on its back. "How much longer you going to keep Grummond's people?"

"Until the INS approves their papers or deports them."

"Which will be when?"

"They start tomorrow."

Blakenship removed the cellophane from a Rum Crook, started to bend to light it in the candle flickering on the table, caught the No Smoking sign on the wall above Buchanan's head and straightened. "Let me put something in perspective for you. I know you think we're nothing but no-account hicks with nothing better to do than bugger sheep and knock up our cousins and I know I already told you some of this, but bear with me. The thing about dairy farming is it's a big investment and to make it work you have to milk on schedule. If you don't, production drops. Diseases set in. And before you know it, you're in a world of hurt. Now your harassment of Jake and his meskins may not seem like much to you, but you could put him out of business."

Blakenship bit a chunk from the end of the cigar and moved it between cheek and gum with his tongue. "You with me so far? This stunt you're pulling with the INS could put him under. And everybody on the western slope will understand that."

"If there's half a million people in this part of the state I'll kiss your ass on the courthouse lawn at high noon."

"You didn't find any drugs, or evidence there of. So you fucked up. You're fucking up worse by holding Jake's people. By virtue of you're incompetence, you're doing serious harm to an innocent citizen."

"The raid was made on sound intelligence."

23

"That so? From who?"

"Two informants with connections to the operation."

"Who?"

"I'm not at liberty to say?"

"You check out their stories?"

Buchanan didn't answer.

"Let me get this straight. You didn't check to see if the snitches had a grudge against Jake or any other reason why they might want to cause trouble for the Grummond dairy."

Buchanan sat unmoved and unmoving.

"I could go on," said Blakenship. "I could tell you I don't get along with Jake. I could tell you he pays his meskins white men's wages — which pisses a lot of people off. He's obstinate, opinionated and not long on the social graces. But he runs the best damn dairy farm in the state. Yes sir. He's rubbed a lot of folks the wrong way over the years. But not one, not a single one, would believe drugs are coming through his place."

"Why'd you go along?"

Blakenship bit another chunk from the cigar. "Didn't think anything would come of it. Thought it might be good training for my deputies."

"And because maybe you wanted to hassle Grummond because he sided with Davis."

"Did some homework, I see. Pity you didn't check out your snitches."

"Your speech on Grummond's virtues has been entertaining, sheriff, but," Buchanan pushed away from the table, "I've got to get some sleep. We start dealing with those aliens at nine."

***

Which was what Jake was explaining to Mary Margaret.

"Honey, I've been through every house and trailer twice and I'm still missing papers." Weariness rimmed her eyes.

"You get a nap?"

Mary Margaret shook her head.

"Why don't you take a hot bath? We'll get a fresh start in the morning."

"Are you coming to bed?"

"Quick as I can." Jake waited until he heard the bathroom door click shut and the water start to run, then half-trotted to the barn. Billy Stanton from down the road and Brian Barnes from the hardware store in Top Hat, the village three miles away, were chatting over the sound of the milking machines as they washed down the next cows.

Billy looked up at the sound of Jake's entrance. "Any luck?"

"Bastards are keeping every man woman and child for the INS to check their papers. Won't start until morning." Jake leaned against the wall and closed his eyes. "Makes you wonder if this is still America." He opened them again. "I want to thank you for your help."

"Forget it," said Brian. "Maybe one day you'll take me to your mountain place so I can get me an elk."

"Who showed you the ropes?"

"Your father was here when we started. Got us organized and went home for a bite to eat and a shower. Said he'd be back before we finished."

"How far along are you?"

"Ain't sure. You got a lot of tits to pull."

Jake looked at the pens. "Looks like you've only got eight full hookups left," he shouted over his shoulder. "Any feed been put out?"

"Not that I know of."

Jake fired up one of the International M's and started for the silage pit. The sick pen was empty and a sinking feeling hit his stomach. He returned to the barn. "You milk the ones from the little pen?"

"What little pen?"

"Never mind." The cows from the sick pen had been milked with the others and that meant the entire day's production had to be thrown out.

He was on his last load of silage when his father clomped around the corner of the barn. "Thought you were going to bring some men home."

"Piece of shit with the funny hair called the INS in. Nobody gets released without their say so."

"Not what he said this morning."

Jake spit at a fence post. "Changed his mind, he said. Supposed to start tomorrow at nine. Supposed to. No telling how long it'll take. For that matter, no telling how many they'll let come back." Jake straightened up. "Mary Margaret can't find all the papers."

Grandpa Grummond leaned his forearms on the fence. "Fucking government assholes." Head half-bowed over his hands, he asked, "What about Eusebio?"

"Lucky there. Found them all. Including the deed to the ten acres out by you. Got every report card for all six children. Some of them go back almost twenty years. Estella's. Doesn't seem that long since she was in first grade. And now she works for a lawyer back east." He meant east of the mountains.

"If we can get Eusebio back by tomorrow noon, maybe things won't go all to hell."

"Take a look at the sick pen."

Grandpa Grummond squinted through the darkness. "Can't see a damn thing, but it looks empty."

"It is."

"Shit." He pounded the ground with his lead pipe. "Shit, shit, shit. I forgot to tell them."

"At least we're getting the milk out."

"Goddammit. We lost a day's production because I had to take a shower. I ain't worth strangling in shit."

"Lost yesterday afternoon's, too. And we're going to lose tomorrow morning's. We'll be lucky to get things halfway straightened out by the afternoon." Jake headed for the barn. "Think about who we can impose on to help tomorrow morning. Which," he glanced at his watch, "is only six hours away."

In the kitchen, Jake rummaged through the refrigerator, settling upon cheddar cheese that he bit straight from the brick and alternated with swallows from the gallon water jug. After the third bite, the cheese seemed to grow in his mouth and he spit it out. He carefully excised his teeth marks with a paring knife and returned cheese and jug to the refrigerator. At the bedroom door fatigue swept over him in a warm thick wave and he had barely enough energy to untie his boots, pull off his pants and get under the sheet.

At the shift of the mattress under his weight Mary Margaret snuggled her bottom against his hip.

Then it was three o'clock and he was sitting on the edge of the bed. The events of the preceding day forced their way into his consciousness and the memory of Buchanan galvanized him to a standing position with a rage so pure and vicious he stood in detached awe of it as it subsided.

Crusty eyes stared from the mirror while he forced himself to shave and he wondered almost without interest who was going to help with the morning milking. Had he asked anyone? Had his father?

His father's truck rolled into the yard at 3:25 with three Mexicans crammed into the cab beside him. "Buddy Rider been owing me a favor for most thirty years. I told him now was the time," his father answered Jake's questioning look. "He still milks a few head and he's got him some experienced hands. Lent them to me for the day. The whole day."

"How do they feel about it?"

"Seem to think it's fine. I'll just supervise them, point out our little peculiarities, while you get some more rest."

"I'm up and shaved. I'll try to sort out the sick ones."

"You think you'll recognize them?"

"I can try."

"And if you make a mistake?"

"You're right."

"Main thing is to get the milk out so's not to hurt production any more."

Mary Margaret had sorted the documents she'd found into envelopes, one per family, and had left them piled on the dining table. Jake carried the stack to the kitchen table, turned on the coffee machine she'd readied the night before and hunted for paper while the coffee brewed.

He found a ruled tablet, laced his coffee with molasses and milk, and began noting the contents of each envelope. When he was done, Jake figured seven families had enough to convince the INS, but all four bachelors and three families looked vulnerable — and two were headed by men from the milking crews.

Refilling his coffee cup, Jake took the skimpy envelopes and crossed the yard. The level of destruction in the Mendoza's trailer took his breath away. Ants and flies foraging a glutinous mixture of sugar and salt and flour and milk and eggs. Holes punched in the paneling. Cushions slashed. Sheets, blankets and clothing tumbled into the hall from the bedrooms.

A quick look at the homes of the others with minimal documentation told the same story. For comparison, he looked into the rest of the homes and found them to be relatively orderly. They had been searched thoroughly, that was clear. But not destroyed.

Jake stopped looking for papers and began listing the damage. At six, with three-quarters of the sun's red ball above the saddle between Mt. Sanders and Tanner Peak, he returned to the house to wake Mary Margaret.

She was at the kitchen table in a clean cotton nightgown holding a full cup of coffee, farm report on the radio and sausages gently frying. She could almost believe it was a normal day — except for the white lines around Jake's mouth.

"I've been to the houses."

She poured coffee into a clean mug and handed it to him. "You should've …"

"Bastards. Bastards going to pay for every goddamn jelly glass."

Mary Margaret studied the man she'd lived with for twenty-two years and known for eighteen before that. Six foot tall, two inches short of his father, a lack she knew bothered him to this day although he never spoke of it. Tanned face turning shocking white halfway up his forehead — proof of always wearing a hat outside. Body so hard from unremitting work that the skin looked as unyielding as a bronze statue. So thick through the chest that, even after all these years, when she hugged him she was surprised at how wide his shoulders were.

Today she felt a rage and uncertainty in him that was entirely new. She shivered and asked how many eggs he wanted.

"Sausage'll be fine. Sausage and a piece of your wheat bread."

She set the sausage patties on a paper towel to drain while she cut slices from a new loaf and set them on a plate near Jake's elbow. She scooped silverware from the drawer, butter from the refrigerator, strawberry jam from the cupboard and arranged them in an arc between her chair and Jake. Then she divided the sausage between two plates and brought them to the table.

All the while Jake sat mug in hand staring at the radio like he'd never heard the farm report before. She touched his arm and he jerked, then smiled and began buttering a slice of bread. "No idea how this is going to go."

"When should we leave?"

"Supposed to start at nine. We ought to be out of here by eight. Ain't going to give them an excuse to hold things up."

"It's only six-thirty. I've got time to do a little more looking."

"I already tried. Couldn't find a thing. You'd be better off taking it easy. We've got a hell of a day ahead of us."

"But I know where I've already looked. If it means keeping someone from being deported, it's worth a try." She carried her plate to the sink and went into the bedroom, a slight hitch in her stride that Jake didn't notice.

She reappeared dressed for town in white jeans and a sleeveless top and went out the door. Fifteen minutes later she was back, fighting back the tears. "I'd forgotten how bad ..."

"Cocksuckers. They'll pay."

Mary Margaret was shocked. Not because she'd never heard the word. Being Grandpa Grummond's daughter-in-law meant you heard it so often it ceased to have any impact —

29

when it came from his lips. But Jake, whose language was as rough as anybody's, practiced a private code in which sonsabitches and fuck and bastards tumbled forth as almost automatic punctuation, while words like cunt and cocksucker were never spoken in front of a woman. This was the first lapse without red-faced apology she'd ever heard him make.

***

When he turned into the high school parking lot at eight twenty-five, Jake was surprised to see three INS vehicles in the shade of the biggest cottonwood. He pulled in next to them, with Mary Margaret pulling the van alongside. Blakenship's Bronco was a minute behind, followed by two plain sedans that might as well have been wearing Day-Glo signs that said U. S. Government.

Jake took Mary Margaret's hand and they walked up and through the double doors. Several INS uniforms were talking to two deputies — neither of whom Jake recognized. They paid no attention to the Grummonds who stood awkwardly, waiting for an indication of where to go. Behind them the door swung open, followed by Blakenship's booming voice. "Raymond, you sorry excuse for a taxpayer's paycheck. Find the Grummond's a place to sit and see if they want any coffee."

A slight, sandy-haired deputy, already balding although he couldn't have been a day over twenty-four, jumped as though stung with a cattle prod. "Yes sir. Mr. and Mrs. Grummond, ma'am — uh, sir. Right this way. Follow me." He skittered down the hall to the coach's office where he seated them in chairs facing the desk and asked how they liked their coffee.

He returned carrying two Styrofoam cups with Blakenship right behind. "Mary Margaret. Jake. How're things today?"

"Been better. A lot better."

"The children, are they all right?" Mary Margaret's look was level and there was only a hint of accusation in her voice. "And Della? The one who got kicked."

30

"Everybody's fine. As fine as can be considering the circumstances."

"Sheriff Blakenship? Ah, here you are. And these are the Grummonds?" Without waiting for an answer, the speaker, a dapper little man with a pencil-thin mustache walked to the chair behind the desk. "My name is Spencer, Gordon Spencer." With bureaucratic self-assurance, he got right to the point. "Do you have the documents?"

"All we could find after the law got through." Jake gave law a special emphasis. No obvious sneer, but it stood out in the flat monotone of the rest of the sentence. "Cecil, I want you to come out and see how your boys left things. And you're going to be getting a bill for damages as soon as I can figure it up."

"There's going to be a lot of folks getting bills before the dust settles on this deal," said Blakenship.

"Excuse me, " Spencer cut the sheriff short, "but in the interests of expediency, perhaps we could get started."

***

Jake was standing by the van explaining to Eusebio and Jesus Garza, who headed the field crew, what needed doing when Buchanan and his agents walked through the children swirling with pent-up relief in the parking lot. A boy of perhaps five bumped into one of the agents and stood transfixed by fear. The agent smiled reassurance and patted the child on the head.

"Wash your hands," Buchanan told him, not in jest. "He's probably got head lice."

Eusebio and Jesus heard him and tensed. So did Jake, who started toward the agent until Eusebio's firm grip on his bicep stopped him. "We must remember the cattle." Eusebio's grip eased a fraction but didn't let go. "We must remember the cattle," he repeated, "but that does not mean we must forget these *pendejos.*"

AUGUST 22 — Late Afternoon

It was almost four before they finished. Spencer's refusal to release the last two families or the remaining two single men offset the small comfort Jake took from convincing him the Arroyo family of five were legal residents.

Anger wrenched his stomach on the drive home, each spasm followed by a lethargy that left him feeling hollow and weak. Pulling in, he saw that the sick pen held animals. Eusebio was reestablishing order — the most reassuring thing he'd seen in two days.

Eusebio heard the truck and met Jake at the barn door. "Production?"

"Not one has given twenty pounds."

"Shit. Mastitis?" The infection could affect any or all of the four quarters of a cow's udder and was highly contagious.

"More than forty. And we have almost two hundred still to milk."

"Any hot?" Hot mastitis, when the udder felt feverish to the touch, was the worst. If treated in time with antibiotics, the cow might survive but would be worthless as a milker. Only thing to do was take it to slaughter.

"No. But it has not been two full days." It took about three days for untreated mastitis to turn hot.

Andy Dawes, the mechanic, caught up to him before he reached the porch. "Two of the International M's are down and Enrique just blew the transmission on one of the John Deere's. I can fix the M's, but the Deere's going to need parts and Vinson says he'll have to special order."

"Sonofabitch. If we weren't ... Shit. Where's Jesus?"

"Far Gate field, last I knew."

The Far Gate field, named because access was through the gate farthest from the main house, was a long dusty mile down the county road. The broken tractor was in the field and Jesus was driving the other John Deere, a truck keeping pace to one side. Jake parked and watched the windrows of hay disappear to emerge as a sepia stream flowing from the chopper into the truck bed.

Jesus made the ninety-degree turn, pulled even with Jake and signaled the truck to stop. He vaulted from the tractor cab and landed, perfectly balanced, on the stubble.

"How's it going?"

"Should be finished by noon tomorrow. Even without the other tractor."

"Good." Jack started to turn the key, then stopped. "How's the family?"

"Maria was crying when I left. The house means very much to her. And they damaged a picture of her parents. The only one she has." Jesus looked at Jake carefully. "They are both dead now." He climbed back into the cab, started the tractor and, with a nod a to Jake, signaled the truck.

Production from four milkings a total loss. Jake did some rough calculations on the drive back. At $1800 per milking, that's $7200, not counting the 20 cents per hundred bonus for solmatic cells testing out below 200,000 per billion. Tonight's production only half normal — if that. Chalk up another $750 to $800. So far the raid had cost better than $8000 in lost milk alone. Figure in antibiotics for the sick cows, damage to the houses and trailers, down equipment and he was looking at a $15,000 hole. $15,000 minimum. And no telling how long it would take to get production back to normal.

Jake parked by the back porch and took in the pens and sheds and outbuildings of the dairy that was the only home he'd ever known. Established by his grandfather who'd moved west from Kansas. Perfected by his father, who'd added three innovations to the way dairy farming was done in this high, semi-arid country. Grandpa Grummond was the first to feed haylage instead of dry hay. He insisted on plenty of sawdust and straw bedding in the pens during the winter that combined with the manure and was worked into the fields. After years of applications, the Grummond fields were the most productive in the valley.

His father's third idea was that if you were raising cattle, in the final analysis, you were raising beef. He grained his cows far more than conventional wisdom held was necessary or even wise for milkers, but, when a cow's production began to drop, he was able to get a third again as much from the slaughterhouse for his culls as any other dairy man in the region.

Even so, the Grummond operation was subject to the fluctuations of weather and market that plagued all agriculture. Jake took those as givens. But this was different. And it wasn't over.

***

It was cool in the kitchen.

Jake's grandmother had her husband plant shade trees as soon as the foundation had been poured. Cottonwoods mostly, but also two blue spruce, one at each end of the front yard — trees that now towered over the sprawling one-story house.

A half-snore, half-whimper drew him to the couch in the living room. It was Mary Margaret lying on her side with her knees flexed, wrists crossed at her breasts. Even in sleep her brow furrowed and her eyes darted under the lids. Saliva drooled from the corner of her mouth to pool on the cushion.

She'd spent hours like this in the months after he'd had to tell her that an out-of-control eighteen-wheeler coming down the west side of Royal Pass had run Paul and the pickup pulling the gooseneck trailer with Elmo Johnson's new Brahma bull off the edge of the road. It was a thousand foot drop and there hadn't been much left of truck, trailer, bull or their nineteen-year-old only child. Got so bad she'd been admitted to the psychiatric ward of the hospital in Union.

Jake's shoulders knotted at the memory of loneliness and impotence and loss.

On the mantle was a framed photograph of Paul on the top rail of a corral, head thrown back in an open-throated laugh Jake could almost hear, black hat blocking out the center of the Elmo Johnson Rodeo Stock sign on the barn in the background.

34

Paul had rebelled at the iron discipline of the milking schedule and yearned to join the rodeo circuit. Jake and Mary Margaret tried to talk him out of it — but how do you tell your son that he's it, that there could be no more?

So they struck a deal. Paul would work the fields as a tractor jockey and he would finish high school. He could practice bull riding at Elmo's in his spare time. He could ride in local rodeos and when he turned twenty, they would sit down as a family and decide whether it made sense to try for the big time.

After a year, Paul had placed in the money three times and spent all his free time at Elmo's.

The clock above the kitchen sink read 6:30. Eusebio could handle the milking and whatever he had to report would keep until it was time to supervise clean up.

Mary Margaret had rolled onto her stomach, right arm cradling her head and legs almost straight, with her toes buried in the space between the last cushion and the arm of the couch. The position was less reminiscent of the troubled months and Jake decided to let her sleep where she was.

With the idea of resting for an hour or so, he retired to their room and the coolness of sheets that carried the faintly acid smell of his sweat and the strawberry bouquet of the shampoo Mary Margaret favored. Later, he felt the springs shift and, without turning or opening his eyes, reached over and half-circled Mary Margaret's waist.

***

His arm was still there when he woke up. Outside, dark branches were outlined against a lighter sky. Call if five o'clock. He checked the iridescent hands on the alarm clock. 5:25. Losing his touch.

He rose, mildly surprised to find he was still fully dressed, and tiptoed to the kitchen. Coffee brewing, he went out to the porch to take the measure of the day. It was overcast which explained why he had missed on the time. Lights were on in the milking barn as they should be. With shock, he remembered he hadn't supervised the evening cleanup.

Pouring coffee and adding molasses and milk, he carried the mug to the barn. The calm efficiency of the men as they washed udders and attached milking machines while they listened to the radio playing lively Mexican polkas made it seem as though everything was normal.

He walked outside to see Eusebio tending to the feeding and that, too, seemed normal until he remembered that Eusebio had also worked the night before. "Sorry about last night." Eusebio nodded. "Clean up go all right?" Eusebio nodded again. "Production."

"It is still very low."

Jake dipped a bigger than usual pinch of snuff, spat between his boots and asked the question he didn't want to ask. "Mastitis?"

"Eighty-two — so far." That meant that almost a quarter of what production they were getting couldn't be sold. "Four were hot," Eusebio continued.

"Shit."

The sun was in full view above the saddle between the peaks now and the sounds of engines being started meant the field crew was beginning the day. Jake reminded Jesus to take grain to the mill and went inside to see if Mary Margaret was up.

She wasn't.

He poured more coffee and, finding the tablet on the table where he'd left it the morning before, sat down to compose a letter to his congressman.

It took the better part of two hours to recount what had happened and to work up a rough estimate of damage and loss. Mary Margaret, still in her nightgown, joined him at the table before he finished.

"You keeping banker's hours now?

She smiled and watched as he wrote in a script that only she could decipher. When he was finished, he pushed it across the table. "Could you type that up by noon? If you've got the time?"

She turned the tablet so she could read. "Do you really think Blair can help?"

"It's worth a try. While you're at it, address copies to Conner and Rheimer." They were the U.S. Senators. Jake had stood on campaign platforms with them and he gave each modest annual contributions.

"I'll get to them first thing." She reached for his hand. "I'm sorry. I don't know what's wrong, but I just don't have any energy." The sound of a vehicle jouncing to a stop followed by heavy steps on the porch and a knock at the door accompanied by Blakenship's boom of a greeting moved Mary Margaret to her feet. "Come in, C. W.," she said on her way to the bedroom. "Coffee's on."

In deference to her voice, the sheriff removed his hat upon entering, then seeing only Jake, returned it to his head.

"Morning, Cecil."

"Jacob." Blakenship waved him to keep his seat and poured his own coffee. "Sorry I didn't make it out yesterday afternoon. Got busy." What he didn't explain was he'd gotten busy with Jessie. Divorced five years, he'd learned never to pass up a moment when potency and opportunity coincided.

"Follow me. You can bring your coffee." Jake led the way across the yard. "Mendozas and Salazars got deported, thanks to your asshole …"

"He ain't my asshole."

"… so you can get a good idea. The Garzas didn't and they've cleaned things up a bit."

Jake led him through the destruction, beginning with the vacant ones and finishing with Jesus and Maria's frame house.

Three young children in the yard stopped playing and stood wide-eyed when they saw the sheriff. Inside, Maria and the oldest daughter were scrubbing cabinets and floors. With everything picked up and being cleaned, the destruction seemed worse than in the others. The jagged edges of paneling, the couch missing cushions, the broken window above the sink and the shattered mirrors in bedrooms and bathroom stood out in sharp relief against the efforts of people trying to reclaim their home.

On the way out Jake pointed to the broken frame and pieces of black-and-white photograph gathered on the kitchen counter. "That was the only picture of her parents Maria had. They've been dead two years."

Except for hello and good-bye, Blakenship hadn't said a word during the entire tour. Now he spoke. "That's not the way we do things in Sapinero County."

"You telling me it was the feds?'

"Bet my pension on it." He stopped in the midst of unwrapping a Rum Crook. "That don't mean some of those deputies Buchanan borrowed from other counties weren't involved. Maybe even a couple of my boys. But the DEA instigated it."

"What about the damage?"

"Can't see how it would hurt to work up a bill." Blakenship handed Jake his mug, climbed into his Bronco and spun in a tight U-turn toward the county road.
Jake set the mugs on the porch rail and went to the barn. He wasn't going to miss cleanup again.

***

The two blocks of Top Hat's business district were visible from the intersection with Rt. 71 and Blakenship decided a drink at Helen's was in order.

Helen's was a hole-in-the-wall on the corner next to the hardware store and across the street from the only grocery store that also housed the post office. The dark room was empty, but the bell on the door rang as he entered and Helen appeared behind the bar before he got to a stool. The short woman of more than mature years regarded him with knowing eyes. "Long time, C. W. Canadian Club, Bud back, or are you on duty?"

"I'm always on duty so I might as well have a drink."

Helen put the beer and a shot glass in front of him, poured the whiskey level to the brim and held out her hand. "Three-fifty."

"Mountain View prices. My, my."

"Don't make any difference to the suppliers how big the town is." She rang up the sale and disappeared through the door to the kitchen. Blakenship emptied the shot glass and took two long swallows of beer.

He was upset. He knew that. But why? Despite what he'd said to Buchanan, there hadn't been any outpouring of outrage on East Mesa. Not yet.

Not yet. That's where the itch was. Jake had been busy dealing with the here and now. How many folks knew about the raid? What it was doing to production? About the damage?

He winced at the image of Maria Garza's torn photograph, the fear in the children's eyes, and took another long swallow from the beer bottle.

Once people got to talking and arguing over coffee or beer or standing in line at the grocery store, what then? Folks had long memories in these parts, memories that would carry to the next election, three years away though it was. A fading "Davis For Sheriff" bumper sticker in the far upper corner of the back bar's mirror did nothing to cheer him up.

Through the fly-specked front window he saw Jake park his Dodge in front of the grocery store and speak briefly to a head protruding half out of a pickup window before going in, carrying three business-size envelopes. The other truck pulled away and Blakenship could have sworn the driver was Johnny Davis.

He left the beer unfinished on the bar and walked across the street. Jake was at the post office window in the back, writing. The sheriff bought two packs of Rum Crooks and went outside to lean against the hood the Dodge.

He was halfway through a cigar when Jake came out. "Make sure you put them in a safe place." Blakenship nodded at the green receipts in his hand.

39

Jake didn't answer and climbed behind the wheel. Blakenship swung around the fender and leaned his forearms on the open window. "One of them going to who I think it's going to?"

Jake didn't say anything.

"Well, you've been one of Blair's longtime supporters," he puffed on the cigar, "just like I have. Hope he can help you out. The others're going to our esteemed senators?"

"Ain't confusing you a bit, am I, Cecil."

"Our representatives in Washington may be able to do something for you with the DEA and the INS, but …"

"Cecil, what the fuck are you driving at?"

Blakenship stepped back from the window. "Damned if I know."

"Let me tell you something. I am going to find out why they raided me."

"And?"

It was Jake's turn to pause. "I'm not sure." He started the engine and shifted into reverse. "But I'll tell you one for damn sure thing. The Sapinero County Sheriff's Posse has got the last dime they'll ever get from me."

***

Jake turned the radio on at the highway. News time. The announcer said something about when Congress would be back in session. Shit. Blair would be in the district, splitting his time between fly fishing and keeping his fences in order.

Once home, he put the receipts in the top drawer of the desk in the alcove off the living room, decided he couldn't wait for some aide to send his letter back to the western slope and looked up the number of the congressman's office in Union, the largest city west of the mountains.

Sitting in the leather chair with the high back he'd never gotten used to, he listened to the voice of a woman he imagined to be young. Not scheduled to be in the office until Monday.

Any way to reach him sooner? Congressman Stewart would call in sometime this afternoon.

"Tell him Jake Grummond needs to talk with him."

She assured him she would and asked for Jake's number, repeating it twice.

Jake stared at the phone, then called the lawyer who'd handled the Grummond Dairy's legal affairs ever since he could remember. According to the recording, Mackey Fitzgerald had gone fishing until Monday.

The house was dead quiet. No country music from the kitchen radio. No sound of Mary Margaret. He looked in the bedroom. No sign. He opened the front door, used not as an entrance but as access to the porch. Cane-bottom rocking chairs looked out on the farm's only area of decorative grass, a well-watered patch of green bordered by a variety of flowers most of which he couldn't name. No sign of her.

Looking out the kitchen door at the spot where Mary Margaret usually parked, he cursed, wondering how he could have failed to register the Ford Ranger's absence when he'd driven in.

The harsh ring of the phone, set loud so it could be heard outside, pulled him through the door.

"Jake. You're home." Mary Margaret's voice was breathless and pitched a little higher than usual. "Your father's had a heart attack."

"What …?"

"He called. Right after you left."

"Where …?"

"At the hospital."

"I'm on my way."

"Slow and easy, honey. Dr. Ben is with him and I need you in one piece."

Mary Margaret was returning a clipboard full of forms to the girl at the desk when Jake got there. She reached for his hand and led him to the slick vinyl of a waiting-room sofa.

"How is he?"

"No word yet."

41

Jake held Mary Margaret's hand and stared straight ahead, the unfamiliar smells and noises bringing cold sweat to his forehead. When was the last time he'd waited in a hospital? Not when Paul had broken his leg in football his freshman year. Dr. Ben had set it in his office and sent him home. The miscarriage. That was seventeen years ago.

He sneaked a glance at Mary Margaret. She seemed calm. As far as he could tell. She felt his eyes and smiled sadly.

It was forty-five minutes before Dr. Benjamin Thomasson, an erect sixty-five proud of his full shock of white hair, joined them. "Bottom line is he's had a heart attack," he began without preamble. "I can't tell how severe yet. He tried to talk but the effort wore him out. He's sleeping now."

"Can we see him?"

"Sure. But like I said, he's sleeping. Was he able to speak earlier?"

"He called and said help." Mary Margaret looked at the ceiling. "When I got there, he was on the floor like he was unconscious. But he opened his eyes when I touched him."

"How'd you get him in the truck?"

"Jesus was working the last of the Far Gate."

"Let's see. He's seventy-two?"

"Closer to seventy-three," Jake said. "In November."

"Active?"

"Fishes three or four times a week. Helps out driving tractor or truck when he feels like it. Looking forward to elk season." Jake took a breath. "Been extra busy these last few days."

"Heard about that. Goddamn shame." The doctor looked from Jake to Mary Margaret then back again. "Nothing you can do here. Best thing, far as I can see, is go home and get some rest. You both look like you could use it. Come back early in the evening. Say around seven."

***

42

The answering machine light was blinking for a single message when they got home. Stewart's office, giving a number where he could be reached. Jake was playing it a second time when running footsteps drummed on the porch.

"Please come. Della is not well." Eusebio's voice carried a note of panic he'd never heard before.

Jake followed Mary Margaret to the Montoya's trailer where Della sat at a kitchen chair with Maria Garza and Mercedes Guerrero kneeling on either side. Red streaked her legs and blood on the linoleum was congealing in the August heat.

Mary Margaret assessed the scene in a glance. "Find Luis and meet us at the hospital."

Jake drove to the Far Gate field. Empty. Cursing because he couldn't remember what was done and what needed doing on his own goddamn operation, he reversed direction. He found Jesus by the mechanic's shed. "Where's Luis?"

"Driving grain to the mill. As you said."

He met Luis on the Top Hat side of the intersection with Rt. 71, had him park the truck full of milled grain by the side of the road and aimed the pickup at Mountain View. Fast as he went, he couldn't catch the Ranger. It was parked near the emergency entrance when they pulled in. Luis jumped out of the truck while it was moving and ran through the hospital doors.

A young girl, young enough for this to be a summer job before her high school senior year, looked up in relief when she saw Jake.

"He's asking about his wife. She came in a minute ago with my wife. Mrs. Grummond."

"Oh. Yes, Mr. Grummond. They're with the doctor."

Mary Margaret came out ten minutes later. She held Luis's hand while she talked. "Della's going to be all right, but it doesn't look good for the baby."

Jake watched Luis's face freeze, just like his own must have done years before. Luis had worked at the dairy for four years, making enough money to marry Della and return with his bride eighteen months before. It was their first child.

"May I go to her?"

"As soon as the doctor says." Mary Margaret reached for Jake's hand and led the two men to the sofa where they sat without speaking on the vinyl, worn and stained through the years by countless others waiting for the doctor.

After fifteen minutes, Jake gently unwrapped his wife's fingers from his. "I'll be back."

"Where're you going?"

"Going to bring Cecil up to date."

***

Blakenship watched Jake check first the bar stools and then the booths. It wasn't good news that had him away from the dairy at this time of day.

"Do something for you, Jake?"

"Remember Della Montoya?" Blakenship neither spoke nor nodded. "She's the pregnant lady that cocksucking Otero County deputy knocked to the ground and kicked. Remember? Right before he kicked Mary Margaret?" Jake stared at Blakenship, forcing a nod. "She's in the hospital. Miscarriage. Their first child."

"I'm mighty sorry to hear that."

"And my father's there, too. Heart attack. Thought you ought to know. The bill's going up." Jake walked out leaving Blakenship wishing he'd never heard of Buchanan or the DEA.

The sheriff looked around for Jessie, but she was taking orders at another booth so he signaled the barmaid directly by holding his empty shot glass above his head until he caught her eye. Jessie picked it up when she brought her order to the bar and she carried it to Blakenship while it was being filled. "Going a little quick, aren't we."

"This has not been a good day." He whistled tunelessly. "Not a good day at all."

By rights he ought to call the Otero County sheriff and tell him. Of course, by rights he should have already called the Otero County sheriff and told him about the kicking. He teased himself by smelling the whisky and taking a sip of beer. Oh well. He'd put it off this long. Putting it off another day wouldn't hurt. He tossed back the shot, caught Jessie's eye and signaled for another.

***

Luis and Mary Margaret weren't in the waiting room when he got back. Down the hall, said the attendant. Last door on the right. They were talking in hushed tones through the mute grief that hung in the room. "The baby?" he mouthed. Mary Margaret shook her head, eyes glistening with unshed tears. He whispered that he was going to ICU.

He met Dr. Ben on the way. "Tough day," the doctor said, peering at Jake through rimless glasses. "Your father's resting comfortably. Vital signs are steady. Haven't run any tests yet."

"What do you think?"

"He's in no apparent danger at the moment."

"What do you mean 'no apparent danger'?"

"I mean cardiac events are hard to predict. If I'd seen him yesterday goddamning his way through the courthouse like he always does whenever he has to go there, I wouldn't have predicted he'd be in ICU today." The doctor shrugged and spread his hands, palms upward. "I'm sorry, Jake. That's the best I can do right now."

Staring through the glass window of the ICU unit at the familiar form of his father festooned with unfamiliar medical paraphernalia, Jake remembered he'd first seen his only child through the glass window of the nursery in this very hospital.

There hadn't been any glass window at the morgue the day he'd had to identify what was left of Paul.

***

Mary Margaret's heat against his buttocks stirred him half an hour before the alarm's setting and the stroking of her hand

45

brought him fully awake and fully erect. "Love me," her breath commanded. "Love me. Now."

He rolled toward her, following her hand's insistence as it led him between her thighs where, with a powerful drive of her pelvis, she seated him within her. She thrashed her hips toward orgasm as if her life hung in the balance, then stiffened at his answering rhythm, a half-stifled moan — pain not ecstasy — escaping her lips as he climaxed.

"What's … what's…," he gasped, supporting his weight on his hands and knees. It was too dark to see clearly, but he was sure her jaw was clenched against some agony and the silver of tears flowed from the corners of her closed eyes.

"Sorry. My back."

"That sonofabitch."

"I'm O. K. Thanks."

She was asleep when he left for the barn, unease at the ferocity of her need and anger at the fat deputy souring his post-coupling satisfaction.

4

AUGUST 24 — Morning

The number Stewart's office had left turned out to be the Hazel Lake Inn, located high in the Presidentials ten miles beyond and two thousand feet higher than a wide spot in the road called Sawtooth, which was distinguished from other wide spots in the road by a long, shingle-sided building housing a gas station, a restaurant and a post office.

Jake reached the Inn shortly after eight, took a seat at a window booth in the dining room and watched the sunlight move down through the evergreens and aspens on the slope behind the outfitter's corral.

Twenty years before, as a present to himself when Paul was born, he'd bought sixty acres on the other side of the ridge. His half-formed notion to build a cabin there when the time came to pass the dairy on to Paul had faded with Paul's lust for bullriding and the accident had erased the idea all together.

"Jake. Good to see you."

He stood to shake hands with a man in his early sixties, short and with pale skin saved from translucence by a splash of freckles across forehead and cheeks. The silver belt buckle was cinched firmly in place above a comfortable paunch and the steel-rimmed glasses sliding down his nose below a stained cowboy hat gave him the look of a banker reveling in his annual escape to the woods with the boys.

Blair Stewart had been a bank vice-president in fact until twenty-three years before when fate in the form of a trout bone choked the life from the incumbent congressman and opened Stewart's path to a quiet career in Washington. He enjoyed restaurants and museums, attended assiduously to his constituents' problems and never embarrassed them by speaking on the House floor or introducing legislation of any kind.

Stewart signaled the waitress. After a discussion about the relative merits of the venison sausage versus the elk steak, he chose both to accompany his eggs and hash browns. With coffee cup full, Stewart pushed his glasses into place and asked Jake how he could be of service.

Voice low, Jake described what had happened in clipped sentences. Stewart listened without interruption, periodically smiling encouragement or nodding in sympathy and even waving away the waitress when she arrived with breakfast.

"Della lost the baby. Dad's in ICU. And I'm losing thirty-six hundred a day. Or more." Jake carefully wrapped his spent Copenhagen in a fragment of paper napkin, packed a fresh pinch between gum and lower lip and stared into his coffee cup.

Stewart waited until he was sure Jake was finished, then signaled the waitress. He cut a piece of elk steak, used it to break the yolk of one of his sunny-side up eggs and unhurriedly chewed the yellow smeared meat. "They didn't find any drugs?"

"Like I said, nothing."

"Strange. Usually they'll plant a little something. Not so much to incriminate as to make them look less foolish." He smiled guilelessly at Jake with gray-green eyes that showed no warmth. "Or so I'm told." He chewed a bite of sausage slowly, as though analyzing the seasoning. "What was their reaction?"

"That I got tipped."

"I thought you weren't a suspect. Isn't that what Blakenship told you?"

"That's right. But that's what that DEA bastard said."

Stewart digested this while he savored another bite of sausage. "Any idea of who pointed the DEA at you?"

"No."

"You backed Davis in the last election. Why?"

"He's from Top Hat. And me and Cecil never have hit it off." Jake sipped his coffee. "But it wasn't Cecil. Not his style. If he thought there was drugs at the dairy, he'd do it himself. Say that for him." Jake looked out the window. The whole ridge was sunlit now. "Nope. On this one, he was just along for the ride. Going along for the ride — that's one of the things he's best at."

"What about his supporters?"

"Blair, we're talking about a race in a county with a total population of 30,000, counting children, Utes and wetbacks.

Cecil doesn't have a campaign organization to speak of. And besides, he won."

Steward looked unconvinced. "Anyone else? Another dairyman? Someone who wants your land? Maybe someone your father angered?"

"Shit. Dad's pissed off more'n half the county, at one time or another."

"Maybe it's someone who doesn't like you hiring Mexicans."

"Maybe. But that don't narrow it down much." Jake waved his empty cup in the direction of the waitress. "Who named me is one thing. What they did when they got there is another. And I want to know what I can do about it."

Stewart considered for a moment. "I'm not sure. It makes a difference whether they were acting on credible information. That's why I asked about the informant or informants. Have you talked to a lawyer?"

"Got a call in. He's gone fishing for the weekend."

"Make sure you talk to him Monday. There's something called the Federal Tort Claims Act. I don't know much about it myself," again the flat eyes above the guileless smile, "but my understanding is it provides an avenue for restitution when agents of the federal government have caused damage to innocent parties." Stewart chewed a mouthful of hash browns. "In the meantime, give a list of the DEA personnel you can identify to Ronnie. You know Ronnie, don't you? I'll get him down here before you go." He motioned for the waitress and asked that someone rouse his aide. "And now," the congressman continued, "perhaps you can tell me what else is going on in your part of the county."

The next half hour passed with questions about friends and neighbors and tax cuts and price supports and food stamps until Stewart's aide appeared, hair still wet from the shower.

Born in Brooklyn and raised in Washington, D. C., Ronald Kenneth Eastman, III, had served as one of the congressman's pages while in high school, had stayed on in one capacity or another through his college years and now into his mid-thirties.

49

"Ah, Ronnie. You remember Jake Grummond? Jake's going to give you the names of DEA agents who raided his place a couple of nights ago. Find out everything you can about the raid and those involved."

Ronnie had never met Jake, but Jacob W. Grummond, Grummond Dairy, Top Hat, Sapinero County flashed up from his mental Rolodex of contributors. He opened a pocket-sized note pad in a well-worn leather cover and cocked his head.

"One in charge was named Buchanan. One that acted like his second in command was called Kiernan. Big man. Like a defensive tackle. Then there was an Eaton — I think. Looked like a southern sheriff except he was wearing a suit. Seems like I heard another called Curtis."

"Last name or first?"

"Don't know. He's a little rat-faced sonofabitch, though. And there was probably five or six more."

"It was a cooperative effort?"

"Yeah. Blakenship from Sapinero County and a bunch of his deputies were there. Deputies from Otero and Collin counties, too. Maybe some others. Bastard that kicked Mary Margaret — and Della — was from Otero."

Jake stared out the window at the memory until Robbie touched his arm. "Just deputies?"

"Say what?" Jake looked from the side to the congressman. "Uh huh. Blakenship was the only high sheriff in the crowd." Jake looked at his watch. "Got to go."

Stewart offered his hand without rising. "Tell your father I know he'll be up and around in no time. We'll look into this, I promise you. But I can't promise what we'll be able to do. It's hard to get the feds to admit they did anything wrong. Just look at that Waco mess. So make sure you talk to your lawyer. Do I know him?"

"Mackey Fitzgerald."

"Mackey Fitz? He's a good man. Although how experienced he is in cases of this nature I couldn't say."

***

50

A mile of winding down hill unpaved road from the Inn brought him to a dirt track on the right that crossed the creek flowing from Hazel Lake to disappear over a low point in the ridge. It led to his sixty acres and on impulse he took it.

It was recently rutted by four-wheel drive vehicles. Outfitters doing pre-season scouting most likely. Bow season opened soon. Jake bounced up and over the ridge where the ruts swung to the right and snaked down through a stand of aspen, some with trunks more than two feet in diameter. At the bottom of the grade it crossed a small park in a lazy arc to climb through successive patches of aspen and mixed conifers.

Three miles of progressively steeper and rockier going brought him to a level stretch where two ridges joined. He was about three miles due east of the Inn, although he'd put eleven miles on the odometer since he left the road.

The track gradually gained altitude for a mile or so, and then dropped abruptly. Jake stopped before the drop-off, shifted into low range four-wheel drive and turned onto a vague set of wheel ruts. After a hundred yards, the ruts passed between two fence posts and he was on his land.

He parked, got out and stretched. Unevenly spaced posts marched away in both directions. No wire was visible and closer inspection revealed that most was on the ground, covered by undergrowth.

When had he last been here? Three elk seasons ago? Four? Longer?

He picked his way through the brush and downed branches, trying to remember where they'd pitched the tents and tethered the horses. Twenty yards from the truck he found the big balsam with the branch stubs protruding from the trunk within easy reach and spaced conveniently for hanging pots and pans. There was the clearing and the fire pit, now half grown over. Tents to the right. Horses to the left. Beyond, the trees thinned to a broad view of hills climbing to snow-capped peaks. BLM land on the other side of the fence and the Bridger

51

National Forest, including the Picket Stake Wilderness, in the distance.

He leaned against the balsam trying not to think, trying to block everything out but the occasional whistle of the wind and the perfume of evergreen resin building in the warmth of the sun now high overhead.

A deerfly's bite on the nape of his neck brought him back. He swatted belatedly and looked at his watch. 11:30.

***

The house was quiet, not even the background lulling of the radio. Jake found Mary Margaret asleep in the bedroom, lying on her side on top of the bedspread, fully clothed except for shoes, breathing easily. He resisted the urge to pat her butt and tiptoed out of the room. Careful not to let the screen door slam, he crossed to the barn, boots kicking up puffs of dust that settled slowly in the brilliant afternoon light.

The barn looked normal, clean and ready for the next milking. The production figures on the clipboard brought reality back and he moved to the door to try to gauge how many head were in the sick pen. He couldn't be sure, but it looked like more than when he'd left in the morning.

The rich smoke of cooking chicken led him to Eusebio standing, beer in hand, turning leg quarters and split breasts on a barbecue pit made from a fifty-five gallon drum cut in half lengthwise. He saluted Jake with the beer and lowered the top. Smoke rose from the chimney and oozed in isolated wisps from spots where the halves joined imperfectly.

Eusebio studied his handiwork with satisfaction. *"Cerveza?"* he asked, pointing to the ice chest.

"No, thanks." Changed his mind. "What the hell," and picked a Busch can from the selection of bargain beers. He flicked some specks of ice into the chest, closed it and popped the top. "Production's still way down."

"Si. And ten more with mastitis."

"Hot?"

52

"Three."

Jake sipped absently, then, surprised at how good the cool tart bubbles felt on tongue and throat, tilted the can up and swallowed freely. He wiped his mouth with the back of his hand and watched Eusebio maneuver two chunks of peach wood through the fire hatch. "How're things going?"

"The field crew they are catching up and we have the feeding back in order."

"I mean, how're the folks doing?"

"Everyone is upset. The baby. The deportations. The destruction. That is why I am cooking chicken — to raise the spirits, perhaps."

"Della?"

"She comes home this evening. Luis has gone to get her. Luis and my wife."

"Anything I can do?"

"At the moment, nothing. Tomorrow? Monday? Maybe. But today you have other things. Your father."

"Crew set for tonight's milking?"

"Yes. The hospital would be best for you, I think."

Mary Margaret had turned on her side but was still asleep so he left a note on the kitchen table.

***

The vehicles in the parking lot ran heavily to dusty pickups. Saturday afternoon was visiting time for folks from the outlying areas. All the shady spots were taken so he took one that the shadow cast by a tall cottonwood would reach within the half hour.

The girl behind the desk looked like John and Betty Sanford's second oldest daughter. He nodded and started down the hall toward ICU.

"Mr. Grummond. Mr. Grummond." She was the Sanford's daughter, but for the life of him he couldn't recall her name. "He's been moved. Your father." She peered down at her list. "He's in 132. That's down at the other end of the hall."

53

"Thank you. Must mean he's doing better."

"I'm sure he is."

Grandpa Grummond lay with oxygen tubes in his nose and IV's in his left forearm like he hadn't shifted position since Jake had last seen him. On the upside, his face no longer had the undercoat of pallor. The click of Jake's heels on the linoleum opened his eyes and he smiled when he recognized his son.

"How you doing?"

"Ain't worth …"

"Strangling in shit. I know."

The reedy whisper was a shock. That and the way he closed his eyes from the effort to speak. Jake squeezed the big hand with its lifetime of calluses that retirement hadn't erased and got a faint squeeze in return. "Don't worry. What with Eusebio, the milking's under control." His father smiled and started to speak. "Don't say anything. Just lay on your ass and harass the nurses." A nod. "Been able to eat?" A faint nod toward the IV's. "Maybe tomorrow. Dr. Ben been by?"

A whispering rasp. "Ain't told me shit."

"Time to take our vital signs." A middle-aged nurse Jake didn't recognize walked around him to the other side of the bed and checked the flow from the IV's. "You must be the son." She went on without waiting for an answer. "Your father's doing very well, but he's still quite weak."

"Will Dr. Ben be by this evening?"

"I couldn't say. But your father's in good hands."

"I didn't mean that. I just wanted to talk to him."

"I don't know his schedule." She placed the probe of the electronic thermometer under his father's tongue and reached for his wrist.

Blakenship was leaning hipshot against the counter chatting with the Sanford girl when Jake returned to the front lobby. He gave a curt nod and pushed through the revolving door. The sheriff caught up with him on the curb.

"Sorry about your father. He doing O. K.?"

"Better'n yesterday. Can't call a heart attack O. K."

"Yeah. Well." Blakenship removed his Stetson and rubbed the mark on his forehead made by the sweatband. "Things back to normal at the dairy?"

"No." Jake let the answer hang between them. The sheriff replaced his hat and folded his arms across his chest. Jake broke the silence. "You find out who tore things up?"

"I'm working on it."

Blakenship waited until Jake had pulled out of the parking lot before walking to his Bronco. He sat in the gathering shade and ran through a mental list of his deputies who'd been on the raid. Would any of them have trashed the houses?

Shit. Were there any who wouldn't have?

Thing to do was talk to Henderson, his senior deputy.

Three blocks on Main then right four and a left brought him to a neighborhood of two and three-bedroom houses built in the twenties and thirties shaded by well-watered trees. He parked in front of a white stucco bungalow with a new red metal roof across the street from a small park featuring manicured grass, picnic tables and a playscape of swings, slides and an arrangement of log stumps of various heights.

Charlie Henderson's father had built the house a year before the stock market crashed. Three children had been born in it. The two oldest had died in successive years, one from the lingering effects of rheumatic fever, the other the only fatality of a school bus accident coming back from a football game with Mountain View's arch rivals, the Elwood Pirates. Henderson had never left home, bringing his bride to live there, moving at his mother's insistence to the big bedroom after his father died, and living alone these last four years now that both mother and wife had passed on.

Patsy Cline's poignant "I've got these little things, but she's got you" floated through the screen of the window that opened onto the porch, entwined with the bubbling aroma of beef stew. Charlie claimed he owned every song she'd recorded and had taped them on three ninety-minute cassettes that he played straight through once a month.

Blakenship knocked and entered. Henderson was at the stove adding a package of frozen corn to the steaming blue enamel pot on the front burner. "Be ready in about fifteen minutes if you're hungry." He got two Budweisers from the refrigerator. "No whiskey. Unless you brought your own."

"Charlie, you know who went on the raid, right?"

"You mean the one out to the Grummonds?"

"How many raids we had lately?"

"Yeah, I know who went."

"What do you think of them?"

"What do you mean?"

"I mean, would any of them flat trash a place out of meanness?"

"I heard some of them talking about that."

"Would they?"

"I don't think any of ours would do it on their own. But any of the ones that went would go along."

"Any of them?"

"Didn't have our paragons of moral courage out on that deal." Charlie took a sip of beer.

"What should I do?"

"About what?"

"About finding out who was responsible for trashing the homes."

"Why do you care?"

"Because it wasn't called for. That's the kind of thing that gives us a bad name. Makes it harder all around."

"Because it might not stand you in good stead come election time?"

"There's that, true enough. But it ain't right, Charlie. You know it ain't right. On top of everything, I told Jake I'd find out." Blakenship sucked on his beer. "Saw him today. At the hospital, checking on his father. You know that crazy old bull elk had a heart attack?" Charlie nodded. "Probably caused by the fallout from the raid. Anyhow. Jake asked if I'd found out anything. So he ain't forgot."

"Not likely he would. What're you going to do?"

56

"Start by you and me seeing what our boys know. Then, we'll see."

Blakenship left Charlie ladling his dinner into a bowl and started toward the Stockman before he remembered that Jessie had a rare Saturday off and he was supposed to meet her at her place.

She lived in a one-room apartment with a small kitchen alcove and a large bathroom above Dunn's Hardware Store. Blakenship rat-a-tatted a shave and a haircut two bits on the door and walked in. Jessie was standing naked, back to him and hair turbaned in a towel, giving a critical eye to her reflection in the mirror above the four-drawer dresser against the wall next to the double bed. The oak of the dresser was a match of the bed's headboard and once again Blakenship wondered if they had been part of larger set, the other pieces of which had been casualties of some storm earlier in her life.

Wondered, but once again, didn't ask.

"I hope you're here to take me to dinner." Jessie spoke without breaking her concentration on the problem reflected in the mirror. Blakenship took the opportunity to admire her back with its smooth columns of muscle on either side of the spine. The cheeks of her ass jutted proudly without a hint of flab and the skin was taut all the way to her ankles.

She half-turned and pouted a kiss. A slight protuberance of abdomen and a bit of sag to generous breasts were the only signs that she was in the fortieth year of a hard life. That and a scar that started at belly button level on her right hip and zigzagged obliquely downward to disappear in the triangle of pubic hair.

The scar was smooth Blakenship knew and he wondered about it, as he always did, but, like his curiosity about the furniture, he never asked.

"Dinner, huh." He slid his arm around her waist. "I thought maybe you were going to give me a home-cooked meal." He bent to kiss the back of her neck just beneath the towel wrapping her hair.

"Stop that." She slapped without meaning it at his hand that sought the cleft between the pouty outer lips of her pubis. "I

57

don't cook. I carry. On my days off, I like for somebody else to carry to me. Feed me and I'll give you more of that than you can handle." She pulled away from his still probing finger.

"Promise?"

"Promise, hell. You know better than that. Unless you've gone senile on me all of a sudden." Jessie began sorting through her lingerie drawer.

"Take your time. Next best thing to watching a woman undress is watching her dress."

"I better be the only woman you watch do either one or you're going to wake up one morning and find one of your favorite parts missing."

"Is that anyway to talk to the man who's going to take you to the Alta and ply you with surf and turf or anything else your little heart desires?"

"The Alta? Guess I'll wear my new bra. It's black and it pushes everything up."

***

They were enjoying coffee and after-dinner drinks when Rudy Mikeska, the Otero County Sheriff, approached the table.

Blakenship had waved with perfunctory courtesy upon entering then steered Jessie to the opposite end of the room when he'd seen his counterpart at a table with his wife, a plump woman with lacquered hair and dimples on each cheek that gave her a false look of constant good nature.

"What's the matter, Rudy? Can't get a steak in Elwood?" Blakenship watched in amusement as Mikeska tried without success to keep his eyes from Jessie's cleavage.

"Martha wanted some fresh peach cobbler without having to make it herself. Besides, if I'm out of the county, I don't have near as many phone calls. Just thought I'd stop by and say how do."

"I've been thinking about calling you, as a matter of fact."

"That so?"

58

"Thought we might get together one of these days and chat about this and that."

"This and that being?"

"Say the raid at Grummond's place you sent some deputies to."

"What about it?"

"About if any of your boys know who tore the shit out of the places Jake has for his people."

"Don't see why you're worried about them wetbacks."

"They're wetbacks in my county, Rudy. Not to mention that the Grummonds have been long time supporters of the Sheriff's Posse. And not to mention them being long time supporters of our mutual congressman."

"If you want to talk, let's do it now."

"May take longer than either of us wants to spend tonight."

"I ain't got a lot of time during the week."

"I think you better make some time for this one. I think we both better make some time.

5

AUGUST 26 — Morning

Mackey Fitzgerald was at his desk adding real cream and two teaspoons of sugar to his third cup of coffee when Jake arrived.

"Do any good?"

"Limited out every day." A strand of faintly yellow hair dangled to the end of his nose and Fitzgerald pushed it to the side with his left hand. "Rainbows mostly. Couple of German browns."

Jake sat down in one of the two worn leather armchairs facing the desk. "You know about the raid?"

"Just a little."

"You know they didn't find anything?" Fitzgerald nodded. "You know they rounded up all my people?"

"Heard something along those lines."

"You know what it'll cost to fix up the houses and trailers? How much production I'm losing? How many head have mastitis?"

"Maybe you better tell me." Fitzgerald took a yellow legal pad from a stack on his desk, centered it on the blotter, aligned two freshly sharpened pencils next to it and with a third, noted date, time and Jake's name on the first line. "Shoot." Fifteen minutes and two pencils later, he looked at his three pages of notes and back at Jake. "That it?"

"I could go on, but you get the idea."

"Let's see. You're innocent. You've sustained considerable losses, losses that are increasing. You allege that the federal government acting through the Drug Enforcement Administration is responsible. You want to be recompensed for all losses and damages, real and emotional, suffered by yourself, members of your household and resident employees."

"And their families."

"And their families." Fitzgerald leaned back and folded his hands across his ample stomach. "That about it?"

"If I followed you right."

60

"The kicking … Mary Margaret and the other woman …"

"Della. Della Montoya."

"Della. There were not only other law enforcement witnesses, there were the EMS personnel …" Fitzgerald trailed off, looking at the ceiling. "She did attack the deputy…"

"Mary Margaret didn't."

"No. Not Mary Margaret." Fitzgerald rose and moved toward his bookcase. "There's something called the Federal Tort Claims Act."

"Blair mentioned it."

"Already talked with Blair, have you? Can't hurt. But the fact is, I'm going to have to do some studying." The lawyer picked up a pair of reading glasses from the corner of his desk. "Check back toward the end of the week. Say Thursday.

***

Blakenship and Henderson sat at a window table in the Chopping Block, the coffee shop across from the courthouse, egg-streaked plates pushed away and drew deeply on a cigar and an unfiltered Pall Mall respectively.

"There's Grummond." Henderson pointed at the figure climbing into the white pickup visible beyond the World War I era howitzer on the courthouse lawn.

"Looks like he got Mackey Fitz off to an early start."

"Speaking of start, when're we going to start what we talked about Saturday?"

"Today. Ran into Mikeska at the Alta after I left you. Kind of promised him I'd be up to talk about it."

"Kind of promised? He that concerned about Jake's Mexicans?"

"O. K. I told him." Blakenship picked up both checks. "My treat."

"You're going to spend a whole $2.52 on me? Why C. W., I'm touched to the heart of my bottom."

***

The Otero County Sheriff was housed in the new courthouse annex, a two-story cube with a veneer of fake log siding. An enclosed walkway connected the second floor of the ornate Victorian courthouse with the annex, an architectural feature that made practical if not aesthetic sense since the jail was on the second story of the old building.

The face of the girl at the desk had the windburned tan of a dedicated skier. A brief smile lit startling blue eyes when he gave his name and asked if Mikeska was in. She pointed to the rear office with one hand as she picked up the ringing phone with the other. Blakenship smiled his thanks to the back of her neck.

Mikeska looked up from a manila folder. "Goddammit, C. W. Haven't you heard about the telephone?"

"You're not going to tell me you're too busy, are you?"

"I can give you half an hour."

"That'll be long enough to get your attention." Blakenship pulled two chairs from the wall, sat in one and propped his feet up on the other. "First thing you can do is tell me the name of the deputy who kicked Jake Grummond's wife. After he kicked a pregnant woman. Who, by the way, had a miscarriage on Friday."

"What're you talking about?"

"That information didn't make it into the report? Maybe that's where we should start. Take a look at what it says."

"None of my men would kick a woman, let alone Mary Margaret Grummond."

"Saw it with my very own eyes."

"What'd he look like? And why didn't you do something about it at the time?"

"Things were moving a bit fast. Besides, it was a federal show."

"Feds keep you from getting his name? Feds keep you from following up on it until, let me see," Mikeska made a show of counting on his fingers, "five or has it been six days?"

"I'm here now, Rudy."

"So you are. Let me ask it again. What's he look like?"

62

"Mid to late twenties. Six-three and heavy — heavy, but soft. Had him a pretty good belly for a man that young. Black hair and a scraggly black mustache. Don't remember seeing him before."

"Sounds like the Donaldson boy. Remember James Donaldson? Used to run some cattle up near the reservoir. Died last winter. Boy of his, Billy, got discharged after four years with the MPs and his mother asked me if I could do something for him. Put him on last spring."

"Any chance of getting him in here?"

Mikeska turned his swivel chair ninety degrees and shouted, "Elvira."

""What?" The red-bronze face appeared at the door. No kid, thought Blakenship. Got to be thirty. Maybe older.

"Where's Donaldson?"

"Let me check."

Blakenship and Mikeska spent the minute's wait in silence, trying not to stare at each other.

"He's on day shift. We got a call about some out-of-state car in an irrigation ditch up the Hays Reservoir Road. He took it. Called about an hour ago for Ricky's wrecker. Should be getting back by now."

"Raise him on the radio. Tell him to get his butt down here. Pronto." At her look, he added, "Please."

"That wasn't so hard, was it?" She vanished, leaving the memory of a smile behind.

"Donaldson's one. Who else you send along with Buchanan?"

"Buchanan?"

"C'mon, Rudy."

"You mean on the DEA raid?"

"What the hell else are we talking about?"

"I was thinking about Donaldson. He really kick Grummond's wife?"

"He really did. By accident, I think. I hope. But kicking that pregnant *chiquita* was no accident."

"That boy's got some explaining to do."

"Rudy, who else went along?"

"Don't know, offhand." Another shout. "Elvira."

"What?"

"Come here. Please." She came no further than the doorjamb.

"Please look up the report on the raid in Sapinero County. Get me the names of everyone who went." Mikeska looked at her. "Dammit. I said please."

"Why don't we just look at the whole report? You know. Read what it says along with the names of who went."

"All right. All right. Elvira."

"Now what?"

"Just bring the whole report. Please."

"I can't find it."

"What do you mean, you can't find it?"

"I mean I can't find it. As in, it isn't here."

"Rudy, ask her if she remembers seeing it."

"Sheriff Blakenship," like a teacher explaining something to a particularly obtuse student, "filing is not my job, so there's no reason why I would see it. But I can tell you there's no report of a raid in Sapinero County in the files."

"Rudy?"

"Get Parker."

"Old Buck finally made senior deputy, did he?"

Mikeska didn't answer, just gazed out the window and drummed his fingers on the dark top of the old oak desk. Blakenship shrugged and fixed his counterpart with a frankly questioning stare.

Five minutes passed before Elvira reappeared. "Parker's at home. Says he's got the flu."

"In the summer?" Mikeska didn't turn from the window. "Bullshit. Tell him to pull his pants on and get his ass down here."

"Sheriff?"

"What?"

"Deputy Donaldson is here."

"Send him in."

64

A not-quite-young man appeared in the doorway, black stubble dotting his doughy cheeks and double chin. His eyes flicked nervously at Blakenship, then fixed on his boss.

"Sit down, Billy." Mikeska indicated the chair from which Blakenship was removing his feet. "You remember Sheriff Blakenship." It wasn't a question. "The Sheriff has some interesting things to say about the raid on the Grummond place. Things like you kicking a pregnant woman. And kicking Mrs. Grummond."

"Look Sheriff, that meskin pushed me and when I put him under restraint, the bitch jumped me and I reacted. The other one, she just got in the way."

"That meskin pushed you because you grabbed his wife. By the tits, as I recall." Blakenship wasn't smiling. "And since when is pistol-whipping called under restraint."

"Tits, eh? Pistol-whipping. And you were surprised? That's why you kicked a second time?" Mikeska's eyes pinned the deputy in the chair. "That the way you learned to do it in the MPs?"

"You had to have been there."

"I was." Blakenship leaned toward the deputy. "That Mexican woman you kicked had a miscarriage. Look at me, boy. A miscarriage. Some folks call that police brutality." He leaned back. "And there's some might call it murder."

"We were on a raid, for crissakes," Donaldson appealed to Mikeska. "We were helping the DEA. Nobody said anything at the time. Not even him." Pointing at Blakenship. "How come it's such a big deal now? Just beaneaters anyway." The last under his breath.

"Because now there's been a miscarriage. Because up to now, I didn't know you kicked two women, one of them being Mrs. Jake Grummond. And because I didn't know that no goddamn report has been filed. Elvira. Where the hell is Parker?"

"Coming up the front steps."

"Keep him coming until he gets all the way into my office."

65

Handkerchief in hand, Buck Parker entered the room, blew his nose and looked for an empty chair. There was none. Mikeska kept him standing. "You really have the flu?"

"What the hell else it could be. Feel like I been rode hard and put up wet."

"Now, Buck, I'm sure sorry I had to jerk you out of your sick bed, but we've got a little problem here. Seems like we can't find the report on the raid down in Sapinero County. You know the one I'm talking about, don't you? You were on it, weren't you?"

"Of course I was. Think that's where I caught whatever the hell it is I got."

"The report, Buck. The report."

"Been working on it at home. Slow going with this shit. Can't focus."

"Can't focus? I'll show you can't focus. What is today? Monday? And the raid was last Tuesday?"

"Wednesday morning."

"I don't care if it was this morning. Get a report on my desk in ten minutes or turn in your badge and spend the rest of your life in bed and by God it won't be a very long life after I get done with you." Mikeska turned to Donaldson as Parker shuffled out the door. "Billy, as for you ..."

"Billy," Blakenship interrupted, "did you search any of the houses?"

"No sir. I was helping guard everyone in front of the main house." He looked at Blakenship reproachfully. "You know that. You was there."

"Did anyone from Otero County search the houses?"

"I don't know. Maybe."

"Think. Try to remember what you talked about on the way home. Or after."

"Mostly we were just doing a job. Andrews was pissed because we didn't find any drugs, but he figured that at least some of those wetbacks would get deported."

"Andrews?"

"That'd be Kenny Andrews. Been on the force five or six years. A good enough officer, although he can get carried away from time to time."

"Let's see." Blakenship enumerated on his fingers. "You and Andrews and Parker. Who else?"

"Parker's report will tell us, C. W." Mikeska studied the deputy who was doing his best not to squirm. "Billy, I don't know what I'm going to do with you. But I'm sore disappointed that you'd kick a woman. Any woman. What would your daddy have thought? Or your mother. For now, turn in the vehicle you've been driving, put your gun away and tell Elvira I said for you to help Cindy with the filing."

"But Sheriff …"

"Get the fuck out of here before I kick you myself."

"And Billy." Blakenship's tone jerked him up short. "They may be beaneaters. But when they're in Sapinero County, they're my beaneaters. Don't you forget that."

On his way out, a sullen Donaldson bumped into Parker, left hand mopping his nose with the handkerchief and right carrying a sheet of paper half-filled with single-spaced typing. He laid the paper on the desk, coughed into the handkerchief and sat down gratefully in the chair Donaldson had vacated.

Mikeska read the report while Parker snuffled softly and Blakenship chewed on the end of an unlit cigar, periodically spitting bits of tobacco in the general direction of the olive drab wastebasket beside the desk.

"Here." Mikeska handed Blakenship the report.

Blakenship scanned it. "Well, at least it says when and where but it's lacking a whole lot of what — as in what happened."

"You know what happened. You was there — which is more than I can say. And it does say who, who from Otero County was there."

"So it does. But let's get back to the what happened part. See, there was a lot that went on that I didn't see. Not until a couple of days after the fact. Mean-ass destruction in some of those houses and trailers. Food spilled — sticky shit like honey and molasses and sugar. Pillows and cushions knifed open. Holes punched in the walls. No call for it. I'd like to know who did it. And better still, who instigated it."

"Why?"

"Because it ain't my style. And I never thought it was yours, either. And also because Jake's really pissed off and he's gone to see Blair about it. He's talking to Mackey Fitzgerald, too."

"He just mad about the wetbacks' trailers?"

"He's mad about the whole fucking mess. Tell you the truth, I can't say as I blame him. Did I happen to mention his father's had a heart attack?"

"Didn't know you and Jake're so close."

"You know better'n that. But it happened in my county. I don't like people coming in and fucking up in my county. Specially not pissy little feds. Your people were there and I want to question them."

"Unless I've been completely misinformed, there was a whole bunch of your people there, too. You questioned them?"

"Planning to start this afternoon."

"Here's the way I see it, C. W. You go back down the mountain and tend to your own people. I'll talk to mine. And I'll get back to you."

"When?"

"When I've got something to say. I've got a department to run and so do you. Besides, you haven't exactly been busting your hump so far."

"I expect things'll start heating up directly."

"Maybe. You work your territory and I'll work mine." Mikeska stood. Time was up. "I will work mine. I don't like the way this deal is starting to smell."

***

Blakenship cocked his chair so he could see the clock on the side wall in the main room. Hands straight up and down at six o'clock. He sighed.

68

"You're late." Henderson grinned at him across the desk.

They'd questioned five of their deputies who'd been on the raid, three of whom had been in on the searches.

Henderson leaned back, hands behind his head. "So far it looks like two of them DEA assholes got our boys going. Of course, Dobbins and Hooper didn't seem to need a whole lot of inciting."

"Dobbin's just a punk kid. Never did feel right taking him on. But Hooper's been around for a while. Think he'd know better."

"Now you do."

"Do what?"

"Know better. About Hooper."

"Question is, what're we going to do?"

"You're the sheriff. There's disciplinary action. There's desk assignments. There's …"

"I don't mean that. I'll tend to our boys by and by. I mean what're we going to do about the DEA?"

"What can we do?"

"We could complain."

"That's shake 'em up."

"We could tell Jake. Or Blair."

"We could. And maybe we should. But was I you, C. W., I'd wait till we finished talking with our folks. And see what Rudy has to say. Visit with the folks in the other counties. Then I'd take a long, hard look at the lay of the land before I got in a pissing contest with federal law enforcement."

"There's also what folks in the county think."

"Election's a ways off. Besides, ain't been much rumbling that I've heard."

"Feds ain't none too popular in the best of circumstances. No matter what folks think of Jake personally, when push comes to shove, he's one of ours."

"What're you going to do if Jake asks?"

"Don't know." He cocked his chair to look at the clock again. While he watched, the big hand clicked over to nine minutes after. "Don't know. But I do know it's time for a drink."

69

Jake watched Mary Margaret prepare supper, trying to gauge her mental state by how she moved between counter, refrigerator and stove. She'd spent an inordinate amount of time napping after Saturday's early morning lovemaking.

She chopped an onion with the smooth precision of long practice and he judged she was all right. He was in the middle of running a mental balance sheet, trying to contain his anger at the mounting costs and the memory of his people being manhandled in his own yard, when Mary Margaret set a plate of pork chops, peas and mashed potatoes in front of him and announced, "Della and Luis are leaving."

Her voice was so light and matter of fact that the words didn't register at first.

"Say what?"

"Salt?" She held up the shaker and Jake shook his head. "I said, Della and Luis are leaving."

Jake watched her butter both halves of a roll still hot from the oven, bite with evident relish into one half and lick the drip of melted butter that had run across her palm to her wrist. "Honey, are you O. K.?"

"You haven't taken a bite. Aren't you hungry? Della told me she wanted to get Luis out of the country before he killed that deputy. I can make you something else if you don't feel like pork chops. But you like pork chops. You always like pork chops."

"They're fine." Jake forced himself to eat. "I'm just upset about Della and Luis. Why didn't he tell me? I saw him three or four times today."

"Maybe he doesn't know yet."

"What do you mean, doesn't know?"

"Maybe Della hasn't told him."

"So there's a chance they won't leave?"

"Oh, they'll leave. And they won't be the last."

"Mary Margaret, what are you driving at?"

"Homes were destroyed. Others will leave." She stood abruptly. "Tired. Going to bed. Clean up in the morning." She shuffled crabwise toward the door, sneakers squeaking on the linoleum, and disappeared into the living room before Jake could reach her. He was at the door when she slipped on the throw rug in front of the Parsons table.

"Silly me." She smiled up at Jake.

"Here, sweetheart." Jake bent down and she put her arms around his neck as he picked her up. He laid her gently on the bed and undressed her while she smiled at the ceiling and lifted her bottom as he pulled jeans and panties off. She sat up as he removed her blouse, raised her arms when he reached behind to unfasten her bra and then, completely naked, rolled onto her stomach and burrowed her head into the pillow.

A blue and yellow splotch spread from the upper swell of her left buttock to the small of her back.

Goddamn. Wife gets kicked and you don't even notice the bruise until five days later. Goddamn.

He shook out a patchwork quilt Mary Margaret's aunt had made for their wedding night and covered her.

He sat at the kitchen table and tried to chew the cold pork chop but the fear that she was going to be like she was after Paul sickened him and he went to the porch for some air.

The sun was hanging above the Sublette Plateau, glowing through purple clouds that thickened over the Presidentials. Good chance of rain in the mountains. Jake watched the sun, fascinated as always by how quickly it dropped out of sight once it reached the horizon. He was about to go inside when two figures emerged from the barn and walked toward him.

Eusebio's soft voice carried across the yard. "A moment, *con permiso.* "

"Sure. Beer?"

"But of course."

When Jake returned with a six-pack, Eusebio and Luis were leaning against the porch railing. He handed each a beer and took one for himself. "So?"

"Luis wishes a word."

71

Uncomfortable, Luis looked at Eusebio, then at Jake, then at the ground, then back at Jake. "Della and I, we will be leaving."

"Why?"

"Della. The baby." He looked Jake in the eye. "We cannot have a family in a place where such things happen."

Leaning against the porch post, Jake closed his eyes and held the cold beer to his left temple. And saw that night, the bright lights and milling people, heard Luis yell and Della scream. Saw Mary Margaret run and the leg swing back. Then he was on top of the pudgy-faced deputy, smelling his sour fear and staring into the non-comprehending eyes that looked back not at him but at his pointing finger.

"Nothing like that has ever happened here before. But I can't say I blame you." He opened his eyes and looked at the two men standing in the gathering dark. "I wish you wouldn't, but I don't blame you."

They sipped their beer without speaking. The laughing shrieks of children wafted in the soft night air. Finally Jake asked the question that had to be asked. "How soon you figure on going?"

"At the end of the week. On Saturday."

"I'll have your money ready. You've been a good hand, Luis. I'll miss you."

"Thank you. We will miss it here, I think. But the baby ..."

"The baby. And that goddamn deputy."

Luis walked off into the night but Eusebio stayed and pulled another beer from its plastic ring. "*Con permiso.* "

"Mary Margaret's starting to act like she did after ..."

"Perhaps it will pass."

"She told me Della and Luis were going to leave. Della told her."

"Women talk."

"She said they won't be the last." Eusebio sipped his beer without expression. "What do you think?"

"It is possible."

A scream of stark terror followed by a thump and then a half-muffled sobbing shocked Jake into a sprint for the bedroom.

Mary Margaret lay crying softly on the floor in a crumpled U as though she'd tried to curl into a fetal position but didn't have the energy to make it all the way. The sobs stopped when she felt Jake's hand on her forehead and she opened her eyes, blinking in confusion at Jake's worried face. "I must have had a bad dream."

Jake helped her onto the bed. "Want something to drink? Water? Tea?"

"Tea would be nice. Iced — no, hot. Hot tea. Here, I'll make it."

She started to get out of bed but Jake held her in place. "Take it easy."

Beer in hand, Eusebio stood by the kitchen door and watched Jake put the kettle on and rummage through the cabinets. Jake found a tray on one of the shelves under the counter on which he arranged cup and saucer and sugar bowl. The bag of ginger snaps on top of the refrigerator caught his eye. He put half a dozen on a small dinner plate and added it to the tray.

The whistling kettle sent spurts of water across the stove because he'd filled it too full. Jake picked up the kettle with one hand, turned off the burner with the other, and, almost in the same motion, filled the cup and began dipping the tea bag. When the color suited him, he put the bag in the sink and carried the tray to the bedroom.

He was back in a minute, still carrying the tray. "She's asleep." He put the tray down carefully on the counter next to the stove. "She always liked these cups and saucers. Said the roses made her think of an English garden. Why an English garden? We've got roses right out front." Jake picked up a ginger snap and looked at it like he'd never seen one before. The cookie broke and Jake looked at the pieces in surprise.

"Good night." Eusebio put his empty beer can on the table and left Jake staring at the crumbs in his hand.

6

AUGUST 29 — Morning

Jake squinted against the sun as he left the bank and crossed the street to the shady side of the courthouse square, the envelope with Luis's final pay protruding above the flap of his shirt pocket.

He sat on the bench and closed his eyes. Mary Margaret with Dr. Ben and twenty minutes before time to see Mackey Fitz — nothing to do but listen to the street sounds of people running errands so they could begin Labor Day weekend by noon tomorrow.

It had been three days since Mary Margaret's collapse. Couldn't call it anything else. For two days he'd tried to believe her moments of clarity meant she was all right, but as each became shorter, he knew she was disappearing again.

Yesterday afternoon he'd found her sitting on the kitchen floor, stark naked, back against the refrigerator door, tongue tip against her upper lip in concentration as she methodically cut newspaper pages into four inch squares. A stack of old papers was by her side and judging by the squares piled like drifting snow from the floor up and across her thighs, she'd been at it for hours.

He'd called the doctor straight away. When he returned to the kitchen, he found Mary Margaret asleep, head pillowed on the stack of papers and the scissors closed and laid carefully against the baseboard. She didn't murmur when he picked her up. The bruise, showing more yellow than purple when he laid her on the bed, brought an angry surge that he contained barely in time to keep from punching the wall above the brass headboard.

A convulsion of remembered rage jerked his head from the back of the bench and yanked him to his feet. The honk of a horn brought him back to where he was and he looked around to see if anyone had seen.

***

Blakenship had seen.

About to leave the office, a question from the deputy at the front desk had stopped him and he'd watched Jake through the lettering on the door's window.

"Going to come apart like a two-dollar watch if he don't watch out." Unnoticed, Henderson had come up behind him. "He'll be by one of these days. Know what you'll tell him?"

"The truth."

"The whole truth and nothing but?"

"Don't know. But whatever I do tell him will be true."

"Maybe if you volunteered some information he'd think more kindly toward you."

"About suing me?"

"Among other things."

"I'll study on it, Charlie." Blakenship pushed through the door and watched Jake climb the steps to the white frame house on the corner that had served Mackey Fitzgerald as an office for more than forty years.

***

"Well." Fitzgerald looked at his legal pad, white this time, on which notes were written in black ink with an elegant hand. "There's a lot to suing the government. Under the doctrine of sovereign immunity, you can't sue the United States unless the United States consents to it. The Federal Tort Claims Act permits suits against the government in certain defined situations." He favored Jake with a wry smile. "As near as I can tell, your case qualifies. Subsection 2680 (h) specifically allows claims when '*they arise from acts or omissions by federal law enforcement officers.*'"

"Thought we knew that."

"Suing the feds is complicated. First, you've got to file a claim for damages with the agency in question. If the claim is denied or the agency doesn't answer within six months, you can bring suit. In any event, you have to act within two years of the incident."

"No problem."

"Now, when you sue, you can't go after more than the original claim filed with the agency. No punitive damages, in other words." Fitzgerald waited while Jake filled a mug and returned to his chair. "It won't be a jury trial. Just a federal judge."

"No jury? Just a judge deciding whether his buddies owe me money?"

"I wouldn't put it quite that way. But yes, a federal judge ruling for or against a federal agency."

"Sonofabitch."

"There's two big hurdles we got to jump. One is whether federal law enforcement officers did the damage."

"The deputies get off the hook?"

"Not necessarily. There's a case cited," Fitzgerald held up a law book, "where a deputy sheriff and a city police officer who," he underlined the passage with an index finger, *"were authorized in writing by the Assistant U. S. Attorney to arrest the plaintiff on drug charges were officers of the United States within the meaning of this subsection, making the United States liable for any claim."* He closed the book. "The 'U. S. Attorney' and the 'authorized in writing' parts have me a little nervous."

"We've got to prove that whoever did it were federal officers when they did it?"

"That's one hurdle."

"What's the other?"

"It's called discretionary function." Fitzgerald opened the law book to another page marked by a yellow tab. *"The United States has a duty to maintain law and order and to enforce the commands of the courts, and just how best to fulfill this duty is wholly within the discretion of its officers, and thus is a discretionary function in regard to which there is no waiver of sovereign immunity."* He looked at Jake. "There is no waiver of sovereign immunity," he repeated.

"So?"

76

"If they were using their judgment as experienced law enforcement officers as to how best to perform their duty, you've got a problem."

"No matter what, they just can't destroy property."

"You'd be surprised what they can do under discretionary function. There's a case," Fitzgerald pointed at the law book, "where the claims of innocent folks in a duplex next to a suspected drug dealer's were disallowed because of discretionary function."

"Innocent people?"

"Innocent people."

"All they did was happen to live in the same building as a drug dealer?"

"As a suspected drug dealer."

"Jesus. What happened to innocent until proven guilty?"

"Welcome to where the rubber meets the road in our criminal justice system. Discretionary function. Which gets us to the question of why they raided you in the first place."

"No idea."

"What's Blakenship say?"

"Says he doesn't know, either."

"A five-term sheriff raiding a solid citizen in his jurisdiction and he doesn't know why? Unusual. Anyway, it's something we need to get a handle on."

Jake took a sip of his coffee and frowned at the taste. "How long's this whole deal going to take?"

"A long time. And remember, the award, if you prevail, will only be for actual and compensatory damages. You can probably document damage to property that happened during the raid. And physical harm to individuals that happened during the raid might — I say, might — be recompensed."

"Della Montoya got kicked and had a miscarriage. And Mary Margaret. She's disappearing again, like when Paul ..." Jake took a deep breath.

"I'm sorry. I didn't know. With the EMTs' testimony perhaps ... But Mary Margaret's prior condition ..."

"Prior condition, bullshit."

"Don't blame the way you feel. But I'm just laying things out as I see them. That's my job. And your biggest monetary loss is lost production and lost livestock. Proving a rock-solid connection with the raid to anyone but another dairyman is going to be tough as hell." Fitzgerald stirred his coffee with the eraser end of a pencil. "It'll take five, maybe ten years before you'll know whether you've won."

"Five or ten years. Goddamn, Fitz. I'm bleeding now."

"Suing the government takes time. They've got it and you don't. That's one of their big cards."

"Land of the brave and home of the fucking free."

Fitzgerald let Jake pace the room. On the third lap he said, "There's another approach. It's called a Bivens action. The time factor may not change. But there are some differences. It's based on a 1971 Supreme Court decision. Case of a narcotic officer violating the defendant's Fourth Amendment rights. That's the one about unreasonable searches, which could well apply in your case."

"Make it quick. I got to pick up Mary Margaret."

"First, you're going after individuals. Second, the remedies include actual, compensatory and punitive damages. And you can have a jury trial."

"That's better. Ain't it?"

"Sometimes, yes. Sometimes, no. With drugs and Mexican nationals involved, it's hard to say. But in order to get something from a defendant, first you have to win and second, the defendant has to have something. And, like I said, it can take a long time."

"You ain't painting a very hopeful picture."

"There's always a chance the DEA will pay up. Particularly if you've got Blair and the senators actively on your side. But it's a long shot. And if you do sue, we're going to have to have another lawyer to help me. Someone who knows his way around federal law. And who's younger than me so there'll be a chance he won't die before it's over." Fitzgerald leaned back, sympathy creasing his face. "He won't be cheap." He sighed from somewhere deep within him. "Sometimes I wonder why I ever got into this business."

"Bastards ain't going to get away with it."

"That mean you want me to go ahead?"

"Means they ain't going to get away with it. As for going ahead — let me talk with Blair. And see what Cecil comes up with. If he ever gets his thumb out of his ass."

***

Dr. Ben was waiting for him. "She's resting." Jake followed the patrician head into the cozy disorder of the office. "I've made arrangements to check her into Crossley Memorial. But you expected that." The doctor carefully clipped the end off a thin, greenish cigar, lit it with a wooden match, and checked the end to see if it was glowing evenly. "You know better than I do how she reacted to the trauma of Paul's ..." He stopped at Jake's flinch. "I'm no psychiatrist, but it looks worse this time."

"Worse? How?"

'She didn't make sense this morning. Not once. Maybe ... Hell, I don't know. Maybe she makes sense and I'm the one who doesn't get it." Dr. Ben turned to the window. "Anyway, she needs people who know what they're doing."

"When's she supposed to be there?"

"You can take her tomorrow. Or wait till the long weekend's over. Up to you. Whenever you go, be ready to spend the day."

"She can come home now?"

"Yes. But have somebody in the house with her at all times. By the way, where'd she get the bruise?"

"The raid. She was kicked by ... Thought I told you."

"She ever been hurt like that before?" The look on Jake's face made him add, "Not by you. Didn't mean that."

"Said after it happened that she'd tried to jump a bar ditch on her bicycle. Didn't make it and that hurt worse. She was nine."

"Maybe it's the miscarriage. Although hers was years ago." The doctor scratched his head with the thumb of the hand that held the cigar. "Maybe … I don't know. Like I said, I'm not a headshrinker. Let's see if she's ready to go home. You going up tomorrow or Tuesday?"

"Tuesday."

"What I figured."

"How's my father?"

"Eating solid food."

Mary Margaret was still asleep, curled in the half-fetal position Jake had come to know too well.

"Think I'll look in on Dad."

***

An hour later, he was on his way to the dairy, Mary Margaret placid at his side.

Seeing his father had left him disconcerted. Nothing he could put his finger on, but twice he'd caught himself looking at the figure in the bed to make sure it really was his father. Just one tube going to the arm and none in the nose. As alert as he'd been since the attack. They'd chatted about milk production and what Vinson had charged for the tractor part and Jake hadn't had to repeat anything.

But the fire wasn't there. Like he was resigned to whatever lay in store.

Eusebio was standing by the swing set in his yard watching two toddlers on the seesaw and talking with Felix Arambula of the field crew when Jake pulled in. Before Jake was halfway to the house with Mary Margaret, the two were by his side. Felix opened the door and waited in the kitchen while Eusebio followed the couple to the bedroom, returning almost immediately to fill a glass with iced tea from the pitcher in the refrigerator.

Mary Margaret smiled as she accepted the glass and took a deep swallow. She drank again, turned to set the glass on the night table but missed by a good three inches. She smiled again at the sound of the glass shattering on the floor, rolled to her side and went to sleep.

Eusebio got a broom and dustpan and began to sweep up the shards of glass and chunks of melting ice cubes. Jake got a mop and bucket from the bathroom and followed where Eusebio had swept.

"That'll do for now." Jake led the way to the kitchen where Felix sat impassively rolling a cigarette. Three others lay on the table in front of him and when the two men came into the room he gave the one he was rolling a final lick, scooped up the others and stored them in a sun-faded Lucky Strike package.

"It is like before?" Eusebio arched his eyebrows in a question.

"Goes to the hospital on Tuesday. Until then, she can't be left alone. I know we got a holiday coming up and I know school started this week and I know some of the older children have things to do and I know everybody's working overtime because we're short-handed, but do you think there's anyone who can lend me a hand when I've got to be out of the house ..." Jake stopped abruptly and filled a glass at the sink.

Eusebio broke the silence. "Some will be able to help. I am sure."

"Thank you." He swallowed some water. "Tell Luis I've got his money. He can pick it up whenever."

"Sunday is the first of the month."

"What? Goddamn. Shit for brains. I'll have the pay on time."

After they left, Jake looked in on his wife. She hadn't moved, as near as he could tell. He retreated to the cool silence of the living room and stretched out on the sofa, the first time he could remember having lain down in the afternoon since grade school.

A lawsuit would take a long time and the only thing he could count on was it would be expensive. Blakenship. What was he up to? Need to prod that sonofabitch. And Blair. What's his aide found out?

81

The phone rang while he was trying to decide who to call first.

"Jake?" It was Stewart.

"Just about to call you. Your guy find anything?"

"Ronnie's learned a few things. Perhaps we could meet to discuss them."

"Things have kind of gone to hell down here. Mary Margaret can't be left alone and I've got to take her to the hospital on Tuesday. I'm losing another hand Saturday and I've got a bunch of things to tend to this weekend."

"It does sound as though you've got a lot on your plate. I was planning to spend part of the weekend at Hazel Lake. Have to be at a picnic in Elwood on Labor Day. Perhaps I could stop by on the way up the mountain."

"Hate for you to go out of the way."

"You're in the district. How's Saturday? Say late morning?"

"I'll be here. Unless another wheel comes off."

"Fine. Saturday it is. Say hello to your father for me." The line went dead before Jake could answer. Three steps toward the sofa and he stopped and went back to the phone.

"Sheriff's office."

"Like to speak to Blakenship."

"The Sheriff's not in. Can anyone else be of assistance?"

"Tell him Jake Grummond called."

Succumbing to the beckoning comfort of the sofa, Jake lay on his back with his arms folded across his chest and tried to organize what needed to be done over the weekend, but he couldn't concentrate.

A thump from the bedroom startled him and he looked at his watch. Three o'clock. He must have dropped off. Getting up was a struggle — like climbing a sand dune — and he puzzled at his weakness.

Mary Margaret was lying diagonally across the bed sound asleep. Her knees were pulled tight to her chest but her ankles were at the edge of the mattress. She must have kicked the wall when she moved. Jake stood by the bed for minutes trying to decide whether he should move her, then gently made room and lay down. As he floated toward darkness, he thought he felt her press against his side.

**

Blakenship had spent the better part of his afternoon with the Collin County sheriff who kept asking why Blakenship cared about what'd happened to a bunch of goddamn wetbacks who were taking jobs away from Americans and corrupting our children with drugs.

Much to his surprise, Blakenship had found himself in a heated defense of Jake Grummond, how he treated everyone who worked for him the same — white, Indian or Mexican — and there weren't many locals anymore who were willing to put up with the grinding hours of dairy farming.

Neither his eloquence about Jake nor his indignant description of the wanton destruction had been persuasive, but when he mentioned Jake had contacted both senators and had already met with Congressman Stewart, he was able to get a copy of the report and a list of the Collin County deputies who had participated.

The modest success had made the drive home almost enjoyable.

The sight of Jake's name on the top message slip of the stack on his desk reminded him how little he really knew and washed away what good feeling he'd had about the day. "Charlie." At the top of his voice. "Charlie." Blakenship stormed out of his office. "Where the fuck is Henderson?"

The deputy at the desk had just come on shift and he snatched up the clipboard with the duty roster. "He went off-duty at 4:30."

"Fuck." Blakenship stomped back into his office then stuck his head out the door. "Get me Henderson at home." He returned to his desk and opened the manila folder he'd brought back from Collin County. The usual bureaucratic prose that obscured more than it told. Nothing new. Except the names of five deputies.

"No answer at home, Sheriff."

"Keep trying. See if you can raise him on the radio." It was quarter past five. Time for a CC and a beer. Fifteen minutes and he was going to the Stockman and Jake Grummond be damned.

What had Mackey Fitz told him? Blakenship had heard of the Torts Claims Act, but he didn't know much about it. Besides, that was federal and he was local. Wouldn't apply to him. Would it? Goddamn feds. Why'd they have to stir things up in his county?

"Henderson on line one, Sheriff."

"Charlie?"

"What's got your tit in the wringer?"

"Had a message from Grummond when I got in."

"So?"

"What'll I tell him?"

"Just like you said this morning. Tell him what you know. As much of it as you want to, anyway."

"That's it?"

"You're a big boy, C. W. Why're you upset?"

"Damned if I know. I spent an hour telling Martin, that Collin County asshole, what an outstanding citizen Jake is. Time I got done I sounded like I was nominating him for Chamber of Commerce man of the year."

"Jake's all right. Look, C. W., see him in the morning. Give him a howdy-do and a progress report. And while you're on about it, maybe you can get an idea of what he's up to with Mackey Fitz and our esteemed congressman. And, C. W."

"What?"

"Go easy. Word is Mary Margaret's going up to Crossley Memorial on Tuesday."

Blakenship had long ago stopped wondering how Henderson got his information. Just accepted the fact he was right nine times out of ten. "Thanks, Charlie. Have a good evening."

84

***

The regulars were at the bar when Blakenship walked into the Stockman and it took him a moment to realize something was different. Eight strangers were whooping it up amidst a welter of beer bottles and half-eaten meals at the big table in back.

As Blakenship made his way to his regular booth, Bucky Chambers, looking like he wanted to be anywhere in the world than where he was, came out of the men's room and started to sit down at the only empty chair at the table. He saw Blakenship and walked to meet him. "Sorry about this, C. W."

"Bow hunters?"

Bucky nodded. "From Chicago. Near as I can figure, they started drinking as soon as they got out of sight of their wives. Every swinging dick was knee-walking drunk when I picked them up. Figured I'd try to get some grease in them before I took them out to my place."

"Christ's sake, Bucky. Ain't that new place of yours made of adobe? They'd do a lot less damage there than here. And why didn't you go to McDonald's or something? Why bring them here where they sell booze along with the grease?"

"I see that now. I'm just trying to ease them toward the door. Shit, how much longer can they last?"

"I don't envy you the next week." Blakenship sat down, accepted the shot and beer Jessie handed him and closed his eyes as he rested the back of his head against the smoke-darkened pine of the divider above the seat back's padding. Feeling a presence, he opened his eyes reluctantly. Chambers hadn't moved. "You better get back to your outdoorsmen."

As Bucky shuffled to his chair, Jessie arrived at the table with a new round and began distributing beers and mixed drinks. When she stretched across the table, the man to her immediate left rubbed her behind in a lingering caress and then encircled her hip with his right arm. Jessie bent down to whisper in his ear. The arm dropped.

85

"What was that all about?" Blakenship's voice sounded whiny to his ears.

"A little touchy aren't we? I told him I'm part Ute and if he did that again I'd cut off his balls and make a tobacco pouch out of the sack — if it was big enough."

"Watch yourself."

"This isn't my first night in a bar." She started to leave and then leaned over and kissed him. "But thanks. You're sweet."

Blakenship caught Bucky's eye and made a cutting sign across his throat. Bucky nodded, signaled for the tab and began trying to get the group's attention by rapping on the table with an empty bottle. He'd made enough progress to start explaining that they still had a long drive ahead and an early start in the morning when Jessie arrived with the check. As she leaned across the table to hand it to Bucky, the same drunk reached out and slid his hand between her legs to the crotch.

Her full arm slap had barely registered when she backhanded the other side of his face and then picked up a beer bottle in the same motion.

"Bitch."

Jessie took a step back — one step, no more — as the drunk struggled out of his chair. Blakenship slid out of his booth.

"Watch it, Joey," one of the others warned, "you've got Wyatt Earp behind you."

The drunk turned to see the barrel of Blakenship's .357 Magnum level with his eyes. "I didn't mean anything. Just having fun."

"Bucky, why don't you take your guests out to your nice, new place and tuck them in. They've had a long day. And they're not used to the altitude."

"That's just what we're fixing to do." Bucky stood and the rest of the group followed in ragged order.

"And Bucky. Don't forget to leave a tip. A big tip."

The group filed out with Blakenship in the rear and milled around next to the van with Chambers' Outfitters stenciled on the side. One of the hunters, a man in his late forties with the drawn cheeks of a dedicated jogger and an air of authority, approached Blakenship. "Sheriff. It is Sheriff, isn't it? I'd like to apologize. I know this is no excuse, but we've all been working hard and looking forward to this trip for a long time."

"I understand. But there comes a time when you've got to pack it up and save it for another day. And for you, that time has come."

"Think you're tough, don't you?" The voice came from Blakenship's right.

"Shut up, Joey."

Joey broke away from the friends trying to restrain him. "Take away the gun and I could wipe the street with you."

"That's why I've got the gun, son. Now go on over by the van and take it easy."

"You want to see tough, you should come to Chicago."

"I don't want to see tough. That's why I live here."

"Give it a rest, Joey" The two who'd tried to restrain him grabbed his arms.

"Get away from me." Joey shook them off. "I'm explaining the facts of life to Hopalong Cassidy."

Quick as a striking snake, Blakenship's left hand closed on Joey's throat, lifted him six inches off the ground and pressed him against the side of the van. "Somebody open the door."

The man who'd apologized fumbled with the handle.

"Son, you've got two choices. You can get in the van like a good boy and go on the hunting trip you've looked forward to for so long. Or, you can give me one more smartass remark and visit the Sapinero County Jail. And, since the judge won't be around until Tuesday, you'll get to know all of us — what was that you called me? Hopalong Cassidy. You'll get to know all us Hopalong Cassidys real good. And we all carry guns."
Blakenship set the man down, spun him around and pushed him through the door. "Bucky. Get the fuck out of here."

***

87

The burning of parched throat and mouth couldn't be ignored any longer. Blakenship swung his legs over the edge of the bed before he opened his eyes. Momentarily disoriented by an unfamiliar alarm clock on an unfamiliar dresser, he looked around the room lit by a three-quarter moon. The mound that was Jessie's hip and the dark hair spread in an irregular pool on the pillow told him where he was.

He moved to the sink in short uncertain steps and drank straight from the faucet, forcing himself to swallow ten more times after he felt full so he wouldn't have to get up again.

2:20.

How long had he slept? Had they made love? He tried to remember, but the pulse in his temples got in the way.

Jesus. How much had he had?

He'd watched Bucky pull away from the curb. He'd had a shot and a beer. Adrenaline had left his stomach too jumpy for food. He remembered that.

Must have stayed until Jessie off work. Nine? Ten? Eleven?

Who'd driven?

He hoped to hell it was Jessie.

7

AUGUST 31 — Morning

The Montoyas left at eight. Jake had shaken Luis's hand, kissed Della chastely on the cheek and retreated to the barn to hide the tears threatening to spill down his cheeks. He was still trying to sort out his emotions when Blakenship arrived.

"Girl in the house said you'd be here." Jake waited. "Got some information if you've got the time."

"Inside. Don't like to leave Mary Margaret for too long."

"Heard about that. I'm sorry."

Maria Elena, Eusebio's youngest at seventeen, was at the kitchen table, schools books spread before her. Seeing the sheriff, she began to gather her things.

"You can work at my desk if you want. Or you can head home. I shouldn't have to be out of the house until evening milking."

"I'll go home. But call if you need me."

"You don't have anything planned?"

"There's a dance this evening, but I'll be home until after supper."

Jake watched the black-haired almost-woman, arms full of books, turn to push open the screen door with her rear. She was wearing a Hard Rock Cafe T-shirt and he shook his head while he poured coffee. "Lived here all her life. Now she's wearing a shirt from a place she's never been. Milk?" Blakenship nodded and Jake handed him a mug then added milk and molasses to his. "Good volleyball player. Better student. She'll get a scholarship to college just like her brothers and sisters. And that means she'll be leaving here in a year."

"Can't stop time, Jake."

Jake finished stirring his coffee. "What've you got?"

"Not a whole lot. But I figure I'd bring you up to date."

"Considerate of you."

"First off, these are some of the deputies on the raid." He slid a typewritten sheet across the table. "Otero and Collin County. And Sapinero."

Jake let Blakenship fiddle with his coffee while he read, mouthing each name as he went. He put the paper down carefully when he finished. "Which ones did the damage?"

"I can't tell you. Not until I know for a fact. Maybe not even then."

"Then why'd you bring me the names?"

"Just trying to keep you informed."

"What else you going to do?"

"Charlie and me, when we know what happened, we'll figure out what we're going to do. Mikeska up in Elwood's doing the same."

"You going to tell me what you find out?"

"Most likely." Blakenship peeled the cellophane from one of his crooked cigars and looked around. Jake gestured toward the top of the refrigerator where three plastic ashtrays, each a different primary color, were stacked next to an assortment of empty jars. "You mind telling me what you're going to do?"

"Tend to Mary Margaret and my father. And the dairy."

"Besides that."

"Ever hear of the Federal Tort Claims Act? Or a Bivens action? Mackey Fitz says they're ways to sue lawmen who fucked up. We're looking into it."

"Them's federal. You just going after the DEA?"

"Like I said, we're looking into it."

"What about Stewart?"

"He's looking into it."

"Connors or Rheimer?"

"Ain't heard from them yet. But I bet they look into it, too."

Blakenship couldn't think of anything else to say. He swallowed the last of his coffee and carried the mug to the sink, telling Jake again how sorry he was about Mary Margaret.

"Let me show you something." Jake led the sheriff to the bedroom where Mary Margaret lay covered with a sheet. She was on her side watching the birds at the feeder by the window and she smiled blankly at the two men, then returned her

90

attention to the two blue jays at opposite ends of the wooden tray.

Jake lifted the sheet and pointed at the still livid bruise on her lower back. "Get my hands on that fat piece of shit ..."

The sheriff left him holding Mary Margaret's hand.

***

It took Blakenship until he'd reached the stop sign to realize it had been Blair Stewart in the passenger seat of the blue station wagon he'd passed half a mile back. He debated turning around, but Helen's was across the way. Shot and a beer first.

Frog Bottom Potts was at the table next to the bowling machine talking with four men Blakenship didn't know. Johnny Davis was leaning against the bowling machine like he'd just been introduced and couldn't tell whether he was expected to join them or not. Blakenship took a stool at the bar, one remove from two cowboys arguing about Monday night's season opener between the Broncos and the Raiders.

Helen set a shot glass in front of him, held up the bottle of Canadian Club and began pouring at his nod. "Twice in the same month. What's the Stockman going to think?"

"Don't want to neglect anybody. And a Bud."

"Been to Jake's, have you?"

"What make's you say that?"

"Figures, that's all."

"You don't really think there's dope going through Jake's, do you?" Frog Bottom's hoarse voice rasped in his ear. "Helen, give me one more, then I've really got to go." He put an empty beer bottle on the counter and turned his attention back to Blakenship. "If you do, you're crazier than a shithouse mouse."

"That was the DEA's play. Never did put too much stock in drugs myself."

"Then why'd you go?"

"Kind of hard to say no to them folks."

"Maybe it's time we get a sheriff who can." This from Davis who'd moved from the bowling machine to stand behind Blakenship.

The sheriff regarded his former opponent's reflection in the mirror. So it's started. "Free country. Vote for who you want. Run for office if you want, for that matter. But you're going to be hard pressed to find anyone with law enforcement experience," he came down heavy on experience, "who'll say no to the feds. Make a habit of that and you won't get help when you need it. Could even find yourself under investigation."

"You worried about an investigation, Blakenship?"

"No, Johnny. But I don't see any reason to have feds poking around Sapinero County any more then we have to."

"Something's wrong when the government can fuck up an innocent man's business just cause they got a wild hair up their ass." Frog Bottom waved his beer bottle in a huge, scarred hand. "Just ain't right."

"Not going to argue with you. Question is, where'd they get the idea there was dope at the dairy?"

"What do you mean?" The speaker was one of the four men from Frog Bottom's table who'd moved to stand between Davis and the sawmill operator.

"The DEA didn't just open the phone book, close their eyes and pick the dairy blind. You can't get a search warrant like that. You got to have probable cause. Where'd they get the idea there was probable cause to raid the dairy?"

"You tell us, sheriff." Davis gave the same emphasis to sheriff that Blakenship had given to experience.

"All I know is they had a search warrant."

The ensuing silence made it clear Blakenship had become the focal point of the entire room. One of the cowboys broke it. "What's it take to be probable cause?"

"Something suspicious. Like a lot of traffic in and out that didn't look to be related to agriculture, for instance. Or some of Jake's people spending more money than he was paying them."

"Shit. Grummond pays all them meskins more than they're worth."

92

"Shut up, Frank." Frog Bottom pointed his beer bottle at the man in his late twenties who'd come in during the discussion. "He pays them for doing the job, same as he'd pay any man."

"Ain't right that he pays them the same as an American. And don't have no white men working."

"Andy Dawes going to be real surprised to learn he isn't white."

"He been there so long, he probably ain't any more."

"Listen, you worthless puke." Blakenship leaned back just enough to plant his shoulder in Frog Bottom's chest, stopping the big man's forward movement. "You had your chance ten years ago, as I recall." Making an effort to be calm. "And you quit."

"I don't take orders from no meskin."

"Seventeen years old and new on the job and you quit cause a man who'd been working there for years and knew more about dairying then you'll ever know told you what to do? That makes sense."

"He was a meskin."

"Fact that it was hard work have anything to do with it?

"I can work."

"How do you know? You ain't ever done much that I heard of."

"There ain't many jobs around here cause of them meskins."

"I had a job at the mill last June. Didn't see you applying."

"You know I can't handle sawdust on account of my allergies."

"Seems you got a lot of allergies whenever it comes to working regular."

"If you really want to work for Jake," Blakenship interrupted, "now's your chance. He had four hands deported after the raid and another left this morning. Then again, Eusebio's still lead man."

"Mexican or not, dairy farming is hard work any way you look at it." The speaker was the man Blakenship didn't know.

"Cows have to be milked every day, Fourth of July and Christmas included."

"Well, kiss my ass. I never thought of that." It was one of the cowboys.

"Course you didn't. You work beef cattle, same as me, and we get lots of days off."

"Don't believe I know you." Blakenship extended his and to the stranger. "I'm C. W. Blakenship. The sheriff, although maybe you figured that out."

"Porterfield. Reg Porterfield."

"Mr. Porterfield and his friends been talking about lumber," Frog Bottom volunteered.

"Building?" Blakenship asked. "Whereabouts?"

"We're looking at the Sheffield place. Trying to get an idea of construction costs and what not. See the whole picture before we make out move."

"Not going into the dairy business?"

Porterfield smiled with the sincerity of a TV pitchman. "Hardly. One summer at my uncle's when I was eleven cured me. We're all close to retirement — George there, one with his back to us, already is. Our plan is to buy some land together and help each other build."

"A compound. Like the Kennedys'?"

"You could say that, although we're no fans of the Kennedys."

"Where you folks from?'

"California. Southern California."

"Should have guessed. How'd you pick Sapinero County?"

"The Colonel …"

"Reg." The voice came from the table. Blakenship couldn't get a clear view but he caught the impression of a straight back and intent eyes.

"Right. Sorry, …" Porterfield swallowed the last word that sounded to Blakenship like it was going to be sir and went back to the table without apology or good-bye.

Frog Bottom drained his bottle and followed Porterfield. "Got to get back to the house by noon," he said over his shoulder, "or my life won't be worth living for a month."

**

Jake was still holding Mary Margaret's hand when the blue station wagon began kicking up dust on the driveway.

"You remember Ronnie." Stewart indicated Eastman with a wave. "I was trying to recollect when I was last here."

"Four years, maybe more. Come in. I'm by myself with Mary Margaret and I don't want to be out of earshot."

"Is there any chance we could look at the damaged dwellings?'

"Let me raise Eusebio." Jake disappeared inside and returned a few moments later. "He'll be right over. Something to drink? Coffee? Iced tea? Beer?"

"I could use a cup of coffee."

"I'll put on a fresh pot. Be ready by the time Eusebio gets done showing you around. What about you?" he asked Eastman.

"I wouldn't say no to a beer."

The aroma of fresh brewed coffee filled the kitchen when Eusebio brought Stewart and Eastman back to the house. "These may be a bit stale," Jake gestured at a plate of cookies on the table. "Mary Margaret hasn't been up to baking of late. How do you take your coffee?"

"Black. You weren't exaggerating about the damage. What's Blakenship have to say?"

"He's not bragging. Matter of fact, he was here this morning."

"Saw his Bronco."

"I got to give Cecil credit for being unhappy about it. Can't say as he's setting any records looking into it, but he did bring out a list of some of the deputies who were along that night."

"That's something. Ronnie, why don't you lay out what you've learned so far."

95

Eastman opened a manila folder and laid two loose sheets of paper on the table, smoothing them unnecessarily with both hands. He took a sip of beer and wiped his mouth on his shirtsleeve. "On August 19, James A. Buchanan applied to U.S. District Judge Bryce Sheets for a warrant to search the Grummond Dairy of Sapinero County — including all vehicles, buildings and other structures located thereon. Buchanan based his request on excerpts from the sworn affidavits of two unnamed informants."

"Unnamed informants? Two anonymous lying bastards started it?' Jake got to his feet, voice rising.

"Jake." Blair's voice, soft but firm. "This will go a lot faster if you let Ronnie finish."

"Sorry. Whole deal's been like fighting ghosts." Jake sat down, then slammed his fist on the table hard enough to make the beer can and Stewart's saucer jump. The congressman had the cup in his hand or coffee would have spilled.

"I know it's frustrating, but bear with us." Stewart's voice carried a quiet authority earned through years of shepherding bills through the labyrinths of congressional committees.

"Buchanan solicited assistance from area law enforcement and flew by government plane with agents Kiernan, Eaton and Curtis to Union where they were met by four other agents."

"Seven DEA?"

"Eight, counting Buchanan. Eight DEA, some thirty deputies from neighboring counties, plus your own Sheriff Blakenship."

"And you got their names?"

"Of the agents, yes. I have information about them, too, and I'll get more. That is, if you want me to." It wasn't clear if the you meant Jake or Stewart.

"We'll see." Stewart smiled at Jake. "When it comes to contacts in federal agencies and knowing how to use them, there aren't many better than Ronnie."

"If you feel that way, we ought to renegotiate."

"Don't push it."

Eastman moved to the second sheet. "No drugs were found, but many of the residents of the dairy were Mexican nationals who could not produce satisfactory documentation. They were detained at facilities in Mountain View and the INS notified." Eastman returned the sheets to the folder. "That was taken direct from Buchanan's report."

"No mention of the damage?"

"Wouldn't expect there to be."

"Then no mention of Della or my wife." Jake refilled Stewart's cup, returned the pot to the warmer, got another beer for Eastman without asking and pushed the can halfway across the table. "Now what?"

"That depends on what you're going to do."

"Meaning?"

"Meaning if you're going to file a tort claim suit, first you have to file for damages."

"That's what Mackey Fitz said."

"If you file, I'll write a letter to the director expressing my deep concern about your situation and urging him to attend to your claim with the utmost care and dispatch. The letter has to be written without any hint that I'm telling him what the decision must be — without any hint of threat, in other words. But I can most certainly call his attention to the matter."

"Will that do any good?"

"It depends. But the fact that the letter comes from a member of the Appropriations Committee and the chairman of the subcommittee which oversees the Department of Justice of which the DEA is a part won't hurt."

"Anything else?"

"If you decide to pursue a Bivens action, Ronnie can be assistance in providing more information about specific agents who were on the raid."

"I've got some already." Eastman riffled the sheaf of papers in the folder. "Here's some of what I've got on Buchanan." He leafed through a packet of what looked like five or six sheets stapled in one corner. "James Albert Buchanan. Born November 25, 1947. High school in Trenton, New Jersey.

Two years at Montclair State with a declared major in Criminal Justice. Father laid off early in 1967. Mother died in June of the same year. Didn't return to school but enlisted in the Army. Tried to get into Special Forces but was rejected. Volunteered for Vietnam and served two tours. Mainly in Saigon, but did get his CIB."

"CIB?"

"Combat Infantryman's Badge."

"No need to read it all, Ronnie. You're going to leave the folder." Stewart looked at his watch. "It's an hour and a half to the Hazel Lake Inn, isn't it?" He stood and extended a hand. "We're going to keep working. And let us know what you decide to do." Jake walked them to the station wagon. "This is all a damn shame," Stewart said as he opened the car door. "I hope things take a turn for the better."

***

A quick look in the bedroom showed Mary Margaret sleeping peacefully. Hungry, Jake dumped a can of tuna fish into a bowl. Chopping an onion or grating a carrot seemed like too much work. He dolloped mayonnaise, sprinkled black pepper, and stirred with a fork. He reached for the bread knife, but cutting a loaf seemed like too much work, too.

Eastman's folder lay open and he began to look through it as he ate from the bowl. The loose sheets didn't hold his attention, but he froze at the picture of Buchanan on the front of the first stapled packet. It had been xeroxed, but the narrow, thin-lipped face and the shocking streak of hair brought the bright lights and children crying in the darkness beyond back in a rush. Della going down and Mary Margaret after her. Buchanan spitting contempt from that slit of a mouth.

Pain followed by a clatter and then the diminishing reverberations of something spinning to a stop opened his eyes and he looked stupidly at blood on the table. The tines of the fork had bent in a U and all four had punctured the skin on the

98

side of his hand. Tuna fish spread across the table and a look behind him showed the stainless steel bowl on the floor.

He must have stabbed out with the fork, hit the bowl somehow, and bent the fork on the Formica top of the table. Cursing softly, he washed his hand at the sink and moistened a sponge to clean the table.

Jake was swabbing the punctures in the meaty edge of his hand with hydrogen peroxide when Blakenship's voice sounded from the other side of the screen door. "OK if I come in?" The squeak of hinges said the sheriff didn't feel an answer was necessary.

Jake closed the folder and carried it to his desk in the other room. "Remember something you forgot to tell me earlier?" he asked as he came back to the kitchen.

"Thought you might have something to tell me, now Blair is gone."

"Not really."

"You mean our congressman spent over an hour of Labor Day weekend with you and you didn't talk about anything?"

"Not what I said."

"True enough. You didn't talk about anything you want to tell me about. Jacob, Jacob. I thought we had an understanding."

"You made it clear you don't feel you got to tell me all you know. And I made it clear we're looking into it."

"Put something away when I came in."

"So?"

"Could be some things have already been looked into."

Jake pulled his Copenhagen tin out and spun it on the table. "Tell you this. Blair said he'd write a letter to the head of the DEA if I decide to file a claim."

"If that's it, that's it." Blakenship heaved himself to his feet.

"One thing, before you go."

"Yeah?"

"What do you know about the search warrant?"

"Just that they had one."

99

"According to Blair's aide, two unnamed informants said drugs were here."

"Unnamed?"

"He'll keep digging. But I wondered if you know."

"No. I don't. Warrant wasn't issued here."

"Know the judge? Sheets. Bryce Sheets. Can you find out who the lying cocksuckers were?"

"Thought the aide fella was going to."

"You might be faster."

"I might be."

"Meaning?"

"Meaning we'll see." Blakenship moved toward the screen door. "See you later. Shame about Mary Margaret."

Jake retrieved the folder from the desk and sat without opening it, listening without focus to the warm quiet of the afternoon broken by the occasional plinks of flies bumping against the window screens and the faint shrieks of children running through the sprinkler on the patch of grass behind Eusebio's house.

With a deep breath of resolve, he opened the folder and quickly turned Buchanan's papers face down. A photo of the big agent was in the upper right hand corner of the next packet. Jake remembered him. Gentle and courteous. Kiernan, Buchanan had called him. He read the name at the top of the page. William Thomas Aquinas Kiernan.

Aquinas? What the hell kind of name was that?

Jake read on. Thirty-three. Michigan State, football scholarship. Accounting and history double major. Academic All American. Alcohol, Tobacco and Firearms immediately after graduation. Moved to the DEA two years later.

The squeal of metal on metal drew him to the door. Billy Stanton was getting out of an eight-year-old pickup with rust starting to show in several fender dents.

"Better get them brakes fixed."

"All I'm lacking is the time." Billy opened the passenger door and accepted the cardboard carton his wife held carefully on her lap.

"Don't you dare tip it," she warned him. "The pie's still hot and the juice will run all over." She smiled at Jake. "Didn't know how you were fixed for food. Hope you don't mind."

"I never mind your fried chicken, Evie. It is fried chicken?"

"Potato salad, too. And a peach pie." Evie Stanton scooched around on the cracked vinyl of the pickup's bench seat and slid to the ground, the skirt of her dress bunching to her ample hips, giving evidence she enjoyed her cooking as much as anyone. A flash of white panties and she stood for a moment, without embarrassment or hurry, to straighten her clothing.

"Iced tea's already made up," Jake told her as she neared the porch. "I think I've got some frozen lemonade. And beer." This last to Billy.

"You wouldn't happen to have any gin to put in the lemonade?"

"Just might."

Evie sat at the table while Jake rummaged in a cabinet at the far end of the counter, emerging triumphant with a half-full bottle of Gordons. "Put the pie on the stove top to cool," she told her husband, "and the chicken and potato salad in the refrigerator."

"Bottom shelf, Billy," Jake directed, "next to the beer. Get one for me while you're at it. How much?" Jake held up the gin bottle and the glass in Evie's direction.

"Oh, about a finger, finger and a half." Evie tasted the drink and smiled her approval, then turned serious. "How's Mary Margaret? Like last time?"

"Worse."

"Can I see her?"

"She's in the bedroom."

Taking her drink, she disappeared toward the back of the house.

"Not meaning to bring up unpleasant subjects, but how's your father?" Billy asked.

"O. K. Considering." Jake took a gurgling pull from the beer can and set it carefully on the table in front of him. "But, I don't know. He seems old."

"He's been out of the egg a long time."

"He never seemed old before. Now, it's like he don't give a shit."

They drank in silence, the unstrained silence of old friends who didn't need the reassurance of conversation. Eusebio's footsteps on the porch coincided with the emptying of beer cans. Jake handed him the stack of pay envelopes. Billy announced it was time they headed home. He followed Jake to the bedroom where Evie sat on the edge of the bed holding Mary Margaret's hand.

She looked up at the sound of the footsteps. "She was awake when I came in and we talked a bit, then she said she was tired." One by one, she unclasped Mary Margaret's fingers and laid her hand gently on the bed. She reached for Billy's hand to help her up and held on until she reached the truck.

"We'll drop by tomorrow," Billy said as he turned the ignition key. "Holler if you need for us to get anything."

***

A mile down the road, Evie started sobbing so hard Billy pulled over. "Hold me. Please hold me." She buried her face in the rough denim of his work shirt. "It was awful. Awful."

"Thought you said you had a nice conversation."

"That's what's so awful. We talked for maybe five minutes just like we always do. And then it was like she wasn't there. Poor Mary Margaret. Poor Jake."

Billy looked across the top of his wife's head to the Sublette Plateau, hazy in the August heat across the valley. "They say the Lord won't pile on more troubles than a body can bear. I sure hope He didn't miscalculate in Jake's case."

He'd meant it as a joke, but it rang hollow in his ears and he felt tears start to well up in his own eyes.

8

OCTOBER 13 — Late Afternoon

The weekend had linked two magical Indian summer days. On the pretext of scouting for elk so he could fulfill his promise to Brian Barnes, Jake had gotten away from the dairy at Saturday noon to spend an overnight on his mountain land. He'd done a lot more looking at aspens flaunting the remnants of their fall brilliance than he had hunting for elk sign.

But the weather had changed. There was heavy cloud cover over the Presidentials when he cleared Long Mesa and dropped to where the four lanes of Rt. 71 ran for thirty miles with barely a curve to Mountain View. Looked like it was snowing heavy in the high country so he wasn't surprised by the occasional snowflakes that spattered the windshield. Nothing to worry about, though.

The same couldn't be said for Mary Margaret. Two hours of talking to her, of holding her hand, hadn't produced a flicker of recognition. She'd gained weight, getting a belly she'd never had, and fat beginning to gather under her chin. But she was clean and well groomed, although he didn't know if that was her doing or the nurse's. And she was polite — short sentences with "pleases" and "thank yous" in the right places most of the time.

But there was no connection. No sense that he'd fathered her son and shared her grief and eaten her cooking and lain next to her almost every night for more than twenty-two years.

How many nights? Jake tried to do the math in his head but the whoosh and sideways wind pressure from an eighteen-wheeler roaring north broke his concentration.

Trucks scared Mary Margaret now. Maybe since Paul's accident. He couldn't be sure. You could see the Interstate from her room on the third floor of the hospital and for the last half-hour of his visit, while he waited for the doctor, he'd watched her while she watched the traffic. "There's a red one," she'd said once. "That's two since lunch." Red what? He couldn't tell and she didn't answer when he'd asked. When a big rig passed, she'd hide her face in her hands. He was sure of that.

When Dr. Allsup finally arrived, he'd asked him, but he didn't have an explanation and Jake got the feeling it was the first he'd heard of it.

Allsup didn't have much to say about anything. "These cases are difficult. It's been less than two months. We have to be patient."

"You mean she's not any better than the day I brought her in?"

The psychiatrist, a small, birdlike man with incongruously large hands that looked like they belonged on a basketball player or stone mason, stared at a spot on the wall slightly above Jake's left shoulder. "The mind is very complex. We gather evidence as we can and try to make sense of it. Then we help the patient cure herself. It takes time."

***

Lights started to dot the gathering dusk for miles on either side of the highway. Almost to Top Hat, he slowed for the upcoming left-turn lane.

Brakes screeched, followed by angry honking. Jake looked into his rear-view mirror to see a dark green sports car swerve violently to pass him on the right. Dark green and no headlights. No wonder he hadn't seen it.

Out of the corner of his eye he saw the driver yelling and giving him the finger.

Jake pressed the accelerator to the floor in furious reflex, flipping his lights to high beam at the same time. His rifle, a Remington 30.06, was in the gun rack above the seat behind him and, with the speedometer climbing past seventy, he reached back with his right hand to swing it down, butt in his lap, barrel pointing toward the door on the right side.

He was alongside the sports car, working the pump. The driver, in his twenties, turned from animated conversation with his passenger, a blonde of similar age, to see the rifle barrel pressed against the window glass of Jake's passenger-side door.

A heartbeat of open-mouthed disbelief and the sports car accelerated. Another heartbeat and taillights lit up, twinkling into the night toward Mountain View.

Jake pulled over to the shoulder. Appalled though he was at what he'd done, the anger kept returning. Asshole hadn't had his lights on. It was a settled area and the prick was driving too fast. Way too fast. And goddammit, he lived here. He'd made the turn a million times. Who was that stranger, who the fuck was he to act like he owned the road?

Jake took a fresh pinch of Copenhagen and rolled down the window to spit out the first rush of tobacco juice. The night air held a hint of moisture from the snow showers. He breathed deeply then turned to the rifle, pushing the release to eject the round in the chamber.

Would he have pulled the trigger?

Working with mechanical care, he ejected the clip, reloaded the cartridge, reinserted the clip and put the rifle back in the rack. Then he spit out the window again and put the truck in gear.

From the end of the driveway, the lights from the houses and barn gave the dairy a cheery look. Even though many were empty now the sounds of children playing mingled with the smells of suppers cooking adding to the relief of being back where he belonged.

Unease returned when he entered the chill darkness of the house. He went directly to the thermostat, flicked the little lever from off to auto and waited until the furnace kicked in. The light on his answering machine blinked for one message. Get it later. Mailed stacked on the kitchen table caught his eye as he headed to the barn. Eusebio or one of his family must have brought it in. He could see insurance company and hospital return addresses. They could wait, too. But before he went out, he put yesterday's stew in the oven to warm.

***

On the second time around the square, the sports car pulled into a space next to a departmental Bronco. The man and woman got out and walked to the only lights that were on in the courthouse.

Blakenship was in his office arguing halfheartedly with Henderson and wishing he were at the Stockman. The flash of blonde hair caught his eye and he watched with growing interest as the couple's conversation with the deputy on desk duty became progressively more heated. "Tried to kill us ... Gun big as ... "

"What do you suppose that's all about?"

"You could lift your ass out of the chair and find out."

Bouncing their story between them like tennis players in a long rally, the couple didn't notice Blakenship until his voice sounded from directly behind the deputy. "What's the problem, Luther?"

"Damn, C. W. You gave me a start." The deputy turned sideways to the desk so he could keep the sheriff and the couple in sight at the same time. "These folks were driving south on 71 and they claim they were threatened."

"Claim, hell. Bastard pointed a fucking gun at me."

"At us."

"Didn't pull the trigger, I take it." Blakenship moved even with the deputy.

"Don't know. I saw the gun and I floored it. Driving a Nissan Twin Turbo 300 ZX," he added as if that explained everything.

"Where did it happen?"

"Ten or fifteen miles up the road."

"The alleged assailant was on foot?"

"No. Of course not. He was in a truck. A pickup. White or light-colored."

"Get the license number?"

"Are you kidding?"

"How many in the pickup?" Blakenship tried not to stare at the woman's nipples lifting the cashmere of the sweater that clung like fawn-colored skin to breasts too firm to be believed.

106

"Just the driver."

"So the driver pointed the gun at you?"

"That's what I've been telling you for the last fifteen minutes."

"What happened before?"

"Nothing. We were just driving."

"Did you pass him?"

"Yeah. He drifted into our lane without signaling and I had to swerve around him."

Swerve to the left or the right?"

"Right."

"You must have been moving right along. Now this was about five-thirty, quarter to six?" The driver nodded. "Have your lights on?"

"I don't remember."

"Don't remember. I see. Anything else?"

"No."

"Let's see if I've got it straight. You passed him on the right after he moved into your lane and the next thing you know is you're looking at the business end of a gun. Pistol or rifle?"

"What?"

"Was the gun a pistol or a rifle?"

"Rifle."

"Were you near a town or anything? Like a left-turn lane?"

"I don't remember."

"How fast were you going?

"I don't remember."

"Fifty-five? Sixty?"

"I don't remember."

"Didn't shoot him the finger or anything did you?"

Neither answered.

"O. K. Luther, get down everything they can remember." Blakenship headed to his office to get his coat. "Come on, Charlie. I'll buy you one."

The pair huddled around Luther looked a lot less enthusiastic when the sheriff and senior deputy went by on their way out. "Uh, and folks," Blakenship said as he opened the front door, "don't get your hopes up. This is pickup country and it's hunting season."

Once settled in his regular booth and with drinks on the way, Blakenship fixed Henderson with a quizzical look. "White pickup with a rifle in a rack making the turn away from Top Hat?"

"Maybe. Since only a couple of transients got made a little nervous, I don't see we should waste any energy on it."

"You're probably right. Still …"

**

He'd set the oven too high and the stew was starting to stick to the bottom of the pot. Jake forced himself to eat, chewing each mouthful like it was a job that had to be done. It was with relief that he left his meal to answer the phone.

"You're back." He'd gotten accustomed to the reedy quality of his father's voice when they talked face to face but it still startled him over the phone. "How is she?"

"Looks healthy enough, but she never recognized me. Not once."

"Like she's got that old-timer's disease?"

"Alzheimer's. Yeah. Maria Elena there?" For the three weeks since his release from the hospital, she'd been cooking breakfast and supper and staying overnight in the cabin, bringing him to the main house on her way to school.

"Yep."

"What'd you have for supper?"

"She's cooking. Smells like pork chops."

"Little late, ain't it? You hungry?"

"I'm working on it. Don't worry. I'll eat. Maria's putting my plate on the table."

"Put her on." Jake could hear the scraping of a chair being slid on the floor followed by a loud, unintelligible outburst.

"Mr. Jake?"

"What's that all about?"

108

"He's mad because I started to cut his pork chops for him."

"At least he's getting mad. That's a good sign. Everything else all right? Warm enough?"

"Yes. The stove works very well."

"I'll be in the rest of the evening so call here first if anything happens." He left what might happen purposefully vague.

After hanging up, he eyed the green light of the answering machine with distaste. It blinked slowly and steadily, the pulse of an electronic conscience that knew it had all the time needed to do its job. He punched the button and felt an unexpected anxiety as the tape rewound.

"Mr. Grummond, it's four-thirty your time. Monday afternoon." His heart rate subsided as Eastman's eastern staccato bounced against the shadows in the living room. "I've got more information. Please call in the morning — say by nine — that's seven your time." With a click, he was gone.

Jake sat in the pool of light cast below the green ceramic shade of the brass desk lamp Mary Margaret had bought when the Top Hat bank had gone out of business six years before and wondered what information Ronnie had and why he wouldn't say it to the machine. He wrote a reminder to call and scotch-taped it to the coffee maker where he'd be sure to see it in the morning.

***

An hour later, Jake stood at the bathroom sink examining the scraped knuckles on his right hand. Blood seeped over and around powdery traces of gray gypsum. He winced as water hit the scrapes and tried to reconstruct what had happened.

He'd been dreaming. That was it. Dreaming about Mary Margaret and the funny little doctor who wouldn't look him in the eye. The smug kids in the sports car. And that Otero deputy. Shifty-eyed bastard. Mean, trashy piece of worthless gutless shit … he caught himself before he tore the basin from the wall. Like

109

all the law — he showed it on the surface, that was the only difference.

He washed his face with cold water, dried it then dabbed at his hand with the towel before pouring hydrogen peroxide.

After examining the hole in the sheetrock above the bed — one more thing to fix — he lay down and stared at the dark. He shut his eyes against the face of the deputy, big pores and black stubble above his hand on his throat.

Only one thing to do. Putting on pants, boots and a flannel shirt over the T-shirt he slept in, he turned on the outside floodlights and went to the woodpile.

The eight-pound maul felt solid and lethal. He set a spruce log on the chopping block, assessed the grain, stepped back and swung. The satisfaction of shock in his back and shoulders overrode the pain in his hand. He worked the maul loose and swung again. The halves fell on either side of the chopping block. He picked one up, centered it on the block and swung again, unnecessarily hard, sending both halves spinning to the edge of the light.

Half an hour later, stripped to his sweat-soaked T-shirt and breathing in regular, heavy gasps, he stopped and measured his handiwork. Stack it? A fluff of wind gave a cold caress to his back and neck, touching off a violent shiver. He peered up at the starless sky then turned on his heel for the house.

***

Blakenship also stared at the starless sky.

He was lying in the bed his father had framed out of rough-cut lumber more than fifty years before, that and a World II-era Zippo the only material legacy he'd received from either parent. Careful not to wake Jessie snuggled on his left shoulder, he eased his backside to a more comfortable position.

It had been a good night. Being Monday, business at the Stockman had tapered early to a hard-core handful and the manager had let Jessie leave at nine. She had had two back-arching orgasms before he'd exploded into her writhing wetness.

Full of male conceit, he relaxed into the warm press of Jessie's breasts against him.

But he couldn't sleep.

It had been Jake. Knew it in his bones.

Jake hadn't done anything. Well, under the law he had. But not really.

Should he drift by the dairy for a talk? Nothing direct. Just see how things were. Answer any questions Jake asked — any he could answer. And somewhere along the way mention the couple. See how Jake reacted.

And then what? Wasn't like he was going to arrest him.

His arm and shoulder were starting to go numb from the weight of Jessie's head and he eased her off as gently as he could. She resisted for a moment then rolled completely over to her other side and snuggled her butt into him.

What should he do? What could he do?

He rolled to his side, nestled his flaccid member against her and tried to will himself to sleep.

***

Grandpa Grummond was at the kitchen table in a rocking chair Maria Elena must have moved from the living room, sipping from a mug. "Don't worry. It's that decaff shit," he said to Jake's raised eyebrow.

"Sleep OK?" Jake asked over his shoulder on the way to the desk.

"Good enough. What's your hurry?"

"Got to call the guy who works for Blair. Supposed to call at seven and it's quarter past." He punched in the numbers and sat down in the leather chair.

"Eastman."

"Grummond."

"Oh. Hi, Jake. You got my message."

"Seems like."

"Something's come up so I can only give you a minute. Main thing is I've got the names of the informants." Jake's stomach tightened and he could feel anger flush across his face. "What? I'm on the phone. Tell him later. Not you, Jake. Some asshole's on the other line. Tell him one minute. Oh fuck. Jake, I'm sorry. I really am. But a deal we had is starting to unravel. I'll call as soon as I can. I promise. You going to be there?"

"Probably. I …" Jake looked at the dead receiver in his hand for a long minute before hanging up.

In the kitchen, his father looked up from swirling the dregs of his decaffeinated coffee. "What was that about?"

"Says he has the names of the bastards who lied to the DEA."

"And?"

"Had to tend to some political shit before he could tell me. Said he'll call back."

"Which will be when?"

"Hard to say. Acted like it'd be today."

His father studied the muddy remains in his mug. "What you going to do when you find out?"

"Depends on who they are."

"And where."

Jake let that one go. "Want another cup?"

Grandpa Grummond grimaced and scooted the mug across the table. "Naw. All it'll do is make me piss. Any signs of pneumonia?"

"Say what?" With his mind still on the abbreviated phone call, the question took him by surprise.

"Pneumonia. It's October. We had snow yesterday." October with its fluctuating temperatures is when primary pneumonia struck the cattle most often. Antibiotics would knock it out if you caught it in time, but every sick cow was production lost.

"No."

"How many hands we down?"

"The four from the raid …"

"None of them came back?"

112

"Just to get their belongings. Then Luis. That's five. And the Arroyos headed off a week or ten days ago. What's that? Six?"

"Six. How many from the milking crew?"

"Three."

"Eusebio and them are probably getting crisp around the edges. You thinking about hiring some new help?"

"If I can find some who know what they're doing."

"What about the Mexican grapevine?"

"Haven't had anybody stopping by."

"You're going to have to hire some hands. Maybe put them on tractors and move the tractor jocks to the barn. But you got to give Eusebio's boys some help or you're going to lose them, too."

Jake took a final swallow of the lukewarm coffee and molasses, savoring the sweetness that Mary Margaret couldn't drink because it made her sick to her stomach. "Eastman calls while I'm in the barn, set up a shout. Don't want to miss him this time."

There was still a chill in the outer room of the barn with its beat-up wooden desk where the records were kept, a chill intensified by the underlay of moisture in the air left over from the snow flurries.

"This the last of the healthy ones?" he asked Renaldo.

"Eight more. Then we start on the sick pen."

"Where's Eusebio?"

"He takes Mercedes to the doctor."

"Call me when it's time to change the pipe." Jake went back to the desk and scanned the feeding charts. Between silage, haylage, oatlage, grain and cottonseed, the herd ate 50,000 pounds a day. Twenty-five tons. A semi load.

When things were right, a semi load of milk went out every other day. Things hadn't been right for six weeks. Maybe he'd better cull the ones that weren't recovering their production. He just hadn't had time.

Hadn't had time. What else hadn't he had time to do? He couldn't remember when he'd last put in a normal day. Shit. He

113

couldn't even remember the last time he'd looked at the bank statements. Felt like he'd been working his ass off, but the realization hit that he was letting the business get away from him.

"*Senor* Jake. The sick pen is ready."

Jake walked to the tank room where Renaldo was detaching the joint on the pipe that ran from the milking machines to the tank and replacing it with a section that dropped straight down to empty into a bucket. Other buckets were nearby.

When the last sick cow was milked, he watched the two men clean and disinfect the pipes and milking machines and reconnect the joint to the tank ready for the afternoon. He started to help them carry the buckets to the calf pens then decided he shouldn't be away from his father any longer. Or the phone.

***

Jake was at his desk trying to make sense of two months worth of bank statements, bills and receipts when he heard Eusebio's pickup make the turn from the county road. A quick look in the spare bedroom showed his father asleep on his back in virtually the same position he'd taken when Jake had helped him from the rocking chair and half-carried him to the bed.

Eusebio's knock and the sound of the back door opening came five minutes later.

"What's wrong with Mercedes?"

"The leg. The blood of the leg."

"She has a blood infection?"

"Not an infection. The trouble is with, you know, the big blue bumps …"

"The veins? She has varicose veins?"

Eusebio nodded. "The doctor gave her special stockings. If they do not work he may have to remove the vein."

"I'm sorry. I know …" He brushed his hand across his eyes. "Anyway. The cows, the ones with hot mastitis — how many?"

114

"There are twenty more."

"About what I thought. Have to cull them. Tomorrow, probably. Anyone around who can watch my father?"

"Maybe Felix's wife."

"If she'd sit here while I drive them, be a big help. Also, if you could get Renaldo to hitch up the goose-neck trailer and help him load — make sure he gets the right ones — that'd be a big help, too."

"Of course."

"Another thing. I don't have to tell you we're short-handed." Eusebio nodded and waited for Jake to go on. "And I don't have to tell you we haven't had anybody come by looking for work. Can you put the word out? For good men. Otherwise, I'm going to have to hunt up some Anglos — and that hasn't worked out too good in the past."

"I can try." Eusebio turned to go.

"One more thing. Any signs of pneumonia?"

"Not yet. But it is the season."

The phone rang as Eusebio was going out the door. "Eastman here, Jake. Sorry about earlier. Anyway, I've got the names — Victor Sanchez and Julio Sanchez. I think they're brothers. Ever heard of them?"

"No."

"Live in Denver, but their father lives in Union. Runs a used-car lot. Seems they'll do anything as long as it's illegal — nickel and dime stuff. One of the things they do is deal dope — marijuana mostly, but harder stuff, too — which is how they came to the attention of the DEA."

"How'd the dairy get into it?"

"When the DEA has somebody by the balls, they usually offer them a deal — leniency if they give up more people. The Sanchez brothers make regular trips to Union, supposedly delivering and picking up cars for their father. But they have a habit of spending more time in Union than they'd have to just to transport used cars. One thing led to another and they got caught with a load — not sure of what."

115

"Still don't see how the dairy figures in."

"According to the statements, the drugs come up from Mexico to the dairy, then they're distributed on both sides of the mountains."

"They say they actually come here and pick them up?"

"I don't know. Understand, I haven't seen the affidavits. This is information a friend of mine at the DEA told me."

"It don't make sense to me."

"I'll keep digging. The congressman wanted me to ask how things are going. How's your father?"

"Dad's doing better. Out of the hospital, at least. Mary Margaret's not doing so good — been in the hospital since the Tuesday after Labor Day."

"I'll pass the word."

"Tell Blair that I thank him. And I thank you, too." He realized he was talking to a dead line.

9

OCTOBER 14 — Afternoon

Blakenship turned off Rt. 71 right behind Jake's pickup pulling an empty stock trailer. An empty trailer meant he'd sold more culls. He wasn't going to be in the best of moods. Turn around? Shit, he'd come this far.

Jake was swinging in a wide arc to pull up next to the calf pen when Blakenship drove in. He parked and walked over with the intent of helping unhitch but Jake was back in the pickup by the time he got there. He gave Blakenship a curt nod as he drove by and was waiting on the porch holding two beers by the time he caught up. "I got maybe an hour before milking." He handed one to the sheriff and took a perch on the railing, back to the afternoon sun.

"Won't take an hour." The sheriff popped the top and watched a hint of white bubbles peek through the opening. When he was sure it would foam no more, he took a sip and lifted his gaze to Jake. "Just wondering how you're doing."

"Doing? In what way? The dairy, you mean? Or you wondering how I'm doing in suing your ass."

"Take it easy. Too nice an afternoon to get your blood up. Especially after yesterday."

"That time of year."

"Speaking of yesterday, funny thing happened. Had a couple, a young couple, transients, file a complaint about someone who pointed a rifle at them. Happened near the turn-off to Top Hat." Blakenship propped the right side of his butt on the railing and leaned against the post. "Hear anything about it? Maybe at Helen's? Was a sports car with Arizona plates."

Blakenship watch a ripple cross Jake's jaw. "Between culls and the hospital, I don't get to Helen's much." Jake swung his left leg over the railing so he could face the sheriff. "Got a question for you. Ever hear of Victor Sanchez? Or his brother, Julio? Father runs a used-car lot in Union."

"Why?"

"They're the bastards who set the DEA on me."

"How'd you find that out?"

"Got my ways." Jake swung his other leg over the rail and watched the afternoon crew move cattle into the barn. "Don't suppose it make's any difference. Blair's aide. Says a friend who works for the DEA told him."

"Probably true, then. I'll run a few traps, see what turns up. As a favor. If you'll tell me why you want to know."

"May learn something Mackey Fitz can use. But goddammit, C.W., I've been fucked, double fucked, but good. I got a right to know who done it. This is America, isn't it? At least I got a right to know."

"I reckon you do." Blakenship put his empty beer can on the railing. "Try to get some rest."

***

"Ain't what you'd call a shocking surprise to find Victor or Julio involved, one way or another." Henderson's voice sounded scratchier than usual over the radio. "Question is, why'd they drop the dime on Jake?"

"Maybe they thought they could claim a tip-off — like that Buchanan asshole did. Maybe drugs are really going through the dairy unbeknownst to Jake. Or maybe somebody's got it in for him and was using them."

"Maybe. Kind of far-fetched, though. It's not like Victor and Julio just fell off the turnip truck. They may not be the brightest lights on the porch, but they been around enough not to get themselves in any deeper — if they can help it. More to the immediate point, what're you going to tell Jake?"

"I'll think of something."

***

The morning frost that had glazed the porch steps when Jake made his way to the barn was gone by the time he returned to the house. He wasn't looking forward to the paperwork he had

118

to catch up on and toyed with the idea of trying to find new help first. No. Two hours at the desk before he did anything else.

He lacked fifteen minutes of his self-imposed minimum when the sound of engine and tires from the direction of his driveway pulled him from the bills, bank statements and adding machine tape strewn across the desk in an organizational system only he could fathom.

A dark green GMC crew cab pickup was halfway between the cattle guard and the house. Johnny Davis. Hadn't seen him twice since the primary — what? Eighteen months ago?

The truck stopped in front of the porch and discharged Davis — slim, mid-fifties, with sandy hair going to gray, although if you hadn't known him for a while it would be hard to tell. Two strangers, one in front, the other in the back seat, disembarked and waited at a polite distance while Davis greeted Jake who was standing at the top of the steps.

"Been too long, Jake."

"You knew where to find me." Realizing how harsh that sounded, he made a conscious effort to soften his tone. "Been busy of late."

"I know. I know. Fucking shame. How's production?"

"Coming back. But it's slow. And the mastitis …"

"I know. Motherfuckers got no idea of what it takes to put food on their tables." Davis turned halfway to the two by the right front fender of his truck. "Got some new neighbors I thought ought to meet you."

The first, a fleshy man of Jake's height and about the same age as Davis — maybe older — advanced, hand outstretched. "Porterfield's the name, sir. Reg Porterfield. And my associate, George Thompson." Thompson, who was leaning against the fender, nodded without moving what looked to be 250 pounds, a lot of it in a belly that hid his belt buckle.

"They're down the road from me," Davis explained. "The Sheffield place."

"That's good land."
"They're not farmers. Just going to retire in a place with clean air and no gangs."

119

"That's right," Porterfield interjected. "There's six of us all told, plus our wives."

"Going to subdivide?"

"No. Oh, we'll build separate houses and all, but we have no intention of breaking up the acreage."

"Shame to take that land out of production."

"We'll do something with it. Raise our own vegetables. Maybe some pigs or steers for our own consumption. Have a few milk cows, chickens. That kind of thing."

"Going for self-sufficiency, are you?"

"Not a bad idea, the way the country's going, don't you think?

"Build houses, you still got to deal with the county."

"Mr. Davis has kindly volunteered to help us in our dealings with the planning commission."

"Wish we didn't have to deal with those assholes at all. Sonsabitches sit there, puffed up like toads, and tell you what you can and can't do with your own land. Same with all them lazy county bastards. Blakenship, the … " Davis spit where years of footsteps had worn away any hint of grass and rubbed the wet spot in the dirt with his boot toe. "These folks have got some interesting ideas on the subject of government. That's why I figured they should meet you."

"We heard about your problem. It's an outrage the way the feds can treat law-abiding Americans and get away with it. No regard for the Fourth Amendment — or the rest of the Constitution, for that matter."

"Makes you wonder what we fought for." This from Thompson in a surprisingly high-pitched voice for a man of his size.

"Having a little get-together of like-minded folks at my place Saturday. Thought maybe you could join us."

"Election's a ways off, Johnny."

"Start planning now, we'll win the sonofabitch next time."

"Maybe. But I got more than I can handle."

"Heard your Dad's not doing so hot."

"He's getting better. Slow, like the cattle. But Mary Margaret …"

"Bastards. Blair any help?"

"We'll see. Got Mackey Fitz looking into it, too."

"It's a shame and a disgrace, Mr. Grummond. Makes you …" Porterfield caught his tone of rising passion. "You have our deepest sympathy."

"Time we should let Jake get back to work." Davis led Porterfield back to the truck. "If you change your mind about Saturday, we'll be gathering around six."

"Thanks, but I don't see how."

"Understand. They'll be other times. Like you said, the election's a ways off."

Jake watched them make the turn on the county road before going inside for his remaining fifteen minutes of paperwork. Irritation at Davis fogged his concentration. If the raid and all was such a damn shame, why wait two months to say anything? Be damned if any politician was going to ride his troubles to office.

Clock read 12:30. Screw it. Fifteen minutes wasn't going to make a whole lot of difference. He went in search of Eusebio, who he found sitting on his porch. "I'm thinking of moving Felix and Jorge to the barn and hiring new hands to work with Jesus."

Eusebio pulled a jack knife from his pocket and carefully cleaned his fingernails. "It would be a help," he said after due consideration.

Neither man was pleased by the switch, but each was willing to do it for the time being. That taken care of, Jake drove to Top Hat.

***

There was a work-wanted ad — firewood, house painting and the like — on the bulletin board outside the grocery store. Jake didn't recognize the name but it was a local phone number so he wrote it down.

Inside, he bought a pack of 3x5 cards and composed an ad of his own, pinning it to the board with thumbtacks he borrowed from Maudie Taylor, the wife of the storeowner, who was in her usual spot at the only cash register. He asked Maudie to spread the word that he needed hands for field work and crossed the street to the hardware store where he repeated the posting of the ad and the request to spread the word.

The bar was next. He pushed open the door and heard Frog Bottom's low rumble of a voice before he saw the sawmill operator's bulk at the bar leaning toward Helen on the other side. They were the only people present and their voices were soft but he caught the words "Porterfield" and "Sheffield place."

Helen looked up at the sound of the bell over the door. "Jake. Been so long I figured you forgot the way." She held up a Bud for his confirmation.

"Just came in to post an ad — if it's all right — and ask you to spread the word that I need a couple of tractor drivers. You too, Froggie. Spread the word, I mean. But I don't guess a beer would hurt."

"Glad to. Best bet's kids just out of high school. Or the service. Anybody much older who ain't working steady ain't going to be worth a shit. Like Frank the asshole." He said it like it was all one word. "I could spare you one of my boys."

"Thanks, but I need permanent bodies." Jake took a swallow of beer and spun the bottle on the bar. "Did I hear you talking about a guy named Porterfield?"

"Yeah. Why?" Helen asked.

"Just that Davis stopped by with two newcomers. One named Porterfield. Forgot the other one's."

"That's them," said Frog Bottom. "I been talking with them about lumber. With six of them wanting separate houses, they'll be wanting a fair amount."

"With Johnny Davis you said? What'd they want?"

"Something about a meeting at his place Saturday. Davis's, that is."

"What kind of meeting?"

"Political, probably."

122

"Ain't heard a thing about it," said Helen. "You, Froggie? Weren't you helping him last time around?"

"Put out some signs is all. But I ain't been invited. Awful early to be worrying about running for sheriff again. If that's what it's about."

"Said them newcomers had some interesting ideas about government and there'd be a meeting of, how'd he put it? Of like-minded people."

"Guess that don't include me. Strange." Frog Bottom studied the Bud label like he'd never read one before. "Whole deal is strange. When you came in, we were wondering why folks with no farming experience would buy five hundred acres of prime land. It's not like they couldn't find some up on the Sublette or in the mountains, like the rest of them Californians. Shit, they could still buy their lumber from me. But five hundred acres down here? That they ain't going to subdivide into ranchettes or whatever they call them?"

"No accounting sometimes. I got to be getting back. Appreciate it if you get the word out."

"Sure will," said Frog Bottom. "Your Dad doing all right?"

"Better. It's slow, but he's coming along."

"And Mary Margaret?" This from Helen.

Jake stiffened. "Not good. Last time I saw her — day before yesterday — she didn't know me at all." His pain was palpable. "And she's scared of trucks. The big rigs. She can see the Interstate from her window and every so often when a semi goes by she hides her face in her hands and starts crying. Like to break my heart."

Frog Bottom and Helen were shocked by Jake's raw emotion. Helen recovered first. "You take care of yourself. And one day soon you come down and let me feed you chicken and dumplings." She walked around the bar and kissed him on the cheek. "I mean it. Soon. This week."

***

Grandpa Grummond was watching the flames dance behind the glass windows of the wood stove's double doors. "Got to admit this is a helluva improvement over any other stove I've ever had."

"That's why you bought it." Jake checked the wood box and went outside for an armload of split pine. "I'm moving Felix and Jorge to the barn and I've got the word out that I'm looking for tractor drivers."

"What's Eusebio think?"

"He's agreeable. Where's Maria Elena?"

"Volleyball practice. She'll be along. Handy, letting her drive Mary Margaret's Ranger."

Jake peered into the refrigerator. "Looks like you're in good shape for the next couple of days."

"Small as my fucking appetite is, I'm in good shape till the end of the month."

"You want anything? Sandwich? Soup? Cup of tea?"

"Cup of tea. That's what my life's down to now. Cup of fucking tea."

"Take it easy, Dad."

"Ain't your fault, Lord knows. You could turn on the TV. On second thought, never mind. All you got on now is them talk shows. That 'how my son's the father of my baby and he won't let me call him daddy' kind of shit."

"You want a dish? Get those movie channels?"

"Shit no. I'm not planning to spend the rest of my life in this goddamn chair."

"You been getting some work done."

"Bullshit. Two days I spend a couple of hours making phone calls. Ain't hit a lick today."

"Takes time."

"Time is something I ain't got much of."

Jake didn't have anything to say to that so he started for the door. "I got to get."

"Any pneumonia?"

"Nope. Production's coming back. If we don't have anymore mastitis …"

124

"Or hoof rot."

"Yeah. Maybe we've turned the corner."

***

Jake thought about Helen's invitation to dinner as he drove back. She must be fifteen years older so it wasn't like she was making a play for him. Besides, she and Mary Margaret were close — some kind of cousins or something. Damn. Known them both pretty near all his life and he didn't know their relationship. Still, be nice to eat somebody else's cooking. Maybe Friday or Saturday.

The mail wasn't on the kitchen table because Maria Elena wasn't back from school yet so he got back in the pickup and drove to the mailbox. Nothing but bills and a letter from the bank which he opened and was shocked to see that his last check to Dan's had bounced. No question but what he had to get his paperwork in order.

There was a message from Mackey Fitz asking him to call in the morning and another from somebody-Leonard asking about a tractor job. Jake replayed the tape so he could write down the number, then dialed and let it ring eight times. Try again in an hour or two, but right now should he eat or lie down? The couch won and he stretched out, promising himself an hour of paperwork when he got up. He was careful to leave his booted feet hanging off the edge. Didn't want Mary Margaret mad at him.

***

The phone rang as he walked in the door after supervising the morning sick-pen milking and clean up. It was Lois Brady, a widow who worked at Dan's Building Supplies. She'd heard Jake was hiring and her oldest boy was getting out of the Army.

"He home yet?"

125

"He'll be home next week. I was thinking of getting him on here at Dan's but it'd be better for both of us if we didn't work at the same place."

"I need help as soon as I can get it, but have him come by when he gets home and we'll talk."

Lois's call reminded him of the unknown Leonard he'd forgotten to call again. This time, a young-sounding voice answered that identified itself as Jeffrey Leonard.

"Jake Grummond here. Someone at this number left a message yesterday about working on my field crew."

"That was me."

"Don't believe I know you folks. You live around Top Hat?"

"Yes sir. We live west of town."

"Been here long?"

"About seven years. My daddy drives truck for Louisiana-Pacific."

"How old are you, son?'

"Eighteen."

Jake winced. Too close to Paul. "Out of school?"

"Yes sir. Been working at McDonald's and your job looks a lot better."

"Driven tractors much?"

"Summers, mostly. Worked for Mr. Sheffield before he stopped farming."

"Sheffield, huh. O. K. When can you show me what you can do?"

"I got to be at work by one. Either tomorrow morning or anytime Saturday."

""Let's say tomorrow at eight. By the way. You didn't ask, but you start at $1000 a month and the hours can be long, depending on the season."

"I'll be there. At eight."

The phone rang immediately after he hung up. Annoyed, he picked up the receiver and gave a curter than he meant to "Grummond Dairy" into the mouthpiece.

"Jake?" It was Helen. "Are you all right?"

126

"Sorry. Didn't mean to bark, but I've been trying to get to the barn and the phone won't let me out the door."

"I'll make it short, then. Dinner tonight. Six sharp. Be there."

***

"My, my, C. W. I never knew you looked so good from that angle. That's your best feature, for sure." The voice was Rudy Mikeska's.

Blakenship was on his hands and knees in his office with his right arm under his desk and his haunches facing the door. "Consider yourself favored. I don't let just anybody see my best." He stretched his arm farther. "Got it."

Rising to his feet, he opened his hand to reveal a vintage Zippo. "Dad carried this across the South Pacific and I'm not about to lose it in my own office." He returned the chair to its accustomed spot in front of the desk and gestured to Mikeska. "Take a load off," and proceeded to demonstrate how that was done. "What brings you out of the mountains?"

"On my way back from Union and I thought I'd pay my respects."

"Neighborly of you."

"That and let you know Donaldson is now relocated in Kansas."

"Good. Although Grummond's probably cooled down by now. As far as bodily harm's concerned, anyhow."

"Speaking of Grummond, what's he up to?"
"Not sure. Jake and me, we've never been what you'd call asshole buddies. But what I can gather, he's filed a claim for damages with the DEA. Which, according to Henderson — and he probably knows — is the first step to suing."
"We're not feds."

"Yeah. But if Henderson's right, since our boys were acting under their direction, we could be in the shit right along with them."

"Fucking DEA. Wish I'd never heard of them."

127

"Speaking of what you have heard of, you hear much about Victor and Julio Sanchez up your way? Or the father?"

"As far as the boys go, just what I pick up talking to folks like you who're closer to Union. Every once in a while someone from Otero County will buy a car from the old man, which means that everyone once in a while one gets repo'd and I hear about it. Why?"

"Seems the boys where the ones who fingered the dairy."

"From what I hear, there's a lot more upstanding people you could deal with."

"DEA don't usually have the option of dealing with upstanding people. That part of what they say is true enough."

"What difference does who did the pointing make?"

"Bother's me. Victor and Julio ain't your solid citizens but they do know that if they give somebody up in order to help themselves, it don't help them if who they give up ain't solid. If you follow me."

"You're saying?"

"I'm saying if drugs weren't coming through the Grummond Dairy, why'd they say there were?"

"You sure no drugs were coming through?"

"Ain't positive, but I'm pretty sure."

"So either someone told the Sanchez brothers an untruth which they passed on as gospel, or they've got out on a limb with saw in hand by their ownselves."

"Way it looks to me."

"Might help if you knew where they were at this very moment."

"You know, Rudy, just every once in a while you make sense. I'll make that one of my top priorities for tomorrow." Blakenship checked his watch. "Because you make such good sense and because it's after five o'clock — way after five — I'll buy you your first drink."

***

128

There were only two cars parked in the entire business section of Top Hat and both were in front of Helen's. Inside, Henry, who ran the gas station out on the highway during the day, was behind the bar, tending to the needs of two log-truck drivers Jake knew well enough to nod to.

"Helen said for you to come on through."

Jake moved around the bar and through the door to the abbreviated kitchen where Helen prepared hamburgers and soup when the mood struck her and the demand justified the effort. Off to the side was a door to the stairs that led to her living quarters. Jake realized that in all the years he'd known her, he'd never been to her home.

The top of the stairs opened on a living area with overstuffed furniture protected by crocheted doilies at the arms and seat backs. To the right was a dining table with cabriole legs of startling delicacy. White place mats set with what looked to be china, antique silver and crystal faced each other across the table and beyond was the kitchen door behind which he could hear the clink of kettle lids.

"Jake?"

"Expecting anyone else?"

"Don't be silly." Helen swung the door open and held it in place with a rubber wedge. She was wearing jeans and a flannel work shirt.

"Glad to see you're in every-day clothes. They way you set the table made me think I'd better go back and change."

"They are my every-day dishes. Might as well get the good out of them before I pass on. What do you want to drink?"

"Beer, if you've got one."

"I own a saloon. Of course I've got a beer." She pulled a bottle of Bud out of the refrigerator, twisted the cap and handed it to him. "Use the glass at your place. Far side."

"Awful fancy for beer."

"Like I said, I use my good stuff for every day. Now let's eat."

Twenty minutes later, Jake pushed back from the table, amazed at the volume of chicken and dumplings and mashed potatoes and peas and acorn squash he'd put away.

"There's apple pie for dessert, but it doesn't look like you can handle it yet."

"Got that right."

"Coffee?"

"I can try."

Helen poured two cups, then sat down across from Jake and stared at him with kindly eyes. "You're probably wondering why I asked you to dinner."

"The thought crossed my mind."

"Reason is what you said about Mary Margaret yesterday."

"What do you mean?"

"About not knowing you. And the trucks and the crying. It got me to thinking." Helen sipped her coffee and set the cup down carefully in its delicate saucer. "You know Mary Margaret and I are second cousins?"

"Something like that."

"I'm sixteen years older than she is and when it became clear that Clement, God rest his soul, and I weren't going to have children — never mind why — we became like mother and daughter. Maybe closer. She could tell me things she'd have had a hard time telling her mother. And when her parents moved to Tucson …"

"I knew you were close."

"Now, the most I know about psychiatry is an introductory course I took my freshman year and that was more years ago than I want to think about. But after her mother's miscarriage," she looked sharply at Jake, "You didn't know?"

"No."

"Happened when she was four, maybe five. Point is, Mary Margaret took it to be her fault. Not an uncommon thing for a child that age to do. Thing that made it worse was it was a boy — at least, that's what Beth and Donald always believed." Helen lit a cigarette and watched the match burn down in the ashtray.

"Anyway, with the two of them hanging onto their grief, Mary Margaret kind of got shut out. Nothing on purpose, I don't mean that. But she felt like a third wheel on a bike. That's the way she described it to me."

"I had no idea."

"To make matters worse, about a year later, her dog got hit by a truck. Out on the highway. By a big rig. Took him fifteen minutes to die. With his head in Mary Margaret's lap. She'd had that dog — a collie — since they were both pups. Over half her life. Slept with her and everything. Dog was her comfort, especially after the miscarriage." Helen picked up the cigarette that had been burning in the ashtray, starting to take a drag then stubbed it out. "After the dog died, she took to spending a lot of her time after school with me. I was working at the bank then and got off at three. Kept it up all through school. She would talk about you."

"About me?"

"Hell yes. She had a crush on you from the fifth grade on."

"Be damned. Took me forever to get her to say yes when I asked her to the homecoming dance sophomore year."

"She didn't want to seem too forward."

"She succeeded."

They lapsed into a silence that wasn't broken until Henry yelled up that nobody had been in the bar for over an hour and could he close up?

"That was all a long time ago."

"Maybe so. But look, Jake. A miscarriage she blamed herself for. Her best friend — literally — killed. Like it was a punishment. Then years later, she has a miscarriage. Then Paul killed — by a truck. I know it was fifteen years after her miscarriage — but... And look at how she reacted. Then the raid and Della's miscarriage and your father ..." Her voice had been dropping, like she'd been talking to herself, and she remembered Jake with a jerk. "I know you've got more to deal with than anybody ought to have, and I sure don't mean to add to your burden. But I thought if you could tell the doctor, it might help.

"I'll tell him." Jake shook his head as though to clear it and glanced at his watch. "I got to get back for cleanup."

10

NOVEMBER 18 — Morning

"Trucks. Miscarriages," Allsup had said. Not really a question. Not really a statement. He looked out the office window, his giving a view of leafless cottonwoods in a small park, and clasped his outsized hands across the top of his head. "Trucks. Miscarriages," he'd repeated as though testing the effect of the words on his tongue.

That had been three weeks earlier and best as Jake could tell all they'd accomplished was to get Mary Margaret to stop talking altogether. Not a single word said the last two times he'd visited. And they'd moved her to a room with no view of Interstate or sky, just a brick wall on the other side of an airshaft.

On the plus side, production was approaching normal on a per head basis. Mastitis had been contained, pneumonia held at bay and none of the other ailments bovine flesh was heir to had appeared. He couldn't afford replacement heifers so they were milking fewer than three hundred, less than two-thirds of the pre-raid number, but light was a dim gleam at tunnel's end. Thank God he didn't have to fight a mortgage payment every month.

The new hands on the field crew — he'd hired Jeffrey Leonard and Lois Brady's son — looked like they were going to work out. The men he'd transferred to the barn were settling in, although he or Eusebio had to keep close watch — thorough wiping of teats and bag wasn't second nature yet.

Jake looked up from the papers and adding machine tape. The fitful snore from his father on the couch raised the question of whether he should wake him before going to the barn or chance it that he would sleep through cleanup.

Chance it.

He looked at his worksheets. Even though the herd averaged better than twenty-six pounds per head per milking — three-quarters of pre-raid production — since the herd was smaller, income was less than half of what it had been. He was a long way from out of the hole. Still, the improved production gave the hint of a spring to his step as he opened the door to the porch. He savored the bite in the November air and studied the snow showing on the mountains. Fourth elk season had come and gone and he hadn't made good on his promise to Brian. Maybe next year.

His father was still asleep when he returned. In the interest of an afternoon nap, he shook him awake. Grandpa Grummond spluttered to consciousness and grasped the back of the sofa to pull himself upright. Swinging his feet to the floor, he leaned back and fixed his son with a questioning look.

"Didn't want to ruin your nap."

"Getting to sleep ain't been my problem lately."

"Get you anything?"

"If I want anything, I'll get it my own damn self." He scratched his armpit vigorously, then adjusted his crotch. "Goddamn briefs. My peckerhead gets caught in the fly and my balls get pinched, some way or another."

"Get you some boxers, if you want."

"Then the equipment swings all over the place."

Jake shrugged and turned to organizing the paperwork on his desk.

"What shape're we in?" Grandpa Grummond struggled to his feet and shuffled to stand behind his son, every second step marked by the muted thump of his lead pipe on the rug.

"Good news is that production's up to better'n twenty-five pounds."

"If that's the good news, we're still belly button deep in shit." Grandpa Grummond thumped his way to the kitchen.

Jake continued to sort through the pile on the desk. Near the bottom he found Eastman's manila folder. He started to open it, but remembered that the first thing he'd see would be Buchanan's picture and put it in the desk drawer.

The folder reminded him that he hadn't talked to either Blakenship or Mackey Fitz for several weeks. Not that there was much to talk to Mackey about — they still had months before they could file suit. But Blakenship had halfway promised he'd find out more about the Sanchez brothers. Speaking of which, he hadn't heard from Eastman, either.

He opened the middle drawer of his desk and rummaged through a tangle of papers until he found his address book. Stewart's Washington office said Eastman would be out until the end of the week. He called the Sheriff's Office to be told, after a thirty second delay, that Blakenship was also out.

"Little early for the Stockman, ain't it?"

"I couldn't say, sir."

"Tell him Jake Grummond called."

***

Blakenship's reason for putting Jake off was simple: He didn't know what to tell him.

He'd run his traps in his law enforcement network and no one knew where Victor and Julio were. Henderson's discreet calls to their known addresses had gotten women's voices saying only that they weren't in. Could mean any number of things, including that they were dead. Blakenship didn't have the manpower or the time to probe any further.

Still, why would two street-smart, raised-in-the-life minor league hoodlums with IQ's above average room temperature, give false information? The question rankled like gristle caught between his back molars. Blakenship propped his boots on the desk and unbuckled his belt — the breakfast *huevos rancheros were* starting to talk back.

Victor and Julio could believe the information was solid. If they really thought drugs were being run through the dairy, they had to have gotten the idea from somewhere. Who else thought drugs were passing through the Grummond Dairy? Or wanted people to think there were?

Same circle he'd been running for days.

He stood up, buckled his belt and hitched his gun in place. He needed to cruise with air hitting him in the face.

***

Gravel crunched under his boots as he walked to the partial shelter of a scrub oak and emptied his bladder of what he hoped was the last of the morning's coffee. It was a clear day, the cloudless sky a picture postcard blue and only a faint breeze coming up from the valley.

He'd left the office and followed the path of least resistance through the moderate traffic, a course that eased west over the Flint River to Jedediah Road and up the Sublette Plateau, driving without hurry, both windows down the better to savor the cool air. As he climbed, he'd taken automatic note of signs offering thirty-five acre "ranch" tracts for sale, of houses under construction, and of fresh tire tracks on the ruts that gave access to BLM land and the possibility of deer or elk.

The new houses, ten he counted, flared arrogant from the hillsides, walls of glass facing the Presidentials, decks soaring above the ground like ship prows breasting heavy seas. They stood in odd contrast to the one-story cabins the old-timers had tucked among the trees and folds in the land to buffer against winds that sped across the valley on winter nights.

He zipped his fly and walked to the guardrail. Spring Valley spread out below, a gold-tinged patchwork of fallow cropland and pastures. Three streams cut it in rough parallel, flowing gently to their respective confluences with the Santa Elena River in the next county. Paved and gravel roads cross-hatched the land with geometric precision while dirt tracks emerged from clusters of tree, houses and out-buildings and wound across the countryside in tune with the land's contours. Ten miles in the distance, the large grove of cottonwoods and willows at the intersection of two paved roads marked Pea Green with its gas station, small grocery store and two-story community hall where Saturday night dances were a tradition that dated from before his parents' courting days.

***

An old Toyota pickup with a flat rear tire was parked on the shoulder about two miles from Pea Green and a tall figure just beginning to fill out from a teenage growth spurt was lifting a three-and-a-half ton floor jack to the ground.

Blakenship rolled the Bronco to a stop. "Handle it?"

"Yes sir." The teenager, he looked to be seventeen or so with stringy hair of indeterminate color poking from a Massey Ferguson gimmie cap, rolled the jack into place.

"You must get flats regular to be carrying a jack like that."

"No sir. Just lucky. Borrowed it from the Grummond Dairy. Dad and I are going to work on Mom's car this weekend."

"I don't believe I know you, son. I'm C. W. Blakenship."

"Jeffrey Leonard, sir."

"Leonard. Leonard. Live out this way, do you?"

"Yes sir. 'Bout a mile down the road and then you take a left."

"Near the old Sheffield place?"

"Yes sir."

"How'd you happen to be at Grummond's?"

"I work there."

"Really?"

"Yes sir. Started four weeks ago. Four weeks ago, Monday," he amended.

"Heard Jake was hiring. What's he have you doing?"

"Driving tractor."

"Not plowing this time of year?"

"No sir. Spreading manure, mainly."

"They always did have the best in the county." Blakenship lit his last cigar. "Fields, that is. How you like working for Jake?"

"Fine. Of course, I don't see him much. Take my orders from Jesus."

"Jake getting things back under control, is he?"

"Couldn't say. I hope so, though. It's the best job I've ever had."

The boy began pumping the jack handle and Blakenship put the Bronco in gear. "Good luck, son."

137

A flatbed truck loaded with dimensional lumber took up all the parking area in front of Rafe's store and gas station, forcing Blakenship to park in front of the community hall. Potts Lumber was painted in fading script on the door, not that Blakenship needed the inscription to recognize the truck, and Frog Bottom himself was at the counter, tearing the wrapper from a fried pie with his teeth.

"Damn, Froggie. How you manage to take up all the parking?"

"Practice, C. W. Practice."

"Looks like you're carrying a full load."

"Taking it out to the Sheffield place."

"Sheffield's? Gimmie a couple of packages of Crooks, Rafe. Sheffield's? I thought … I remember. Those California retirees who're going to build them a cooperative or something. Ones with you at Helen's a while back."

"Them's the ones."

"Didn't get the idea they were going to move this quick."

"Me neither. But I got a call a couple of weeks ago. This is my second load."

"They straight with the county?"

"Davis helped them out, way I understand it."

"Davis, huh? Might just follow along and say how do."

"You're welcome to tag along."

"I appreciate your giving me permission, Froggie."

"Didn't mean it that way. It's just that every once in a while you act like a real person and I forget you're the law."

Five miles later and five minutes behind the truck, he turned onto a dirt road newly rutted by all-terrain tires and drove to the cupola-topped two story house the first Sheffield had built many years before to remind him of his native New England. A newly scraped track continued at an oblique angle a half-mile past the barn to what looked like a foundation from which floated the cracks of a nailing gun.

Head out the driver's side window, Froggie was talking to a man of average height who pointed in the general direction of the barn. Blakenship pulled up on the other side of the stranger.

138

"This here's C. W. Blakenship, Sheriff of Sapinero County and all that goes with it. This here is …"

"Clarence, Sheriff. Clarence Petersen. Most people call me Pete." C. W. reached across the seat to shake the hand extended through the open window. Petersen was wearing rust-covered overalls so new they still had the creases from the box. "To what do I owe the pleasure?" Petersen's voice rasped like machine parts in need of oil and there was an inflection to his vowels Blakenship had never heard before.

"Just driving around and thought I'd say hello." Blakenship got out of the Bronco and leaned against the hood of the lumber truck. The nailing gun had stopped and the westerly breeze carried only the smell of freshly turned earth. Blakenship eyed the spots of gray clay stuck to Petersen's work boots, which looked like they weren't long out of the box, either. "Smells like you been plowing, but I don't see where."

"Say what?" Petersen was mildly startled. "Don't notice it anymore. Not plowing, though. Cleaning out the barn. Getting the old manure and straw and what-not cleared out before we pour the floor."

"The lumber go here like last time or up to the new house?" Froggie shifted into gear.

"Here. We'll sort out what's what."

Froggie started the truck rolling forward. "How 'bout in the barn out of the weather?"

"Nope. Not done yet."

Blakenship and Petersen watched without speaking while Frog Bottom maneuvered the truck and dropped the load neatly next to the weathered barn wall. In the distance, a motor coughed and caught. Blakenship watched a pickup jounce toward them from the new building.

"Looks like they're moving right along. Unusual to get paperwork through the county that fast."

"John Davis …"

"Johnny helped. I know. Whose is that one going to be?"

"The Colonel's. He …"

"Better cover it tight." Frog Bottom interrupted, handing Petersen a clipboard and following with a ballpoint pen he pulled from in front of his left ear, held in place by the brim of his stained khaki hat. "You want to check, see if it's all there, before you sign?"

"We know where to find you if there's a problem."

Frog Bottom drove off and Petersen turned to find Blakenship standing at the barn doorway. There was a small Bobcat bulldozer in the middle of the floor, a fresh clod clinging to the bottom right corner of the blade. The floor of the main section had been lowered six inches, maybe more. A backhoe stood where the stalls had been and next to it a cement mixer.

"Going to put down about three or four inches of gravel, then some rebar and pour," Petersen explained. "Then we'll rewire."

"Why the backhoe?"

"We'll be putting in water and electric to the other houses as we build. Used it for the Colonel's septic tank. Didn't do too bad, considering it was my first time."

"Sort of looks like you're going to use it in here." Blakenship indicated what looked like an eight-by-ten rectangle staked out in the cleared part of the barn floor. "What's it going to be?"

"A shop, mainly. And storage. Seems like the best way to use this structure. We're not farmers, after all."

Behind them, an engine died, followed by the slamming of two doors. Blakenship watched two men approach, both wearing faded military fatigues with spots not quite as faded where the nametags had been. Both had the lean build of long-distance runners and moved with straight-back efficiency.

"Everything O. K., Pete?" It was the man from the passenger side who spoke. "You must be the Sheriff." He extended his hand in a no nonsense shake. "My name's Burns."

"The badge does give that away. C. W. Blakenship." Where had he seen him before? Helen's. The voice that had brought the other one — Porterfield? — back to the table. "Making good progress, looks like. The others, they here?"

140

"Went back to California. We're trying to get my place dried in by the end of the month. Pete here took some vacation time to help out."

"An unusual arrangement you got here, Mr. Burns. Or should I say Colonel?"

"Ten years retired, call me Bill." Burns looked at his watch. "Probably should keep moving, Pete, if you're going to finish before you have to go back to collect your gold watch. And we'd best keep moving, too."

Petersen moved toward the Bobcat while Burns and the driver — who'd spoken not a word — walked on either side of Blakenship to his Bronco with a purposefulness that encouraged no lingering. Men with no time to waste. But when Blakenship made the turn onto the county road, the truck hadn't moved.

Now why, he thought, if the plan was to get the new house dried in, was Petersen working in the barn?

He tooted his horn, but got no wave in return.

***

Two mornings later, Blakenship pulled in as Jake was coming out of the barn.

"You got something for me, Cecil, or you just need a cup of coffee?"

"Thought I'd pass along what I found out about the Sanchez boys. But I wouldn't say no to coffee."

At the kitchen table, Blakenship sniffed the steam rising from his cup and smiled. "Actually, I don't have much. Called their houses and got their wives — I think they were their wives — anyway, got some women who said they weren't home and they don't know where they are. Checked with police and sheriffs and neither one is in custody in any jurisdiction in the state."

"Try their father in Union?"

"My, my, Jake. You haven't been doing a little detecting on your own, have you?"

"Just what Blair's aide told me."

141

"Haven't tried the father. But it's not a bad idea."

"They're nothing but crooks. But you know that by now. Probably knew it all along."

Blakenship's look carried a hint of amusement along with a tinge of wariness. "Can't fool you for a minute, can I?"

"Oh, you can fool me all right. But you go denying what you know don't make me feel like I can trust you." Jake drained his mug and set it down harder than he'd intended to.

"Tell me, Jake, how'd the delay hurt you? It ain't like you were going to take any action."

"My lawyer might. For all you know, he's already doing something and what you know could help him out."

"Way I hear it, if you sue, you'll be suing me, too."

"If that's the way you see it, then there's no reason I should trust you at all, is there?" Jake picked up his coffee mug, realized it was empty and set it down, without a sound this time.

"My job is to keep the peace in Sapinero County, not help you make a case against the federal government. Or me, either, for that matter. Anything I do along those lines is strictly voluntary."

"Justice have anything to do with your job, Cecil?"

"Justice is supposed to come out of the whole system. I'm only one part."

"We'll see." The sound of a pickup being started broke the silence. "That'll be Eusebio taking Mercedes to the doctor. Her legs." Jake walked to the door. "Too many doctors. Lately, there's been too many goddamn doctors."

**

The next morning the phone caught Jake as he was on his way to the barn.

"Sorry I've taken so long to get back to you, but it's been busy around here." It was Eastman.

"I know something about busy."

"I bet you do. Can't tell you any more about Victor and Julio than I did last time, but..."

142

"Don't know where they are, then?"

"I have their home addresses. Why?"

"Sheriff says nobody knows where they are."

"That's interesting. Let me get back on it. Do you want their addresses, too?"

"Might as well."

"I've got more information about the DEA agents. I'll fax it."

"Don't have one. Can you mail it?"

"Sure. How're things otherwise?"

"Some ups and some downs."

"Your wife?"

The image of Mary Margaret sitting silent and lumpish in the chair by the window that looked out on the brick wall blotted out everything in the room.

"Jake?"

"She's one of the downs."

"I'm sorry." Jake was about to hang up when Eastman added, "By the way, the Congressman will be in the district over Thanksgiving and wonders if he could drop by."

"That's what? Next week?"

"Thanksgiving's a week from today. Probably be Friday or Saturday."

"He'd better call first. Between Mary Margaret and my father, something might come up."

***

The weekend went by without incident. On Monday, Jake supervised the morning cleanup and watched the tanker collect three milkings' worth of production before he drove to Union for his weekly visit with Mary Margaret. There'd been more than 28,000 pounds in the tank which meant that per head the herd was better than 90% back to its summer average. He pulled into the hospital parking lot feeling more cheerful than he had since the raid.

143

Two hours of talking to a non-responsive Mary Margaret took care of that.

He'd tried everything he could think of. He'd even started to ask her about how to make sausage dressing for Thanksgiving but stopped when his lips went numb and trembled and his eyes began to tear because this would be the first holiday in twenty-two years that they'd been apart. He fought the urge to cry all the way back to Top Hat.

Helen called on Wednesday to invite him to her place for Thanksgiving. No good. He was working both milkings to give Eusebio a break. Helen said shit, she'd come out there and bring dinner with her.

Dinner had been good. Not like Mary Margaret's, of course, but it was nice to have company. His father'd had one of his better days and kept up a running banter with Helen during the football games while Jake nodded off in a chair. Billy and Evie had stopped by late in the afternoon, Evie bearing a mince and a pumpkin pie and they'd visited until time for the evening milking.

Midway through, Helen came out to the barn to tell Jake that Stewart had called and would stop by in the morning. She pecked him quickly on the cheek and said she'd drive Grandpa Grummond to his cabin.

It had been past eleven o'clock when Jake had finished clean up and the alarm had rung four hours later. He hadn't worked two full shifts in succession for years, let alone three, and he groped his way around the barn with a wooden headedness that refused to abate. The fact that Eusebio wasn't there and Paco — from the field crew who was subbing for Jorge — was also operating in a fog caused in equal parts by inexperience and holiday beer, made it a rough and clumsy operation all around.

It was with an undeniable sense of relief that the car Jake heard pull up a little after nine proved to be carrying Blair Stewart.

"Didn't mean to be this early, but something came up and I've got to fly back to Washington tomorrow. Means I have to cram all my appointments here into a day and a half. Ronnie sent this." Stewart handed Jake a large, thick envelope. "He didn't want to trust it to the mail."

"Let me holler at Paco."

When Jake got to the house, the congressman was at the table reading a document attached to a manila folder which he held at a forty-five degree angle, the bottom supported by his thighs and the back resting against the table's edge. Stewart looked up at the sound of Jake's footsteps. "Sorry. A piece of pork-barrel legislation to derail if we can do it without upsetting a number of delicately balanced apple carts." Stewart closed the folder. "So. How are things?"

"Like I told Eastman. Some ups and some downs."

"Tell me."

"On the downside, Mary Margaret hasn't recognized me since the day we put her in Crossley Memorial."

"That was shortly after my last visit, wasn't it?"

"Tuesday after Labor Day. At first she'd talk, at least. Carry on a conversation even if it only made sense to her. But the last four weeks or so, she hasn't done anything but sit. Not while I was there, anyway."

"And your father?"

"He has his good days and his not-so-good days."

"What's a good day?"

"When he feels like doing a little paper work. Or getting on the phone and goddamning folks at the CO-OP or Dan's. But he hasn't got much strength and I'm beginning to think he never will."

"And on the upside?"

"Upside is that production is starting to recover. We're better'n 90% per head of where we were before the raid and we've got the mastitis beat back. Of course, I'm milking a hundred less head than I was then and I've lost six hands. But I've hired a couple of kids who look like they might work out."

"And how goes your attempt at restitution?"

"We filed a couple of months ago. But you know that."

"Yes. I wrote expressing my strongest hope that it would receive careful and expeditious attention."

"So?"

"So we'll see. Have you begun preparing any legal action? I ask because the climate in Washington is very much pro law-and-order at the moment. Particularly in the case of drugs or the suspicion thereof. And the involvement of Mexican nationals doesn't help. Even with my letter, the chances of your claim being honored are not very good. And in any case, law enforcement agencies are notoriously loathe to admit any mistakes or liability."

"Mackey Fitz's is working on it."

"What about an attorney who's more experienced in these types of suits?"

"Fitz talked about that from the beginning. But he hasn't done anything yet, that I know of."

"I may be able to point him in the direction of able co-counsel. Ronnie's been getting information to you?" The rumble of a truck drowned Jake's answer. "What's that?"

"Milk tanker."

"I've been in Washington too long. Ronnie's been a help?"

"I guess so. Found out it was a couple of small-time crooks who told the feds. But nobody knows where they are."

"Nobody?"

"What Cecil says."

Stewart picked up the folder. "Didn't realize you and the good sheriff were working together so closely."

"Not the way I'd put it. He drops by from time to time and tells me what he thinks will keep me quiet. Like giving a pacifier to a baby."

They stood together on the porch and watched the driver of the tanker uncouple and coil up his line. Paco came out of the barn and Jake called to him, asking if he'd fed the calves the milk from the sick pen.

Paco gave the classic palms-up shrug of bewilderment.

Jake felt a tightening begin to sicken his stomach. Paco was new to the barn. He jumped the three steps from porch to ground and sprinted to the tanker, reaching it as the driver swung into the cab. "Hold on a second, Greg. We may have a problem."

He came out of the barn short minutes later. "Have to dump the load."

"Sick pen?"

"I don't guess I was your first stop today."

"Sorry, Jake. At least it didn't contaminate everything at the CO-OP."

"That's something."

"What's going on?" Stewart's tone said he knew he should be concerned but he didn't know why.

"I just made a seven or eight thousand dollar fuck up."

"How?"

"Left an inexperienced man to finish milking and clean up. He either forgot or never knew he was supposed to separate the milk from the cows in the sick pen. Not only do we lose the production from our last three milkings, I've got to pay for the milk Greg'd already picked up."

"Jesus. If I'd come a little later ..." Stewart's voice trailed off.

"Maybe. And if I hadn't worked three straight shifts. But those are reasons, not excuses. Ain't no excuse. I been in this business all my life." Jake spit his snuff in an arc that just missed the fender of Stewart's car. "No fucking excuse."

11
THE NEW YEAR

The Grummond Dairy got through the weeks between Thanksgiving and early January without catastrophe.

Eusebio brought Mercedes home after four days in the hospital and the pre-Thanksgiving schedule was reestablished.

Grandpa Grummond's routine tracked the football games. Monday and Tuesday he rarely left the cabin. Wednesday he'd come, but mostly napped on the couch. Thursday and Friday were his best days — he could manage up to three hours on the phone. Saturday morning brought him early where he'd drink decaf and fidget until it was time for the first game of the day.

Jake plodded along with leaden determination. Every Monday at noon he pointed the pickup toward Union and the hospital where he'd spend an hour by the clock talking to Mary Margaret. On rare occasions he was rewarded by a smile, but mostly she just sat, a lump getting bigger every week: stomach beginning to strain at the buttons of the simple housedress that had become her uniform; cheeks puffing with fat; eyes shrinking to brilliant blue dots of blank clarity.

Afterward, he went for his consultation with Allsup, an exercise that either sparked a barely-containable urge to beat the doctor's head against the desktop or left him feeling profoundly sad and helpless.

The second Friday in January brought a letter from the insurance company with "URGENT" stamped in red on the envelope, front and back. Jake eyed its bright insistence while he fixed a sandwich and ate half. He opened it to the expected — insurance had run out.

What about this Medicare shit? Or was it Medicaid? He lumped them with all the other government handouts that made his taxes too high. The idea was repugnant, but what was a man to do? If it hadn't been for the goddamn government Mary Margaret wouldn't be in the hospital.

How did you find out about this shit, anyway? Hospital? Courthouse? Who do you talk to?

Start with the hospital. He finished the second half of his sandwich and went to his desk. Make an appointment for Monday with somebody up there.

***

"San Francisco or Dallas?"

"Don't ever bet against San Francisco on their home field."

"Home field didn't do them much good two years ago."

"Didn't say it was a lock. All I said was don't bet against them." Blakenship reached across the table for the front section of the *Mountain View Bulletin*. "You done with this?" he asked Henderson and took it without waiting for an answer.

They were sitting at a table by the front window in the Chopping Block hungry for the homemade cinnamon rolls to go with the coffees that sat before them in oversized ceramic mugs. The cafe had changed hands in early November, bought by a couple from Minnesota who did their own baking, the quality of which had so impressed the two lawmen that the nine o'clock break had become an indelible part of their routine.

Absorbed in the coverage of Sunday's upcoming league championship games, Henderson didn't register Blakenship's low-pitched whistle. "Look at this, Charlie."

"Say what?" Reluctantly, Henderson lifted his eyes to squint at the small headline midway down the page Blakenship held before him. It was a story about a one-car accident on the Interstate in the mountains between Shotgun and Anton. "Hold it steady, dammit." Henderson frowned in concentration. "I'll be. Bet they were driving a car off their father's lot."

The waitress brought their rolls and refilled their mugs. "I wonder where the hell they've been?" Blakenship scratched his cheek absently with the fork handle.

"Now that you know where they are, could be you could drive over and ask them." Henderson scanned the column again. "Says there're in serious condition."

149

Blakenship finished his roll in two bites and dabbled his fingers on the plate to get the last of the frosting. "Time we earned the money the good citizens of Sapinero County pay us."

***

Blakenship got a cordial but not particularly informative response from Sheriff Sam Phillips, in whose county the accident had occurred. A trucker had radioed in the wreck at ten-thirty in the evening. Vehicle, a '91 Thunderbird with dealer plates, totaled. No, he didn't know yet whether either alcohol or drugs were involved. It was at the county yard. No, they hadn't examined it. In fact, he'd just gotten off the phone with a DEA agent asking him to leave it untouched until he got there. Name? Buckman. Buford. Something like that. Buchanan? Could be.

Blakenship thoughtfully gnawed a ragged patch off his left thumbnail. Buchanan. He dialed his counterpart in Anton.

Wendell Darling knew even less than Sam. The brothers were going to be moved out of ICU. Yeah, he had a deputy with them until somebody from the DEA got there. Wouldn't have if they hadn't called. The name? Buchanan. Due in mid-afternoon or thereabouts. Sure. No problem. Be in touch.

Blakenship scratched his head vigorously. Curiouser and curiouser.

***

Buchanan cleared the top of Granger Pass in the right lane of the Interstate, clinging to the steering wheel with both hands in white-knuckled concentration. Traffic whizzed past, attacking the downhill grade with blithe indifference to the possibility of ice, but he held the needle below sixty, a caution born not of his status as an officer of the law but of the fact that the piece of shit the motor pool had issued him developed a teeth-rattling shimmy at sixty-five.

Buchanan's long awaited promotion and transfer to Washington, DC had not come through. Grummond's complaint

150

and Congressman Stewart's interest had put both on hold. "Keep a low profile," he'd been told, "and you'll be back on track."

"Keeping a low profile, it turned out, meant being shunted to a windowless cubbyhole while William Thomas Aquinas fucking Kiernan was promoted to his old command.

He now had a bitter wife fully capable of giving tongue to her feelings. She had never adjusted to the expanse of western horizons that made her feel she could blow away at any moment and not be missed. Transfer to Washington meant salvation and having the promised land slip away had raised the tension in the Buchanan household to the breaking point.

The only way to get peace was to get back on track and he was convinced that the only way to get back on track was to bust the pipeline that ran through Sapinero County.

A drug pipeline ran through Sapinero County. He was sure about that, if nothing else. When the raid had come up empty, he'd had every intention of squeezing Julio and Victor's balls until they gave up everything they knew or had ever imagined about drugs. But it had taken him three days to finish in Mountain View and by then they were gone.

He'd heard about the accident by chance. He still maintained a working friendship of sorts with a sergeant in the narcotics squad of the metropolitan police and, since life at home was decidedly unpleasant, he'd taken to spending one night out of three with him. They'd been drinking coffee when the accident report came in. Seeing the name Sanchez, the sergeant had handed it to Buchanan with the comment that it looked like his snitches had reverted to form.

Almost noon. He made a quick calculation. As long as none of these speeding piece-of-shit-ought-to-be-outlawed foreign cars caused a pileup, he should be at the hospital by two-thirty. Three at the latest.

He couldn't wait to get his hands on those lying-greaser-fucking-wetbacks. If they were conscious, he'd start right in, no matter what the doctors said. If they weren't, they first thing they'd see when they came to would be his smiling face.

151

The conversation with the hospital administrator hadn't made Jake feel any better. Neither had the meeting with the psychiatrist. There had been a lot of talk in jargon that hadn't meant a thing to him, but as near as he could tell the best thing was to put her in the state hospital.

The funny farm.

Commit Mary Margaret? Couldn't happen.

Keep her at home? That was his decision, of course. But without professional care, without monitoring and supervision around the clock, there was virtually no chance of recovery.

"So I got three choices. Take her home, which I can afford — but she won't get better. Leave her with you — which I haven't got the money for, even with help from all those alphabet soup agencies your bean counter told me about — and there's a chance she might improve. Or, I can have her committed, but that's where she'll stay until she dies."

"I appreciate the difficulty of your position, Mr. Grummond."

"Appreciate my ass."

Allsup winced. "Let me talk with the office. Perhaps I can work something out. At least buy you some time while you evaluate your options." He stood, and with marked courtesy, escorted Jake to the door — the first time he had done so in all the months of weekly meetings.

***

Just before lunch, Blakenship called Phillips and Darling again. Neither Buchanan nor anyone else from the DEA had been by.

"You know, we got our tails in a crack cooperating with them last summer," Blakenship told Phillips. "If I were you, I'd check out the vehicle myself."

"Been thinking along those lines. But why're you so interested?"

"Might be connected with what went on down here. Those boys been making that run for years. Funny they'd pick this time to have a wreck."

"The vehicle is in my jurisdiction. A body might think I was derelict in my duty if I didn't take a look. What do you think I might be looking for?"

"Well, those boys were mules, so you might look for illegal substances of a recreational nature."

"I figured."

"And they were also snitches, so you might look for a mechanical irregularity, if you get my drift."

Darling didn't have much to report, either. Julio and Victor were in stable condition. Both had regained consciousness, but neither was saying anything. Not even to ask for their lawyers, an interesting omission given their prior experiences with the law. Oh yeah. Neither had tested positive for alcohol or drugs.

"If I drove up your way this afternoon, think you might have time to take me by?"

"Depends on when you'd get here."

"I'm out the door."

***

Blakenship beat Buchanan to the hospital by fifteen minutes, time enough to ask each brother what had happened and where they'd been since August and stare into their obsidian eyes as they refused to answer.

Had their father been notified?

He'd called about mid-morning. Seen the story in the newspaper. Sounded relieved that they were going to live. Said he'd try to see them this evening. "Seemed real upset about the car," Darling added. "Wonder why?"

"Runs a used-car lot in Union and I expect it was one of his." Blakenship led the way outside to their vehicles, parked side-by-side. "I suggested to Phillips he might look it over for

153

mechanical irregularities, seeing as how they came back clean for booze and drugs."

"I can see where he might be upset if a car of his was boogered and his boys almost died."

"Yeah. On the other hand, it's not like he don't know what his sons were involved with. And if the car didn't meet factory specifications, he ought to have some idea of the why of it." Blakenship removed his Stetson and let the wind riffle his hair. "My, my. Look who's here."

"Who?"

"See that skinny sonofabitch in the top coat? The one getting out of the puke-green Chevy with the soft left front tire? That's James Buchanan of the DEA. You and fate might have a serious talk about his showing up in your little corner of the world."

Buchanan splashed through the melting snow in short, rapid steps, kept from a run only by the footing. When he reached the shoveled sidewalk, he did break into a run. Darling and Blakenship watched him, moving so fast he had to wait for the automatic sliding doors to react before he could disappear inside.

"Maybe we should tag along," said Blakenship.

When the elevator door opened on the third floor, they could see Buchanan face to face with the deputy on duty, jabbing him in the chest with a rigid forefinger.

"Got a problem, Gabe?" Darling called.

"This guy wants to see the Sanchez brothers. Says he's DEA."

"Well, is he?"

"Don't know. He hasn't shown me any ID." Buchanan cursed under his breath as he fumbled in his inside jacket pocket. The deputy stared at the ID for a full thirty seconds. "Says he's DEA, sheriff. Name's Buchanan."

"He's Buchanan." Blakenship spit the end of an unlit Rum Crook in the general direction of a wastebasket against the wall.

The DEA agent focused on Blakenship. "I know you. You're the sheriff from ..."

154

"Sapinero County. Hard to remember if you're not from this country. Although for a body here to see the Sanchez brothers, it shouldn't be all that hard to come up with."

"And you are?" Buchanan asked Darling.

"Wendall Darling. Sheriff of Packer County. The Sanchezes are in my jurisdiction. You are, too, come to think of it."

"I need to talk to them. Now."

"So do I. But we're waiting for the doctor's say-so."

"You haven't talked to them?"

"Just a little bit."

"And?"

"And nothing. They just lay there. Eyes open, mouths shut."

"Seeing me might open things up."

"That's what we're hoping," said Blakenship.

"This isn't your jurisdiction," Buchanan snapped. "What're you doing here?"

"What you see here is cooperation between fellow law enforcement officers," Blakenship answered mildly.

"You see, son," Darling added, "I don't know how it is where you come from, but out here we try to help each other as much as we can. Now, while we're waiting for the doctor, maybe you can tell us why you're interested in Victor and Julio."

"That's government business."

"Funny. I always thought we were government. Didn't you, C. W.?"

Buchanan flushed. "I mean federal."

"As I recall, you feds were glad to call on us locals back in August." Blakenship trimmed some more of the soggy end of his cigar with his teeth and spit it at the wastebasket.

"They'd been cooperating with us on one of our investigations — then they dropped out of sight."

"You couldn't find them, either."

"What do you mean, either?"

155

"Been trying to have a chat with them ever since I found out they're the ones who sicced you onto Jake's place."

"Why?"

"Lots of reasons. One of them being why they told such an outright lie in the first place."

"Maybe they thought it was true when they told it, C. W." Darling shushed Buchanan with a wave of his hand. "Or maybe they're protecting somebody."

"If they're protecting someone, they wouldn't be in the hospital." Buchanan's assurance sounded forced.

"You mean you don't think they were drunk?"

"It's not like them."

"Know them well, do you?" Blakenship brushed passed Buchanan to the water fountain and rinsed the remaining flecks of tobacco from his mouth. "As it happens, you're right."

Darling leaned against the wall and folded his arms across his chest. "They may have been protecting folks, but somebody didn't get the word. Just knew they'd been talking to you."

"Interesting," said Buchanan. "What's taking the doctor so long?"

"He won't be by until five or so."

"Five? Five? Why the fuck didn't you tell me? I'm going in now."

"Mr. Buchanan," said Darling, "let me tell you how it is as clearly as I can. We are going to wait for the doctor. If you put up an argument, I'll have to run you in and at the very least you'll be tied up at my office until way past five. So the quickest way for you to talk with them — or try to — is to be patient."

"Can I make a suggestion, Wendall?"

"Sure, C. W."

"Why don't we give Sam a call? See if they've looked at the car."

"I told him not to touch it until I got there." Buchanan was quivering all over.

"Car's in his jurisdiction. His responsibility to find out what happened."

156

They rode the elevator in silence, Blakenship and Darling standing at the back, comfortable with each other, Buchanan in a front corner, shifting nervously from foot to foot. It was spitting snow as they got into Darling's Cherokee — the two sheriffs in front and Buchanan in the back behind Darling — and waited for the dispatcher to patch them through to Shotgun.

Blakenship and Darling chatted about the weather while the radio crackled before springing to life with the metallic voice of Sheriff Phillips.

"Wendall here, Sam. What're you, on one of them damn speaker phones? Sounds like you're talking from the bottom of a well."

"That better?"

"Yeah. We're sitting here in my vehicle listening to you on the radio."

"Who's we?"

"Me and C. W. and that Buchanan fellow from the DEA."

"Good. Save me from having to repeat myself."

"Finished, have you?"

"Nope. Still got a ways to go. But I did find something kind of interesting, C. W. Remember your thought about — how'd you put it? — mechanical irregularities?"

"Yeah."

"Brakes. Fluid low. Real low. So low they'd had to have noticed it right away."

"Unless ..."

"Unless the reservoir had been topped off with water."

"Which boils away. My, my." Blakenship unwrapped a cigar. "Does that mean the father had a hand in trying to kill his sons?"

"Maybe. Maybe not," Darling answered. "But it sure as hell means who did it knew which car they were going to take. And had the time and opportunity." Darling picked up the microphone. "Esther. This is Wendall. See if you can raise Homer Underhill over in Union for me." He replaced the microphone and glanced at his watch. "Most five. Why don't you two go on and see if the doc'll let you in."

***

The snow was heavier as Jake started the long, gentle downhill to Top Hat. State hospital. Home care. Had to decide by the weekend. He drove past the turn to the dairy and continued to Fritz Bonham's new nursing home on the highway with a half-formed notion of checking on costs. But when he pulled into the parking lot, the raw earth next to the new building looked so forlorn in the gathering twilight he couldn't bear to go in. Tomorrow. He'd talk to Fritz tomorrow.

***

The doctor had finally showed up at 5:30 and he'd allowed them fifteen minutes, not that they'd needed that much time. The only acknowledgment of their presence either brother gave was a flutter of Julio's eyelids when Buchanan mentioned water in the brake lines. Otherwise, they lay there with reptilian impassivity even through Buchanan's threats of federal hard time.

Buchanan had held his tongue until they got outside, then he'd blown up. Blakenship and Darling had waited until he'd run down, and then walked him to his car. The two sheriffs stood side by side, their respective breaths streaming in alternating plumes like locomotives waiting to pull from the station, while they watched the Chevy turn in the direction of the Interstate.

"Strange fellow," remarked Darling.

"By himself, too." Blakenship spit reflectively. "Last time I saw him, he was ramrodding a crew. Don't look like the world's been kind to him since August."

***

Thursday, Allsup left a message on the answering machine. The best he'd been able to do was reduce the rate for Mary Margaret to $1000 a week, payable weekly. Would Mr. Grummond contact him as soon as possible?

Jake heard the message at five-thirty and tried to reach the doctor at his office. He hung up when the recording came on, then thought better of it, redialed, and waited patiently for the beep so he could leave his own message. The phone rang halfway through a bowl of leftover stew he hadn't bothered to reheat. Much to his surprise, it was the psychiatrist.

"Dr. Allsup here, Mr. Grummond. You got my message?"

"A thousand a week is out of the question."

"Do you want me to make arrangements to transfer her to the state hospital?" When Jake didn't answer, he repeated the question.

"She can go to the state hospital any time. Can't she?"

"True."

"What I think I'll do is bring her home. For the weekend, anyway. See how it goes."

"That's your choice. But I cannot stress too much that she needs attention twenty-four hours a day."

"I understand."

"Perhaps we can talk when you pick her up. Do you know when?"

"Saturday at the earliest."

"I won't be available then. But please give me a call next week."

Around-the-clock care. How was he going to manage that? Jake surveyed the living room like he'd never seen it before. Dust on the tabletops. Dust balls under the sofa. Had to get somebody to give it a good cleaning.

He pushed the bowl aside and put on his down vest. There was a bite in the air when he stepped onto the porch. Jake shivered, then stiffened and headed toward the yellowish square of light spreading from the door of the barn.

***

159

He'd gotten a late start to Union. His father was in a foul mood because it was the first Saturday without a football game. A real game. Them fucking all-star games didn't count. He'd fussed around the main house, trying to help Maria Elena with mopping and vacuuming, doing such a poor job she had to do it over again. Jake finally took him back to his cabin.

Since he wasn't sure how Mary Margaret would act, he'd taken the van with the seats removed and a mattress with pillows and blankets laid out in back. Much as he hated to ask for help, responsibility overrode pride and he'd enlisted Helen to accompany him.

Helen was shocked when she saw Mary Margaret. It wasn't like Jake hadn't tried to explain. She'd asked him an innocuous question when they'd barely left Top Hat and it had opened up something. He talked all the way to Union.

But nothing he'd said had prepared her for actually seeing her cousin. How passive — how stupid — she'd become. How much weight she'd put on — pudge blurring the classic angles of cheek and jaw, belly pushing against the buttons of the housedress.

It was all Helen could do to keep from crying. As it was, she'd gasped audibly when she'd walked into the room and realized that the thickening body with the expressionless face had been the lithe and lively woman she'd known for more than forty years.

Jake and the nurse had gotten her into the wheelchair and they made their way to the elevator. Just before going outside, Helen tried to button Mary Margaret's coat against the January chill, but she was sitting on the coattails and began to whimper when Helen tried to free them.

"Never mind," said Jake, "with the heater on, she won't need the coat."

Getting her into the van was a chore because she didn't have any idea of what they were trying to do — moving in response to pressure but stopping once the pressure ceased.

Finally Jake picked her up like a groom carrying his bride over the threshold and laid her bodily on the mattress.

Neither Jake nor Helen said a word until they were halfway to Top Hat.

"People are hard to figure."

Helen was sitting half-turned in her seat with her back against the door so she could keep an eye on Mary Margaret. "What do you mean?"

"The psychiatrist. He paid for Mary Margaret's last week."

"From what I understand, psychiatrists make good money."

"Ain't saying it would break him. But he didn't have to do it."

They rode the rest of the way in silence. At the intersection, Jake turned into Top Hat.

"Don't you want me to come out to the dairy?"

"Eusebio's there."

"But I can help her get comfortable. Wash her face. Things like that."

"You've done enough. Don't want to impose on you any more."

"Impose hell, you dumb bastard. She's my cousin. I as much as raised her."

Jake pulled up in front of the tavern and let Helen's anger sink in. "Don't know what I was thinking." He backed away from the curb and made a U-turn.

The number of pickups and other vehicles parked along the shoulder of the road told Jake something was wrong before he made the turn into the dairy. Then he saw both of the volunteer fire department's pumpers and the brush truck.

"Jesus Christ."

Men were standing around the smoldering remains of the mechanic's shed.

Jake sat white-faced and rigid, trying to put together what had happened. Frog Bottom, slicker still buckled against the

161

wind, walked over. "Got the call about three-thirty. Lucky we got here in time to keep it from spreading."

Jake looked at the black pile of ash where the tractors and other equipment had been worked on ever since he could remember. Then he looked at the barn. No lights.

"Fire knock the power out?" He knew without waiting for an answer because the pole that carried electricity to the shed was gone. "Milking time and I ain't got electricity."

12

JANUARY 17 — Late Afternoon

Electricity to all the buildings ran off the burned pole. Jake lit a fire in the wood stove and found two Coleman lanterns last used at elk camp many seasons ago, while Helen made up the bed in the guest room. He and Eusebio got Mary Margaret inside and propped her on a bed she'd never slept in before.

When Helen returned to the cold dark room, she found her staring at the shadows flickering on the wall, silent tears streaming down her face to puddle in the folds of neck and bosom. One look at her cousin and Helen walked to the phone.

"Fritz, this is Helen."

"I recognize the voice."

"Any room in that new home of yours?"

"You mean the nursing home?"

"Only new home you got, isn't it. Or have you cut another deal in the last twenty-four hours?"

"Why? Age creeping up on you?"

"Not me, you idiot. Mary Margaret."

"Grummond?"

"Of course."

"Thought she was in Union."

"Insurance ran out. Jake had to bring her home today and ..."

"The fire."

"Right. House is as cold as a tomb and Jake's got things to do."

"We've got room. What shape's she in?"

"She doesn't say anything and she doesn't do anything. Doesn't even make any noise when she cries. And gaining weight. You remember how she weighed the same as when she was in high school?"

"Mary Margaret always was a trim-looking woman."

"She must have put on sixty pounds. Maybe more. Keeps going at that rate, she'll look like a beached whale by Easter."

Helen started to sob, a sound so unexpected from the woman he was talking to that Bonham was startled into compassion.

"I'll have someone pick her up as fast as I can."

"Better send two. And one of those stretchers on wheels. It's hard to get her to go the way you want her to."

"Two it is."

"And Fritz. I'll pay."

"We'll talk about it later."

Jake was talking to a raw-boned kid with a wispy smear of a mustache. He wasn't talking exactly, more like listening through the boy's snuffles.

"Jake," Helen called from the porch. "Fritz is sending someone to pick up Mary Margaret."

Jake turned stiffly, like a gate with hinges in need of oil. "Say what?"

"I said, Fritz is sending some people out. She can't stay here."

"Right." Jake turned back to the boy. "From the beginning, Jeffrey."

"Yes sir. Mr. Grummond, sir. Like I said, when I went to hitch up the manure spreader, I saw the bar, the one the hitch is on, was cracked pretty near all the way through."

"Cracked where?"

"On the curve. You know, just up from where it's welded on the tractor. That was one of the last jobs Andy did before he left. Welding the bar on, I mean."

"I remember."

"Anyway, I figured I better fix it 'cause if I didn't the whole works might come undone when I was out in the field, so I drove it into the shed. Over near the east wall where the light's better. I got the welder out and fired it up. But there was some spilled solvent on the floor. You know, from the bath where you soak parts. I hadn't noticed it before. And …" Jeffrey choked to a stop.

"And?"

"It caught fire." He stopped again.

"And?"

164

"I ran for the fire extinguisher. I knew I had to get it before the flames reached the rest of the solvent. But when I swung the extinguisher around, I must have hit the glass bowl on the tractor."

"The fuel filter?"

"Uh huh. It broke and gasoline started running all over the place and it caught on fire and then it reached the solvent and …" He was crying full bore now, with no attempt to stem the tears streaming down his face or wipe the mucous bubbling from his nose.

Jake let him stand there for minutes that seemed like all the time there ever had been or ever would be. Then he let out a great exhalation of air and walked in a slow circle through the mucky clay of the barnyard until he was back where he started in front of the boy. "Best thing for you to do is leave. Because if I see you again tonight, I don't know if …"

"Mr. Grummond, I …"

"Go." Jake wiped his hands across his eyes. "Just go."

***

That had been six hours earlier. The crew from Sapinero Rural Electric arrived at eight-thirty and jury-rigged lines within the hour. The foreman promised they'd be back on Monday to put in a permanent pole. It was pushing midnight now and Jake leaned against the wall watching Eusebio and Jorge. Production was down.

Jake walked through the barn and opened the door that led to the pens. The chill air carried the sounds of shifting feet. They're like me, he thought. Sleepwalking through what has to be done at the wrong time of day.

Has to be done. Why does it have to be done? What's the point? He remembered the story about the dairyman who'd been fighting mounting debt and an unsympathetic banker. The farmer called the banker at home at four o'clock one morning and told him if he wanted to save his herd he'd better get out here and do his milking.

Why not quit? Why not tell Eusebio to forget it and go to bed?

Can't do anything now. Best sleep on it.

***

The gray of first light slanting across his face opened his eyes to the sight of his booted feet pointing toward the ceiling. Further inspection revealed he had on what he'd been wearing in the barn.

He swung to a sitting position and eyed the smears of dried adobe on the bedspread without concern or curiosity. Through the window, darkening layers of clouds promised snow before the day was out. The alarm clock read three-thirty, mute proof he'd forgotten to wind it.

The kitchen clock showed a quarter after six. Jake got the coffee started and went to the porch while the pot filled. The blackened earth and scorched metal piled where the mechanic's shed had been brought yesterday back with a rush and he stood motionless for a good two minutes while he beat back anger and fought to regain a sense for the sequence in which things had happened. He pulled his eyes from the cold evidence of the fire to the cattle standing hunched against the wind.

Time to cut his losses.

It came to him with a clarity as pure and unequivocal as his anger.

Time to sell the herd.

He went inside and poured coffee while he thought about who to call first. His father? Neighbors who might want to pick up some bargains?

He started by calling Barry Willis out Pea Green way who said he'd be by with a gooseneck trailer before nine. Three other area dairymen had similar responses. It was a little after seven when he finished calling everyone he could think of. He started to dial the number of James "Silver" Dollar who ran the region's largest auction company, but, it being Sunday, decided he'd best wait until eight.

Eusebio had been up late. Give him another hour.

His father. Hadn't seen him since he'd been such a nuisance cleaning up the house. Had it really been less than twenty-four hours?

Where had he been during the fire? Surely he'd heard the trucks.

By the fourth ring, he was sure of the worst when the faint rasp of his father's voice sounded in his ear. "Yes, goddammit."

"You all right? Where've you been?"

"Been right here. Where'd you think?"

"I don't know. What with the fire and all ..."

"Then the fire was at our place. What went?"

"Mechanic's shed. Welding set some solvents on fire and ..."

"Damn. Never knew Andy Dawes to make that kind of mistake."

"Andy left before Christmas."

"That's right. Got his own repair business."

"How come you didn't come down?" The silence stretched toward half a minute. "Dad?"

"Didn't figure there was anything I could do." Another silence. Then, "Guess I didn't want to find out if it was us. Don't know as I can take any more bad news."

"It's bad news all right. Almost ten before we could start milking."

"Shit. Shit, son. I ..."

Jake could barely hear him. "Want me to come over?"

"No." A pause. "What're you going to do?"

"Sell the herd."

"We out of the dairy business?"

"Don't know for sure. But we got to cut our losses."

"You might ought to think it over."

"I have. Willis and some others are coming this morning to see if there's any they want. I'm calling Silver Dollar at eight."

"Equipment, too?"

"Haven't thought that far ahead."

"What about Eusebio and the rest?"

"Like I said, I ain't thought that far ahead."

"Mary Margaret?"

"At Fritz's new place."

"Permanent?"

"Don't know that, either."

He reached Dollar a little after the hour, who said he'd have his trucks there by noon. They could talk about everything else then.

That left Eusebio and the crew.

If anything, the sky was darker now than it had been when he'd first gotten up and it look like snow was falling on the Sublette Plateau. The adobe of the barnyard and road, churned by all the trucks and feet from the day before, had frozen so hard during the night that the clay ridges didn't crumble under his weight.

Mercedes opened the door at the creak of footsteps on the frozen boards of the porch. "He is in the shower."

"Please tell him I'd like to see him."

"It is not good?"

"No. It is not good."

"Will we have to leave?"

"The ten acres. They're yours."

"Yes. But …" Mercedes let her voice trail away, the concern about work and paychecks clear. "I will tell him."

Eusebio found him standing over the scarred desk in the barn with Barry Willis going over each cow's individual production record.

"You wished to see me?"

Jake straightened up from the desk and rubbed the small of his back. "Guess you know why." Eusebio nodded. "Haven't got the details worked out. Willis here may buy some of the best. Probably be a few more by this morning to do the same. The trucks for the rest, except for the calves, will be here after lunch." Eusebio showed no expression except for the resigned sorrow of his eyes and a slight quiver of his upper lip. "I don't know how this is going to work out," Jake continued, "but everybody will be paid through the end of February."

***

A dairyman named Edwards from the western part of the county had just finished loading ten milking head and five heifers carrying their first calves when a dark blue Lincoln nosed to rest next to Jake's pickup. A tall, rail-thin man unfolded from behind the steering wheel to reveal that the faded overalls he was wearing were at least a size too big and had a tear at the right knee.

"Damn shame, Jake," said Silver Dollar, extending his hand. "Sometimes I feel like an undertaker, showing up when folks are going through a hard patch."
"Not your fault."

"That's what Maggie always tells me. Trucks will be along in about half, three-quarters of an hour. They all go?"

"Except for some of the calves and young heifers. Going to let my people take their pick of them. May want to feed them out for the freezer. Or keep a cow to milk."

"We still talking about three hundred head?"

"More or less."

"What about equipment?"

"Don't know yet. Things been happening so fast I haven't had time to figure out whether this is just temporary or if I'm out of the dairy business permanent."

"Fair enough. No particular hurry for things that don't eat or get sick."

***

The Presidentials were still hidden in thick folds of snow-bearing clouds, but in the valley the heavy overcast had broken a bit, letting a thin mid-afternoon sun through. Jake leaned against the post to the left of the porch steps, its powdery paint leaving white marks on his jacket. His father, lead pipe in hand and

169

thighs pressing against the railing for support, stood next to him. Shoulders almost, but not quite, touching, they watched the last cows being loaded.

With the tailgate up and the driver revving plumes of black smoke from the chrome stacks, Grandpa Grummond finally spoke. "Now what?"

"Don't know. A lot'll depend on what the auction brings."

"How much from Willis and them?"

"Have to check. Think it's pushing $30,000."

"That ain't much for fifty head of prime milking stock."

"They ain't prime. Not at the moment, anyway."

"Suppose not. How much we owe?"

"Have to add it up. But first, I'm going to sleep." Jake spit into the yard. "After I check on Mary Margaret." He looked at his father and tried to brush the paint powder off the old man's jeans. "Been meaning to paint the house."

His father made his way down the steps to his pickup, leaning heavily on the lead pipe every step of the way. "Never thought I'd see this day. Never." He put the truck in gear and drove slowly down the still-frozen adobe ruts to the county road. Jake watched the taillights brake red as the truck turned right and kept watching until it was out of sight. The unnatural quiet, broken only by occasional bleating from the calf pen, disoriented him and he retreated into the house.

The answering machine's blinking caught his eye. Helen's voice. "Jake, I know you're busy, but give me a call. I'll be home until four. That's when I'll check on Mary Margaret."

He let it ring six times and was about to hang up when Helen's out-of-breath voice sounded in his ear.

"Just got your message."

"I was on my way to Mary Margaret. What's going on?"

"Silver Dollar just finished picking up the herd."

"Oh Jake, I'm sorry. Somebody said they saw cattle trucks headed your way. What now?"

"First thing, I'm going to get some sleep. Then I'll start figuring. Since you're going to check on her, I think I'll wait."

"I'll call you when I get back."

170

"O. K. No. Better let me call you. Don't know how long I'll sleep. It's not like there's any milking to get up for."

He had drifted into a half-dream populated with cows and cattle trucks and the questioning faces of the men and their wives and children when footsteps sounded on the porch and Evie Stanton's voice echoed through the empty house.

When he got to the kitchen, Evie was pulling dishes from paper sacks. "Didn't figure you'd have time to cook. This here is macaroni and cheese. And there's green beans and a saucepan of venison chili all you have to do is heat up and there's some rolls and …"

"Anything I can do?" Billy asked.

"Don't know. I've got a lot of sorting out ahead of me. But thanks."

"How's Mary Margaret?" Evie asked.

"Not good. She's at Fritz's."

"Can I see her?"

"Suppose so. But I doubt it'll be worth the trouble. She hasn't recognized me for months. Look. I got to get some sleep."

Billy pulled Evie toward the door. "Call if you need anything. Any time."

Jake was on the bed before the pickup's motor sounded. The crunch of its tires pulling away from the house was the last thing he remembered before morning light.

***

Blakenship hadn't learned of the fire until late Saturday night when he picked up Jessie at the Stockman. They'd spent a quiet afternoon together, leisurely lovemaking followed by cuddling in front of the TV watching a cassette of "Red River". It was one of his favorites and ever since they came out with movies on video, he made a point of watching it once a year.

When the time came for Jessie to begin her shift, he'd dropped her off and driven home to nap for a couple of hours. It was ten before he was up and if he hadn't overheard a conversation at the bar as he pushed his way through the

Saturday night throng, he might not have heard of the latest catastrophe at the Grummond Dairy until Monday morning.

If the fire was as bad as the Stockman barflies made out — and his call to Frog Bottom bore out that it was — then Jake was in his deepest hole yet. And, according to Froggie, Jake had brought Mary Margaret home and she was in bad shape.

Sunday restlessness brought him to Henderson's door by mid-afternoon. "Wake you up, did I?" Blakenship gestured at the shirttails Henderson was trying to tuck into his pants without undoing his belt.

"No. But two minutes earlier and you would have. What brings you away from Miss Jessie's comforting arms?"

Blakenship started to sketch what he'd heard about the fire when Henderson interrupted. "Word is Jake's sold off his herd. Jimmy Reese said cattle trucks rolled onto 71 coming from the dairy with Silver Dollar's Lincoln right behind."

"Sold off the herd." A calendar on the wall behind Henderson sported a photograph of a skier jumping from a rocky promontory and Blakenship wondered why anyone would do such a thing. "Now what?"

"You asking or just making noise?"

"Making noise. But since you brought it up, I'll ask. What's Jake going to do?"

"I haven't the foggiest, C. W. Except he's going to have time on his hands and he's not a happy man."

***

Mary Margaret hadn't gotten out of bed for a week.

Jake had been to see her every day and every day it was the same. Sometimes lying on her back, sometimes on her stomach, and on two occasions raised to a sitting position by an attendant. Usually awake. They'd tried to get her up and walking, Fritz told him, but she acted like her legs were paralyzed. Ran tests and everything checked out. But she wouldn't use her legs. They could get her standing with an attendant on each side, but once they let go, she collapsed to the floor. And then it was hell getting her back in bed.

"I hate to say this, Jake," Fritz had told him, "but she's the next thing to a vegetable."

They'd been standing in the nursing home's back yard, the most active of the residents enjoying the warmth of the afternoon sun, when Fritz made his blunt assessment. "Think you ought to schedule a couple of sessions a week with a physical therapist. There's a couple who moved to Mountain View last summer. Set up shop and work with the hospital — and us, when we've got the need."

"They could come out to the house as easy as here."

"They could. Although you got to remember she needs a lot of checking on. Shit, Jake, she won't even use a bedpan. She's in diapers."

He almost threw up at the thought of Mary Margaret in diapers. After he'd regained a modicum of composure, he told Fritz he'd think on it. That had been two days ago and he wasn't any closer to knowing what to do.

He was at the kitchen table on his fifth cup of coffee and listening to the quiet he couldn't get used to when the phone rang. Mackey Fitzgerald. "Got a letter from the DEA," the lawyer drawled. "You should've, too."
"Mail hasn't come yet."

"They rejected the claim."

"So much for Stewart's letter."

"Blair may be the reason we got the letter, which is really permission to sue, a month ahead of schedule. And don't forget the information his aide dug up."

"Wasn't anything I didn't have a right to know."

"Can't argue. Thing is, if we're going to sue it would be a good idea to talk to another lawyer. I happen to have the name of one who comes highly recommended. He's in Denver. You and me could drive over one day and have a talk with him."

"When?"

"The sooner the better. When have you got some time?"

"I got nothing but time."

173

"I'll see what I can set up."

Fitzgerald called back less than an hour later to say the appointment had been made for 3:30 Friday afternoon.

"The day after tomorrow?" asked Jake.

"That's Friday, isn't it?"

"Need to be on our way by eight. Reckon we should spend the night?"

"See how we feel. And what the weather is."

"I'll drive."

"Was hoping you'd volunteer. But we can take my Grand Cherokee."

***

The meeting with the lawyer, H. Harold Griffin according to the gold lettering on the door, had started a half hour late and had lasted well past 5:30. Although Jake had mainly listened after describing the raid and the destruction while the two attorneys went over Fitzgerald's file and discussed points of law, he'd left the session drained.

Mackey Fitz was tired also, too tired to drive back, and had made reservations from Griffin's office for rooms at a downtown hotel he favored. They were now seated at his favorite steak house, a room of dark wood and brass that had been elegant in the 1890's and which still carried for him the cachet of a big city celebration.

When they'd ordered drinks, Jake had George Dickel and water — the same as Fitzgerald — and when they'd ordered food, he'd duplicated Fitz's order, except for having his porterhouse done medium well. He hadn't mimicked the older man because he was intimidated by the restaurant — he'd hardly given it a second thought.

Thinking was the problem.

The meeting had laid out everything that had happened since the day of the raid in one sweeping presentation. With some notable exceptions, Jake had been able to cope since the raid by doing what had to be done. But to sit for two hours while

174

other people unrolled his recent history had unnerved Jake more than he could say.

"Another?" Fitz indicated the empty cocktail glass.

"I guess so."

The waitress took the order and disappeared.

"So," said Fitzgerald, "what do you think? Griffin's good. Very good."

"Still, I'm looking at a long time with short odds of recovering anything."

"True."

"Did I hear right that he didn't think Mary Margaret's ..." he groped for the right word.

"The problem he was raising was how she reacted to Paul's ...," Fitzgerald winced at Jake's involuntary tic. "Be like what the insurance companies call a 'pre-existing condition.'" The fresh drinks came. "Look, Jake. Connections are going to be one of our big issues. Your father's heart attack. Della's miscarriage. Even the lost production and lost animals."

Jake tinkled the ice in his drink for a long time before answering. "You're saying I can only sue for damage to the houses and trailers."

"No. I'm saying that that's where the connection to the raid is clearest."

Jake went on as if he hadn't heard. "Even if I get it, ain't a drop in the bucket of what I lost. And Griffin's not going to come cheap." He set the glass down. "How long before I got to give him an answer?"

"Think about it. But not forever."

Jake nodded and brought the heavy-bottomed glass of whiskey and water to his lips then slammed it on the table hard enough to startle the waitress bringing their salads into almost dropping her tray. "Cocksuckers," Jake exploded, loud enough to carry throughout the room. Then "cocksuckers" again in a whispering hiss.

***

It was almost ten when Fitzgerald signed the credit card slip and waved away Jake's proffered cash with an irritable shake of his head. Pedestrian traffic was moderately heavy on the sidewalk despite the biting wind. They were four blocks from their hotel, four blocks of once top-of-the-line restaurants now interspersed with adult book stores, pawn shops and topless bars, the sign for one — a neon silhouette of a naked woman — prompting a jolt of sexual warmth that made Jake pause in mid-stride.

How long had it been? He stood, trying to make the calculation until Fritz asked him what was the matter.

"Nothing. Just had a thought. Nothing that makes any difference."

They continued toward the hotel, hunched against the wind and occasionally veering out of the way of small clots of men trying to decide which topless joint to spend their money in first.

They were pinned momentarily between two such groups when he saw him. A tall, softly heavy figure greeting the doorman of one of the strip joints with loud familiarity.

That Otero County sack of shit.

He was introducing a younger, slightly smaller version of himself to the doorman who ushered them inside with practiced conviviality. They disappeared into the smoky dimness, bouncing in awkward rhythm to the whirl of some rock song Jake didn't recognize. He looked up to the marquee, the same impossibly large-breasted silhouette that had jolted him moments before, and read the blinking script: Sugar's. Where Every Dream Is Sweet.

"If you want to go in, it's all right with me." Fitzgerald was looking at Jake with amusement. "But I'm a little old and way too tired."

"Say what?" Jake turned, startled. "It's not that. Thought I saw someone."

***

176

The hotel room was too hot and he couldn't figure out how to adjust the thermostat or open the window. Couldn't get comfortable on the firm mattress of the strange bed, the pillows that didn't have enough give to them.

He stood at the window in his underwear, a glass of ice water in hand, studying the trail of neon lights marching toward Sugar's.

Donaldson. That was the name on Blakenship's list. He hadn't been able to erase the sight of him. The self-proud familiarity of his greeting to the doorman, his sweaty eagerness to get to the naked women, the screams and violence of the dusty August night. He could smell the man's fear — sour and acid — feel the veins in his throat pulsing in his left hand.

He could have squeezed the life out of him then. Could have watched his eyes bulge and the swollen purple obscenity of his tongue protrude from his gross lips.

13

JANUARY 31 — Late Afternoon

"She's just not here anymore, Jake." Helen put a Bud in front of him and began wiping imaginary puddles on the bar. "And I don't think she's ever going to get any better." She threw the bar towel in the sink and began cleaning her eyeglasses on the tail of her blouse.

Jake had gotten back shortly before three. After skimming the mail and calling his father — who grumbled about being awakened from his nap — he drove to the nursing home. He'd come in while the therapist, a vigorous, full-bodied woman in her late thirties, worked Mary Margaret's limbs and massaged her back. When she was finished, she introduced herself as Adrienne and washed her hands with a surgeon's pre-operation thoroughness. "That's all I can do until she decides to respond. I wish I could be more encouraging."

After she left, Jake watched Mary Margaret stare at the ceiling, her familiar profile rising above the ever-thickening mass of her neck and shoulders. Where's the fat coming from? Was she really eating that much? Was it the lack of exercise?

He needed air.

The cold slap of the gusting north wind drove away the lethargy brought on by the overheated nursing home. Almost dark. Time for milking. But there was no milking. When he reached the county road, he'd turned left and pulled up in front of Helen's.

Jake toyed with the beer bottle but didn't pick it up. "Allsup was pushing the state hospital. What do you think?"

"Jesus, Jake. That's a hell of a thing."

"What other choice is there? Can't take care of her at home and Fritz is going to want his money sometime."

"It's just …" Her voice faded as Fritz Bonham came into the bar.

"Helen. Jake." Bonham shucked out of his jacket, draped it over the bar stool and sat down on it. "Jack Black and water.

Please." He turned to Jake while Helen built the drink. "Saw your truck. Figured it was time we had a talk."

"What do I owe you?"

"We can work that out later. Question is, what're you going to do?"

"That's what we were talking about." Helen set the drink in front of Fritz. "And we ain't got very far. Except the state hospital."

Fritz broke the silence that had settled after Helen's assessment. "She hasn't shown a sign of getting better. Getting worse, if anything. I don't mean she's a whole lot of trouble. Just have to remember to change her diapers — although heavy as she is, that can be troublesome. Sorry," he said at Jake's involuntary flinch. "Thing is, we can't do more than tend to the basics."

"We know." Helen leaned on the bar midway between Fritz and Jake. "You have anything new to add?"

"You want me to get her out?" Jake spun his stool to face him. "I can do that right now, if that's what you want."

"Take it easy. It's just I had half an idea. You know the Normans? Tom and Alice?"

"Of course."

"Alice, she's from California. Tom met her when he was stationed at Fort Ord. Anyhow. Alice has got an aunt who's come to live with them. Early retirement. Get out of the rat race. That kind of thing."

"Get to the point."

"Seems she's a psychologist. Also appears that time is starting to hang heavy on her hands. She called, asking if I needed a counselor. Said I'd just got up and running but I'd keep her in mind. You might want to give her a call." Fritz reached between his legs to his coat and pulled out a notebook. "Name is Taylor. Bridget Taylor, Ph.D."

"She staying with Tom and Alice?"

"For the time being." Fritz swallowed the last of his drink, laid four crisp dollar bills on the bar, stood up and put on his coat.

They watched Bonham close the door behind him. "Not like Fritz not to get the financial details settled, preferably with a wad of your cash in his pocket. Don't suppose he's going soft in his old age?"

"Not likely," Helen answered. "You know how most folks at his place are paying?" She answered her own question. "With their land. And you have some of the best land between Mountain View and Union."

"Think I'll get things straight with Fritz quick." Jake pushed the barely touched beer toward Helen. "Don't seem to be in the mood."

"Fritz's idea about the aunt might work. Just 'cause he's greedy don't mean he's wrong."

***

Blakenship saw Fitzgerald's Grand Cherokee in the driveway of the frame house that served as both the lawyer's office and residence. Which meant, if Charlie was right, he and Jake were back from seeing the big-time lawyer.

He pulled into a parking space near the end of the Stockman's block but the radio crackled and a static-fuzzed voice called his name before he could switch off the ignition. "Luther. This better be good," he grumbled.

"Sheriff?"

"Who do you think?"

"Sorry. So much static I didn't recognize your voice. Someone from the DEA just called. Says he'll be in Mountain View tonight and wants to talk to you."

"He got a name?"

"Buchanan, I think he said. Wasn't he the guy honchoing the raid last summer?"

"He was indeed."

"Said he'd be in by eight. At the Alta."

"O. K. I'll give the Alta a call. Wait. You make the call. If he's in, call me at the Stockman. If he's not, call me anyway."

180

Inside was smoky and warm. Blakenship made his way through the Saturday night crowd to the only open booth, two down from his regular one. Wendy behind the bar waved the telephone receiver in his direction before Jessie brought his first shot and a beer. Expecting Luther, he was startled by Buchanan's nasal rasp. "Guess you're checked in already."

"Just got here. Your deputy called while I was registering."

"Must be some important to bring you to our part of the world on a Saturday night."

"Why don't we discuss it over dinner?"

"You buying?"

"Yes."

"I'll be there. Say," Blakenship squinted at his watch, "quarter to nine."

Jessie was putting his CC and Bud on the table when he got back to the booth. He slipped his arm around her from behind and bent to kiss her ear. "Don't wait too long between rounds. I got to meet that DEA prick in less than an hour."

"How long will that take?"

"No telling. But if it goes past closing time, I'll swing by your place. Or would you rather go to mine?"

"You rent any movies?"

"'The Searchers.'"

"John Wayne again?"

"It's a classic."

"Not to this Ute."

"Hell, you'll be too tired to watch after work anyway."

"If that's what you think, I'll go home."

"Can I come by?"

"Don't wake me up."

***

Blakenship found Buchanan studying a map at the same table where they'd had their last conversation of the summer. He peered at the legend. "A map of Sapinero County? My, my."

181

"CC, Bud back, Sheriff?" The waitress had padded silently behind him. "Another?" she asked Buchanan without waiting for Blakenship's answer.

"No." She started to walk away when Buchanan added, "I'm ready to order." He chose a rib eye, medium well, fries and Thousand Island dressing.

"Sheriff?'

Blakenship ordered a green chili cheese steak.

"How can you eat that crap?"

"Try it. You might surprise yourself."

"No beaner shit's ever been in my mouth and it never will."

"Thanks, darling." Blakenship smiled at the waitress as she set his drinks on the table. "Tell me, Mr. DEA agent, why I should spend the best part of Saturday night with you or I'm out of here." He sipped from the shot glass. "After I eat the beaner shit you're buying me."

Buchanan's lips twisted like a challenged Doberman, then slackened just as quickly. "I need your help."

Blakenship could only guess at how much it cost him to say those four words. "Last time you wanted my help, it didn't turn out so hot. Especially for Jake Grummond."

Buchanan blinked, then continued as if Blakenship hadn't spoken. "Drugs are being run through your county. But if they're not going through the dairy, then where?" He stopped when their salads arrived and didn't begin again until the waitress was half way to the kitchen. "We know it's a Mexican connection."

"How do you know?"

"We've been on this a long time."

"With those public-spirited citizens we know as the Sanchez brothers?"

"No. We didn't identify them until last year. We learned of the route from an informant in Sonora. Although he claimed he'd never participated, he told us his village was a debarkation point for drugs going to the mountain states."

"He name names?"

"A few. Reluctantly."

"And you questioned them?"

"Only after a lot of groundwork."

"Shame you didn't put the same effort into my county."

"That's what I'm doing now."

"Little late from Jake Grummond's point of view. Had to sell his herd. Father's not coming back real good after a heart attack. And his wife … Word is he's fixing to sue your happy ass."

Buchanan blinked again, but, again, didn't respond. The entrees came and neither spoke until they finished eating. Blakenship took a sourdough roll from Buchanan's basket and used it to mop the last of the melted cheese from his plate. He popped it into his mouth and fixed him with a faintly amused stare.

"I imagine you know about the potential suit." He smiled. "Probably the reason why you ain't leading a herd of agents and you're driving that worn out Chevy. Just what is your status, exactly?"

"What difference does that make?"

"You come poking around in my county and asking for my help, I need to know who I'm dealing with."

"I'm on special assignment."

"Special assignment. I see. And that assignment is?"

"To get to the bottom of the drug problem in Sapinero County."

"Drug problem? We don't have much of a problem with drugs here. Marijuana, sure. A little speed. Our main problem is too few jobs at too low pay and too much booze on Saturday night."

"I mean the way station."

"You ain't convinced me there is one. Although the accident with the Sanchez brothers indicates there might be something going on somewhere in this geographic area — broadly speaking." Blakenship leaned back and chewed on a post-prandial cigar. "Who do you report to?"

"Why do you want to know?"

"Because I'm going to check you out. If you're legit, I'll maybe help you. If you're not, I'm going to run your ass out of this county before you do any more harm."

Buchanan, hands on the table, stared across the dirty dishes at Blakenship, a quiver starting in his arms and spreading to his shoulders. "Kiernan," he spit out finally.

"Kiernan?"

Buchanan nodded.

"Wasn't he ...? The big one?" Blakenship rolled the cigar with the fingers of his left hand. "I see. Raid didn't do you any good, either. " He pushed his chair away from the table and stood to look down. "You meet me at my office tomorrow. Say at one. Then we'll see if we can reach Kiernan."

"Tomorrow's Sunday."

"If we can't reach him tomorrow, we'll just have to try again on Monday. And you just sit tight until we talk to your boss."

"He's not my boss."

"If you report to him, that's close enough for me."

One of the Alta's owners was talking to the desk clerk as Blakenship made his way to the door. The sheriff motioned him to come over. "See the guy sitting under the No Smoking sign? Name's Buchanan. I'd take it as a personal favor if you could tell me what room he's in."

In the parking lot Blakenship lit his well-chewed cigar and looked up at the black velvet sky dotted with the cold brilliance of distant stars. Then he opened the Bronco door and reached for the mike. "It's me, Luther. Patch me through to whoever's working sector three." He sat down sideways in the driver's seat while he waited, a position that gave him a good view of the main building.

"This is Duane. You wanted me, Sheriff?"

"You remember the DEA guy with the funny hair?"

"Hard to forget."

"He's checked into the Alta Vista. Room 110, building on the left, last door on the left, ground floor. And he's driving a Chevy, light green."

184

"Government plates?"

"You got it. I want you to kind of check on him. See if the car stays put. Spend a little time, see if anyone other than him goes into the room."

"You want a regular stake out?"

"No. Make your rounds. But stop by the Alta. Often. And tell your relief to do the same."

***

Blakenship got through the night undisturbed. He'd returned to the Stockman well before closing time, much to Jessie's pleasure. They repaired to Blakenship's where the question of "The Searchers" never came up. Blakenship felt so good when he awoke that he surprised Jessie — and himself — by making buttermilk pancakes and elk sausage and serving her in bed.

The phone rang at ten while they were sipping what each vowed would be their last cup of coffee. "Damn." Jessie sat up. "Oh well. I need to brush my teeth."

"Blakenship, just what the fuck do you think you're doing?"

"Finishing breakfast. Why?"

"Putting me under surveillance."

"You're in my county. If you got a problem with that, you can leave. Otherwise, I'll see you at one."

"I'm a federal law enforcement officer, goddammit, and no hick …"

"Like I said, you can leave. Or you can have another cup of coffee and enjoy the view of our mountains. It'll soothe you and you'll be surprised at how much better the afternoon will go."

"Very good," Jessie mumbled through a mouthful of foaming toothpaste. "I bet I even have time for a shower first."

"There's room for two."

"So there is. So there is."

Blakenship found a not-noticeably soothed DEA agent in his office at 12:42.

"See," he said, waving at the wall clock, "ahead of schedule." He hung his jacket on the coat rack in the corner of his office. "You got a number for this Kiernan?"

Buchanan slid a fragment of paper across the desk. "If he's not in the office, and it's not likely at this time on a Sunday, ask to be patched through to his cell phone."

"You don't have that number?"

Buchanan gave a quick negative shake of his head.

"I see." A hint of a smile twitched the sheriff's lips before he began punching in the telephone number. "Yes. I'd like to speak with Agent Kiernan, if he's available. Blakenship. C. W. Blakenship. I'm Sheriff of Sapinero County. Yes ma'am." He cocked the receiver between shoulder and head and leaned back to put his feet on the desk.

"He's in the office," speaking around the mouthpiece to Buchanan, sullenly erect in the chair on the other side of the desk. "Yeah. Last August. Look, I've got Buchanan here in the office. Says he's on special assignment to investigate the same operation .... Don't want a cluster fuck like before ... I want at least one of my men with him at all times." Blakenship handed the receiver to Buchanan, "Wants to talk with you."

Buchanan put the receiver to his ear without changing expression. "Yes...I understand...I will."

He passed the receiver back to Blakenship. "Good... Keeping posted is a two-way street. If it's got something to do with my county, I want to know...Right."

The sheriff replaced the receiver and took a deep breath. "So. You'll work with one of my men at all times. Right?"

Buchanan nodded.

"And we'll keep each other — and Kiernan — informed. Right?"

Another nod.

"And Kiernan will keep us informed." This last to the ceiling. No leverage there. Just Kiernan's word. He brought his feet down from the desk with a moderate thump. "O. K. How do you want to start?"

"Like I said last night, the drugs come out of Sonora. So, we're looking for a place with a fairly high number of Mexicans. Workers. Visitors. Customers. Given the way our informants say they operate, it would probably be in an outlying area. But not difficult to get to."

"Like a dairy."

"Yes."

"But it could be an orchard. Or a chicken farm. Or a slaughterhouse."

"Perhaps."

"Doesn't even have to be agricultural. It could be a used furniture store. A body shop. A restaurant."

"Possibly."

"Doesn't narrow it down much." Blakenship studied the water stain in the acoustic tile of the ceiling. "You're saying it's a place where meskins come and go without attracting attention. We're a long way from the border. Plenty of time for your good old Americans to get in on the act."

"According to our information, this is entirely a Mexican operation until it gets down to street level."

Blakenship shifted in the chair so most of his weight rested on his left cheek. "Why'd you raid Jake? Even if drugs were being run through the dairy, hitting it would have only caused a minor delay. Why not wait until you could shut down the whole shooting match?"

"There were other constraints."

"Pressure from above, huh." Blakenship smiled when Buchanan didn't answer. "No matter." He broke the cellophane on a fresh pack of Rum Crooks and lit one, his first of the day he realized with mild surprise. "Why are you still interested in Sapinero County?"

"I want to finish the job."

187

"If that's your story, that's fine by me. You learn anything from the Sanchez boys, now you know where they are?"

Buchanan bristled, then shrugged his shoulders. "Nothing. They haven't said a word."

"They're still in the hospital?"

"Yes."

"Learn anything about the alleged accident?"

"Nothing conclusive."

"But I'll be the first to know. Right?"

"That's the deal."

"O. K." Blakenship rose and walked to the county map pinned on the wall. "Let's begin with outlying areas."

***

On the telephone, Bridget Taylor's voice carried a youthful lilt that belied Jake's image of a lady in her retirement years. In person, while the incongruity was not as pronounced, she looked far younger than he'd expected. Close-cropped curls, light brown with hints of gray, framed an unlined face set off by dimples that showed when she smiled, which was often. With uncharacteristic forwardness, he asked her age.

"Fifty last June."

"Little young to be retired."

"It's a combination of things. Burn out. A third divorce. Air quality. The realization that I'd been doing the same thing at the same place for twenty years and if I didn't make a change that's what I'd be doing until the day I died. Change is invigorating, don't you think?"

"Not in my experience." They were seated at the kitchen table and the wide swing of Jake's arm toward the porch implied the empty barn and blackened remains of the mechanic's shed. "To get to the point, is there anything you can do for Mary Margaret?"

"I have no idea."

"Well, at least you're not trying to bullshit me."

188

"Frankly, from the way you described her condition, it's going to be very difficult."

"If that's the way you feel, why are we talking?"

"It's not that I'm not interested. I just want to make sure you know the odds aren't very good."

"I've been watching her go downhill since before Labor Day. Either I try to help her or I let her die."

"I understand. And I hope you understand that no matter what I do — we do — she may stay this way until she does die."

Jake played a soft tattoo on the tabletop with the fingers of his right hand. "Before we go any further, how much are you going to cost?"

"I'm not sure. My previous rates were based on the California economy." She pulled gently on the turquoise-and-gold pendant dangling from her left ear. "What did you pay the men who worked for you?"

"A thousand a month. Plus housing."

"O. K. For one thousand dollars I will spend an intensive month with your wife. Then we can see what changes need to be made — or if I should continue at all."

Jake disappeared through the door to the living room, returning with his checkbook. "That's Bridget Taylor, Ph.D.?" He tore the check from the page. "What's first?"

"I'd like to meet her."

***

Mary Margaret was much as Jake had left her the day before. He bent to kiss her forehead and whisper her name but nothing registered. Bridget watched for a moment, then approached the bed. "Mrs. Grummond, my name is Bridget. Bridget Taylor. I'm going to be seeing you every day and I hope we'll have lots of things to talk about."

Mary Margaret made no response. The psychologist grasped her right hand that was lying on the white cotton blanket that covered her and squeezed. "Her circulation seems to be normal." She bent to place her cheek against Mary Margaret's

189

forehead. "Temperature, too. Has she been getting any exercise?"

"Just the therapist who moves her arms and legs."

"The weight. She didn't have a weight problem before?"

"Weighed the same as when she graduated high school. Proud of it."

"A therapist sees her. And the staff. Anyone else? Besides you, of course."

"There's her cousin, Helen. Evie Stanton can't bear to see her like this. Neither can her other friends, when it comes to that."

Bridget walked to the window that looked out on fallow fields and bare cottonwoods and, in the distance, the upward slope of the Sublette Plateau. She took a stick of gum from her purse, unwrapped it and popped it into her mouth, carefully folding the foil into a tight rectangle and then folding the paper wrapper around it. "How to stimulate ..." she murmured to herself. "Stimulus. Stimulus."

"What do you think about moving her back to the dairy?"

"What?" Startled, Bridget turned from the window.

"I said, what do you think about moving her back to the dairy?"

"Let me work with her for a week or so and then we'll see."

Jake checked his watch. "I need to look in on my father."

"Is he here, too?"

"He's home. At his cabin," he added to her questioning look. "It's a long mile from the big house but still on the farm."

They drove back in silence. She refused his lukewarm offer to come in and went directly to her car, a blue Acura with California plates. "I'll be talking to you. A lot." She started the car and put it in gear. Rolling down the window, she called, "What was the name of the doctor and the hospital?"

"Allsup." Jake spelled the name for her. "He's at Crossley Memorial."

He followed the little car to the road then turned right, driving slowly and trying not to stare at the stubbled fields that

190

should be getting fertilized in preparation for spring planting. His father's truck was parked so close to the porch that the front bumper was over the first step. It didn't look like it had been moved for days.

Grandpa Grummond was asleep in the recliner, the last minutes of the Pro Bowl flickering on the television. A four-day growth of gray-white stubble fuzzed his face and the skin of his neck hung in loose folds. A paper towel with a sandwich neatly bisected sat on the arm of the couch next to the chair. Two bites had been taken out of one half. Jake picked it up — egg salad and the bread dried half way through.

What else had he eaten that day? Or that week? Three plates, two coffee cups and a handful of silverware stood in the drainer. Congealed fat floated on the water in the frying pan in the stainless steel sink. Jake sniffed and couldn't detect any smells of recent cooking.

He opened the refrigerator. An egg carton with four eggs gone. A package of bacon carefully wrapped in a plastic baggie. Most of a loaf of bread. Several small plastic containers holding the remnants of beans, corn and tomatoes.

Need to get Maria Elena in again.

Jake opened a can of cream-of-mushroom soup and added water, taking care to put in a little at a time and stirring so it wouldn't be lumpy. When it was ready, he poured some in a clean coffee mug and carried it his father. "Game's over, Dad."

Grandpa Grummond's eyes opened at the sound of Jake's voice but it took him a while to focus. "That you, Jake?" With effort, he maneuvered the recliner upright.

"Here's some soup. Don't look like you pigged out today."

"Say what?" Jake held up the sandwich. "Oh, that. Must have fallen asleep. Nothing happening in the Pro Bowl to keep a body awake." He accepted the mug and took a swallow. "That's good." He swallowed again. "Won't be a game worth watching till Labor Day."

"Don't college games start before that?"

"A week, maybe. Big deal." He cradled the soup on his lap. "No football and no cows. What the fuck we going to do?"

"Not sure. Maybe I'll find a job. See if Frog Bottom needs a driver."

"And suing? You got a chance of winning anything before you die?"

"Don't know about that either. But I ain't going to roll over."

***

The sun was low through the office window as Buchanan gathered up the lists of farms, ranches and other businesses with a high proportion of Mexican employees or clientele. The phone rang and the deputy at the front desk answered. "He's here. They're both here." She held her hand over the mouthpiece. "It's Sheriff Darling."

Blakenship took it at his desk. "Wendall. Yeah. Do say. I'll be in touch." He replaced the receiver and gave Buchanan a look. "It seems Victor and Julio are no longer patients at the Anton Hospital. Left without paying their bill or leaving a forwarding address."

14

FEBRUARY 1 — Late Afternoon

Blakenship's words had frozen Buchanan immobile, back bent like an old man giving way to the weight of every year he had lived. "What?" he croaked. "When? How?"

"When was sometime after three. How they got no idea about."

"Two and a half hours and they just found out?"

"Found out around four. Being as they were in custody — sort of — they've put up roadblocks and already searched the father's house. Took a little longer to call me." Buchanan started for the door. "Where you going?"

"To Anton."

"What can you do there that isn't being done?" Blakenship let the thought settle. "Best thing is to think about where they might be headed. Luther," he called, "should be a description of two fugitives by now. Two meskins. Victor and Julio Sanchez. Tell our boys to keep their eyes peeled. And get Henderson." He turned to Buchanan. "Sit down," he told him, not unkindly. "Leaving aside the question of how they got out, but assuming they've got a vehicle, where would they go?"

"It would help if we knew their physical condition."

"I expect we will, by and by."

"What's got you in such an uproar you had to interrupt my Sunday? Good thing I was coming in anyway." Henderson sat down in the remaining chair and put his feet on the desk.

"Victor and Julio. They left the comfort of their hospital room without telling anyone where they were going."

"Could be they figured if someone tried to kill them once, might try twice."

"And who might that be?"

"Got to be about this drug thing. Only thing big enough to make it worthwhile. Except for that, they've been penny ante all the way."

"Who helped them? Couldn't make it alone, shape they're in."

"Family. I say the wives. One or both."

"They've always kept the wives out of it." Buchanan assertion broke the rhythm of call and response between the Sapinero lawmen.

"I'm just supposing to be supposing," said Henderson. "You got a better idea?" Buchanan didn't answer. "O. K., C. W. Nothing you haven't thought of your ownself. Question is, where'd they go?"

"The same place they went last summer." Buchanan's voice cracked with frustration.

"Maybe. Maybe not." Blakenship leaned back and put his boots on the desk opposite Henderson's. "Not that it makes much difference since we don't know where they went then, either."

"What if they were abducted?" Buchanan leaned forward, a vein pulsing in the center of his forehead.

"Possible," Blakenship agreed. "But why? Lot of trouble to get two guys who don't want to go out of a hospital on the peak visiting day of the week. Why not take them out right there?"

"Killing is messy." Henderson got a cigarette without removing the pack from his shirt pocket. "Abduction or killing, if I was going to do either one, I'd pick a better time than the middle of Sunday afternoon." He lit the cigarette. "I vote for the wives."

"Where the fuck were the guards?" Buchanan glared. "How hard is it to guard invalids in a hospital room?"

"Settle down. All we know is they're gone. We don't know how or if anyone got hurt."

Luther walked in with the printout and handed it across the desk.

"What's it say, Blakenship?"

"That they disappeared. Victor's head is shaved and bandaged. Julio's left arm's in a cast. Looks like they'd stand out in a crowd."

"Means they're not going to hide in plain sight." Henderson removed his hat and massaged his forehead where the hatband had been.

"Gives their wives's names. Victor has two children and Julio doesn't have any. If it was a wife, it was most likely Julio's." The phone rang on Blakenship's desk and he listened without comment for several minutes. "That was Wendall. Seems the deputy on guard was knocked out. All he remembers is a young Hispanic woman wearing a nurse's aid uniform asking for help. Found him in a linen cart."

"What's she look like?"

"How old?"

"How tall?"

Henderson and Buchanan glared at each other.

"Anywhere from eighteen to twenty-eight. Between five foot and five-two. Near as Wendall can tell, his deputy spent most of his time trying to look down her dress. He was right eager to help when she asked."

"Not much to go on."

"He did say one other thing. Both wives are at home."

Henderson shrugged. "Doesn't change things much. Woman involved, odds are against abduction. Bet you she's a lot closer to eighteen than twenty-eight. Younger than the wife at home."

"Let's do some more supposing, Charlie. Suppose they've got a hidey-hole in the county. Where might that be?"

"They could go to ground in the mountains for a long time."

"Snow in the high country."

"There's plowed roads."

"Only on school bus routes."

"There's snowmobiles. Go the rest of the way by Arctic Cat."

"Leaves tracks."

"So? It's winter. Lot of snowmobile tracks in the high country."

"Have to be provisioned regular. Wintering in would be pretty rough for boys used to the bright lights of the big city. And they're hurt."

"Another option is to hide amongst some meskins."

"Risky. More who know, more who might talk."

"Don't mean they'd talk to us, C. W. We don't have the best rapport with meskins. It wouldn't hurt if we had a meskin deputy or two. Might be you should tend to that before the next election."

"Mexicans can't vote," Buchanan interjected.

"Mexican nationals can't. But we've got a fair number of naturalized citizens. We even got some whose people were here long before this part of the world got attached to the U. S. of A."

"They ..." Buchanan sputtered and fell silent.

"Whatever, C. W., it'd help if we could find the girl. Could be by tomorrow that deputy'll remember something besides her tits."

***

"You got to realize how boring it is." The deputy's soft brown eyes pleaded for understanding. "I know somebody tried to kill them, but who's going to try on a Sunday afternoon? The place was packed. People everywhere, with flowers and books and candy."

Blakenship unwrapped a cigar and chewed on the end. They were in the Packer County Sheriff's Office, which had a strict no smoking policy. "Tell me about the woman."

"Cute little *chiquita*. Went by me a couple of times pushing the cart with the juice and stuff. Tight little ass and she knew how to move it."

"And big tits, from what Sheriff Darling tells me."

"Yeah."

"Anything else you remember?"

The deputy closed his eyes in concentration. Shit, he didn't look to be a year out of high school. "There was a necklace with a gold cross. Hung there with the bottom part

196

between her tits. You know. Like it was pointing where she wanted you to look. And when she bent over …"

"What kind of shoes was she wearing?"

"Shoes?"

"Shoes."

"The same kind most nurses wear. White. With wedge soles."

"They look new?"

"New?"

"Like brand new?"

"I don't know." He thought for a bit. "They were white and clean. Didn't look old. But I couldn't say if they were brand new or not."

"Her teeth. Straight or crooked?"

"I don't remember."

"Nose. Big or little?"

"Man, I wasn't looking at her nose."

"What about her hands? Any rings? Wristwatch? Bracelet?"

"I don't remember … Wait. On her hand, the one she handed me the drink with. She had a couple of lines between her thumb and finger. Right here." He pointed to the spot on his own hand.

"Lines?"

"Like a tattoo. You know. It was like she started to get one of those homemade tattoos Mexicans have, but changed her mind."

"Or someone stopped her." Blakenship bit a piece of cigar. "So. After twitching her ass at you for an hour or so and giving you a drink from her cart and letting you look down her dress, you were only too happy to give her a hand, even though it meant leaving your post."

"Yes."

Looked me in the eye. Give him credit for that. "Tell me what happened."

"I followed her to this closet or storeroom. When I went in, somebody grabbed me around the throat."

197

"From behind?"

The deputy nodded. "Choke hold. That's all I remember. Doctor says they gave me a shot."

"Sedative be easy enough to find in a hospital. If you knew what to look for. Bring your own in, as far as that goes." Blakenship stood. "Keep thinking about the girl. Something may come to mind."

***

"She sat up. Of her own accord." Bridget Taylor sat down at the kitchen table strewn with manila folders. "Taxes?"

"Information for a lawyer." Jake pushed the yellow legal pad away. "She sat up by herself?"

"She most certainly did. I thought about getting her to stand, but she's awfully big and I wasn't sure I could keep her from falling. The therapist and I are going to try tomorrow." She crossed her forearms on top of some folders and leaned forward. Her perfume, a spicy scent that was new to Jake, brought home how long it had been since he'd been close to a woman and sent a flush through his loins. "Can you be there?"

"What time?"

"Around two."

"I can do that." Jake stretched back. "Any idea why? Her moving, I mean. Why now?"

"I don't know. I said 'Hello, Mrs. Grummond,' the same way I do every day and she sat up. She gave me the sweetest smile and then lay back down. But she looked at me when I spoke and her eyes followed me around the room." Bridget moved to the sink for a glass of water. "It's like she's known I was there the other days. Like she's been listening. So when she heard my voice today, she sat up because that was one of the things I've been asking her to do."

"I've been asking her, too. And so has the therapist. So has Helen, for that matter. What did you do that's different?"

"Timing, probably. It's possible she's ready to acknowledge the outside world again and I happened to be the

198

one there." She drank the water in small rapid swallows. "She must have been very beautiful."

"She was." Guilt at his feelings of lust kept Jake's eyes focused on the calendar above the refrigerator. "The prettiest woman in the county."

***

It was dark when he placed the last sheet in a new folder. The telephone rang as he was on his way to the refrigerator for a beer and he answered curtly.

"What's got your bowels in an uproar?"

"Sorry, Dad. Been getting stuff together for the new lawyer."

"Watch the news?"

"Like I said, I've been shuffling papers all afternoon."

"Victor and Julio Sanchez escaped from the hospital in Anton."

Jake took a moment to gather himself. "What do you mean, escaped?"

"Seems they were in an accident a few weeks ago only the law wasn't sure it was an accident. Had them under protective custody. They were also known to be 'police characters' and the DEA has been interested in what they have to say."

"How long you say they been in the hospital?"

"Couple to three weeks."

"Wonder if Cecil … You think that sonofabitch'd be surprised if I told him?"

"Take it easy, son."

"Cocksucker."

"Take it easy."

"I'm going to call that shit-eating bastard and …"

"What good'll that do?"

"Shit. Mackey could have talked to them. Taken a deposition or whatever they call it." He fell silent. "The news give a description?"

"Had some old pictures. Did say that one's head was bandaged and the other's arm's in a cast."

199

"Pictures'll be in tomorrow's paper, wouldn't you reckon?"

"Likely. Why? You're not going to try to hunt them up, are you?"

"Catch them again, I'm going to make sure we get to talk to their sorry asses."

"Don't do anything foolish. You're all I got."

***

"So that's what they look like." Henderson smoothed the front page of the newspaper. It was dominated by pictures of the Sanchez brothers. "Heard their names every now and then but never seen them."

"Don't forget to add a bandage to that one." Blakenship tapped Victor's picture.

"Could have taken it off by now."

"Then erase the hair."

"How about a wig? Shit, he could make one out of that mustache." Henderson nudged Blakenship and pointed to Jake coming toward the Chopping Block with the stiff-legged strides that meant he was fighting for control. Jake looked at them through the lettering on the plate-glass window without slowing. At the entrance, he held the door for an elderly couple on their way out, then marched to stand over them.

"The Sanchezes ain't news to you, I see," Jake said, pointing to the newspaper. "When did you know where they were?" His face was blank as chiseled stone except for the twitch of his jaw muscles.

"Sit down, Jake, and stop grinding your teeth. It ain't good for them."

"Never mind my fucking teeth, Cecil. How long?"

"Seems like we knew the day after it happened. It ain't a secret. Read it in the paper — just like you could have. About three weeks ago, wasn't it, Charlie?"

"Didn't think it was something you could tell me about?"

"Figured you can read, just like me. Not my job to help your legal work."

"Wasn't your attitude last fall. Or maybe your were just blowing smoke then. What about catching them? That your job?"

"If they're in my jurisdiction."

Jaw still twitching, Jake stared unseeing at the blackboard with the day's menu for a full thirty seconds. "As long as you do your job."

Blakenship and Henderson watched his stiff-legged progress to the other side of the square. "Going to Fitz's, most likely." Blakenship's tone was of a long-suffering man used to being unappreciated but wishing that someone, sometime, would understand things from where he sat.

"Lucky Buchanan wasn't with us." Henderson drained his coffee and swallowed the last of his cinnamon roll. "Not likely Jake's forgot what he looks like."

***

"The Sanchezes don't affect things that much. The main thing we have to prove is that federal authorities — or those operating under their command — caused you serious damage because they acted improperly. Of course, if you could find them, maybe they'd explain why they fingered the dairy." Fitzgerald eyed Jake with growing concern. "Sit down before you wear a hole in my carpet."

Jake stopped pacing, sat down, started to speak, then jumped to his feet. "Seeing those bastards in the paper ..." He sat down again. "Before they were just names."

Fitzgerald gave him a minute before turning to business. "Let me review this material. I'll be in touch by the end of the week. We'll see Griffin again." The lawyer's voice stopped Jake at the door. "How's Mary Margaret?"

"Got a psychologist working with her. Said yesterday that Mary Margaret had sat up. By herself." Fitzgerald made no attempt to hide his shock. "You didn't know? She's been nothing but a lump since the fire. Or before.""

"I had no idea."

"Gained weight and just lay there. Might as well be dead. But, according to this Bridget Taylor, she sat up by herself. Sat up and seemed to listen to her when she spoke. Watched her, anyway."

"I'm sorry."

"Don't be. This is the first sign of progress since the raid."

***

Grandpa Grummond opened the door before Jake was out of the truck. "Let's set out here," he said, pointing to the bench that backed against the cabin wall. "In the sun. Don't get outside enough." His jeans and shirt looked fresh and Jake caught the slightly flowery scent of laundry detergent.

"Shaved with a new blade, I see." Jake touched a dab of blood-spotted toilet paper stuck to his father's chin.

"Seemed like the thing to do when I got up."

"What'd you have for breakfast?"

"What I wanted, goddammit. I've been eating for seventy-three years. I know what I'm doing." He glanced sideways at his son. "No coffee." He leaned his head against the logs and closed his eyes. "Sun feels good."

Jake leaned back and closed his eyes, too. "Been to see Mackey Fitz."

"See the newspaper?"

"I saw them." He didn't add that the pictures were taped to his refrigerator door.

"See C. W.?"

"Sitting in the Chopping Block like he didn't have a care in the world."

"You didn't do nothing foolish?"

"Just asked why he hadn't told me about them."

"And?"

"Said he figured I could read the paper same as him. Seems the wreck they were in was reported three weeks ago. I guess I missed it."

"What did Mackey say?"

"That the Sanchez boys weren't that important."

"Even though they started the whole fucking thing? Fucking law."

***

Eusebio must have been watching because he was halfway across the barnyard before Jake got out of the pickup. "May we talk?"

The kitchen felt inhospitably cool. Eusebio choose the chair facing the porch while Jake rinsed the coffee pot. "Be ready in a minute." He studied the serious man's ageless face. "What is it?"

"The others, they are leaving. Except Jesus."

The coffee maker bubbled invitingly while he digested the news. He took the tin of Copenhagen from his shirt pocket and rolled it back and forth on the table. "What about you?"

"Maria Elena must finish school here. She already has one scholarship for college. One thousand dollars from the vegetable growers. I will try to find work."

"In the valley? You can live here as long as you want."

"*Gracias*. But what if you were to sell? The new owners …" He shrugged. "I was thinking. My ten acres, they are next to your father. He already has water and the electric. Perhaps I could put a trailer on my land. That way it could be easily separated if you sell."

"Shouldn't be very hard to extend the power. Might could tap into Dad's well. You'd have to put in the septic, get permits. But you could do it." Jake tried to scratch a spot in the middle of his back. "What about Jesus? He's got ten acres, too."

"They are thinking."

***

Jake parked between Bridget's Acura and a Lexus that still had paper dealer plates. The Lexus was Bonham's. He'd put money on it.

In the hall, he could hear Bridget's voice. "That's it. That's it. Now turn."

Mary Margaret had both arms on the psychologist's shoulders and her face was screwed in eager-to-please concentration as she struggled to turn and balance herself on the edge of the bed. The nightgown had ridden high on her thighs revealing flab the color of raw biscuit dough hanging from her knees.

"Am I late?"

"If anything, you're early." She placed a pillow on each side of Mary Margaret's hips, reached up to gently remove the hands from her shoulders and, still holding them, stepped back a pace. She smiled and Mary Margaret gave a tentative smile back. "That's excellent. Look who's here."

"It's me." Jake moved closer. "It's me. Jake."

Mary Margaret's eyes flicked over Bridget's shoulder toward the new voice then quickly sought the reassurance of the familiar face.

"Well, look at you." The professionally cheery greeting from the physical therapist startled everyone and Mary Margaret reacted by pulling Bridget closer. "Sorry. Here's the wheelchair."

"It's your friend Adrienne. We're going for a ride in the wheelchair. Won't that be fun?"

Mary Margaret's expression said she wasn't so sure it would be at all fun and she started to lean back, pulling Bridget with her.

"What do you figure's the way to do this?" Jake had moved up to Bridget's left, keeping his voice soft and low.

"With the chair here," said Adrienne, moving it about a foot behind Bridget and setting the brake, "then you get her right arm over your shoulder and I'll get the left. We'll get her to

204

stand and put some weight on her feet. We'll try to get her to take a step or two, turn around and sit down."

Jake moved the pillows and set down next to his wife. Adrienne did the same on the other side. With Bridget giving encouragement, they lifted the soft bulk.

"She's off the bed. How are her feet?"

"I can't tell," said Bridget. "Can you lower her?"

They did and Mary Margaret let her legs give way.

"Can you stand, dear?" Bridget asked. "I bet you can. Just like you sat up. That's right. Stand and take a step toward me."

Bent so as not to lift Mary Margaret off the ground and conscious of the contrast between Adrienne's muscled arm pressing against his and the fat breadth of the back they spanned, Jake fought the urge to swing his wife bodily into the chair.

"That's it. Now another."

With three-quarters of her weight supported by Jake and Adrienne, Mary Margaret had moved her right foot forward. She was breathing heavily and kept her eyes focused on Bridget.

"Very good. Very, very good. Now stop. Bring them together. That's it. Rest. Catch your breath. That's it. Now, Jake and Adrienne are going to turn you around. You can help if you want. Good. That's it. Fine. Now they're going to sit you in the wheelchair."

Jake and Adrienne carefully removed Mary Margaret's arms from around their necks and straightened up. Both were breathing heavily, from tension more than exertion.

Bridget draped a bathrobe over Mary Margaret's shoulders. "There. Let's go for a ride, shall we?"

***

"It's the best she's been since I drove her to Union."

"You could have knocked me over with a feather when I saw her in the wheelchair." Helen sat on the bar stool next to Jake. "Don't know how it'll play out, but so far that Taylor woman has earned her money."

"Don't know what she's doing different than we did, but whatever it is, it's working."

"Maybe it's just that she's new." Helen considered her glass, still full of water and enough scotch to give it an amber tinge. "I've got to admit it feels funny to have a stranger be able to accomplish what we couldn't. With our own kin. It's like Mary Margaret's scared of me. Always looking to her for reassurance whenever I touch her or say something. Helen took an imperceptible sip. "You get that feeling?"

"Sometimes."

"I wouldn't say this to anyone but you, but I'm feeling a little bit jealous."

"Main thing is, she's the only one who's been able to do anything. That's what we got to remember, no matter how we feel."

***

Blakenship was in his usual booth at the Stockman with Henderson and Buchanan crammed together on the other side, each sitting stiffly and excusing themselves with exaggerated politeness whenever they shifted position.

"That's it?" A couple of lines tattooed between her finger and thumb?"

Blakenship ignored Buchanan. "Charlie, you know what I want, right?"

"A list of all the nurses aides and volunteers and such like who've worked at the hospital during the last year."

"Wouldn't hurt to include cleaning folks. In fact, it wouldn't hurt to include everybody but full-blown nurses and doctors." He raised his empty shot glass in the general direction of Jessie who was coming from the kitchen with a full tray.

"It's a long shot, C. W."

"I know. But what the hell. She knew her way around a hospital. We got a hospital. It's possible and we might as well check it out."

"You don't figure she's still working there?"

206

"Maybe yes, maybe no. The deputy wasn't sure, but he didn't think her shoes were brand new. And there's the dress — which he says fit her. Point is, she's probably young and with some experience."

"She could have come from anywhere in the state." Buchanan's skepticism was palpable. "Or out of state, for that matter."

"True enough. Thanks, darling." Blakenship accepted the shot glass Jessie proffered and tilted his head for a peck on the lips. "But we're here. Besides, you're the one who's sure drugs are coming through the county. If we do happen to find her, we may be able to start sorting things out."

"Like why they fingered the dairy in the first place." Henderson stirred his coffee. "I been thinking about that every now and then. And it occurred to me that maybe Victor and Julio thought they were giving good information. You know, Jake's a hard man. Not as wild as his daddy, but he's got his way of doing things and he don't bend much. He went through a bunch before he settled on the ones who work for him. Could be there's a party with a grudge who figured this would be a good pay back."

"Whatever. But put somebody good on the hospital. First thing in the morning."

15

FEBRUARY 7 — Early Morning

"You ready?" Billy Stanton's voice boomed from the porch, followed by Frog Bottom's deep rumble. "It's already pushing eight."

The kitchen clock read barely seven, but Jake didn't care. Through the window he could see Froggie's pickup with a trailer carrying three snowmobiles. It'd been years since he'd ridden but when Billy invited him for a day in the high country, it hadn't taken long to say yes.

Billy pointed at the thermos on the counter. "If it ain't got schnapps, we'll leave your sorry ass here."

"You can rest easy."

They rode three abreast on the pickup's bench seat. "Might snow," Frog Bottom observed as clouds obscuring the sloping ridge leading to the Hazel Lake Inn came into view. "Got Randy's helmet if you want." Long as it had been, he'd remembered Jake preferred stocking cap and goggles to the confinement of helmet and face shield.

Most of the Inn's winter customers were snowmobilers and, early though they were, the tracks of several vehicles marked the two inches of fresh snow on the narrow road. "Hate to meet some hotdog coming down," said Billy. "I hear they average a wreck a week on this road."

"Most ain't serious. Besides," Frog Bottom snorted, "I drive these sonsabitches for a living."

A quarter of a mile higher and they were in the clouds. Tiny flakes, in no hurry to reach the ground, swirled in the breeze of the truck's passing and the three men rode in silence as they climbed into the land of tall trees and deep snow.

"Man, they're pretty," Billy breathed. "You ever have second thoughts about cutting them down?"

"Why I do selective cutting. And you got to understand they're living things that'll die sooner or later. All you got to do is see how many topple over on their own account to figure that out. Jake, you got any Cope?" He helped himself to snuff without taking his eyes off the road. "Thing is to do it so they keep coming back."

The road leveled onto some two hundred acres of flat with the Inn at its proximate center. The flakes were thicker and angled by a southwest wind, but visibility was still clear enough to see there were only three pickups and trailers in the parking lot.

They pulled up next to a truck with 4x4 lettered on its side. "You take Evie's Jag," Billy told Jake. "It's got electric start."

"Whatever. I never even seen one with electric start."

"They got a lot more bells and whistles now."

"Still have the throttle on the right and the brake on the left, don't they?"

"Main thing is we got to keep Froggie and his new Mountain Max in sight. That sonofabitch's got a set of balls."

"I'll take it easy on you boys." Frog Bottom had his leather suit, emblazoned with the Yamaha logo, slung over his shoulder and his helmet, gloves and lined boots in his hands. "I'm going inside."

"Of course," Billy added in a stage whisper meant for Frog Bottom's ears, "powerful as that sled is, it don't seem to keep him from getting stuck. He'll take it easy so we'll be close enough to help when he buries it."

***

"This is why I don't want to live anyplace else." Billy chased a bite of sandwich with a swallow of schnapps-laced coffee. "We've got the bluest sky in the world."

They were in a park almost at timberline, having broken out of the clouds some ten miles from the Inn. It had taken Jake about thirty minutes to reacquaint himself with snowmobiling in general and to learn the tendencies of the unfamiliar machine, but it had come back and he looked with satisfaction at the looping tracks he'd cut in the snow of the broad alpine meadow.

He'd even followed Billy over a jump without doing damage to either the sled or himself.

Frog Bottom took two steps from the rough triangle formed by the three machines and sank through the crust up to his knees. "Fuck it." He unzipped his suit and fumbled for the fly in his thermal long johns. "That's better."

"Damn, Froggie," said Billy. "I always heard about pissing like a racehorse, but this is the first time I ever knew what it meant."

Frog Bottom ignored him. "What say we run in the general direction of the stone bridge?"

***

Jake stopped next to Frog Bottom, cheeks burning from the cold wind rushing through the upraised visor of the borrowed helmet and the elation of having almost kept up with the Mountain Max on a downhill slalom through a mixed stand of spruce and aspen. They were in the middle of a large clearing that in the summer was a blackberry patch.

Billy pulled up between them. "You look like a kid set loose in a chocolate factory." He touched the tip of Jake's nose. "Turning white. Best warm it up."

"That's why they put shields on these things," Frog Bottom added.

"Never have liked them."

"You've always been a hard-head. That's one thing age ain't changed."

Jake groped inside his jacket to the shirt pocket for his snuff, took a pinch and offered the tin to the big man.

"Thanks." Frog Bottom loaded his lip. "About two-thirty, ain't it? Way I figure, we can drop down to that bit of flat and then switchback our way to the top of the ridge. If I calculate right, the Inn ought to be just below. Shouldn't take more than forty-five minutes — an hour."

"And if you figure wrong?" Billy asked.

"Still have two and half hours of light."

"He's right," said Jake. "Unless I'm all fucked up, we're right above my sixty acres." He squeezed the throttle, caught air over a small drop-off he hadn't seen, landed on one ski, righted the sled and raised his left fist in triumph. Billy and Frog Bottom waved, then Billy started down.

"Hoo haw." Billy slid up next to him. "Look at Froggie."

Jake turned from trying to locate his property in time to see the Mountain Max start the downward course of its arc, land in a cloud of snow and emerge on the other side. "What if there'd been a rock?"

"Might have had to tow him."

"Lot of work."

"That's why you don't see other tracks around here. Most folks tend to stay on the maintained trail. Close to, anyway." Turning to Frog Bottom, Billy continued, "Which way the Inn?"

"There's an old logging road goes up and over the ridge. If you look real careful you can see where the gaps in the trees are too straight to be natural." Frog Bottom pointed. "See?"

"I think so," said Jake. "But it's going to be soft. Soft and deep."

"We'll make it. Me first, you in the middle. Stay in the tracks and keep up your speed. Weight forward and lean into the turns."

Half an hour later, they were at the top, looking down at the Inn's filled parking lot and the overflow lining one side of the road. "Damn," said Jake. "Look at them all. And we haven't seen anybody all day."

"I bet the Shadow Lake trail looks like an L. A. freeway at rush hour." Frog Bottom started his machine. "It's not getting any warmer up here."

***

The harsh jangle of the phone at six-thirty tightened a knot in his stomach. His father. Goddammit. Should have checked on him last night.

211

The relief at hearing Bridget Taylor's voice was short lived.

"Didn't you get my message?"

Jake looked guiltily at the blinking light on his answering machine. "Got in late and didn't check."

"It's Mary Margaret." Jake waited. "She had an accident. It's not serious," she added hurriedly, "in and of itself."

"What happened?"

"She was getting into the wheelchair. You know how she's enjoyed it all week. And how we park it a little farther away from the bed each time. Well, yesterday we had it about ten feet away ..."

"I thought you weren't going to do that unless I was there."

"She walked just fine. Adrienne and I hardly had to give her any support at all."

"What happened?"

"Evidently we forgot to set both brakes. When she sat down, it rolled away a little bit and she went all the way to the floor."

"How bad's she hurt?"

"She was half in the chair when the left side rolled, so it wasn't like someone pulled it out from under her. Still, it was a pretty good thump. But the physical injury isn't the problem. She hasn't moved of her own volition or acknowledged anybody's presence since it happened."

Jake fought to keep the anger out of his voice. Goddammit. First relaxation since the raid and this happens. "So she's back at the beginning? Like nothing happened all week?"

"Outwardly, I'm afraid so. But I can't believe she's regressed totally. When you come today ..."

"Will you be there?"

"Of course."

"When?"

"Whenever you say. I suggest the earlier the better." She waited for Jake to say something. "They're finished with breakfast by nine. Perhaps then?"

"Nine it is."

He took a step toward the bathroom and felt his leg tense to kick the parson's table. Breathe, he ordered. Ten breathes. Count them. Motherfucker. Breathe.

He filled the basin with cold water and stuck his face in as far as it would go, sputtered and did it three more times.

Now get dressed. That's it. Underwear and socks. Pants and boots.

He was tucking his shirt in when his right leg tensed again and before he could stop it, it kicked a bentwood chair across the room.

Half an hour at the woodpile depleted him enough to feel he could handle the nursing home. He washed face, hands and armpits, donned a clean undershirt and made breakfast from a leftover ham and cheese sandwich.

***

Mary Margaret was lying on her back, eyes closed, breathing regularly. Her lids were puffy like she'd cried through the night.

"It's me, sweetheart," he crooned. She surprised him by turning toward the sound. Her eyes remained closed, but she turned. "I'm sorry I wasn't here yesterday, but everything's going to be all right."

She kept her head turned to him as though she was trying to see through the veil of her lids. Jake reached for her hand and squeezed. He was surprised again when she gave a faint squeeze in return. "Everything's going to be all right."

"Hurt."

The sound of her voice shocked him to momentary paralysis. "It hurts? Where?"

"He hurt me." The words came haltingly and after she said them she turned her face to the ceiling.

"I'm sorry I'm late." Bridget Taylor's breathless voice pulled Jake's amazed stare from his wife. "Alice's car was parked behind mine and the battery was dead so…" She stooped

213

when she realized Jake wasn't paying any attention. "Is something wrong?"

"She talked to me."

"She what? She spoke?"

"Twice."

"What did she say?"

"First she said 'hurt'. Then she said 'he hurt me.'"

"That's wonderful. Amazing." Jake thought she was going to hug him. "Wait a minute." She stepped back. "There was only Adrienne and me here. There wasn't a man present." She circled the room, twin frown lines creasing the space between her eyebrows. "Did she say where she hurt?"

"I asked, but she turned on her back and that's when you came in. She got kicked during the raid. Piece of shit ... Sorry." The psychologist stopped her circular pacing. "You didn't know?"

"It wasn't in any of Dr. Allsup's reports and you ... Begin from when you got here."

"She was lying just like she is now. Except her breathing was shallow. Regular, but shallow. I could see her eyes were red and puffy, like she'd been crying. I said something like it's me, honey and she turned her head ..."

"She turned her head? At your voice?"

"Surprised the shit out of me."

"Did she open her eyes?"

"No. It was like she was trying to look at me but she forgot she had to open them to do it."

"Go on."

"I held her hand and squeezed and she gave me a squeeze back. Not strong, but it was a squeeze. Then she said 'hurt' and I asked where and she said 'he hurt me' and that's when you came in."

Bridget resumed pacing, mumbling to herself. "Awfully recent ... Maybe a childhood ..." She stopped abruptly. "Is it too early to call Helen?"

"Not hardly."

Bridget left the room and Jake returned to watching his wife. He folded her right hand in his. They were still the slim, competent hands he remembered, vestiges of the real Mary Margaret.

"You are the husband, yes?" A middle-aged Hispanic woman stood in the doorway.

"That's right."

"I'm going to give her a bath. It won't take long. There is coffee at the lobby, if you would like." She filled a basin and arranged soap, washcloth and towels with brisk efficiency. "Although perhaps you could move her before you go."

With Jake at her shoulders and waist and the attendant at her knees and ankles, they rolled her on to her left side and the woman unbuttoned the back of her nightgown. When she moved to the other side of the bed to free Mary Margaret's right arm from the light garment, Jake had an unobstructed view. The livid coloring of a new bruise glared from the base of her spine.

He had the fat deputy by the throat again. Everything wrong with his world was concentrated in that mean, slack-jawed face. "Bastard. Cocksucker."

The woman jerked upright. "*Senor* ?" She saw where he was staring. "Oh. *La pobrecita.* It was not there yesterday." She leaned forward to examine it, tracing the outline of the bruise ever so lightly with her forefinger, moving lower and applying gentle pressure at the base of the spine. Mary Margaret made neither move nor sound and she pressed a little harder. "*Mira.* She has no pain. It looks worse than it is." She began to wash the expanse of white skin in gentle arcs.

"I apologize for my language."

"You were upset. It is natural. And I have heard those words before."

***

The purpling twilight had settled enough for headlights when Jake broke over Joseph Pass. Before him lay the treeless expanse of the San Marcos Valley, average elevation 8000 feet,

215

across which the highway angled for a gently undulating thirty miles before reaching the trees and the steep climb to Royal Pass. Lights from crossroads gasoline stations were beginning to dot the valley floor and smaller glows in the foothills signaled the end of another workday on the surrounding ranches. The sky and snow-capped peaks along the Continental Divide glowed deep orange and another time Jake might have stopped by the side of the road to enjoy the sunset.

But today he was in no mood to enjoy anything.

Mackey Fitz had come down with the flu so he'd had to drive by himself the night before. Not that he minded driving alone, but a heavy snowstorm predicted by no forecaster had left vehicles strewn on both sides of the pass, causing a two-hour delay. More snow and the glare of homeward-bound commuter headlights had compounded the difficulty of finding his way through the urban maze to the hotel.

The meeting had not gone well. Griffin had left him cooling his heels for an hour. When he'd finally been admitted to the inner sanctum, the lawyer'd stayed on the phone for another five minutes. When he hung up, he moved abruptly to the business at hand without so much as an acknowledgment of the delay, let alone an apology.

And what he had to say wasn't good. Since there'd been a search warrant, winning anything under tort claims was going to be very difficult. Going after individuals might be easier, but whether there'd be any money was another story. If Jake wanted him to proceed, he would bill at $200 an hour — half his usual fee. A $10,000 retainer would be required.

"I thought the statute limited lawyers' fees to 25%."

"That's the limit on our share from the judgment. But we can set any terms we want with the client. It's called freedom of contract."

"If I pay you $200 and hour, you still going to take the 25%?"

"If we win, yes."

216

"And if we don't, you still get $200 for every hour you say you worked?" Griffin nodded. "Looks to me like you can't lose and I've got my ass hanging out."

"You came to me." He spun his chair to look out the window at the golden dome of the capitol six blocks away, then spun back. "Didn't Fitzgerald explain this?"

"Not quite the same way. But then, he's a friend." Jake stood and stretched his arms to the ceiling. "Am I paying you for this meeting?"

"Yes."

"My appointment was for ten-thirty. You kept me out there for more than an hour and talked on the phone for five minutes after you let me in." Jake looked at his watch. "The way I see it, you owe me two hundred bucks. How about we talk for an hour. Then we'll call it even and I'll go home and talk with Mackey and we'll let you know."

The lawyer looked intrigued. "Your time's worth $200 an hour?"

"It is to me. What I'm trying to find out is what your time is worth."

"To you."

"To me."

They shook hands and pored through Jake's material. Mary Margaret? Since she'd had a similar episode in the recent past, the court might treat it as a pre-existing condition. The mastitis? A common affliction of dairy cows. His father? In his seventies. They worked through the stack until Griffin pointed at the clock. "We're even. Let me know what you decide."

Jake left angrier than he'd been while waiting in the outer office. The weaknesses — wrapped in phrases he'd heard only on TV — seemed to be lawyers' tricks that had nothing to do with justice and he'd come away with a profound sense that the government would protect its own at all costs. By the time he'd fought through the Friday afternoon traffic to the first tier of mountains, his frustration had gelled to an abiding fury.

He also needed to move his bowels.

With the sun going down and a wind picking up, roadside bushes didn't appeal. Only ten miles to the next glow of lights and the rest room of a gas station.

He pulled up next to the gas pumps less than ten minutes later. There was enough in the tank to get home, but it never seemed right to use a station's facilities without buying something.

Gas pumped, he went inside to pay, getting a shy smile from the teenage Hispanic girl behind the counter when she told him the men's room was outside and handed him the key.

Comfortable again, he washed his hands and stepped into a stiff breeze. The plate glass window of the store wrapped about three feet onto the side wall and as he went back to return the key, a large figure carrying a six-pack walked into his line of vision. Jake stared. He'd seen that soft bulk in his dreams.

Donaldson.

The former deputy must have said something to the girl because she gave an angry shake of her head as she counted his change. Donaldson grabbed her hand with one of his and reached to fondle her breast with the other.

Jake was through the door and had Donaldson on the floor without conscious decision, left hand on the throat and the right hand pummeling the unshaven face with half a year's pent up fury. He was dimly aware of high-pitched screaming and of footsteps sounding around him. But stopping never occurred to him. Splat went the right hand on the bloody mush that had been a nose. And the left hand squeezed. Crack went the right hand on the left cheekbone, splitting the skin like an overcooked sausage. And the left hand squeezed. Crack again, this time above the eye, splitting skin and tearing away half the eyebrow. And the left hand squeezed.

Then there was a forearm across his throat and hands on his arms and voices saying *Basta* —Stop, *hombre* — It is enough — Stop before you kill him.

The hands on his arms kept him from hitting and other fingers pried his from the throat and the arm on his throat pulled

218

him back and hands lifted him up and leaned him against the counter and he caught his breath in ragged gasps.

"We thank you for protecting our sister." The speaker was Hispanic, shorter than Jake but with a shoulder span at least the equal of his. Two younger versions stood on either side.

"I can't abide that lowlife sonofabitch." Jake's breathing was starting to even out but a tremor began to ripple his legs as the adrenaline rush subsided. "Bastard did almost the same thing last summer at …" He spat at the head lying unconscious in widening pools of its own blood and aimed a kick at the closest knee.

"That is enough," said the eldest brother and stepped between Jake and the body.

"Is he dead?" Jake asked.

One of the younger brothers bent to the former deputy's neck. "He lives."

"Bastard kicked my wife." Jake filled his lungs and exhaled through his mouth. "Suppose I ought to call the law."

"That won't be necessary…" A moan from the floor caused the man in front of him to pause for a moment. "When he is able to hear what we have to say, we will tell him what will happen if we ever see him again." The older brother smiled. "We are the Ortegas — Juan," he pointed to the one who had felt for the pulse, "Miguel" who nodded at Jake, "I am Ricardo. And, of course, our youngest sister, Melody."

"Jake Grummond." He held out his hand. "From Top Hat. Near Mountain View," he added, unnecessarily.

"As you see, we were not far away, but we thank you being first to stop the attack on Melody. And now, perhaps you would like to wash your hands."

Jake looked with surprise at the scraped knuckles welling blood and flexed the hand. It was beginning to swell. "O. K. And I best put some hydrogen peroxide on. Hell of a note if that piece of shit — excuse me — gives me an infection."

"Melody," said Miguel in a voice of soft concern. "If you are all right, show Mr. Grummond to the sink."

When Jake returned, the brothers watched while their sister sponged his knuckles with cotton balls soaked in peroxide. Donaldson had been propped to a sitting position against one end of the counter, red-tinged bubbles frothing his lips every time he exhaled. Someone had given him a rag that he pressed against the left side of his face, covering his eye.

Finished with Jake, Melody got a bucket, brush and sponges and began cleaning the blood from the floor. Miguel moved to stand in front of Donaldson. "Is there anything you wish to say to him?"

Jake studied the beaten man. "I ever see you again, I'll ..." He tried to read the one dumb eye that looked up at him. "Fuck it. He's all yours."

16

FEBRUARY 14 — Morning

He woke from a dream of Mary Margaret lying on her side in the nursing home bed watching him punch Donaldson and mouthing 'he hurt me' with each blow.

The sky was lightening so he got up, started the coffee and stepped into the shower. Back and shoulders were sore from the unaccustomed violence of movement. He turned the faucet to as hot as he could stand. The water stung the abrasions on his right hand and he clenched it at the memory of the fat hand on the young breast and the nose exploding beneath his fist. But the clenching intensified the pain and he swore at the trouble the deputy was still causing.

He was looking at a bloodstain on his only sport jacket when his father called. "You must have got in late. Morning meeting wasn't it?"

"Noonish."

"Well?"

"He'll be expensive, win or lose. And he wasn't encouraging."

"So?"

"Going to talk it over with Fitz. You eat?"

"Yeah."

"What'd you have?"

"I mean I'm fixing to eat. Stop by after your talk."

Bridget Taylor rang as soon as he hung up the phone. "You're back."

"Seems like."

"I've been talking with Helen. She told me about the miscarriage two years after Paul was born and how Mary Margaret couldn't have children after."

"I told you all that."

"But not from a woman-to-woman point of view. I'm trying to get a fix on why her reaction to Paul's … accident … was so severe. What caused the relapse.. Such a serious …" She trailed off. Jake waited for her to continue. When she didn't, he'd said he'd get by the nursing home sometime in the afternoon and had the receiver away from his ear when her voice sounded again.

"Say what?"

"I said I'd like to take her for a drive."

"A drive?"

"She's been confined so long it's like she's frozen. Driving by familiar places might … maybe seeing Top Hat, or Mountain View, or the dairy, or the school … you know, might trigger … break the logjam.   '

"Fresh air'll do her good, whatever else."

"I'll have her back by four."

***

"A possible what?" Blakenship en route to the coffee pot had overheard Daryl talking with Henderson.

"For the girl who helped the Sanchez brothers disappear."

"Talk to me."

"Felipa Ruiz." Daryl flipped through his notes. "Lives in Top Hat. Senior in high school. Worked last summer at the hospital. Now, she works part time at Taylor's grocery."

"Well, you got sex, age, ethnicity and hospital experience."

"I stopped by the store yesterday evening for a pack of cigarettes. Meskin girl was stocking shelves. Had a cross on a chain around her neck and what looked like they could've been tattoo lines. Right here." He indicated the flesh between thumb and forefinger.

"Tits?"

"More than a mouthful."

"How'd you find her?"

"Noticed that my sister's oldest wasn't on the list the hospital gave us. Seems they forget to give us the names of the summer and part-time employees, so I got them to print them, too, and I ran down every girl with a Spanish name."

222

"Follow me. You too, Charlie. Let's do a little thinking out loud." They waited while their boss squirmed his butt comfortable and propped his feet on the desk. "Okay." The sheriff fixed on the younger man. "What you got is interesting. But what connects her to the hospital in Anton?" He pulled out a pocketknife and began working on the nail of his left thumb. "Put another way, what connects her to the Sanchezes?"

"Ruiz?" Henderson leaned back and focused on the ceiling. "Wonder if she's kin to Abel Ruiz? The one Jake fired … when was it? … Six, eight years ago? Maybe longer. That was a hell of a set to."

"You recall what it was about?"

"Something to do with wanting what's his name's job — Eusebio. Or maybe just an argument between the two, argument that got physical."

"How'd we get involved?"

"Somebody called. One of the wives, if memory serves. Anyhow, I happened to be in Top Hat and got there before Jake killed the sonofabitch."

"Wonder where Ruiz is now?"

"Union, last I heard. Of course, that was a while ago."

Blakenship turned to Daryl. "What's the next step?"

Daryl leaned forward with his arms on his knees. "See if she's related to Abel Ruiz. Then, I guess, we try to find a connection to the Sanchezes."

"How'd we get the description of the girl in the first place?"

"Shit." Daryl leaned back. "We could show that Packer County deputy a picture."

"Even better, we can see if he's got time to come down here and buy a pack of cigarettes." Blakenship smiled. "You think you can find the number for the Packer County Sheriff's Department?"

***

223

He was shocked by how frail his father looked. "You haven't had another attack? A little one?"

"If I did, I got enough sense to call the doctor."

"What is it, then?"

"Nothing. Nothing I can put my finger on. Just don't feel like much of anything."

"You eating? Has Maria Elena been out?"

"Yeah. She was here a couple of days ago. Had her cook up a big pot so's she wouldn't have to come back 'til today."

Jake opened the refrigerator and lifted the lid of the pan on the top shelf. "*Carne guisada.* Don't look like more than a couple of spoonfuls gone. Used to, you could eat that whole pot and ask for dessert."

"That was then. This is now."

"You got to eat. Want me to heat some up? Might be the smell will make you hungry." Jake set the pan on the burner. The aroma of beef and onion and cumin and chili and oregano began to fill the room. "Damn," Jake said. "Think I'll have some myself."

"What'd Fitz have to say?"

"I asked him if he could do it himself. Can't afford that high-priced bastard and I don't feel like doing nothing."

"Don't know if it's worth the trouble." Grandpa Grummond pulled himself to his feet and shuffled to the radio. "Most time for the farm report. Don't know if it's worth the trouble, either. He going to?"

"He's going to think about it over the weekend." Jake filled two bowls and set one in front of his father.

"What'd you do to your hand?"

Jake looked at the scraped knuckles. "Nothing."

"Don't shit a shitter. Who was it?"

"The deputy who kicked Mary Margaret. And Della," he added as his hand clenched involuntarily.

"What were you doing in Elwood?"

"Wasn't. Happened at a gas station. San Marcos Valley. Piece of shit reached for the tit of the girl who worked there — just like he did with Della. Next thing I knew her brothers were

224

pulling me off him." Jake shut his mouth abruptly, surprised by the flow of words.

His father eyed his son across the table, waiting for him to go on. When the silence continued, he dipped a spoon in the bowl and savored the aroma. "Can't say as I blame you." He swallowed. "But you if you don't remember jumping the sonofabitch, you better watch out. It ain't a good idea to be doing things you don't remember doing." He ate another spoonful. "Won't bring the law down on you, will it?"

"Not likely. Don't think he's still a deputy." Jake swirled his spoon in the bowl before him as though getting the perfect mixture was the only thing that counted in this life or the next. "Besides, the brothers said they'd take care of it."

"Meaning?"

"I didn't ask."

***

Blakenship got the call from Mikeska when he walked into the office after his monthly haircut. The Otero County sheriff had received a courtesy call that morning from the manager of the clinic that served the San Marcos Valley. Seems that Donaldson had been found in the parking lot. In his pickup. Beat up too bad to have driven there himself. Say what? No, he wasn't talking. Not about anything. Yeah, he'll live.

"Why tell me?" Blakenship couldn't keep a tremolo of concern from his voice.

"Might have something to do with the August raid."

"Happened in the San Marcos, didn't it?"

"Near as anyone can tell. And, Lord knows, he's capable of pissing off any number of folks. Never liked the sloppy bastard. Or his father before him, come to that."

"I appreciate you keeping me informed, Rudy." Blakenship hung up and stared out the window until a deputy brought in some papers for his signature. He watched her leave, butt so skinny he wondered how she kept her britches up.

The answering machine light was blinking when Jake returned from seeing Mary Margaret.

He'd gotten there just as they were getting back from the drive and had helped get her out of Bridget's low-slung car and into the wheelchair. She smiled like she had a secret all the way to her room. Once in bed, she'd closed her eyes and dropped into a deep sleep, lips still curled in her secret smile.

"I'm sorry I tired her out." Bridget's voice carried more satisfaction than apology.

"You really think this will lead somewhere?"

"It's far too early to tell, but my gut feeling is yes. We need to talk. Not now, though. I've got a dinner engagement."

"A date, huh?" Jake meant it as a joke and was surprised by what could only be a twinge of jealousy.

"I'm not sure I'd call it that. But yes, a gentleman invited me to the Alta Vista."

Jake had followed her down the hall, jealousy turning to anger he didn't recognize as such and which changed to equally unrecognized self-pity on the way home.

Billy Stanton's message asking if he wanted to go snowmobiling the next day perked him up enough to rummage in the freezer and the hot crackle of a frozen steak being force-thawed in the frying pan pushed his malaise into the shadows.

***

Jake watched the clouds thicken above the Presidentials while Billy drove with one hand and tried to keep his coffee from spilling with the other. "Ought to fix these shocks." The truck sliding to a stop by the shoulder broke Jake's concentration on the high ridges. "Jesus. Will you look at them sonsabitches." Billy pointed to a herd of elk moving in unhurried trot across a field on the other side of the road. "Where were they last fall?"

"Snow must be real heavy higher up."

"What they been saying. More elk and deer down low than in a long time. Froggie says he sees them all the time. Big horns, too. Came around that hairpin this side of Concho Pass and there was herd on the bank. Some even standing on the pavement." Billy drained his coffee and put the truck in gear.

A mile on the other side of Sawtooth they caught up with an older pickup laboring under the weight of two snowmobiles in the truck bed.

"Fuck," said Billy. "Don't know where I can pass. Hate to have to follow them all the way to Hazel Lake."

As if he'd heard, the driver signaled a right turn and swung onto the plowed road that, in the summertime, went the twenty plus miles up to Doyle Reservoir. Jake caught a glimpse of a girl with long, black hair in the passenger's seat as they passed.

***

"He coming Monday?" Blakenship fixed Daryl with a hard eye.

Yesterday, the deputy had told him Abel Ruiz was the girl's uncle — her father's youngest brother — and that he'd returned to Union about a year ago after spending four or five years in parts unknown. He'd also announced that the Packer County deputy was coming down the next day. Unfortunately, he had forgotten to find out whether she'd be working and had been embarrassed later to report that she had the afternoon off.

"Late. But that's O. K. She's supposed to work from after school to closing time."

"The uncle. Abel. He been in the county any?"

"Visits the family — parents and a brother," the deputy checked his notes, "brother Felipe."

"Felipa and Felipe. Interesting."

"I guess. Stays with Felipe when he comes."

"Felipe Ruiz. What's he do?"

"Works on cars. Has a one-man shop west of Top Hat."

"On the Pea Green road?"

"Uh huh."

"I think I know it. Just a step up from a shade tree mechanic."

"What I'm told, he does a lot of work for the meskins around the county."

"The whole county?"

"What I'm told. Supposed to be real good."

"And brother Abel is a frequent visitor?"

"I don't know how often. Just that that's where he stays when he comes."

"How do you know all this?"

"I have my snitches." Daryl grinned.

"Snitches, bullshit. Answer me."

"I can't blow his cover. Why do you need to know, anyway?"

Blakenship stared at the ceiling. "Fuck me, sweet Jesus. Can't blow his cover. Why, he asks me." He stared at the deputy. "There's lots of reasons. To see how good your information is. To try to get an idea if maybe your," he worked his tongue like he had a bad taste in his mouth, "snitch is snitching to the other side. To see if you've got the sense God gave a syphilitic goat on a cold winter's morning. But most of all," Blakenship stood to his full six-foot-two and kicked the olive-drab wastebasket across the room where it hit the wall with a clang and reverberated dully on the floor, "but most of all because I asked you and I'm your goddamn boss." Blakenship returned to his seat. "I'm not confusing you, am I?"

"No sir."

"That's better. Now answer the fucking question."

"Gabriel Munoz."

"Who he?"

"Guy I went to high school with ..." Blakenship rolled his eyes. "Works at the Safeway but he wants to get into law enforcement and has an application in with the state police."

"You see him much?"

"Not in public. But yeah, we get together and talk. He's always wanting to hear what it's like being a deputy."

"And in return he tells you what he knows is going on in the county. Discretely, of course."

"Right."

"So we've got a wannabe cop who also happens to be a meskin. He know anything about drugs?"

"Not that he's said."

"You have asked him?"

"Once or twice. A couple of weeks back. When that fed was here."

"Buchanan."

"Buchanan. Gabe didn't say he didn't know anything. Just wanted to be sure first."

"Meaning?"

"I took it to mean he was doing some investigating on his own."

"And you didn't see fit to tell me about any of this?"

"Didn't have anything to tell you. Until now."

"What's going on?" Henderson leaned against the doorjamb.

"Daryl maybe got us something to play with." Blakenship indicated the empty chair with a tilt of his head and the senior deputy pulled it up to the desk. "Hokay," Blakenship let his breathe out with a whoosh, "we got the Sanchez brothers here." He put his finger on the desktop. "And we got the Grummond Dairy here." He moved it a couple of inches. "And we got a direct line between them 'cause we know they dropped the dime that set off this mess."

"And we got a direct connection between Abel and Jake." Daryl marked another spot. "And a direct connection between Felipa and Abel and between her and the brothers ..."

"We ain't sure about that one yet."

"No sir. Not technically. But I'm thinking we will be by Monday night."

"Go on."

"So — where did the Sanchezes get the idea to name the Grummond Dairy? From Abel."

"Keep talking."

"We know Abel's been in Union where the father lives and where the brothers visit. And we're pretty damn sure Felipa was the one who sprang them from the hospital."

"You figure Abel's in on the drug thing?" Henderson fumbled with a fresh pack of Pall Malls. "Reasonable working hypothesis, I reckon. It's not like what we know of his character would preclude the possibility out of hand."

"That and Sherlock here tells me he's got a snitch who says Abel comes to the county and stays with his brother on the road to Pea Green."

"Felipe?" Every meskin in the county gets his vehicle fixed there."

"If Abel's working with the Sanchezes, why'd he give them Grummond's place when he knew it wouldn't hold up? Come on, Charlie, help me out."

"Maybe he figured he could plant some dope and screwed up some way. Or maybe he wanted to bring the boys down — take their place in the organization. Or maybe he wasn't thinking any too good and just wanted to get back at Jake."

"Then there's the question of who fixed the brakes on their car and got them in the hospital in the first place."

"There is that."

"What I'm thinking," Blakenship scratched his ear and stared off into space, "what I'm thinking is we nail down Felipa at the hospital. And," dropped his gaze to look directly at Daryl, "we politely ask your friend Munoz to have a talk. Soon."

"I don't know …" Daryl stammered.

"I do. That's what counts right now. I do."

***

"Is that smoke? Wood smoke?" Jake turned as Billy pulled up beside him and killed his engine. "Flip up your visor."

"Smells like it to me."

"Where you reckon it's coming from?"

They were about ten miles from the Inn, having started out on the Shadow Lake trail and turning off on a less-traveled route that followed a ridge through BLM land. They could see the highway from where they sat, a two-lane blacktop winding out of sight beyond the shoulder of the ridge they were on.

"How far to the highway?"

"Hard to judge. Fifteen miles?"

"Ain't that the Doyle Reservoir road? You can see some brown coming down the grade where it's plowed to the dirt."

"Could be."

"Look." Jake pointed a gloved hand. What appeared to be two snowmobiles were making their way down the far slope in the general direction of where the plowed road might be if it followed the logic of the land's contours. He traced the tracks back to a mixed stand of aspen and evergreens. A thin strand of smoke was visible just above the treetops before a gust of wind erased. "That's what we smell. Hope they didn't leave it burning."

"Could be they've got a good stove."

"If it's the meskin boy and girl we passed, they can't have been there more than hour, hour and a half. Why build a big fire for just a little while?"

"Might be that clothes got in the way of what they were doing."

"Long way and a lot of trouble for some nookie."

"You never was much of a romantic, Jake."

"Maybe not. But if I was, I think I'd try something other than driving more than an hour, unloading two heavy snowmobiles from a pickup — they didn't even have a trailer, for crissakes — then breaking trail for ten miles to get to a cold cabin where there ain't any running water, then building a fire and waiting for it to warm up enough to shed the clothes, then screwing and turning right around and getting back on the sleds."

"Put it that way, it don't seem near as romantic." Billy hit the electric start on his machine. "But whatever they're doing and why, we got to get a move on if we're going to make the top of Baldy before it gets dark."

231

They were a mile beyond the turnoff to Doyle Reservoir on the way home when they passed the same Chevy pickup going the other way.

"No snowmobiles."

"Say what?" Billy gave Jake a quizzical look.

"Same pickumup. Looks like they kept the fire going because they were coming back."

"Maybe they went for groceries."

"You'd have thought they'd have brought them the first time in."

"Maybe they didn't know they were going to stay the night."

***

It was dark when he woke up, too dark even to make out the branches of the shrub just beyond the bedroom window that Mary Margaret had planted in the first year of their marriage. What the hell was it called? He lay on his back and tried to remember, but the name wouldn't come.

Thinking about the bush made him think of her smile when she returned from her ride. Maybe that Taylor woman was on to something.

He rolled to his side to get an angle on the alarm clock. Getting on toward six.

He showered and shaved then stood irresolute in the kitchen. Maria Elena had cleaned while he'd been in the high country with Billy and he was loath to dirty any dishes. Breakfast at Alma's, that was the ticket. Couldn't remember when he'd had one of Alma's Belgian waffles.

There was no sign of activity behind the plate glass windows of Alma's Cafe. He squinted at the door, trying to read the hours painted in small script above the handle. Cursing automatically, he got out and walked closer.

6:00 AM to 8 PM Mon. thru Sat.

8:00 AM to 2 PM Sun.

He found himself heading west through Top Hat's few blocks of residential district, over the Flint River and up to West Mesa. The road ran straight as an engineer's rule for two miles before it curved to follow a cottonwood-lined stream wending its way to Pea Green. The sun had cleared the mountains now and glinted off the metal roof of Felipe Ruiz's garage nestled under bare limbs where the road turned.

Jake slowed for the curve. The garage doors were padlocked and there was no more sign of life than there'd been at Alma's. He reached to flip the passenger side visor down to cut the glare of the rising sun. On his left, clouds were gathering over the Sublette Plateau and he turned the radio on to see about the chances of snow. Not that it made a shit.

Static. His fiddling with the tuning made it worse so he turned the radio off with a goddammit that carried no conviction and pulled the snuff tin from his shirt pocket.

Lip loaded, he was balancing the tin on top of the steering wheel trying to put the lid back on when a yearling steer bounded from the bar ditch. Brakes locked up, the pickup fishtailed sideways, sending the snuff flying across the cab. The cow stopped momentarily on the pavement before crossing the road where it dropped its head to the grass between gravel shoulder and fence. Jake rolled down the window to spit and swore at the animal, this time with feeling.

The snuff was beyond salvaging. Maybe Rafe was open.

He pulled into the Pea Green store as Rafe was finishing mopping the porch.

"What brings you this way so bright and early?"

"Need some Cope."

"In the beer cooler. Top shelf, on the right."

Jake removed a tin from the shrink-wrapped stack, started for the counter, changed his mind and got another. "Way I been going today, better get a spare."

"Heard you sold off the herd. You out of the dairy business permanent?"

"Hard to say."

233

"Goddamn shame. Hate to see agricultural land get turned into residential. Speaking of which." A blue Suburban pulled up to the gas pumps. "Californians." Rafe spit at the wastebasket behind the counter. "Although to give them credit, they are making noise about putting in a garden and maybe feeding out a calf."

They watched in silence as the driver, large and soft, stretched expansively while the passenger, a wiry man of efficient movement that spoke of a lifetime of physical work, set the nozzle and cleaned the windows all around.

The driver said something to the other that was acknowledged with a curt nod and walked with heavy strides up the steps, fumbling in his jacket all they way. "This country will fool you. You don't realize how cold it is until you try to do something with your gloves off," he said as he laid a wallet on the counter and blew on his hands.

"You'll get used to it." Rafe slid the credit card through the machine.

"And how are you this morning, Mr. Grummond?"

Jake looked blankly at him.

"Porterfield. Reg Porterfield. We stopped by your place last fall."

"You the folks who've got the old Sheffield place?"

"That's right. Heard about your misfortune and I don't mean to rush you, but if you're selling any of machinery, we'd certainly be interested."

"Haven't thought about it."

"Perhaps we could drive over someday and take a look."

"Can if you want."

"Perhaps later in the week." Porterfield bent to sign the receipt. "What brings you out this way?"

"Waiting for Alma's to open so I can get a waffle."

"Waffles? We'll have to give them a try."

"Just don't plan on eating before eight on Sunday."

There was a Chevy pickup parked to the side of Ruiz's garage when Jake retraced his route back to Top Hat. It hadn't been there on the way out. They were back early, but he guessed they'd had plenty of time for passion in front of the fire.

17

FEBRUARY 17 — Late Morning

"He say it was her?" Blakenship eyed Daryl over the toes of his boots.

"Ninety per cent sure."

"Close enough for now." Blakenship caught himself reaching for a fresh cigar with one still burning in the ashtray. "When're we going to have a chat with your snitch?"

"He says after work. But not here. We usually meet at his house. Sometimes mine. If it's his, I drive my own car."

"Of course." Blakenship nodded gravely. "He live alone?"

"With his parents."

"Don't think it would be a good idea if I showed up there."

"How about my place? Nothing strange about my boss stopping by."

"Tonight?"

"I'll have him there by seven."

***

"The way I see it, we have two points of attack." The lawyer knitted his fingers together on top of his head and leaned back in his high-backed leather chair. "First, we can challenge the validity of the information which was presented to the judge who issued the warrant — and whether an experienced officer of the law should have known it was shaky. Second, we can challenge the appropriateness of their conduct during the raid itself."

"What about the INS bullshit?"

"I'd group that with their conduct during the raid."

Jake worked the snuff from one side of his mouth to the other while he thought. "How're we going to challenge the warrant?"

"Depose the agent in charge — Buchanan, wasn't it? — and perhaps some others…"

"Fucker'll lie."

"Perhaps. It would also help if we could obtain statements from the informants themselves — or their associates."

"How do you reckon to do that?"

"Didn't say it would be easy. If I were you, I might start with the father."

"Me?"

"Jake, I'm willing to take this on because your father was one of my first clients. He trusted this green kid fresh out of law school. Also, you're getting screwed by our alleged public servants about as bad as I've seen in forty years of practicing law — which goes against everything I believed when I chose law in the first place, if I can remember that far back. And I'm willing to do it for expenses and the legally allowed percentage of the award, if there is any. But I'm sixty-six years old. I'm a small town lawyer with one secretary who comes in thirty hours a week. The leg work is up to you."

Jake absently added fresh snuff without spitting out the old. "It's not like I got anything else to do."

"Understand, your job is to find out what happened. Why the Sanchez brothers said what they were represented as saying. Who instigated the destruction in the dwellings. Find some people who'll talk to you — deputies, relatives or friends of the informants. We'll get subpoenas when — or if — we decide to file suit."

"Think it'll work?"

"No idea. But it's the best I can come up with."

***

The afternoon sun had thawed the rutted adobe of driveway and barnyard to a gumbo consistency that clung with malevolent persistence to tires and boots. The sun had also warmed the sheltered area of the porch to shirtsleeve temperature and Jake sat with his back to the wall going over the list of names Blakenship had provided months before — had it been that long? — hat brim pulled low against the glare.

He was trying to decide whether to start with the Sapinero deputies or drive to Union and the used-car lot when the sound of an engine revving over lost traction drew him from the papers.

A blue Suburban slogged to a stop next to his pickup. Porterfield and three he didn't know, although the thin one looked like the one who'd pumped gas a Rafe's.

"Hope we're not disturbing you." Porterfield's question was tentative enough that maybe he really did hope he wasn't. "We were coming back from Mountain View and since we were this close we thought we'd see where you stood about selling equipment."

"Ain't decided yet. But you can look. Everything's over there," he gestured beyond the milking barn. "Go on over. I'll be along soon's I put on my boots."

He picked his way through the mud to the men clustered by a John Deere. "See anything you like?"

"Waiting for you. We're out of our league." The sweep of Porterfield's arm included them all. "This is Pete Petersen," the gas pumper extended his hand, "Bob Walsh," lean and weathered he raised his hand in half salute, "and Colonel Burns" who gave a curt nod and fixed flat blue eyes on Jake in an unblinking almost-stare.

Jake looked at each man in turn. "What're you thinking about doing?"

"We hope to be as self-sufficient as possible. Vegetables. Fruit trees. Maybe chickens, once we get settled. Perhaps a steer or two. That kind of thing." Porterfield's voice exuded confidence but he seemed to eye Burns for approval after each statement.

"Then the John Deeres are too big."

"John Deeres?"

"What you're standing next to."

It took the better part of an hour to show them the International M's, letting each start one and drive around, and another half hour while they examined several trailers.

"It looks like two of the small tractors and two trailers," Porterfield said, "But before we buy …"

"Haven't said I'd sell them."

"Ah, yes." Porterfield swallowed and went on. "Could we prevail upon you to come over and see what we have in mind? Bribe you with dinner."

"When?"

"No time like the present."

"Not today. Got things to do."

"Saturday, then? Say mid-afternoon so you'll have plenty of light?"

Eusebio and Jesus mounted the porch as he watched the Suburban negotiate the driveway. "Get a job?"

"I will know in two weeks."

"And you?" Jake asked Jesus.

"I have a *primo* at the Martin Orchard in …"

"I know where it is."

"He says they need another for full time."

Jake turned back to Eusebio. "What about Maria Elena? She told me she will graduate from high school. Here in Top Hat. No matter what."

"That is what she told me, also." Eusebio smiled. "If my father were here, he would think she is beyond redemption. Almost eighteen and not even one child. And she tells me what she is going to do. He would not believe it." He shook his head. "I am very proud of her. She will stay here. If not in the house, then with friends."

"You want me to buy back your land?"

"No. We wish to build."

Jake looked at him with surprise. "You're not leaving for good?"

"We have spent too many years here. Our children …" His voice broke and he turned his head.

"Well." Jake drummed his fingers on the porch rail. "Like I said before, you can probably tie into Dad's water. Septic and power, you've got to do." He spit towards the front bumper of his pickup. The sun was dropping and the adobe was starting to harden. "Then there's permits."

"The permits, that is where we would like your help."

"When you thinking about breaking ground?"

"In the summer."

"We'd better get started. Damn county takes forever to do a simple thing that shouldn't need doing anyway. Not out here."

"I am thinking maybe a doublewide."

"Let me know."

***

Henderson used his hand to shield his eyes from the slanting morning sun as he entered Blakenship's office. "Damn, C.W. Haven't you heard of venetian blinds?"

"I like the light, Charlie. Get here when I do, you won't have that problem. Besides, it won't last long."

Henderson dragged a chair to the side of the desk in the shadow cast by a bookshelf lined with manuals and three-ring binders that hadn't been disturbed for years. "What came of the talk you had with that Munoz kid?"

"Nothing solid. But he's heard you can get dope at Ruiz's garage. Could be Buchanan's right after all. Drugs come through and they get a cut to retail."

"Can't be much of a cut, considering that possession is way down on the list of crimes and misdemeanors we deal with."

"That might be changing." Blakenship sighed. "Last night, Jessie told me that Minnie told her that she'd caught her only boy with a baggie of white powder."

"Minnie Fletcher? The manager of the Stockman?" Blakenship nodded. "What'd she do with it?"

"Flushed it down the toilet."

"Say where he got it?"

"Not that she told Jessie."

"Shit. Support your local sheriff." Henderson's tone carried the weariness of four decades in law enforcement. "This

Munoz, he know you can score at Ruiz's garage, or is it just what he hears?"

"Not the type to push. Kind of a mama's boy. One of those meskin Baptists — real proper."

"Why the hell's he want to be a state cop?"

"Sees it like a calling. Sort of like being a minister."

"Lord save us."

"That's his hope, I reckon. With him helping the Lord along. Anyhow, he gave us enough to justify having the garage watched."

"Hard to do, it being out all by itself on the Pea Green road.

"There's that."

"Of course, you might could put somebody with a pair of binoculars up in the dobies." Henderson grinned. "But you already thought of that."

"You're a hard man to fool, Charlie."

"And the girl?"

"That one's a little trickier."

"Let me study on it."

***

Jake pulled into a convenience store on the outskirts of Union. None of the three telephone booths had directories so he went inside and got one from the clerk. Together, they pored over the city street map until they pinpointed the site of the Sanchez used car lot.

Logic said his odds of learning something Mackey Fitz could use were higher canvassing deputies than criminals — or at least relatives of criminals. But the brothers' lies had started the chain of disasters and their unfeeling expressions in the photographs on his refrigerator was building in him an overwhelming drive to confront them. By seven he was on the way to Union, stopping only to look in on Mary Margaret, who was more animated than usual, although, as near as he could tell, seeing him didn't have much to do with it. He remembered that she was going riding with Bridget Taylor and felt another of the pangs of jealousy that were becoming more frequent.

The Sanchez lot was on the far side of town in a welter of strip malls, junkyards and small industrial parks. Three or four men dressed in slacks and shirtsleeves were clustered around the coffee pot — salesmen, he supposed. One approached with a practiced smile and hearty greeting that carried the optimism of a new day.

"Is Mr. Sanchez around?"

The smile faded. "He hasn't been in for weeks. Not after the accident. They say he had a stroke. Or a heart attack."

"What accident?"

"You didn't read about it? His sons. And they were driving one of the cars from the lot. It was in all the papers."

"I'm from down Mountain View way. They were killed?"

"No. Badly hurt."

"They're in the hospital?"

"Not now. They disappeared." The man frowned. "It was after that that Mr. Sanchez …" He stopped when he noticed a man standing, arms crossed, in the doorway of the farthest of the paneled cubicles that lined the interior wall. The plate above the door read Manager. "What kind of car are you looking for? Perhaps I …"

"That's O. K. Think I'll have a chat with your boss."

The manager uncrossed his arms as Jake neared and shifted his weight slightly to the balls of his feet like a street fighter who wasn't sure if trouble was coming. But his voice held the same practiced joviality as the salesman's. "How may we help you today? If you're driving that Dodge Ram Charger, I can get you in a '93 Ford 350 for the truck and a little pocket change."

"Not today. I was hoping to see Mr. Sanchez."

"He hasn't been in for a while. Health. If you're not looking for a vehicle, just what is it you want?"

"Actually, I was trying to get some information about his sons."

"Which ones."

242

"Victor and Julio."

The man rubbed a hand through the salt and pepper of his hair and fixed Jake with a steady look. Scar tissue, faded now so you didn't see it at first, marked the ends of both eyebrows, Jake noticed. Don't let the belly fool you. This was one to watch. "You're not a cop." It wasn't a question. "If you're not a cop and you're not a customer, you can get the hell out of here."

Jake didn't move, debating whether to explain about the raid while the manager tried to stare him down. No point, he concluded. This sonofabitch wouldn't care one way or the other. "Thanks for your help."

There was a familiar pickup parked nose up to a metal building at the back of the lot. A man was leaning ass against the fender, listening to another in mechanic blue coveralls talking with animated gestures. Jake backed from his space and turned toward the pair. The one against the fender saw him coming and disappeared into the building.

Jake swung passed the pickup, raising his finger in lazy salute to the mechanic who watched him go by without acknowledgment or expression.

The last time he'd seen that truck, it was parked at the garage on the Pea Green road with two snowmobiles in the back. And there was something about the one who'd disappeared. Something about the set of his shoulders.

He was halfway back to Top Hat when it came to him. Abel Ruiz.

The sonofabitch.

The memory of coming into the barn to find Eusebio backed against a stanchion with Ruiz's forearm across his throat came back so vividly he had to stop on the shoulder, get out and walk along the fence. It took the better part of a mile before he felt able to drive.

Abel Ruiz and the Sanchezes. Could it be?

***

243

"You mean you haven't questioned the boy or the mother?" The echo of the speakerphone didn't mask the incredulity in Kiernan's voice.

"Getting around to it. I've known Minnie Fletcher for twenty-five years. She ain't going anywhere. Besides, if I don't approach it right, it could mean Jessie's job and jobs for Ute women over forty ain't that easy to come by. Men either, for that matter."

"Still."

"To get back my question, what white powder would be in a baggie?"

"Could be any number of things, the most likely being cocaine or speed. Maybe heroin. I'm more interested in the quantity. If it was a small, could hold a gram or maybe an eight ball — that's an eighth of an ounce — that's one thing. But you start getting into an ounce or more — that's a lot of money for small-town kid. Could mean he was getting ready to deal." Kiernan cleared his throat. "Mother's name is Fletcher, you said. Strange. This thing's been Mexican all the way to Denver and from what you say about the Ruiz garage, what retailing they're doing is to Mexicans. Of course, they could be expanding."

"Whatever. Drugs never been a problem here, outside of a little marijuana or pills."

"That you know of."

Blakenship ignored him. "How do they use this shit?"

"Shoot it, snort it or smoke it. If it's speed, somebody may be making it right in your very own county."

"Now there's a happy thought."

"In any event, it may be time to raid that garage."

"I'd rather let my boys watch it for a while. All we've got right now is the word of a wannabe cop and as I recall, the last raid we had didn't turn out so well."

"How is Mr. Grummond?"

"Well, he's lost the dairy, his father hasn't come back from a heart attack and his wife is in a nursing home doing a pretty good impersonation of a vegetable. How the fuck do you think he is?"

244

"Easy. Sometimes shit happens. You've been in law enforcement long enough to know that. I hear he may sue."

"That's what I hear, too. And since he's coming up the sidewalk right now, I may learn a bit more."

"Keep me posted. Buchanan should be back your way in a couple of days."

"I can hardly wait. And, Kiernan."

"Yes?"

"We're not going to have a raid — any raid — in Sapinero County until I say so."

"I can wait. But not forever."

Henderson leaned forward in his chair to stub out his cigarette. "He may be more reasonable than Buchanan, but he's still a fed."

"Yeah. And we're going to have to deal with Buchanan pretty soon, it looks like."

"Good to see you're hard at work." Jake took a step into the office. "The both of you."

Blakenship couldn't tell if Jake's tone meant contempt or good-natured ribbing. "The ins and outs of law enforcement ain't always apparent to the inexperienced eye, Jake. Have a seat and tell us what we can do for you."

"You any closer to finding the Sanchez brothers?"

"Why?"

"Because my lawyer wants to get statements from them."

"So you are going to file suit."

"Maybe."

"Can't help you there."

"What about the father?"

"What about him?"

"Yesterday, I went up to Union. Went the day before, too. To the car lot. Folks there said he hadn't been in for weeks. Health, they said. But one of them let slip that his health problems coincided with his sons dropping out of sight."

"So?"

"So this morning, I drove back to Union. Went by the house. Wasn't that hard to find — he's in the phone book. It's closed up and the neighbors said nobody was home."

"Interesting. Maybe I should give Homer Underhill a call."

"You telling me this is news to you."

"Yep."

"I was right. You have been working hard. Let me tell you some more news. I saw Abel Ruiz at the car lot. He ducked out of sight when he saw me, but it was him all right. You tell me if putting Abel with the Sanchez brothers don't mean something."

"Such as?"

"Like why I was raided in the first place — or don't you remember the set-to I had with that slimy bastard?"

"Now that you mention it, something does come to mind. And that's important because?"

"Because it means that piece of shit fed didn't have valid information for the warrant."

"You mean because there might have been a personal vendetta?"

"Stop jerking me off, Cecil. You're not that stupid."

Blakenship let that go by. "What you say is right interesting and I can see where it might could help your case, but what's it got to do with me?"

"If you can't figure that out, then you are stupid." Jake spun on his heel then stopped at the door. "Tell you what may have something to do with you. I'm going to be talking to the deputies on the list you gave me."

Blakenship and Henderson watched through the window as Jake stomped down the sidewalk to his pickup, stop with his hand on the door handle then jaywalk across the street toward Fitzgerald's office.

"What do you think, Charlie?"

"Think he's starting to get het up. If he's just doing legwork for a lawsuit, then O. K. But if he gets frustrated with the speed that wheels of justice turn and decides to take direct action … and we know he's capable of it — by bloodline, if nothing else."

246

"At least he doesn't know about the girl."

"Maybe. All we know for sure is that he didn't mention her."

"You do have somebody watching her?"

"When she's at work. Watching the house ... that's a tough one."

"And the garage."

"Covered. All twenty and four hours."

"O. K. Hope we get something to pop before Jake does."

"Or Buchanan."

"Him, too, Charlie. Him, too."

***

"I can give you fifteen minutes, Jake." Mackey Fitz gestured at the papers spread across the desk in creative disarray. "Got an appointment at two."

"I know why I got raided. Abel Ruiz."

"Who's he?"

"Low life piece of shit I fired, I don't know, seven, eight years ago."

"How does he fit in?"

"Went up to Union day before yesterday looking for the father. Like you said. Father wasn't there — or home, either — but I saw Abel at the car lot. Slid out of sight when he saw me."

"That's it?"

"Shit. Makes sense, don't it. When the brothers needed a name, Abel gave it to them."

"You may be right. But that's nothing I can take into court."

"Can't you depose him?"

"Not until we file suit and are in discovery. I doubt he's going to come forward voluntarily and a subpoena has to be served."

"Meaning?"

"Meaning you have to find him first." Fitzgerald smiled. "Still and all, it's more than we had two days ago. Now if you

247

could just find the Sanchezes. Get them in custody, we'd know where to serve them."

***

"So what're you going to do?" Jessie's words got lost in the graying mat of chest hair pressing against her cheek.

"Say what?"

A hair worked its way inside a nostril, beginning the tickle that would build to a sneeze. She raised her head to slide her hands under her chin. "What are you going to do about Minnie?"

"Going to have to talk to her. And the boy." Blakenship shifted his position so that Jessie's head flowed naturally to his shoulder. "That's better. I'm not going to arrest him or anything, but I need to know where he got it. She didn't say how much there was?"

"Just a baggie."

"You reckon she meant a sandwich-sized one or what?"

"Don't know. Why?"

"According to Kiernan, it makes a difference. If it was an ounce or more, could mean the kid was dealing — or getting ready to. And that opens up a whole new level of problems."

"Minnie's really upset. She doesn't know whether to keep it quiet or come to you — doesn't want Lonnie to get in trouble, but…" Jessie rolled to her back and lay with hair spread across the pillow looking at the ceiling. "Why don't I suggest she talk to you?"

"With or without the boy?"

"Let her decide."

"O. K. For starters. But I'm going to have to see the boy, too. Soon or sooner." Blakenship sat up and shifted his pillow higher on the headboard and scooted to a semi-inclined position. "Last thing I need is a drug problem."

"You're right. This is different."

"Different? What do you know about drugs?"

248

"Shit, C. W. There's always been drugs in the county. Pot. Pills. Biker speed brought in by truckers. And whatever the Mexicans do among themselves."

"How do you know that?"

"I work in a bar. Lots of things you hear in a bar, even if you are the sheriff's old lady. But all that was kind of personal and low key. Low key enough for you to ignore it. This could be something else."

"Meaning?"

"If you're right, that Lonnie was going to deal — see, before, if you were white you either had to have a friend or relative bring something in for you — from Union, maybe. Or Denver or — wherever."

"What about Felipe Ruiz?"

"Just Mexicans. No Anglos need apply. Or Utes." She gave him a half-grin. "That's what I'm told."

"What's to stop the boy from having someone bring in the shit for him to sell?"

"Could be. Maybe he's working for someone who wants to supplement his income — in a big way. I don't know. But it's a change. The county may be catching up with the rest of the country."

"That's progress I don't need."

FEBRUARY 22 — Early Evening

"Sure you wouldn't like a toddy?"

"Beer's fine." Jake watched Porterfield add water to his glass until the color of the bourbon suited him. It didn't take much water.

They were sitting in what had been the parlor, formal with horsehair sofa when Mrs. Sheffield ruled the house with inflexible propriety. Now a large-screen TV dominated one wall and the furnishings ran to Naugahyde.

"Well, what do you think?"

"How many of you did you say there's going to be?"

"Six couples. Three bachelors. No children. Visitors from time to time, of course."

"I don't see you need more than one of the M's. Unless you just want to have two. I still ain't decided to sell, though." Jake sipped the beer. "You've got a lot of building to do."

"That we have. Although some will probably stay in RV's or house trailers at first. Speaking of house trailers, are any of your for sale?"

"Ain't made my mind up about that either."

"If you decide to, keep us in mind. The women will start coming in the spring."

"You want a garden this year, have to have your seed in the ground no later than Memorial Day." Jake padded in his stocking feet to the gun cabinet next to the TV and stared through the glass at a short-barreled shotgun with a dull silver finish.

Porterfield watched him from the armchair. "Are you a gun fancier?"

"Not really. Just that I never saw one like this."

"It's a Mossberg. Military. Fifteen rounds. Sixteen, with one in the chamber. 12 gauge, of course." Porterfield opened the cabinet door and handed it to him.

"Light." He put it to his shoulder. "Not legal to hunt with."

"Made for a tight spot. Close range. Which is not to say I haven't popped a cap at a pheasant or two, just to see. Now with this," Porterfield took out a long-barreled rifle with the biggest telescopic sight Jake had ever seen, "you can count the veins in a fly's wings." Porterfield aimed through the window toward the barn where a light glowed above the double doors. "See for yourself."

Jake nestled his cheek along the stock. The weapon seemed to settle into place automatically, coming to horizontal where it waited patiently for him to pull the trigger. The sight brought the flaking paint and exposed nail heads of the siding on the barn into sharp relief and he wondered how the white stripe in that DEA prick's hair would look. He worked the bolt and nodded at the silky noiseless action. "Not much call for one of these around here."

"A hobby. That's all."

Jake walked to the window. "What're you going to use the barn for once you're done building?"

"A shop. Most of it at any rate. There'll always be something that needs work."

The afternoon tour had included a cursory look inside the barn and he'd noticed an enclosure against one wall with what looked like a steel door. He also noticed the recently leveled floor, the poured concrete over half the surface area with stakes and string marking out where forms were to go for more.

Steps on the porch announced the arrival of what proved to be Burns and Petersen. "What's on the menu tonight, George?" Burns threw over his shoulder as he made his way to the collection of bottles on the table next to the gun cabinet.

"Ham and au gratin potatoes," came the answer from the kitchen.

"You're in for a treat, Mr. Grummond." Burns dropped ice cubes into a tall glass and reached for a half-liter bottle of George Dickel. "George won mess awards just about everywhere he was stationed. Isn't that right, George?""

"Just about, Colonel," the kitchen voice answered.

"And dessert?" Burns added water to his glass until it was several shades lighter than Porterfield's.

"Choice of cherry pie or German chocolate cake."

"With food like that, we have to work to keep the weight off."

"Looks like work won't be your problem. Not for a while, anyway." Jake drained his beer and set the bottle on the floor between his feet."

"Another?" Without waiting for answer, Burns said "Ben" and nodded toward the kitchen. Another man — was it one of the ones who looked at the tractors? — had entered the room soundlessly.

"Interesting place you're setting up here. Don't think I've seen anything like it."

"I suppose not. But it's quite simple, really. As you've probably guessed, we're all retired military. By pooling our resources, we can get more for our pension dollars than any of us could individually."

"Why here?"

"Price was right." Porterfield was back at the table, refilling his glass — but not from the bottle of Dickel, Jake noticed. "That was a major consideration. And we all wanted to get out of Southern California. Away from the traffic, the air pollution, the race riots, the crimes, the drugs ...."

"Dinner's on, Reg." Burn's soft voice stopped the flow of Porterfield's words as effectively as a sock stuffed in his mouth.

Conversation dwindled to the essentials of passing of food and condiments as they fell to a meal with the habitual single-mindedness of men without women who had eaten in the company of men without women for much of their adult lives. Main course and dessert were as good as advertised and the cook, who turned out to be the fat man who'd been with Porterfield on their first visit to the dairy way back in the fall, accepted the compliments with the air of a man receiving his just due.

"Six couples, you say?" Jake smiled thanks as Porterfield refilled his coffee cup. "They all going to have their own houses?"

"Eventually." Porterfield settled comfortably into his chair. "That's why we're interested in your house trailers. Each couple will make their own decision, of course. You know how women are." He stopped awkwardly at Jake's involuntary twitch. "Sorry."

"No matter. It's a fact." Wishing it were molasses, Jake stirred sugar into his coffee and tapped the spoon on the lip of the cup. "For sure you got room enough. What about the county? Can't just slap a house up where you want. Not like the old days."

"John Davis has been helping us in that regard. Got approval for the Colonel's place already and he seems to think we'll be ready for the rest by April. May at the latest."

"Good luck to you on that. County has a way of slowing things down. But with Johnny on your side? Maybe. He can be a help sometimes. Although I haven't seen him lately."

"He told us about your unfortunate situation." Burns rose and started, coffee cup in hand, to the parlor. The others followed suit as quickly as though it had been a voiced command. "It gave us pause. That's the kind of thing we're trying to get away from."

"Goddamn cops." This from the man who'd brought the beer. "Local or federal, they fucking never…"

"You're on KP, aren't you?" Burns watched until he disappeared through the kitchen door. "He gets worked up, sometimes. Had some bad experiences. On the other hand, he's right. The government is hardly paying lip service to the Constitution. Things keep going the way they are, it won't be long before they drop all pretense. Don't you agree?"

Jake felt his jaw torque. He put his cup and saucer on the couch arm and willed the knotted muscles to relax before he spoke. "Don't know about the Constitution. But the bastards fucked me up for no reason."

"And are you able to get any satisfaction."

Jake flexed his right hand. The scabs were almost gone. His lips twitched in what could have been a smile.

"Satisfaction? Not really. But I'm not done yet. Not if I can find those lowlife motherfuckers who lied to the DEA." He rose to his feet. "Appreciate the meal. But it's time I was going."

Porterfield walked him to the door. "You'll let us know if you decide to sell."

"You'll know when I know."

***

Hard to figure what to make of them, not that it made a shit. If he was going to sell off equipment, they could buy it same as anybody else.

He braked for the first of the ninety-degree turns that formed the zigzag on the Pea Green road, headlights catching a sheriff's department Bronco waiting where the track started that led to the high dobies. What kind of crime wave they having up there?

Lights on bright glared in his rear-view mirror as he gained speed after the turn by the garage. Red and blue flashing lights followed. Jake lifted his foot from the accelerator and edged toward the shoulder. The Bronco shot past, giving a glimpse of the shield painted on the door. The flashing lights went off once it was clear of Jake.

When he pulled into Top Hat, he saw the Bronco parked in front of Alma's and he felt a flash of gut-tightening anger at the arrogance of flashing lights just to get to a hamburger a little faster. He rolled slowly through the next block, undecided about what to do. Frog Bottom's pickup in front of Helen's made up his mind and he swung left in a wide arc to pull in beside it.

Froggie was sitting hunch-shouldered on a bar stool, talking to Helen. Two couples at a back table took turns at the bowling machine and a long-retired logging truck driver was at another table, eyes unfocused on a TV basketball game.

Helen saw him come in out of the corner of her eye and pulled a beer from the cooler. "What brings you this time of night?"

"Been out. On the way home."

"From?" Frog Bottom spun the stool halfway around and rested his back against the bar.

"Them new folks out Pea Green way. Wanted me to tell them what kind of equipment they needed, then sell it to them."

"You selling equipment?"

"Haven't decided." Jake took a sip of beer. "They're a strange bunch."

"Know what you mean." Frog Bottom stretched his arms to the ceiling, one at a time. "Damn. Stiffen up faster than I used to. Been delivering dimensional out there. Still, long as they don't bother anybody, no skin off my ass." He pushed a couple of dollars toward Helen. "But this valley's changing. Too many people. Too much land being taken out of production."

"People who build houses buy lumber."

"I ain't saying it's hurting me. But I liked things the way they were."

***

"Sheriff?"

The tentative voice spun Blakenship from the window and his contemplation of the church-going traffic. "What?"

"I finished my surveillance report from yesterday. You want it?" Daryl proffered what looked to be two sheets of single-spaced typing.

Blakenship waved them away. "Sit down and tell me."

"O. K. I took over about mid-morning. According to Allen, her father had dropped her off right on time. Nothing happened until about noon or so when she came out. At first, I thought she was going to lunch, but she walked past Alma's, past that little old post office to the park, you know, with the merry-go-round and …"

"I've been to Top Hat, Daryl."

255

"Yes sir. Anyway, there was a pickup at the park —
looked like a '79, '80 Chevy, white. She walked straight to it and
got in."

"You see who was driving?"

"Just a glimpse. See, I was up on the second floor of the
building they're remodeling. Charlie's cousin is doing the work
and he, Charlie that is, asked him if it would be all right for us
…"

"I know the drill."

"Right. Looked like a Mexican behind the wheel, but I'm
not sure. Funny thing is, the pickup had two snowmobiles in the
back."

"Snowmobiles? Two?"

"Uh huh. Anyway, the girl gets in the truck. It looked like
they talked for a bit and then the truck takes off. I waited until it
got to the highway. When it turned toward Mountain View, I ran
down to where my truck was parked — Charlie said for us to use
our own vehicles and we'd get per something …"

"You'll be reimbursed."

"Right. Anyway, it didn't take me too long to catch up, it
carrying a fair amount of weight and all. I didn't get too close,
just kept them in sight and …"

"I don't need to hear about your technique. Where'd they
go and what'd they do?"

"Right. They drove up past Sawtooth, turned off at the
Doyle Reservoir Road, drove to where the school bus turns
around, unloaded the machines and rode into the mountains." He
paused to catch his breath. "And they stayed the night. At least,
they hadn't come back at six when my shift was over."

"Who took over?"

"Nobody. Jerry was supposed to but he's sick and Charlie
didn't want to put anyone else on the job."

"Need to talk to Charlie." Blakenship spun back to the
window. "Doyle Reservoir Road. Pretty good work. We know a
little more about Felipa Ruiz than we did before. I don't suppose
you checked the truck?"

"No sir. I was in Otero County and I didn't figure …"

Blakenship sighed. "The license plate? You didn't happen to write it down, did you?"

Daryl brightened. "Yes sir. I'm waiting for the report."

***

Sunday morning, Jake got to the nursing home just as Bridget was closing the passenger-side door for a seat-belted Mary Margaret. "You're getting an early start."

"She wants to go, so ..."

Jake looked through the window to his wife who favored him with a brief smile. The skin under her chin seemed tauter than it had in months. Was she losing weight? Why hadn't he noticed? He checked the impulse to open the car door and feel her belly. "Where you headed?"

"I thought we'd go by the school again and maybe the old house and then up on the Sublette. The idea is to give her ample time to talk if she wants. Plus let her actually get to a place she's been looking at through the window for so long."

"Any idea of when you'll be back?"

"That depends on Mary Margaret. I can't imagine it'll be more than two, three hours at the most."

"I'll look in around four."

***

"Harold was the best you could do?" Blakenship had caught up with Henderson at the deputy's house. "Shit, Charlie. How do you think he can keep from getting seen, big and dumb as he is? Every month I talk myself out of firing his sorry ass and I can't tell you why I do."

"Fact that his uncle's a county commissioner have anything to do with it? Look, C. W., I got him up on a roof with binoculars. Getting seen shouldn't be a problem. More like will he see anything? His attention has been known to wander."

"Ain't we got anybody better?"

257

"Not who hasn't pulled more than a full shift this week. Besides, who'd you rather have freezing his ass off on a Sunday?"

"There's that. Maybe he'll freeze to death and relieve us of a problem. But Charlie, since Felipa works every day but Saturday afternoon and Sunday, shouldn't we have our best people on duty then?"

"What about the garage? Our manpower's not unlimited."

"I don't know, now that Daryl's turned up snowmobiling near Doyle Reservoir. Not what you'd expect someone like her to do of a Saturday afternoon."

"And night. If Daryl's right."

"If he's right, there must be a cabin." Blakenship swore. "And if there's a cabin, it might be occupied."

"Sanchezes."

"We could follow the tracks."

"Which tracks? There's a number of high country snowmobilers who put in on the Doyle Reservoir Road. Not to mention it's in Otero County. Not to mention it's snowing up that way, if you hadn't noticed. Supposed to hit the valley later on."

"We could scout for the cabin without attracting attention."

"How're we going to know which cabin?" Henderson jumped to the whistle of the teakettle and the skittering pop of water on the electric burner.

"Send somebody up to the Otero County courthouse to check the tax rolls for that part of the county."

"That's something Darlene could do. She's pretty thorough about things like that. What's she looking for?"

"Won't know until I see it. Need for her to copy everything you could reach by snowmobile from the Doyle Reservoir Road. Send her tomorrow. And Charlie. Keep it between the three of us." Blakenship was at the door when Henderson spoke.

"Occurs to me that the cabin, it'd be occupied in the middle of the working week. That would cut the possibilities down considerable."

"That it would, Charlie. That it would. Why don't I try to round us up some machines? Maybe we could set out Tuesday or Wednesday."

"You still want me to send Darlene to Elwood?"

"More than ever."

***

After going over the list of Sapinero County deputies, Jake decided he'd start with Harold Dobbins and Riddle Hooper. What kind of name was Riddle, anyway? He checked the telephone book, finding several Dobbins but no Harold, so he wrote them all down. There was a Riddle Hooper on 12th Street. O. K. Start tomorrow.

Too early for the nursing home. He turned the TV to the NBA game because the moving bodies and announcers' voices provided non-demanding companionship, stretched out in the recliner and woke up three hours later to an infomercial for an exercise machine that looked like a cross between a bicycle and a pogo stick.

Across the way, the houses and trailers loomed bleak and lonely under a darkening sky. There'd be snow tonight and it looked like it was already hitting the high country.

Mary Margaret was asleep with Bridget standing by the bed, a pleased half-smile twitching her lips.

"She just dropped off." The psychologist patted her shoulder with an easy familiarity that sparked a throe of envy in the pit of Jake's stomach.

"How'd it go?" was all Jake could manage between clenched teeth although Bridget didn't seem to notice.

"She talked more than she ever has, but I've got to think about it before I know what it means."

"What about?"

"This and that. Nothing very coherent. On the surface. As I said, I've got to think." She patted Mary Margaret's shoulder again, gathered her purse and coat. "Tomorrow? Same time?" and was out the door before he could say he wasn't sure, he had things to do.

***

The only light at the dairy was a single window in Eusebio's house glowing faintly in the afternoon gloom. His pickup was gone. Where was he? For that matter, where was Jesus?

For reasons Jake couldn't explain to himself, he moved to where he could look in the window. Maria Elena sat at the dining room table, head down over paper, open books scattered on the table. He could hear the beat of some kind of music and wondered how she could concentrate. He watched for a long minute, watched her stand and stretch, sweater riding up to reveal a belly button centered in a taut stomach.

His knock brought Maria Elena to the door.

"Didn't mean to bother you, but I wanted to talk to your father."

"He and mother went to Denver. To see Estella and perhaps look for work."

"Say when they'd be back?"

"No. But they will telephone, if not tonight then tomorrow. Do you want me to ask?"

"If you think of it. Got a few things for your father to tend to. For pay."

"I will tell him." She started to close the door, then stopped. "Do you want me to cook you something for dinner?"

Her nipples poking erect through the thin material of her long-sleeved T-shirt shook him with an ache of desire. He swallowed the yes in his throat. "That's all right. I've got plenty and you've got work to do."

In the house, he made two cheese sandwiches and started to open a beer, changed his mind and poured two fingers of Jim

Beam in a coffee cup. A glance out the window showed the light across the way. Flushed, he carried sandwiches and whiskey to the living room where he flipped through the channels, settling for a program about wart hogs on the Serengeti Plains.

***

"I'm outa here, Charlie. Jessie ain't going to be happy I spent most of her day off with you."

"That ain't going to cheer her up any." Henderson gestured out the window where a sickly-green Chevy with government plates had pulled into the slot next to Blakenship's Bronco. A top-coated figure with an all-too-familiar streak of white hair was locking the car door.

"Damn. Oh well, it ain't like Kiernan didn't warn us."

Both men watched as the DEA man picked his way through the cluster of desks in the outer room. He reached the office door and began shrugging out of his topcoat. "When are we going to hit it?"

"Say what?"

"Come off it, Blakenship. Kiernan told me about the garage." He hung his coat on the rack in the corner. "I can have five agents here by noon tomorrow."

"Can you now. Kiernan say so?"

Buchanan flushed. "Yes."

"Kiernan also say that no raid is going down in this county without my say so?"

"That's why I'm here."

"Well, we've got a few things to tend to before we do something as dramatic as another full-blown raid. Last one wasn't what you could call an unmitigated success."

"If not tomorrow, when?"

"Maybe this week. Maybe next. Maybe not at all. We'll just have to wait and see."

"Jesus Christ." Buchanan coiled like he was going to leap across the desk at the sheriff. "I've heard of slow, but this is ridiculous."

"That's the way it's going to be. If I was you, I'd head on back where I came from. I'll let Kiernan know when it's time. I can't stop you from booking a room at the Alta, of course — assuming you've still got expense money— but I'd rather you wouldn't because then I'm going to have to put a deputy with you and we're kinda short-handed at the moment."

"I'm staying."

Blakenship let out a heartfelt sigh. "Was afraid of that. Duane — you remember Duane? — he'll meet you in the dining room at 7:30 tomorrow morning. Be a nice gesture if you could buy his breakfast. Anything you want to add, Charlie?"

"Nope."

Both Sapinero lawmen rose and took their jackets from the backs of their respective chairs. "Been here too long for a Sunday," said Blakenship. "Don't intend to be back here until eight tomorrow. At the earliest." He plucked Buchanan's topcoat from the rack and half handed, half tossed it at him. "There is one thing. Have any thoughts about the bag of white powder Minnie Fletcher found in her son's sock drawer?" He smiled at Buchanan's blank look. "Kiernan forgot to mention it? Interesting."

***

"She's nervous." Jessie, mollified by a bowl of venison chili Blakenship had thawed and served with cheese, onions and jalapenos, snuggled against his shoulder while the cassette in the VCR rewound. "Wants to talk with you first."

"When?"

"Maybe tomorrow. After the lunch rush."

"Tell her not to worry. I don't have any evidence other than what you told me she told you." The VCR indicated the rewinding was complete and he gently moved her head to the back of the couch and went to eject the tape. "On second thought, let me tell her."

"You said that Kiernan told the other one — Buchanan — about Felipe's garage but not about Lonnie Fletcher?"

"Didn't even tell him Felipe's name. Leastways, Buchanan never used it."

"Why?"

"Don't know. Maybe he don't think Buchanan can handle more than one thought at time. Maybe he doesn't want him loose in the county. Maybe it's some kind of bureaucratic politics that this country boy can't understand."

"Why tell him anything at all?"

"I don't know. One thing I do know, though, is that I'm not going to think about drugs, or Buchanan or Felipa Ruiz or the Sanchez brothers until tomorrow morning."

19

FEBRUARY 24 — Morning

It snowed in the high country all Sunday night and continued into the next day, the fall working its way ever lower until by late morning the valley was being pelted by the heaviest storm of the year.

Henderson had dispatched Darlene to Elwood before the snow hit Mountain View but she'd run into trouble a mile from the top of Morris Pass and had slid off the road, there to stay until the tow truck arrived.

Jake had started the morning with the intention of looping through the country west of Mountain View trying to locate the various Dobbins residences, but heavy snowflakes sticking to his windshield turned him toward town and they were coming so thick and hard by the time he reached the light at Flint and Main he gave up on finding Riddle Hooper's home as well.

He parked near Fitzgerald's office and got out of the pickup into a snowfall so heavy he couldn't make out the lawyer's sign at the end of his sidewalk. What the hell was he going to tell Mackey Fitz anyway? He looked around. White accumulation was piling on the parked cars lining the street and lights shone dimly through the windows of the stores on the square. Maybe it would stop as fast as it started. And if it didn't let up, at least the snowplows would have a chance to do some work. He crossed the street towards the dim beacon of the Chopping Block's front window.

Jake wasn't the only one who thought to wait out the storm. Four tables were occupied with people lingering over coffee and three men stood near the cash register chatting with the female half of the new ownership. The steamy warmth bordered on oppressive but the aroma of baking was a comfort.

He hadn't been in the restaurant to eat for months, and took his time studying the menu chalked on a blackboard behind the counter before ordering a bowl of split-pea soup and a grilled cheese sandwich. He carried the soup to a small table against a wall, hung his jacket on the back of a chair and sat so he could watch the snow through the plate-glass window.

The sandwich arrived halfway through the soup, as did three deputies — two men in their twenties still with the half-cocky, half unsure air of high school ballplayers and a girl who barely looked old enough to have graduated. The three placed their orders and took the table next to Jake without giving him a look — the men ragging the girl for having to get pulled out of a ditch.

"What I don't get is why Henderson sent you to Elwood in the first place," said one.

"I told you," the girl answered, mixing teenage coyness with the tone of a teacher dealing with a particularly obtuse student. "To copy the tax rolls for the western half of Otero County."

"But why?"

"Henderson didn't say."

"But you got an idea," said the other deputy. "You've been working in the office and I know for a fact you ain't deaf."

The girl leaned forward to speak in what she thought was a conspiratorial whisper. "I think it's got something to do with the Sanchez brothers. The ones that disappeared from the hospital in Anton."

Jake's full attention focused on the table.

"You know that Felipa Ruiz girl?" she added.

"That they been staking out?"

"Well, Saturday Daryl followed her and a Mexican man to the Doyle Reservoir Road. Said they snowmobiled into the mountains and he thinks they spent the night."

"What's the girl got to do with the Sanchezes?"

"Because the girl helped them escape from the hospital. The deputy from up there identified her."

"So that's why she's being watched."

"Duh."

"Don't forget the garage."

Ruiz? Abel ducking out of sight. And the garage near Pea Green. Forgot it's his brother's. Felipe? That's it. Snowmobiles and escape from the hospital.

Jake tried without success to put a face to the girl. Maria Elena — maybe she'd know.

"I don't see why they've got us watching. What's any of this got to do with Sapinero County?"

"From what I can tell, it all goes back to the raid last August."

"On the Grummonds?" The other deputy set his coffee cup back in its saucer with a rattle. "Shame about Mrs. Grummond. You were on that raid, weren't you, Harold? Never found any drugs, did you?"

Harold? Dobbins? The deputy's back was to him so Jake couldn't read the nametag.

"Found a bunch of meskins. Reason enough, far as I'm concerned. They're going to take over the county if we don't watch out and it's people like Jake Grummond who're causing it."

Jake listened with half an ear while the world narrowed to a crystal cube in which figures stood tantalizing close, only to fade mockingly away. Abel Ruiz. The photos of Victor and Julio taped to his refrigerator door. Buchanan. Donaldson. And the pickup with the snowmobiles straining uphill.

"That DEA guy's in town?" Harold's voice rose above the conspiratorial.

"He was in the office early this morning," said Darlene. "Sheriff wasn't happy. Told him to go back to the Alta, he'd let him know when they learned anything new. Buchanan didn't want to go and I thought Blakenship was going to throw him out."

"Sheriff ought to take a few lessons from him. No doubt who's running the show when he's in charge. He thinks right, too. Knows who made this country great." Dobbins — Jake was sure it was Dobbins — got louder as he warmed to the subject. "At the Alta you say? I'd like to talk to him."

266

"You going to apply to the DEA?" The other man gave a snort that was hard to interpret. Their food arrived and the waitress's comment about the weather turned the conversation to the storm and the condition of the roads.

Jake took advantage of the moment to leave, shrugging into coat and pulling his hat low before making his way to the front door. There was better than two inches on his windshield and hood that he swept off with his gloved hands. A glaze of ice remained and rather than bother with the scraper he started the engine and waited for the defroster to do its work.

Three figures emerged from the Chopping Block, heads tilted so the broad brimmed hats that said they were deputies could shield their eyes. Two went into the Sheriff's Office. The third got into a Bronco at the far end of the row of official vehicles. Exhaust floated down from the tailpipe and the figure — Harold, no doubt — reappeared to brush the windshield. Paying no attention to mirrors or side and rear windows, he got back in and eased from the curb.

A good time to ask him about the raid? Jake followed the Bronco around the courthouse square.

The traffic light at Flint and Main glowed faint red. Lights flashed on the roof of the Bronco and Dobbins turned right, skidding into the oncoming lane. There were no moving cars and Jake couldn't tell whether the deputy was having fun or was just a piss-poor driver. Either way, Jake dropped back as far as he could and still see the Bronco's taillights. Traffic had been light — hardly enough to tire mark the accumulation — and the snow on the road combined with the poor visibility brought even Dobbins down to a crawl.

A mile past the John Deere dealership, the Bronco slowed at the sign for the Alta Vista Lodge and turned without signaling, almost hitting a Jeep pickup with a snowplow that was clearing the parking lot.

Jake coasted to a cleared space distant from the deputy who had pulled into a No Parking area directly in front of the walk to the main building. A man wielding a snow shovel raised his head as though to complain, saw the sheriff's insignia and went back to work.

Follow him inside? And then what? He's not going to answer questions without a little persuasion. Jake watched the snow fill in behind the man with the snow shovel. Dobbins reappeared and started slogging along an unshoveled path toward the far rooms. Same one that Buchanan bastard had stayed in before.

The urge to pound Buchanan's face to a pulp convulsed Jake without warning, easing only when he became conscious of the pain shooting up his forearms. He willed his hands to loosen their grip on the steering wheel and sat flexing them while he felt the anger recede to an abiding ache across his abdomen.

When he felt it was safe to drive, he turned the key and backed with infinite care away from the curb.

***

"Fucking snow." Blakenship stared bleakly out his office window. "No tracks to follow. No tax rolls to study. Going to slow us down two days, maybe more."

"Sanchezes ain't going anywhere in this shit." Henderson grinned. "If we can't move, just think about them."

"No indication that moving is what they want to do. Assuming they're where we think they are." Blakenship spat soggy tobacco flakes at the wastebasket. "Where the hell ever that is."

"Sheriff."

"What, Daryl?"

"The report on the pickup plates came back."

"Took their sweet time. Well?"

"Belongs to a David Martinez of," he looked at the scrap of paper in his hand, "of 3845 Willow Street in Union."

"Union. And he loads up two snowmobiles and drives all the way to Top Hat so he and little Miss Ruiz can go riding off the Doyle Reservoir Road." Blakenship took his feet from the

268

windowsill and swiveled to look at the young deputy. "Now that we got a name, what do you think we ought to do next?"

"See if he's got a record?"

"Why don't you do that."

"I'm already on it."

"And?"

"They'll get back to me."

Blakenship watched Daryl's departing back. "They're up there, Charlie. Ruizes here and in Union. Abel and Jake. Felipa and Martinez — from Union — and snowmobiles. They're in the mountains all right."

"I had Allen Canton lined up for Wednesday."

"The outfitter? The one who works out of the Hazel Lake Inn?"

"Yeah. But with this snow pushing us towards the weekend, I don't know that he'll have the time."

"Start thinking about backups. And don't forget to send Darlene up when the roads're clear."

"You been reading my mail."

"Question is, what do we do with Buchanan on this deal?"

"If we bring them in, we got to tell him."

"No shit."

"What'd you tell him this morning?"

"Nothing about Daryl's report. Helped that the snow started and we got busy. Even he had to agree it made sense to get back to the Alta while the getting was good. Although not without some persuasion." Blakenship shook his head. ""Duane followed him. Make sure he got there."

"Or went there."

"That, too."

"Seeing as how Buchanan ain't exactly your winter outdoorsman, I don't see you having a problem leaving him behind. If we bring them in, then you tell him like you would under any circumstances."

***

269

Jake had driven home in four wheel drive, never going faster than twenty-five and it had taken him over an hour. It had been especially slow after the turn at Top Hat — no plows had been through and if it hadn't been for a lifetime of driving the road, he'd have ended up in the bar ditch.

A light was on in Eusebio's house and the Ranger was parked by the porch. He guessed Maria Elena was safely home but he slogged through the snow — must be ten inches — and knocked on the door. "Don't worry about my father," he told her when the door opened. "I'll check. Don't want you to get stuck."

"Thank you."

"Hear anything from your folks? They aren't driving back in this?"

"No. I called when I got home to make sure."

"Well, okay," and slogged his way toward the house, stopping to get his gun from the rack.

A quick phone call assured that his father was warm and had more than enough to eat.

Jake regarded the rifle on the kitchen table. He wasn't sure why he'd brought it in from the pickup, but as long as he had, he might as well clean it. Couldn't remember the last time.

He arranged rod and patches and Hoppes No. 9 solvent and began. His parents had given him the rifle on his twelfth birthday and he'd taken it apart to clean it so often during his teens that his hands worked automatically, allowing him to think about the Sanchezes and Buchanan and the pickup with the snowmobiles and Dobbins and the snowmobiles below him in the valley and the smell of wood smoke ...

Of course. Should have figured it out in the Chopping Block. He lifted his eyes to the newspaper photographs on the refrigerator. The brothers gazed back, the face on the right fleshy and clean-shaven, that on the left thin and with mustache and chin whiskers. But eyes, nose and the shape of the lips showed a family resemblance.

Jake looked out the window. Still snowing. He looked at the clipping again. He looked at the rifle on a layer of newspapers to soak up any spills.

Heat and moisture had swelled the door of the walk-in storage closet off the kitchen enough that Jake had to brace his left hand against the doorjamb for leverage. Inside, the air was musty and the neatly ordered rows on the shelves — rows of everything from canned goods to motor oil — wore a blanket of dust.

He found what he was looking for right where he remembered — a Marlin lever action .30-.30 carbine in a saddle scabbard hanging from nails on the back wall and below it two revolvers — a Ruger Vaquero replica of the 1873 Colt Army .45 and a Ruger Blackhawk Single Six .22 magnum version of the same model — both in western-style holsters and pistol belts with cartridge loops.

They had been Paul's. He'd liked them because of the nineteenth-century cowboy image, although when he hunted, he used a Remington .30-.06 that was the twin of Jake's.

Where was it? There. In the gun case on the third shelf.

Jake flipped up the fasteners. It lay as Paul had last put it away, clean and with a faint sheen of protective oil.

He closed the lid. Leave it here, like Paul left it. He carried the carbine and the pistols to the kitchen. The rifle was dusty but free of rust. Whenever it was that Paul had last used it, he'd put it away well oiled, like he knew it would be a while before he got it out again. The same was true of the pistols.

It was dark outside when he replaced the cylinder in the Blackhawk and spun it to feel the action.

He turned the porch light on to check the snow. Ten inches on the hood of the pickup. He'd cleaned it off in Mountain View. Ten inches since lunch and still falling. Fiddling with the radio dial brought a weather report. Storm system moving east. Front range bracing for the worst storm of the year, but tomorrow should be a clear, sunny day over the western part of the state. Clear and cold.

He wondered how much they'd gotten in the high country. It took eight rings before anyone picked up at the Inn, the delay caused, the voice on the other end of the line explained, because they were shoveling snow off the roof. How much? Pushing three feet. Looked like it was over, though. Snowmobiling? Best to wait until afternoon. Wednesday would be better. Have the trails busted out.

Ellie answered at the Stantons. "I was going to bring over a ham casserole, but with the snow …"

"I got plenty, Ellie. Billy around?"

"Hang on."

"What's up?" Billy mumbled around a mouthful of what was probably the casserole.

"Wonder could I borrow one of your snowmobiles for a day or two. New snow made me think cruising would do me good."

"No problem. I'll bring one over tomorrow. Early?"

"No hurry. The Inn said it'll be better Wednesday."

"Have it over there by lunch time. Want the trailer or you going to put it in the back of your truck?"

"Whichever's easiest for you."

"Hell, they're on the trailer now. Why don't I just bring it over and you can hitch it up. That way, you can take your pick."

"Appreciate it." Jake hung up and went back to the storage closet to look for ammunition.

***

How's the road to Elwood?" Blakenship turned from the glare of the mid-morning sunlight bouncing off the snow-covered lawn to give Luther a questioning eye.

"Clear. According to my wife's sister, the one married to Norm who works for the highway department, he, that's Norm, been working straight through since yesterday morning. That is, he hasn't been home since then. They take breaks and all and get to sleep …"

Blakenship held up his hand. "Your sister-in-law, she says the road's open?"

"Huh. Oh. No. Highway patrol."

"Thank you. Tell Henderson to tell Darlene …"

"She left forty-five minutes ago."

272

"Good. Send Charlie in."

"No need." Henderson set his coffee down on the corner of Blakenship's desk, settled into the chair across from the sheriff and lit a cigarette. "Bright out there."

"But cold. Doubt we'll get any melt today. You call Allen Canton?"

"Been trying since eight, but he ain't made it to the Inn and nobody answers at the house. Phone company says the line's down."

"What about …"

"It's a bright, sunny day at the Inn, just like here only about twenty-thirty degrees colder and they've got a wind that's playing merry hell with plowing the parking lot."

"How much they get?"

"Three foot plus."

"What about the road up?"

"Being bladed as we speak. Think it'll be open from the highway by noon. Not that they expect many. Not today. Figure by tomorrow, every snowmobiler in the state who can get away from work at mid-week will be out."

"Where's that leave us?"

"First, earliest we can do anything is tomorrow."

"Even I can figure that out."

"Never know. Second, won't know if Allen can let us have any sleds, let alone guide us, until then."

"Charlie, we don't have to go up to Hazel Lake. We'll be taking off from the …"

"Doyle Reservoir Road. I know. I'm going to see if Monty over at the Yamaha place can loan us some machines."

"Which deputies? Ones that ride and know that country up there'd be best. And that can keep their mouths shut."

"First two ain't hard. It's the last that's giving me pause for thought."

"Think it through, Charlie. Think it through and get back to me."

***

273

"There," Billy said as he rose from his knees after attaching the safety chains to the bumper of Jake's pickup. "Wish I was riding with you."

"Maybe this weekend."

"Nah. We got to go to Union. Wedding. They're gassed and two of the five-gallon cans are full. Here," he added, handing Jake a gallon of two-stroke engine oil. Billy drove away, waving at Maria Elena, who'd come out on the porch of her house. Snow had closed school.

Jake circled the trailer. A four-year-old Arctic Cat 440 and last year's Skidoo 600. He peeled the cover from the front of the newer, bigger machine and raised the hood then lowered it to almost closed and tried to estimate clearances along the sides and the front.

In the kitchen, he broke down the carbine to stock and barrel and measured them with a length of twine. Back outside, he found several places for the barrel, but the broader stock was a problem.

Maria Elena's voice startled him. "My parents will be home tomorrow."

Jake masked his surprise with careful attention to fastening the hood. "Didn't hear you. How'd you walk through a foot of new snow without making any noise?"

"I made noise. Like this." She took a couple of steps closer to the trailer.

"Must be going deaf. What time tomorrow? Your parents, I mean."

"By supper."

"Tell your father I'd like to talk with him Thursday."

"O. K." Maria Elena stepped closer to the trailer and gingerly reached out a hand to touch the snowmobile. "Are they fun?"

"They can take you places in the winter you never thought you could go."

"Is it as pretty in the winter as the summer?"

274

Jake folded the canvas cover back over the windshield and handle bars and walked around to the front to stretch it over the machine's nose, pulling the slack out and making sure that the elastic at the cover's edge was under the body all around. "Maybe prettier."

Maria Elena peered under the snowmobile. "The track grabs the snow?"

"Sort of like a bulldozer. Except there's only one. You steer with the skis." Jake looked at her. "Want to go for a spin?"

"A ride? When? Where?"

"Now. Here. There's plenty of snow. " Jake removed the cover he had just put in place. "You'd best get the warmest jacket you have. And some gloves. It can get cold on one of these." Maria Elena ran toward her house, awkward in the deep snow. "And a hat," he shouted after her.

He started slowly, weaving around the empty cattle pens and equally empty trailers with Maria Elena behind, hands resting on his shoulders and demurely trying to keep her breasts from pressing into his back. The seat was short — the Skidoo wasn't designed for two riders — and Jake was acutely conscious of the warmth from her crotch.

"Hold on." He squeezed the throttle and Maria Elena yelped in delighted surprise as the machine jumped forward, sending a spray of fresh snow up the curve of the hood, passed the windshield and into Jake's face. Thumb on the throttle and mouth stretched in a grin below the goggles, Jake accelerated until the speedometer passed fifty and the cottonwoods along the irrigation ditch loomed close.

"How'd you like that?"

"How fast were we going?" He breath came in laughing gasps.

"Over fifty."

"It felt faster."

"Snow in your face will do that. Ready?" Jake gained speed, swinging away from the fence by the road, accelerating toward a mound in the far corner of the field, turning before he got to it and accelerating toward the road again. Maria Elena realized they were making a series of large W's in the direction of Grandpa Grummond's cabin.

The unfamiliar sound of the snowmobile brought Grandpa Grummond to the door. "Where'd you get that idiot machine?"

"Billy."

"Figures. Come on in. You two probably need to thaw out."

It felt oppressive in the cabin even though the window in the stove showed only the dull glow of fading coals and they quickly shed the top layers of their clothing.

"Make you some tea if you want." Grandpa Grummond raised the lid of the wood stove and dropped in a piece of split spruce.

"I'll make it." Maria Elena started toward the kitchen area.

The ride back was slower and more direct. Maria Elena watched Jake run the snowmobile up the angled trailer and helped him tip it back to horizontal.

"Have fun?"

"Very much."

Jake pushed the cotter pin in place. "You know a girl named Felipa? Felipa Ruiz?"

"Felipa? Yes."

"She's Abel Ruiz's niece?"

"He is her uncle, yes. Why?"

"Something came up. Maybe nothing. How well do you know her?"

"Not well. We were friendly when we were young. But after you … After the fight … She works at the grocery store after school." Maria Elena helped pull the snowmobile cover over the front of the hood.

"I guess I've seen her then. Short. Short but pretty."

***

He purchased two boxes of .30-.30 cartridges and two of .22 Magnums at the hardware store. Target practice, he explained. Target practice, now that he had time on his hands.

276

The grocery across the street was still open, with four customers lined up at the only checkout stand. The girl at the cash register must be Felipa — short and busty with an easy smile. Unusual for Zeke to let a non-family member handle money.

Jake hunted through the aisles for something to take on tomorrow's ride, settled on granola bars, and took his place at the end of the line. When his turn came, he asked for two tins of Copenhagen and five pieces of homemade elk jerky. He laid a twenty-dollar bill on the counter and watched while the girl made change. Nothing in her manner was any different than the way she'd treated any other customer.

It was like she didn't know who he was.

20

FEBRUARY 26 — Early Morning

The stars shone impassively at four the next morning and the sliver of a new moon over the Sublette Plateau kept them cold company. Jake pulled back the cover of the 600 and opened the hood. The carbine's stock went on the underside to the right of the motor, the barrel on the left above the clutch shield. He lowered the hood, jiggling it slightly to settle properly and fastened the latches.

Have to remember to get all traces of duct tape off before he gave the machine back to Billy.

In the kitchen, he filled the stainless-steel thermos with coffee and set it beside the granola bars, jerky and the .22 Magnum. Figure an hour and a half to the Inn.

***

Save for occasional small patches of ice, the highway was clear all the way to the Hazel Lake turnoff. The road up the mountain had been bladed to an even snow pack maybe two inches thick — no problem in four-wheel drive. He opened the window to let the air play across his face. It felt like zero, maybe colder.

The pink of the sun was faint in the sky above the ridge when he crested the rise into the park. He could see a light from the Inn. Another went on, then another. He checked his watch. Not quite 6:30.

A Ford 250 with a four-up snowmobile trailer and four identical V-Maxes ranked neatly beside it showed that at least one group of riders had gotten in yesterday. Jake parked next to the Ford and unloaded the 600.

The revolver got five rounds, double checking to make sure the hammer rested on the empty chamber, and went into the storage compartment next to the thermos. Extra cartridges and food would go in jacket pockets.

He was shivering when he finished. He returned to the truck and shrugged into the leather snowmobile jacket Billy had insisted he take.

He threw the Skidoo's choke lever to full and turned the key. The engine roared to life on the second try — Billy kept his equipment in top shape — and he quickly cut it to half choke. Kneeling on the seat, he eased the machine next to the truck where he collected the trouser half of the borrowed snowmobile suit and rode to the front of the Inn. Coffee and a piss before he put on the overalls was all he had intended, but the seductive aroma of frying bacon reminded him he'd forgotten breakfast.

A scrubbed blonde in her early twenties smiled as she walked past on her way to the kitchen. "Sit anywhere."

A cup of coffee was waiting when he got back from the men's room. "You didn't ask, but you looked like you could use a cup. Something to eat? Choice of eggs and hashbrowns or pancakes. Bacon, ham or sausage with either."

"How about eggs and pancakes?"

"I expect we could do that."

Plate mopped clean of egg yolk with the last bite of pancake, Jake settled a pinch behind his lip. A man with a weathered face took a seat in a chair at the far end of the bar and began leafing through papers on a clipboard. Jake walked to him. "You the outfitter?"

"Allen Canton." He offered his hand. "And I'm booked till Monday."

"Just wondered what shape the trails are in."

"The Elwood Club groomed the trail to Shadow Lake yesterday. Haven't got to the others yet, although everything's still well marked — far as I know." Canton smiled his thanks at the waitress for the coffee she set in front of him. "What're you riding?"

"Skidoo 600."

"A Summit? You shouldn't have any trouble. Not unless it gets real soft later on. And according to the weather report, that ain't supposed to happen today."

Outside, the hairs on the inside of his nose froze when he breathed in. A glance at the thermometer by the door confirmed it was five below. The Skidoo started on the first try, however, and he rode to the pickup for the helmet and extra gas with confidence in the machine.

Now, could he find the wood smoke?

A lazy circle past the Inn led to the Shadow Lake trail. Slow as he was going — it couldn't be twenty miles per hour — the wind burned to numbness. He flipped the helmet's windshield down to the sealed-in condition he disliked. Couldn't hear. Couldn't smell. No sense of the world around him. But it was warm. Had to give it that.

The trail was as smooth as a newly paved parking lot, sunlight making the surface flash like sequins. He thought he was going slow but a glance at the speedometer showed the needle above fifty. With no wind in his face he'd better be careful.

The trail began a gentle climb through leafless aspens and snow-laden evergreens, then, as it got steeper, switch-backed its way to the shoulder where it followed the contour in a southwestwardly course. The cold was penetrating, numbing his hands. He worked the fingers of his left hand free from the fingers of the glove and balled them against his palm, but the right hand was losing feeling, especially the thumb on the throttle.

He stopped to warm them. Ahead, he could see the sun in a broad open area. Below, the land and trees dropped away in steep folds. He flipped the helmet shield up to spit out spent snuff, appreciating the rush of fresh air.

He was putting the lid back on the snuff tin when he saw the switches, one next to the choke lever, the other on the opposite side of the handlebar column. Warmers — one for the handlebars, one for the throttle.

Dumber than dirt.

He road across the open space relishing the heat radiating through the gloves. Another patch of trees, then the trail broke into the open again, giving a clear view of the highest peaks of the Presidentials framed against a deep blue sky.

Jake wasn't looking at the scenery. He could just make out the last of the plowed portion of the Doyle Reservoir Road below. He pulled to the side of the trail, turned off the snowmobile and raised the shield. Deep breaths through the nose. Still cold enough for the hairs to freeze. Couldn't smell a thing. He heard snowmobiles behind him.

Four V-Maxes broke from the trees and fanned out on the uphill side of the trail in a wild, looping race to nowhere but the pure pleasure of speed. One detached from the pack and cruised toward Jake. "You all right?"

"Enjoying the view." Jake gestured toward the snow-capped chain that he had paid no mind to up to that point.

"Hell of a day. Going to Shadow Lake?"

"Probably. See where my nose takes me."

"Well, have a good one."

Jake scanned the valley below for a plume of smoke. Nothing. Had to have a fire. If they were there. Clear and cold and still as it is, smoke would go straight up. Dry wood and a hot fire, there wouldn't be much.

But there had to be something.

Had to be.

Jake road slowly, shield up, eyes locked on the valley.

Then he saw it.

A faint line rising ten feet or so above a grove of aspen and balsam before it dissipated in the sunlight. With the smoke located, the slope of a roof and a bulk beneath it took shape.

A light touch of thumb on throttle moved him along the trail until he was directly above grove and cabin. He eased onto the new snow, crusted from the night, and started down, pausing halfway in a small depression to look uphill. Riding on the crust, the snowmobile had left only the hint of tracks that the wind was already scouring away.

Solution to a problem he hadn't thought of.

281

He charted a route to a pair of snow-covered humps at the fringe of the grove that looked too regular to be natural. Wood piles, maybe. Or derelict vehicles. Getting to them took ten minutes, uniting rifle stock and barrel three minutes more. He levered a round into the chamber and set the safety.

The pistol was a problem — it wouldn't fit in the jacket pocket and the bib of the overalls made sticking it in the waistband of his jeans a slow and clumsy process. He put it there anyway. What the hell — if he needed a quick draw, he was going to be shit out of luck no matter what.

He picked up the carbine with his gloved left hand and caressed the trigger guard with his naked right index finger. Heat from the engine had made the weapon almost hot to the touch when he'd removed it, but it had cooled rapidly. Have to watch for skin sticking to metal.

He poked the barrel into the mound closest to the cabin. Woodpile. Stepping lightly so as not to break through the crust, he moved to its edge. The cabin was a simple rectangle set on a foundation high enough so the top of the stem wall was still above the snow line even after the winter's accumulation. Siding curved to look like logs, green metal roof and a door with steps that plunged straight to the snow. Rail and deck partially visible on the side to his right.

The angle from the other end of the woodpile afforded a better view of the deck that continued around to the front of the cabin. Wood piled along the wall under the eaves. A trodden path led from the door down the middle of the stairs to another woodpile where the circle tramped in the snow attested that someone had been busy the day before.

The door opened while he watched, releasing the sound of a song in Spanish and a man stepped out to stand in the sun for a moment before bending for an armload of wood. The thin one, head bandaged and wearing only a long-sleeved thermal top and jeans stuffed into high-top rubber boots like the ones Jake wore in the barn.

The sight of the kind of boots he didn't need to wear anymore tightened his fingers on the Marlin and he raised it halfway to his shoulder.

Get a grip. Remember why you're here.

Jake waited for Sanchez — Victor, if he remembered right — to go inside, then circled to the front. The snow beneath the trees hadn't been softened by the afternoon sun of the day before. As a consequence, it hadn't formed as strong a crust and every so often a foot broke through, sending the leg knee deep. It took fifteen minutes to reach a vantage point behind a mature balsam.

The deck was twice as wide in front, with mounds of snow spaced across it in clusters. Deck furniture, most likely. Wide stairs with a railing on each side led to a broad clearing that must be the parking area in the summer. A picture window stretched across the center two-thirds of the wall providing a view across the valley to Mt. Sanders and several lower peaks.

The window also provided a view into the cabin. The two brothers were seated across from each other at a table, talking. Arguing, more like, judging by the way they waved their arms, even the one with a cast.

Keeping an eye on the brothers, Jake picked his way to two young spruce growing so close together their branches intertwined. The argument was heating up, if anything, with the fat one — Julio — waving his cast with abandon.

Twenty-five feet of open space to the side stairs. Could he make it without being seen or heard?

Have to try. He flipped the safety off, took a deep breath, then moved around the spruce and, keeping an eye on the window, stepped with strides as long as he dared until the corner of the cabin blocked his vision.

He forced himself to wait for a count of twenty, eyes fixed on the door.

Nothing.

He made the rest of the way to the stairs in as much of a run as he could manage in the snow. Stopped for another twenty count, then up the stairs to the deck. Twenty count, then across the deck and through the door in a rush.

At the table, the fat one stared in open-mouthed bewilderment as Jake burst into the cabin and leveled the rifle at him.

Where was the other one? At the stove, coffee pot in hand. Coming toward him. Duck.

The pot bounced off the his helmet, scalding coffee running down his back that he didn't feel thanks to Billy's leather jacket. Jake took a step towards Victor, whose momentum had carried him forward, and jabbed the barrel of the rifle into his stomach as hard as he could. Victor went down in a writhing heap on the gray linoleum of the kitchen floor, fighting for breath. Jake turned toward Julio who was halfway out of his chair and squeezed off a round into the floor at his feet.

"Sit down." Jake levered another cartridge into the chamber. "Sit down. I just want to talk."

Victor was regaining his breath. Jake stepped beside him and prodded him with the rifle. "You, too. Up and at the table."

Jake waited while Victor struggled to his feet and, bent at the waist, stumbled to a chair across from his brother. Keeping the rifle in his right hand aimed at a point between the two, he removed the helmet with his left, wincing as it pinched past his ears, and set it on the counter. "My name is Jake Grummond."

Neither face made a sign but he thought a light of recognition flickered across their eyes.

"Doesn't mean anything to you?"

Neither spoke or moved, except the eyes shifting between the gun barrel and Jake's face.

"It should. Because you have caused me more trouble than I can tell you. I've got one question: Who told you to tell the DEA that drugs were coming through my dairy?"

"Fuck you." Julio spat at Jake, the globule landing a yard short. He had barely wiped his mouth when Jake was on him, barrel coming down on the cast hard enough to bring his head forward, a raw scream choked to a whimper when Jake caught

284

the top of his head with the rifle butt, blood flooding from the hair to cover the table.

"Here's the situation." Jake fought for control. "Your only chance is to talk. Because if you don't tell me and if you don't repeat it to my lawyer when the time comes, I got no problem with killing you. One or both."

"Why do you think we will talk to your lawyer?" Victor looked with no apparent emotion at his brother who was sitting upright, blood streaming through the fingers of the hand he held to his head.

"Because I'm going to tell the sheriff where you are and you'll be in jail where he can find you." Jake tossed a dishtowel at Julio. "See if that helps. You've got no phone. No snowmobiles. You ain't going anywhere."

"We talk to you and go to jail. Not much of a deal."

"If you don't, you die."

"Fucking Buchanan. Fucking Abel ..."

Julio's head exploded before Jake heard the sound of breaking glass or the report of the rifle. A second shot took Victor in the throat, blood spewing a fountain across the rug before subsiding to a bubbling flow.

Jake lay behind the kitchen counter with no memory of how he got there and waited.

No more shots. No steps on the porch.

He waited.

Just the sound of the wind coming through the shattered window.

He waited, knuckles going white on the carbine, butt of the pistol poking into his side above the pelvic girdle.

The sound of a snowmobile growing fainter.

He waited.

When he'd decided it wasn't a ruse to draw him into the open, he stood up. Maybe they couldn't see him. Didn't know he was here.

He looked at the brothers. Now what?

The metallic gleam of his spent shell against the baseboard caught his eye and he stooped to pick it up.

Now what? Talk to Mackey? Have to think.

He retrieved the helmet and struggled it over his ears. Pick up the Marlin. Close the door.

He tried to follow his tracks back to the snowmobile. Once behind the woodpile, his stomach rebelled and he emptied all that remained of the Inn's breakfast. Shaking from a cold he'd never felt before, even though the sun reflecting off the snow of the woodpile had created a comparatively tropical oasis, he fumbled to retape the carbine under the Skidoo's hood. Then he started the machine and rode uphill with exaggerated care.

**

Eusebio's pickup was next to the Ranger when he got home.

He'd ridden back to the Shadow Lake trail, the crust softening a little in the late morning sun so he left a bit more of a track than he had on the way down. From there he'd turned toward the Inn, riding back five miles or so to intersect the trail that led to the high meadow.

His intent had been to drop over the east side to his land and return to the Inn the way he'd done with Billy and Frog Bottom. But when he'd stopped for coffee and jerky, his hands shook uncontrollably and it was all he could do to unscrew the thermos top. When he finally poured a cup, the coffee came back up on the third swallow.

He spent the afternoon stretched out on the machine near the edge of the high meadow trying, without success, to put the pieces together. Who was the killer? Somebody in the drug deal most likely. Had the killer followed him? If so, why was he still alive? If not, did he know Jake had been there?

The two men dead — so much for their story. Could it have been the DEA? Report to Blakenship? Tell Mackey? How far did lawyer-client confidentiality go? A real cluster-fuck.

The chill of encroaching shadows had roused him and he'd made his methodical way to the Inn. Now he was home. Be just his luck if Eusebio came out as he was untaping the carbine.

286

Have to remember. Can't let Billy get the trailer with it still there.

***

Blakenship watched Monty Broderick from the Yamaha dealership unload the last of four snowmobiles from the long trailer. A fifth was in the bed of the pickup. It was mid-morning Friday and they were standing at the school bus turn-around that was as far as the plows went on the Doyle Reservoir Road.

Mikes turned from watching one of his two deputies unload three sleds from the trailer behind an Otero County Cherokee. "My guys have rifles, C. W. You?"

He held up his Winchester. "All but Charlie. He's got a riot gun."

"You thought out how we're going to do this? Eight machines, going to be hard to sneak up."

"Got to find it first. Once we see what it looks like, we'll figure out what to do. Oh, shit."

"What?"

Blakenship pointed to the top of the rise a quarter of a mile up the road where a nondescript sedan glanced off the snow bank, moved to the center of the road and took dead aim at them. "Buchanan. Wonder how he found out."

Buchanan stopped in the middle of the turn-around and was out of the car before the two sheriffs reached him. "Blakenship ..."

"Something I can do for you?"

"What's the idea of going after the Sanchezes without me?"

"Why should I bring you along?"

"They're my case."

"Fugitives ain't exclusive property, last I heard. More to the point, have you ever ridden a snowmobile? You sure ain't dressed for it. Your ass'll freeze to the seat before we get a mile."

287

"If they're up there, we'll bring them down," said Mikeska.

"Who are you?"

"Mikeska. You're in my county now."

Blakenship blew cigar smoke in the agent's general direction. "We're going to see if we can find where I think they are. Don't know how long it's going to take, but it's perfectly all right with me if you sit here until your dick freezes solid and drops off." He spun on his heel and joined Broderick by the exhaust-belching snowmobiles.

"Wouldn't hurt to get started. Might snow." Broderick pointed to the overcast sky. "Let's get oriented."

Blakenship spread a map across a snowmobile seat. "According to the tax rolls, there's a five-acre tract with a cabin that belongs to one Miguel Martinez of Union somewhere around here."

"That's about ten miles." Broderick bent closer. "Ten miles and two, maybe three miles off the reservoir road." He straightened up. "There's three, maybe four cabins in the area."

"Any used in the winter?"

"All of them, I think. Not regular. Weekends now and then." He pointed to the tracks cutting the snow at the edge of the turn-around. "Looks like somebody's been in and out since the last snow."

"How many?"

"Just one machine, one round trip."

"Not enough to get both Sanchezes out." Blakenship folded the map. "If they're up there. When we get close, say within a mile, stop and we'll think things over."

They set out, Broderick breaking trail. The air felt like snow any minute and the low barometric pressure kept the exhaust unpleasantly close to the ground. Twenty minutes from the turn-around brought them to the top of a rise. The land sloped into a valley, then rose on all sides.

"O. K.," said Broderick. "See on the left? Where the trees stop about a quarter of the way up the slope? That's where the cabins are."

288

"Looks like that's where whoever was here earlier in the week was headed." Blakenship checked the safety on his rifle. "Rudy, you reckon your boys can get around back before we brace them?"

"Guess we'll find out."

They followed Broderick single file to the edge of the woods. "Not being an officer of the law, I'm going to let you take it from here. Just follow the tracks — as far as you can. Who rode it knew where the road was and stayed on it."

"What'd you think, C. W.? Bottom to top or top to bottom?"

"Figure we get to the top, look for signs of life and work our way down. Ought to leave Henderson here with Monty. Catch anyone making a break."

"Catch, hell." Henderson lit a cigarette. "Only if they're afoot."

Mikeska led the way, following the faint tracks just fast enough to maintain enough momentum to keep from sinking in the soft snow. A half to three-quarters of a mile of uphill slogging, Mikeska gestured with his left hand at a sign nailed to a tree. The Bear's Den it read and the notched logs of a cabin corner were visible some hundred yards beyond.

Mikeska continued up hill, standing up and gunning the engine every so often when he threatened to bog down. A second sign, this time to the right, and then an expanse of whiteness became visible through the edge of the woods. They were near the tree line.

Mikeska stopped and dismounted, the others following suit in single-file behind him. He walked to Blakenship and motioned to the deputies to join them. "Cabin's up yonder." Mikeska pointed to a gray shape in the trees maybe two hundred and fifty yards away. "Why don't my boys get above it in the open, your men stay here, and you and me ease in from the front. When they're set above, we'll hello the house."

The two sheriffs watched Mikeska's deputies weave through the trees to the open. "Might should have had them unsling their rifles, Rudy. They don't look like run-of-the-mill snowmobilers with the barrels sticking up over their shoulders like that."

"Not much we can do about it now."

They followed the faint tracks to where they looped in a circle just before a large spruce with four or five saplings clustered around it.

"Didn't go in. Now that's strange." Blakenship unslung his Winchester. "But it looks like it stopped here. How far you reckon?"

"To the cabin?" Mikeska shaded his eyes. "Fifty yards? No more than fifty-five."

"No smoke." Blakenship stepped to where the snowmobile tracks they'd been following indicated a stop. "Couple of footprints. Didn't get far from the machine." He looked up at the cabin. "Clear sightline into the cabin. Don't see anything … except the window. Looks broken."

The lawmen looked at each other. "Let's go," said Mikeska and they gunned their machines in a dead heat to the cabin stairs.

21

FEBRUARY 28 — Late Morning

The Sanchez brothers had neither moved nor been moved. The fat one, Julio, lay shattered head toward the kitchen counter; his brother at an oblique angle to him, face down in a clamshell-shaped puddle of frozen blood that fanned from his butchered throat.

"Don't look like they knew what hit them." Blakenship wished he'd brought a flask of Canadian Club. "With that cast and that head bandage, looks like we found the Sanchez brothers. A little late. Pending positive identification, of course," he added absently.

"Yesterday or the day before, I reckon," Mikeska offered.

"Say what? Oh. Yeah. Same as the tracks we been following."

"Bert. Harry. You boys come on in," Mikeska yelled to his deputies. "You, too," he hollered in the direction of the Sapinero County contingent.

Blakenship was kneeling by Julio's head. "Hell of a shot." He moved to Victor without standing up. "Shots," he amended. "And it looks like the second shot came so fast the other didn't have a chance to move."

"Makes you think it wasn't the first time he'd done something like this."

"Could have been two of them."

"Only one set of tracks."

"True. I'm going to see what else is here." Blakenship moved behind the counter. "Why don't you see if you can raise Henderson. Get him up here. And send for a meat wagon." Blakenship moved through the door to the back of the cabin. "And a couple of cargo sleds for the bodies."

Mikeska was putting his radio back in its holster when Blakenship reappeared. "Well?"

"Two bedrooms, bath in between. Both been occupied." Blakenship fumbled under his jacket for his shirt pocket for a cigar. "No other bodies." He circled through the kitchen, opening cupboards and the refrigerator, lifting the lid of the trashcan. "Haven't dug too deep into the canned goods left by the owners. Not much trash. I'd guess they had company most every week." He paused to study the cards laid out in a game of solitaire on the dining table. "No TV. Hardly any books or magazines."

"No telephone, either."

"Wonder what they did for fun."

"Isn't there a girl involved, one way or another?"

"That there is."

"Sheriff." It was one of Mikeska's deputies at the door.

"What?"

"There's footprints going and coming. Looks like they circle from over there," he pointed to the snow-covered rectangle, "past those trees and then a beeline to the steps."

"Why don't I take a look, Rudy, while you see what's going on with the body bags and all. If it's not too late, ask them to bring along a camera."

Blakenship was sweating profusely and gasping for air by the time he reached the squared-off mound — the snow was softer than it had been for the mystery man and he'd broken through to the knees at every other step. He rested one hand against the pile — unsplit firewood, like he'd figured — and unzipped his parka halfway. There were snowmobile tracks to and away from the wood — faint scours on top of the snow and the sides folding in from wind and sun, but a snowmobile without doubt.

Tracks seemed to be pretty much straight up the slope. Maybe they looped toward the road. Couldn't be sure.

Blakenship bent to inspect a faintly discolored blotch near the corner of the pile. Might be the remains of his lunch. If the mystery man barfed at dead human beings ... ain't likely he's a hardened killer. So... What was he? And who? Coming down the slope — if that's the way he came — means he didn't know the usual route — no, means he didn't follow the usual route. Whatever — but most likely means he wouldn't have been a welcome visitor.

The muffled roar of a snowmobile drew his attention. Charlie. He started to wave to be picked up. No. Old fart hadn't been on a sled in years. Get him in this soft shit and he'll bury it deep enough would take three of us and a young mule to get it unstuck.

A snowflake hit his forehead, then another and it was snowing straight down and heavy. Going to cover everything real good within the hour.

He started the slow walk back to the cabin, stopping every five steps to catch his breath. Ain't careful, going to need a cargo sled for me. Maybe Jessie's right. Drink too much. Not enough exercise.

***

Blakenship watched the Saturday morning sun make fast work of yesterday's snowfall while he listened to Mikeska's voice crackle and pop from the speakerphone. "Say it again, Rudy."

"I said, have you questioned the meskin girl yet?"

"Going to."

"Slow, ain't you?"

"She's got no reason to think we know about her." Blakenship looked at Henderson and raised his eyebrows. "I apologize since this is technically your case, but I asked Union to round up the father. Abel Ruiz and David Martinez, too, if they can. Buchanan's headed that way."

"What about the other Martinez? The one that owns the cabin?"

"Miguel. Him, too."

A click followed Mikeska's last words. Blakenship looked out at the water spreading from the snow banks that lined both sides of the street. "Going to be some fun tonight after the sun goes down."

"There's something that bothers me." Henderson stared at the joint where the ceiling met the wall. "We're assuming whoever got them also watered the brakes. Associated, anyway."

293

"Well?"

"Could be. But when you think of drugs, you think of Uzis and assault rifles. They were taken out by one shot each. Like a man hunting elk."

"There's hunters who live in Union. Even have some in Denver, I'm told. Besides, he could have been ex-military — a sniper, maybe."

Henderson ground out the stub of his cigarette, clasped his hands behind his head and leaned back to reexamine the wall and ceiling joint. "Tape's working loose."

Blakenship followed Henderson's gaze. "Need to talk to the county."

"It wasn't that Martinez. First off, he's been working to save their ass. Second, he'd been coming there regular, so, if he was going to take them out, he'd have waited till he got inside. Spray with automatic fire, just like they do in the movies if he had to."

"Whoever killed them knew the way to the cabin. Which brings us to the mystery man."

"You say he puked by the woodpile?" Henderson didn't wait for an answer. "Means he was there when it happened, or shortly thereafter."

"If he was there, why wasn't he killed, too?"

"Maybe they couldn't see him?"

"And what was he doing there anyway?" Blakenship rubbed his eyes. "Fucking drugs," he muttered. "Why did he come down the mountain?"

"He didn't want to be seen?"

"Killer wasn't seen."

"Didn't know where the cabin was? Not exactly."

"How'd he find it then?"

"By the smoke?"

"You figure he went bouncing around the mountains trying to find a cabin with a fire going?"

Henderson shrugged. "What did Monty say about the route?"

294

"Three or four ways, if you know the land. Including from the Inn."

"Might be we should talk with them."

"Maybe we should." Blakenship stood and stretched. "But first we talk with the Ruiz girl and her uncle. They might be surprised to see us, but considering last night's news and the front page of this morning's paper, they're not going to be surprised about the Sanchez brothers' untimely demise."

***

Jake hadn't been surprised, either, although he hadn't expected the law to be that close to finding the brothers. Of course, if they were looking at tax rolls, they probably had a name.

The day was warm and he sat at the kitchen table watching the trickle of water from the eaves that would soon build to a steady stream. He'd been doing a lot of sitting the last two days, sitting in a lethargy that made it hard to sort things out, a lethargy broken by momentary twitches of rage that the brothers had allowed themselves to get killed.

So close to an answer.

He had been surprised by what he saw as his weak-kneed reaction to the killings. Dead animals were nothing new — over the years he'd gotten up many a morning to find a cow down in the pen, lips pulled back to show teeth in a death grimace, calf nearby staring in wide-eyed bewilderment.

Was it because he'd seen it happen? Because he might be next? Because he'd been talking to them at the time, so the fact they were creatures like himself was undeniable?

Fuck. Can't sit here all day. He dialed the cabin and accepted without question his father's assurance that he was fine, Maria Elena was coming later, not to worry.

He got in his pickup and found himself in the parking lot of the nursing home without remembering how he got there. Mary Margaret? Gone riding with Bridget.

He drove into Top Hat with half a mind to stop at Helen's, but the thought of a beer brought what little breakfast he'd had to the back of his throat and the revulsion at the prospect of having to carry on a conversation almost finished the job.

He pointed the truck toward Pea Green and the snow-covered undulation of the Sublette Plateau beyond. Be back in time to see Mary Margaret by three. Four at the latest.

***

Felipa wasn't working at the store and she wasn't home. She'd made arrangements early in the week for someone to cover her shift, and her mother told them she was spending the night with friends.

Henderson opened the passenger door of the Bronco. "Looks like the garage."

Five or six vehicles were parked in front of the open doors and about twice as many men were drinking beer. Blakenship and Henderson stepped from the Bronco, Henderson leaning against the door, the sheriff picking his way through the mud. A man straightened from under the raised hood of a '74 Dodge.

"Felipe Ruiz?"

"Yes."

"Got a couple of questions I'd like to ask you." Ruiz waited. "Be better if this was between you and me." Blakenship turned toward the door and looked back. Ruiz hadn't moved. "This doesn't have to be hard. But it can be." Ruiz followed, stopping where the gravel met the mud. "Mr. Ruiz, have you ever heard of Victor and Julio Sanchez?"

"No."

"Let me put it this way. Did you watch the news last night? Or listen to the radio this morning?"

"No."

Blakenship sighed. He lit a cigar. "Have you ever heard of Felipa Ruiz?" He sucked on the Rum Crook. "Before you say no, let me tell you I know she's your niece. Do you know where she is?"

"She works at the store."

"But she's not at the store. And she's not at home. And since she sometimes goes riding on a snowmobile with a man named David Martinez who lives in Union and drives to Top Hat in a 1980 Chevy pickup and since that very same pickup has been seen parked by this very garage, you can see why I might think you'd know where she is. Can't you?" Blakenship smiled around the cigar.

Ruiz scuffled his feet. "David Martinez. I know him. But he is not here today."

"You expect him? And Felipa?"

Ruiz shrugged. "Here? No."

"Where is she?"

"I do not know."

"How about your brother? You expect him?"

"Which brother? I have five."

"Abel. Brother Abel."

"No. I do not expect him. Although maybe he will come. He likes to visit *la famila*."

Blakenship looked over to the house set back among the bare cottonwoods. "Maybe your wife knows something. Charlie." He jerked his head toward the two-story building.

"There is no one there. She and the little ones have gone to Mountain View. Shopping."

***

Felipe waited until the Bronco was well down the road before going back in the garage. "Abel." He motioned to a man standing against the wall in the shadows, partially screened by four others drinking beer, and led the way through the mud to a cluster of rusting car hulks behind the garage.

"*Chinga.* I just bought these shoes."

Felipe ignored him. "The sheriff. He knows about Felipa and David."

"How?"

"He did not say. But he knows. He also asked for you."

"Why me?"

"I don't know. But when he talks to Felipa …" He stared at the Sublette Plateau. "First the brakes, now this … It is not good. And a shipment comes next week." He gave his brother a measured look. "Go back to Union and be difficult to find. I will be in touch. Through the cafe."

***

Blakenship turned toward Pea Green. Where the road angled sharply left, he made a right and shifted into four-wheel drive before following the slick ruts of a track up a gray adobe escarpment dotted with *chicos* and an occasional juniper. Halfway up, Henderson reminded him they'd pulled the stakeout.

"Time to put it back. Who've we got?"

"When?"

"Now. When the hell you think?"

"If it's now, it's Harold."

"Harold?"

"Only one on duty doing something we can pull him off of. Can put Daryl on tomorrow."

At the top, Blakenship swung the Bronco in a U-turn and parked next to a rock bracketed by juniper on either side. Below, the land stretched all the way to Mountain View and with the naked eye they could see people among the cars parked by Ruiz's garage. The sheriff got out and pulled a leather case from behind the seat. He put the binoculars to his eyes and rested both elbows on the hood. "Radio Harold. Tell him we'll be waiting so he'd best hurry."

***

Blakenship was not happy. No sign of Felipa. Sanchez the father had been in parts unknown for weeks. Martinez, father or son, were not forthcoming, beyond apparently solid alibis. Abel

298

Ruiz was not at his apartment or usual haunts in Union. Should have moved faster.

Harold had nothing to report from the stakeout. He'd told him to stay for another hour or so, and count the headlights pulling in or out. At least he'd know where the dumb bastard would be.

He left the warmth of the Stockman after one shot of Canadian Club and three cups of coffee. Skim ice was already forming on the sidewalk and in the gutters. There'd be fender benders and folks in the ditch before the night was out. Ought to be a law banning Saturday night when the roads were like this.

Time to try the parents again. Or the friend she was supposed to be staying with. Might be time to squeeze Felipe Ruiz. Could raid the garage.

He didn't welcome the prospect of another raid, but ... did have enough for probable cause. Have to talk with Kiernan.

There wasn't much traffic on the road to Top Hat, which he took to be a good omen. Maybe tonight wouldn't be so bad. Of course, he thought, as the digital clock on the dashboard turned seven, it's early. Plenty of time for his constituents to get out and get fucked up.

He turned into a small patchwork of gravel lanes lined with small frame houses and house trailers, an occasional doublewide marking the more prosperous among Top Hat's Hispanic population. Left. Right. Left. This was it. White picket fence on the corner, the only one in the neighborhood. Chain link fence at the end of the lane.

Blakenship climbed stiffly from behind the wheel to unlatch the gate, drove in far enough to clear it, got out and relatched it. No telling what needed keeping in — or out.

A motion light came on as he drove the remaining distance to the house. Hilberto Ruiz met him on the porch. "I told you this afternoon, Felipa, she is staying with a friend."

"So you did. So you did. And you told me the friend's name. Thing is, the friend wasn't home, either. In fact, nobody was home."

299

"Perhaps they went shopping. It is Saturday. Maybe they went to the mall in Union."

"The whole family?"

"Yes. Why not?"

"If that's where they went, when do you guess they'll return?"

"Maybe by now. Maybe later. Who can say?"

"Speaking of Union, have you seen your brother lately? Abel?"

"No."

"When was the last time?"

"Around the holiday. *Navidad.* ."

"Surely he's been to Top Hat since then."

"It is possible. Maybe to see Felipe. They are closer in age. I, I am the oldest and we were never very much friends. I was working. I had a family long before he got out of school."

"How often does Felipa spend the night with her friend — what was her name?"

"Julia. Julia Rojas. Often. Almost every weekend it seems. Since the New Year." Ruiz produced a pack of Marlboros. "We do not smoke in the house," he said over hands cupping a match and exhaled with evident pleasure. "It is difficult to raise children today. Especially girls. They do not have the modesty. They do not obey their fathers as before."

"She's in school and has a job."

"Yes. But I worry." He puffed on the cigarette, staring past Blakenship at some puzzle in the night sky. "Tell me. I did not ask this before. But now I ask. Why do you wish to see her?"

Blakenship regarded the lined face of this man worried about his daughter and wished he could tell him the truth. "Just some leads we're running down."

"Drugs?"

The bluntness of the question startled Blakenship. "Why do you ask?"

"Because you asked about Abel. Some say he sells drugs. Along with Felipe. It is not something I know of. But I hear.

Because she is their niece, do you think my Felipa is selling drugs?"

"No. I don't think she's selling drugs. But the connection with Abel and Felipe … and some other things. We need to ask her some questions."

"I have always tried to live properly. I became a citizen twenty-five years ago, two weeks before my twenty-first birthday. I was very proud. And my children, they were all born here. But now it is hard. Because of the newcomers with money, it is hard to buy land. It is hard to pay rent." He spread his arms outward, palms toward the sky. "But this I will tell you. Felipa will speak with you. You have my word." He opened the door and disappeared inside.

Blakenship painstakingly backed and turned, remembering to stop far enough from the gate to have room to open it. First the meskin freeze out, then volunteering to bring his daughter in. Almost. He pulled forward, closed the gate and retraced his path back to highway. Why make it complicated? Probably doesn't like drugs. Wants to get his daughter out of a tough situation before she gets in deeper.

Right before the town center. Left at the third side street. He stopped in front of the Rojas house, two-story clapboard with Victorian ginger breading along the eaves that dated from the turn of the century. The paint was fresh except for the gleam of raw lumber on two of the porch steps. Two bicycles and a wagon lined neatly on the porch. But the house was dark.

The dashboard clock turned to eight. An acid burp burned the back of his throat, a reminder he'd had only coffee and one whiskey since breakfast. He hoped Alma's was still open.

***

It was dark when Jake drove through Top Hat, down from wandering the Sublette and on his way to the nursing home. It had taken most of the day to formulate a tentative course of action. Don't tell Mackey about going to the Sanchezes' cabin. Fact that they were dead and so was their story was all he needed to know. Concentrate on the deputies. Which ones and in what order? And how? Tell Blakenship? Ask him? Have to think some more.

And what about the killers? What the fuck to do about them? Besides watch his back and keep a weapon handy.

Mary Margaret was asleep. Should have guessed.

Loathe to go home, he turned towards Helen's, but with half a beer left after an hour, he gave it up. He nodded good-bye to Frog Bottom and Helen and went into the night, almost falling when his feet hit the film of ice on the sidewalk.

Flashing red and blue lights by the side of the road about two hundred yards before the intersection with the highway slowed him. The Ranger was parked in front of a sheriff's department vehicle and someone was standing, hands on the hood, legs spread in the position known by every child of the television age.

Maria Elena. It had to be Maria Elena, although Jake couldn't see her because the uniform deputy was standing behind her close enough for his crotch to be welded to her butt and it looked like his hands were wrapped around … the cocksucker was feeling her up.

The deputy started to pull away when Jake turned his headlights to bright and he jumped back a foot and a half when he heard the brakes squeal. Jake boiled from the cab, grabbed the deputy by the jacket and half-lifted, half-pushed him against the truck bed. He'd hit him once, the heel of his open hand coming up to catch the point of the deputy's chin, snapping the head back with brain-rattling force and was about to do it again when another set of lights slowed, then stopped.

"Jake, I'm assuming you've got good reason to be manhandling one of my men."

"Piece of shit stopped Maria Elena so he could cop a feel."

"Let him go, Jake."

"Sheriff, it was just a routine …"

"Shut up, Harold."

Harold? In the dark and the fury of the moment, Jake hadn't recognized him. Right hand tried to grab the close-cropped hair to bring the face into full view.

"That's enough, Jake." Blakenship's pull on his arms was gentle but undeniable. "Take care of the girl." The sheriff moved until his face was within a short two inches of the deputy's. "Don't say a fucking thing until I ask you." He turned toward Maria Elena. "Excuse my language, miss. Why don't you tell me what happened?"

"I was in the store. Getting things for Mr. Grummond. The father. I look after him, you see. And with the snow and volleyball, I couldn't buy food earlier. For tomorrow," she explained to Jake, "I made his dinner before I left for the game. All he has to do is ..."

"It's all right."

"Go on," said Blakenship.

"The deputy, he came into the store and began to follow me around. You know. With his eyes. And then he'd be next to me. He would go down another aisle. Then he would be next to me again."

"Did he say anything?"

"No. He'd just be next to me."

"Sheriff, I was just ..."

"Shut up, Harold. Don't make me tell you again. Go ahead, miss."

"I got in the truck and he followed me and turned on the lights. He told me to get out. I asked him why? He said, 'Just do what I say you spic bitch.' I got out and then he ..." Maria Elena's voice, which had been as emotionless as a farm reporter reading livestock futures, broke and she began to cry.

Jake put his arm around her and she buried her face in his shoulder. "Well, Cecil?"

"Sheriff, she's a meskin. Driving a good truck. I just wanted to make sure everything was in order."

"Lots of folks drive stolen trucks to grocery shopping. That right, Harold?" Blakenship sighed. "Here's the way it's going to be. As of now, you are suspended. That means you give

303

me your gun and your badge." Blakenship held out his hand. "Now."

"Now?"

"Now." Blakenship waited while Dobbins handed him the automatic. Waited some more for the badge. "O. K. Now you will drive the department's vehicle straight to the courthouse. Straight back. Slowly. And the reason I know that's what you're going to do is because I am going to be right behind you. And if you go over the speed limit or do anything else other than drive slowly back to the courthouse, may God have mercy on your nasty ass. Because I won't."

Jake and Maria Elena watched them go. "Can you drive?" Jake asked.

"Yes. I think so."

"Go slow. I'll follow."

"That deputy. He was on the raid. He searched the houses."

"I know." Jake spit at where he'd been standing. "I know."

22

MARCH 2 — Early Morning

Jake woke up tired and angry. Sleep had been a long time coming. Couldn't position his arms so they wouldn't go numb just as he dropped off. Dobbins obscene against Maria Elena jerking him awake.

He stayed in bed until the seven o'clock sun roused him from a half-dream of driving back and forth over the deputy, Maria Elena jumping and dancing like a high school cheerleader at the homecoming pep rally, and the Sanchez brothers watching from the truck bed with the enigmatic wisdom of the dead.

Eyes gritty and mouth dry, he barely recognized the face in the bathroom mirror and grimaced at the white line of dried froth rimming his lips. Repeated double handfuls of cold water cured froth line and eye grit. He bent to the faucet again and drank greedily.

Two aspirins followed by two cups of coffee later, he drove to the cabin. Smoke was rising from the stovepipe so at least his father was up and about enough to stoke the fire.

"Close the door." His father sat in the leather chair by the fire, shawl across his shoulders and blanket across his legs, staring at the roaring orange of the flames visible through the stove's soot-streaked windows. "Cold out there."

"Warming up fast. Like yesterday."

"I was cold yesterday. Cold all the time seems like."

"Had breakfast?"

"Some of that decaf shit and toast."

"I'll fix some eggs." Jake opened the refrigerator. "Eusebio and Jesus will be leaving. End of the week, probably."

"Not surprised."

"But they aren't leaving for good. Want to build on their land. Probably start in the summer."

"Next to me?"

"Yeah."

"I'd enjoy the company."

"Seems to me they could tap off your well." Jake waited for a response that didn't come. His father was leaning back open-mouthed, a whistling snore assuring he was still alive. Jake stirred a cup of decaf shit while he waited for the eggs to congeal. Grandpa Grummond jerked awake as the eggs finished and the toaster popped up. "What did you say about Eusebio and Jesus?"

"They're leaving."

"No. Had something to do with water."

"Asked if they could tap off your well. It's running good enough, ain't it?"

"Plenty good. But if they're leaving, what do they need water for?"

Is it Alzheimer's? Jake wondered on the way back to the farmhouse. It had taken twenty minutes going over the same ground and he still wasn't sure it had sunk in.

***

The phone rang while Blakenship was in the shower. "You got that, honey?"

Jessie groaned an affirmative and groped toward the nightstand. "It's Darlene. Says a Mr. Ruiz called. His daughter is home."

"Tell her to call Charlie."

"Does that mean I can go back to sleep?"

"Looks like."

***

Hilberto Ruiz opened the door and led them to a living room filled to overflowing with two sofas, three easy chairs, a number of straight-back chairs and cabinets with glass-faced shelves crammed with knickknacks, religious figures and family photographs.

He indicated two of the upholstered chairs in front of a brand new big-screen TV and walked through the room's other door. Ruiz conducted himself with such an air of quiet authority that both Blakenship and Henderson sat without speaking in their appointed places, hats balanced on their knees.

Ruiz returned in less than two minutes, shepherding Felipa before him. Her long black hair had yet to see comb or brush and her eyes had the red-rimmed look of a night spent crying. She was wearing a flannel bathrobe that reached from neck, where the pink and blue of a nightgown peeped out, to ankles covered by heavy wool socks. Despite the thick clothing, breasts and buttocks moved in unconsciously seductive rhythms. Blakenship understood how the Packer County deputy could have been distracted.

"This is Senor Blakenship, the high sheriff of Sapinero County." The father half-pointed at the sheriff, who stood involuntarily and offered his hand. "This is the Sapinero County Senior Deputy …"

"Henderson, miss." He had also risen to his feet. "Charlie Henderson."

"These gentlemen have questions they wish to ask you. You will answer them. You will tell them the truth." Ruiz to a seat in a straight-back chair to the right of the TV. "I will be here."

"I don't …" Blakenship began, but the look on Ruiz's face stopped him. "Tell me how you knew Victor and Julio Sanchez."

She acted as though she'd been expecting the question. "I really know … " she wiped her eyes on the sleeve of the bathrobe, " I knew Victor. He came to visit with my Uncle Abel and they bought cigarettes at the store."

"And?"

"And we became friends."

"Just friends?"

She glanced at her father and didn't answer.

"Was it Abel who asked you to help get them out of the hospital?"

"Yes."

"And you've been seeing him once a week or so. Taking them supplies. Maybe spending the night?"

"Yes."

"Do you know what Victor and Julio do? Did," he amended. She nodded and wiped her nose on the sleeve of the bathrobe. "Do you have any idea of who wanted them dead?" She shook her head. "No idea at all?"

She shook her head again. "I know they had something to do with drugs, but that is all. I just wanted to be with Victor."

"No idea who they were hiding from?"

"From you. From the law. From the DEA."

"That's all? They weren't hiding from others, too?"

She raised her eyes, then returned her attention to the floor. "I don't know."

"You met Victor with your Uncle Abel in the store where you worked … when was that, by the way?"

"Before Christmas."

"How much before?"

"Two, maybe three weeks."

"You met Victor with your Uncle Abel in the store on a Saturday three weeks before Christmas," he paused and waited for an affirmation. She nodded and he continued, " and you became …" he paused momentarily to set the word off, "friends. Is that right?" Head down, she nodded again. "How often did you see him? After you first met."

"I saw him the next day. And again the Saturday between Christmas and New Years."

"In Top Hat?"

"Yes."

"Did you ever see him in Union?"

"Once. For a few hours on a Sunday. I was supposed to be going to the mall with Julia." She looked guiltily at her father, then refocused her attention on the rug.

Blakenship started to remove a Rum Crook from its cellophane but a glimpse of Hilberto Ruiz out of the corner of his eye changed his mind. "How many times did you see Victor before you helped him leave the hospital?"

"Six. Perhaps seven." Her voice became flat and lifeless.

"Now the hospital. Tell me what happened."

"What do you mean?"

"Who told you they were hurt? Who asked you to help? Who planned it? Who told you what to wear?" Blakenship stopped his hand moving for a cigar. "And why did you want to get them out? Seems to me a hospital's the best place to be if you're hurt."

"Uncle Abel told me. He said they had been in an accident but that the DEA would find out and there would be trouble so we needed to move them someplace safe. Said to wear my nurse's aide uniform. David picked me up ..."

"David?"

"David Martinez. From Union. He picked me up Sunday morning."

"You went straight to Anton?"

"No. We stopped in Union. At a cafe. Uncle Abel was there. And two men I did not know. They explained the plan. What I had to do. The two I did not know, they had scrub suits ..."

"They were the ones who moved Victor and Julio?"

She nodded. "I was to attract the attention of the guard."

"Who took care of the deputy?"

"One in the scrub suit. He knows the martial arts."

"Then?"

"Uncle Abel had a van — with no windows ..."

"Like a delivery van?" Henderson leaned forward like a teacher coaching a nervous student.

"Yes. There were mattresses for Victor and Julio to lie on."

"Did they take them straight to the cabin?"

"The next day."

Blakenship nodded. "And you saw them again the next weekend. At the cabin?'

"Yes."

Henderson cleared his throat. "Tell me, Felipa. Did they want to be there? Out of the hospital and in the cabin? Did they think it was a good idea? It sounds like they might of halfway been prisoners."

309

Felipa looked from Blakenship to Henderson, her eyes confused, then wary, then suspicious.

"Just something to think about."

Blakenship broke the ensuing silence. "This has been a shock." He spoke in soothing tones. "But we've got two murders here and I know you want whoever did it to be captured and punished. So I'm asking you to come to my office tomorrow morning and look at some pictures."

As the father led the way to the door, Blakenship looked back at the girl sitting back erect, with silent tears coursing down her cheeks. "Maybe you don't know, but that accident was no accident. The brakes had been tampered with."

***

Jake studied the list of Dobbins he'd compiled from the phone book. There were a fair number, but no Harold. They seemed to be clustered west of Mountain View in Spring Valley and up the Sublette.

Jake turned to the phone book, leafing through the pages for the addresses of the other Sapinero County deputies on Blakenship's list. He found about half and wrote them down on a separate sheet. Tucking both in his right shirt pocket, he headed for the pickup.

A sheriff's Bronco with what looked like Blakenship at the wheel turned south as he approached the highway and he waited at the stop sign until it was a fast-disappearing speck before going on. At the outskirts of Mountain View, he turned across the Flint River and into the undulating country of fields not yet plowed and animals pawing for something edible under the melting snow.

The road angled up across the scarp of a ridge, then ran along the crest for a long mile before dropping into Spring Valley. Jake stopped at the beginning of the descent and tried to put names to the roads crisscrossing the valley floor in a wide-spaced grid. He hadn't been out this way for a long time, but if he remembered right Whitfield Road was the second one he could see and the first Dobbins place, let's see, listed for Herschel Dobbins, was along there somewhere.

Dobbins was freshly painted on the mailbox.

He slowed as much as he dared. Old house, paint flaking. Smoke from the chimney. Two well-traveled pickups and a '78 Chevy sedan with a pronounced ding in its right rear fender ranked in casual order by the side porch. Small house trailer across the way not far from what looked to be an empty chicken coop. Muddy tire tracks next to it, but no vehicle. No livestock, although the horses grazing in the pasture just ahead might be theirs.

He continued at a methodical pace, checking each crossroads sign against his list on the seat beside him.

Sundown found him near the fringe of a new development on what had been a potato field the last time he'd been this way. In the distance he could make out the white rails of Elmo Johnson's corral. With a jerk of the wheel, he turned toward Mountain View, the brilliance of the setting sun in his rear-view mirror erasing the sight of the stock ranch but not the memories.

He stopped in Mountain View for gas and to check the list. One was nearby — Riddle Hooper. Again he wondered at the name.

Maple, named a century before by people yearning for familiar shelter, was three streets before the courthouse square. Not knowing which way the numbers ran, Jake hesitated at the intersection before doing the easiest thing and turning right. The first house number he was able to read told him he was in the fifteen hundred block. As usual, the easiest thing was the wrong thing. He arced a U-turn at the first intersection and began looking for 1109.

Ahead, in what should be the eleven hundred block, he could see two men, young men by the look, leaning against the tailgate of a mud-spattered compact pickup in the driveway of a modest two-story stucco house. A sedan of indeterminate make and vintage was parked in front of the pickup and a five-year-old Ford F-150 was along the curb.

Jake cruised by, headlights picking up a glint of beer cans. Both were wearing civilian clothes, but the big one was Harold Dobbins, no doubt about it. He fought the sudden urge to hit the brakes and finish the business of the night before.

Think it through. Brace them now?

No. Separately would be better. And just how to do it so as to get answers Mackey Fitz could use?

When the two were no longer visible in the mirror, he turned right then right again, intending to head home. The street dead-ended at a park. Another right brought him to Maple. He waited for headlights to pass. They proved to belong to the Ford pickup, Dobbins behind the wheel.

Better to be lucky than good.

Almost no traffic, not at this time of a Sunday. Jake kept the taillights in sight, even with a quarter mile of separation, as Dobbins led him on a faster and shorter version of the route he'd taken earlier. The taillights turned at the first Dobbins address and stopped next to the tiny trailer house.

Now?

Better talk with Mackey Fitz. First thing in the morning.

***

The lawyer was pouring a cup of coffee when Jake entered the office and he motioned him to the empty cup next to the sugar bowl.

Jake shook his head. "Seems like all I do these days is drink coffee and my kidneys are starting to feel the strain." Jake sat down in the chair across from the desk.

"With the Sanchezes gone, I guess we're going to have to concentrate on the deputies." Fitzgerald moved to his seat behind the desk.

"What I figured. Problem is, I don't have a handle on how to get them to talk to me, let alone tell me anything we could use." He felt a twinge in his forearm and looked down, surprised to see his right hand in a white-knuckled fist. "Thing is compounded by a set-to I had with one of them Saturday night."

312

"What kind of set-to?"

"Was driving home from Helen's and one of those cocksuckers had Maria Elena up against the Ranger. He was copping a feel."

"And?"

"I threw him up against the truck. Blakenship came along just then or there's no telling what I might have done." He flexed his fingers several times. "Dobbins. Harold Dobbins. Maria Elena says he was one of the ones who searched the houses."

"What did C.W. do?"

"Suspended him. Made him turn in his badge and gun right there. I doubt he'll be happy to see me real soon. Neither will his buddies, for that matter."

"We've got their names and we know where they are. If we bring suit, we can depose them during discovery." Fitzgerald eyed him thoughtfully. "Technically, you've got more than a year before you relinquish your right to sue. But the longer you wait, the easier it will be for them to have memory gaps."

"Without the Sanchez brothers — assuming they'd have told us anything we could use — this things looking like pissing into the wind."

"They could have been useful, that's true. And you know there's some who'd say you got off easy. The DEA didn't confiscate your farm and claim it was bought with drug money."

"Jesus Christ, Fitz. My grandfather started the dairy back in 1908."

"DEA doesn't have much of a sense of history, I'm told."

Jake stared at the lawyer for a long minute, then got to his feet. "I'll let you know."

***

Felipa and her father had appeared in the doorway to Blakenship's office promptly when the hands of the clock on the wall pointed straight at nine and she had spent almost a full hour

313

looking at pictures to no avail. She did, however, sign a statement implicating the Sanchez brothers and her uncles.

"The Ruiz girl said they were dealing drugs?" Kiernan's voice echoed from the speakerphone sitting in a pool of morning sunlight on the desktop next to Blakenship's boots.

"Yep."

"Put that with what your informant, what's his name?"

"Munoz. Gabriel Munoz."

"Put that with what he said and what your deputies have seen and we've got probable cause."

"I'll get the warrant this time."

"If you want." Kiernan's voice carried a shrug. "I don't want to get in a jurisdictional pissing contest over this. We'll call it a joint operation."

"You going to be here?"

"Absolutely."

"Buchanan?"

"Uh huh."

"Fuck."

"He'll be under my command."

"Thought you said this was a joint operation."

"Between you and me. Look Sheriff, you can be the titular commander if you want, but my people will work a lot better if they get their orders through me."

Blakenship sighed and recrossed his boots. "Probably so. But I'm warning you — no destruction of living quarters this time. And absolutely no harassing women and children or I'll bring charges against you and your men my ownself."

The pause at the other end of the line was long enough that Blakenship didn't think the DEA man was going to answer. When the answer came, Kiernan's tone carried an edge. "It's a garage, not a dairy. And there's only one family."

"As long as we understand each other. You keep your men under control."

"And you'll be responsible for yours."

Blakenship gave him the same silence he'd gotten a moment before, then said, "I'm figuring on tomorrow night."

"Friday'd be better. Odds are they'll have product on hand for weekend sales. Pay day and all."

Blakenship chewed his cigar. "Giving them a lot of time."

"You haven't done anything to scare them."

"Stopped in at the garage Saturday asking after Felipa. Mentioned brother Abel."

Kiernan seemed to asking a question of somebody in the office. "Just a minute, Sheriff." Voices mumbling, then Kiernan was back on the line. "O.K. Tomorrow it is. We'll be there no later than noon."

Blakenship looked at the dead speakerphone then at his senior deputy. "Another fucking raid. Just what we need."

"No way we can let it go, C.W. Not with what we got. Including two murders." Henderson moved toward the door. "I'll start picking men."

"Pick 'em careful this time, Charlie. Pick 'em careful."

***

A sharp hunger pang struck Jake as he closed Fitzgerald's outer door and led him past his truck to the Chopping Block across the street. At twenty minutes before the noon hour there were only three customers gathered at a single table.

The taste of the soup didn't register with the first spoonfuls, only the warmth flowing down his throat to his midsection. When his stomach's insistent demand had subsided, he tasted the potato and leek soup quizzically and after due consideration added a dash of Tabasco and a generous sprinkling of black pepper.

A copy of the tabloid weekly shopping guide lay on the table and he leafed through it, the ads for used farm equipment catching his eye. Maybe he should stop by Silver Dollar's auction yard on the way home.

He was full by the time he finished the soup and half the grilled ham and cheese sandwich but he'd never been able to abide wasted food, so he kept on eating, slowly chewing each bite and washing it down with water. A gust of wind rustled the guide's pages and drew his eyes to the door. Three women — two in deputy uniforms — came in, deep in hushed conversation. He'd almost finished his sandwich when four more deputies — men, all in uniform — entered. The shortest bore a marked resemblance to the beer drinker with Dobbins. Riddle Hooper.

If he could read their nametags, he'd bet they were on the list. All four had the mean-as-a-snake eyes he'd learned to be wary of when he was in the seventh grade and two eighth graders with that look had jumped him in the restroom.

No reason. Just meanness.

As it turned out, they'd picked on the wrong guy. Both had to be carried out on stretchers — one with a broken jaw and the other's right eye hurt so bad they were afraid he was going to lose it.

The principal had spoken with sad understanding when he'd been brought to the office, along with his father. "I know they started it, Jacob. I know those two are heading for prison just as fast as they can get there." He was talking to Jake but his eyes kept shifting to Grandpa Grummond. "But you hurt them so bad I'm going to have to suspend you for a week." Now he was looking directly at Grandpa Grummond. "I can't have people think that there're no consequences for physical violence. You see that, don't you?"

The feeling of outrage came back with a rush, the picture of his father towering over the principal, yelling that no goddamn son of his was going to let two pissant pukes push him around.

Jake watched the four line up at the counter making comments that the three women from the department did their best to ignore. Orders placed, they descended on a table near Jake and after a fuss of removing coats and ostentatiously adjusting holsters, picked up the conversation interrupted by the business of ordering meals and offending their female co-workers.

"Sheriff took his gun and badge right there."

"Just for stopping a *chiquita*?"

316

"Knowing Harold, he was probably copping a feel."

"Shit. That's one of the few benefits of this godforsaken job. If you can't do a thorough," exaggerated drawing out of syllables accompanied by rolling of eyes and probing hand motions, " a thorough frisk, might as well join the army."

"Yeah. It's not like they mind. Not really. Them meskin girls, they like to be appreciated for what they got."

"Harold never did have no luck with women."

"Part of the problem was Grummond. The bitch works for him and he come along and caught Harold while he was in the middle of his search. Threw him up against the side of the truck and …"

"Harold threw Grummond?"

"No, dumb ass. Grummond threw Harold. Harold says he was just about to throw down on him when Blakenship arrived."

"Sheriff or no, no fucking civilian would do that …" The speaker stopped when he realized the others were looking at a spot over his head. He craned his neck around and up to find Jake's eyes boring down at him.

"If you boys don't know, I'm Jake Grummond. I'll tell you this once — don't fuck with my people." He stared at each one in turn, memorizing faces and nametags.

***

Smart. Put all those assholes on notice. Never get them to talk now.

The turn to Silver Dollar's auction yard was fast approaching and Jake debated going in.

No. No hurry. Could sell equipment anytime.

Selling made him think about the offer to buy trailers from those new folks out Pea Green way. Could he sell or would they be needed as evidence? Another thing he'd have to ask Mackey Fitz.

Since he'd messed up with local deputies, maybe he should try some on the Otero County list. Should he talk with the sheriff — what was his name? Mikeska, that's it — or just do it? Ask Cecil? That would do a lot of good.

But maybe it would.

Investigating was complicated.

He made the turn from the highway to the nursing home in time to see Bridget Taylor's car turn left out of the driveway and head toward Top Hat. The passenger looked enough like Mary Margaret to convince him to reverse direction and go home.

Now what?

He missed the comfort of the dairy's unremitting schedule.

23

MARCH 4 — Morning

Blakenship awoke with liquid rumblings in his abdomen that sent him repeatedly to the toilet before he could get dressed. The demands from his lower tract continued through a sparse breakfast of coffee and toast, and it was eight-thirty before he felt secure enough to leave for the office.

He hoped to hell everything would quiet down by the evening and the raid.

Darlene handed him a message as he walked past the front desk. Henderson was seated across from his desk when he came in and watched Blakenship while the sheriff read. It was from Kiernan: he and four agents would arrive by government plane before one. Buchanan would pick them up and they would go directly to Blakenship's office.

"Looks like we'll be meeting and planning most of the afternoon. You got every one picked?"

Charlie nodded.

"No Dobbins?"

"He's suspended. Wouldn't have picked him any way."

"What about Hooper?"

"He's with the group on Road 58.50."

"Don't know as I want him where he'd think shooting was called for."

Charlie shrugged. "We only got so many deputies, C. W. With any luck, won't none get that far."

"You got a sketch of the premises worked up for ..."

"Can I have a word with you, C.W.?" Jake leaned left shoulder against the office door.

"Not today, Jake." Visibly annoyed that a civilian could have overheard their plans, Blakenship moved to shut the door. "We got a shit pot full of things to tend to. Try me tomorrow afternoon."

Fucking Cecil. Fuck Cecil. Jake tromped between the desks in the main room, out the door and across the street to his truck. Go on up to Elwood my ownself.

He sat behind the wheel for a full two minutes, letting the anger die, then turned the key, put the truck in gear and pulled away from the curb as sedately as he could manage.

He had the list of Otero County deputies Blakenship had provided and he'd found addresses for most of them. Question was, should he talk to Mikeska first, or try to talk to them one-by-one on his own.

He debated the question from the light at Main and Flint until he passed the turn off to the Hazel Lake Inn. Shit. He didn't know their schedules and he didn't know Mikeska. Better stop in first.

***

"And your name?" The startling blue eyes that held his were non-challenging but businesslike, although the veiled twinkle in them gave promise that a smile and a laugh were never more than a heartbeat away.

"Jake Grummond. From down Top Hat way. I expect my name will ring a bell."

"Let me check. " The woman, Elvira if he read the name tag right, disappeared through a heavy oak door of late nineteenth-century design that clashed with the functional economy of the new building. She reappeared momentarily. "You're in luck. He's got twenty minutes before he has to talk with a county commissioner who he'd just as soon never see again in this lifetime, at least. This way." He followed, enchanted by the dazzling smile, brief though it had been.

Mikeska sat behind a desk that was the twin of Blakenship's but without the boot-heel scars decorating its surface. He rose as Elvira led Jake into the room and extended his hand. "Mr. Grummond. Your name rings more than a bell." He waved at a wooden armchair opposite him and returned to his seat. "I would hazard a guess that your visit has something to do with the unfortunate affair of last summer."

"Unfortunate." Jake sat down, turning his head at the sound of Elvira discretely shutting the door. "That's one way to put it."

Mikeska ignored the sarcasm. "What's on your mind?"

"You know your boys put me out of business."

"I've heard you've had problems. But I remind you, my deputies were only part of a large federal operation and .." "Not here to argue about that. Not at the moment, anyway. Thing is, I got permission to sue the DEA. You know how that works?"

"Vaguely."

"Right. Anyhow, I was hoping I could get statements from your deputies."

"Statements?"

"About what happened. Who tore up my property — my people's houses. Things like that. I got a list of who was there." Jake reached inside his tan jacket with the quilted lining and extracted a sheet of paper from his shirt pocket.

"A list. Where'd you get that?"

"From C. W."

"Blakenship gave you that, did he?"

"Blair Stewart's office gave me the same list."

"Heard you contacted our esteemed Congressman." Mikeska didn't sound as though he was sure he'd decided what esteemed meant. "Why come to me? If you're pursuing a lawsuit, you can subpoena them during discovery. Or, you could approach them yourself and see if they'll talk out of the goodness of the heart."

"First off, I thought it'd be polite to let you know what I'm doing. Second, I figured I might get better results if I had your blessing — official or otherwise."

Mikeska spun his chair to the right, then to the left, and looked at the ceiling. "Could get them all together for you," he muttered, more to himself than to Jake. "Goddamn DEA." He turned to face Jake. "I ain't happy about what happened, Mr. Grummond. I'll make no bones about that. But helping you build a case that could potentially hurt my department ... my people

… I don't know." He looked at his watch. "But right now I've got a county commissioner out there who's got a list longer than yours about what's wrong with this department and my running thereof. So let me think about it. Give me a call at the end of the week."

"Like you said, I can always talk to them on my own."

"You can always try."

***

Jake spent the better part of the next two hours locating as many addresses as he could, then turned the truck west. It was four o'clock when he cleared Mountain View and twelve minutes later when he made the turn into the nursing home. Helen and Bridget Taylor were talking in the parking lot as he pulled up. The psychologist gave him a brief wave, got in her Acura and drove away. Helen walked over to him.

"No point in going in, Jake. She's deep into a nap. With a smile on her face."

"Been driving again?"

"Yep. And it seems to be working. Why don't you let me feed you supper and I'll fill you in."

"Got to go by the place. See how Dad's doing."

Helen turned Jake's wrist so she could read his watch. "Shouldn't take more than two hours. Say seven?" At Jake's nod, she added, "You can use the outside stairs around back if you don't want to see anybody at the bar."

***

Fresh from a shower and shave, Jake patted some Old Spice on cheeks and neck and dressed in fresh jeans and shirt. Buckling his belt as he moved through the living room, he eyed the unblinking red light on the answering machine with something akin to relief, shrugged into his winter jacket and headed through the door. Once behind the wheel of the pickup he began an unbidden mental debate as to whether he should

322

return to Elwood and try questioning Otero county deputies on his own.

He had come to no decision when he reached Top Hat's main street and drove to the back of Helen's building. He climbed the outside stairs to the intensifying aroma of roasting chicken wafting through the slightly open kitchen window that erased Otero County deputies from his mind.

Hungrier than he'd thought he was. Had he eaten lunch?

Helen opened the door before his knock and hugged him, then led him inside and pointed to the recliner in front of the TV. "Sit down. You want beer, whiskey, coffee or tea?"

Jake surprised himself with his answer. "Tea."

"Lemon?"

"I guess."

"Lemon," Helen said firmly. "Lemon and honey."

They ate without talking. When they were done and the dishes cleared, Helen motioned him back to the recliner. "You want to talk about Mary Margaret?"

"Didn't you say she went to sleep with a smile on her face? Like the drives are doing some good?" At Helen's nod, he leaned back and closed his eyes. "I feel tired, for some reason or other. Let me see for myself tomorrow, then we can talk."

"O. K. Want me to put some music on? You're not going to watch TV with your eyes closed. What do you like?"

"You choose."

A faint smile flitted across his lips as the first notes of Eine Kleine Nacht Music filled the small living room. "That's nice."

"Mozart."

"Mozart?"

"Something I got a taste for in college. Music appreciation course. Daddy died before I could finish and I had to come home and help Mama. But I always remembered the music and started building a collection as soon as I could. It's something special for me. Just me."

She stood by the sideboard holding the teapot and watching the man in the recliner. As the music rolled over him,

323

the lines in his face seemed to relax and she detected the hint of a snore.

***

Blakenship watched the men file into the room and group themselves according to their affiliation — DEA agents to the right towards the copying machine, his deputies on the left around the coffee pot. The last two to enter were Buchanan and Kiernan in that order.

Blakenship waited while the anxious chatter died down and the jockeying for position had ebbed to a nervous shifting of feet, then cleared his throat. Before he could begin, Buchanan moved to the blackboard that had been wheeled from its usual position against the far wall to a spot in front of the door to Blakenship's office. "O.K. men. The balloon is about to go up. You've all spent the afternoon …"

"Goddamn it, Kiernan," Blakenship exploded. "I thought we had an understanding."

"He's right," the big agent spoke softly but his voice could be heard in every corner of the room hushed by the sheriff's outburst. "I thought I'd made that clear this afternoon. This is Sheriff Blakenship's operation. If any of you federal officers have questions about his orders, I will clarify them. Me. Me alone. That clear, Buchanan?"

"Jesus Christ, Tom, I've been on this crew for two and a half years and I'm not going to let …" The vein running vertical up the agent's forehead pulsed with fury and frustration as his tongue failed him.

"I'm your superior now." Kiernan kept his voice soft but there was no give in it. "You may not like it, but that's the fact. You will obey Sheriff Blakenship — or me. I don't have to remind you how a reprimand for endangering an operation will look in your personnel jacket." Kiernan stared at the quivering Buchanan until the older man turned his head. "O.K., Sheriff."

Was it a question or an order? Blakenship couldn't tell.

324

"We've spent the afternoon going over everything, so I'll just hit the high points. We'll leave here in a caravan, me in the lead. We'll stop in the CO-OP parking lot in Top Hat. From there, we'll wait until Rob and his men radio they're in position off the 58.50 road. We will then proceed quietly — let me say that again — quietly — to the garage where you will take up your positions and wait for my orders. And remember this — there are women and children in the house so do not fire a weapon until I give the order. Do not pull a trigger without my say-so. Is that clear?" His eyes swept the room. "O. K. Get your gear and assemble by your vehicles."

Outside, Hooper, at the passenger door of the last Sapinero Bronco lined in the reserved parking spaces nearly pissed in his pants at a loud whisper from the large shrub immediately behind him.

"Riddle. Hey, Riddle."

'Goddamn it." Hooper felt his crotch to make sure it was dry. "What the fuck. Is that you, Harold?"

"Yeah. What's your assignment?"

"Blakenship's put me on the 58.50 road. Case any of them beaners go running across the fields."

"58.50?"

"What're you, deaf?" At that moment, the engines started in ragged order. "Got to go." Hooper slammed his door, and the Bronco backed and turned to take its place in line, so the deputy didn't see Dobbins sprinting across the lawn to his truck parked by the World War I cannon.

***

"Two-hour nap. Not bad. Here." Helen's hand extended toward him with a teacup in it. "This'll clear your head enough so's you can drive home." Jake struggled the recliner upright. "Careful. It's hot."

He sipped gingerly, then set the cup on the floor between his feet and stood to stretch toward the ceiling. "Time I was going."

Dew had settled on the pickup since he'd parked, settled and frozen. He started the engine, pushed the lever on the panel to defrost and rummaged under the seat for the scraper.

He'd finished the windshield and was working on the passenger-side window when the sound of an engine pulled his attention to the main street. A pickup gleamed in the light cast by one of Top Hat's two street lamps, a pickup that looked very much like the Ford 150 now linked indelibly with Dobbins in his mind.

Dobbins in this end of the county? At night? He turned after the taillights, twin red spots already across the Flint River and climbing up West Mesa on the Pea Green road, gaining speed.

The spots glowed a brighter red — slowing for the turn by Ruiz's garage. He soon did the same and when he straightened out, the lights were no longer in sight. He sped through the straight, braked for the ninety-degree turn to the left, and accelerated — the lights far in the distance.

They glowed and disappeared. Turned on 58.50? Jake sucked pensively on the snuff tucked into the lower left quadrant of his lip. Probably taking the long way home. He slowed as he passed the T intersection. No lights. Boy must be really moving.

***

"Okay, gentlemen. One last time." Blakenship looked at the men grouped in a rough semi-circle in the parking lot of the Top Hat CO-OP. "Rob, Ralph and Hooper will go first and set up along 58.50. Kiernan, you get some of your men in back and put the rest on the right near the garage. Daryl, your crew will set up on the left. Charlie and me and Kiernan will be in front." He pointed to two young men who looked like this time last year their biggest concern was making the district basketball playoffs. "You two stay with me and Charlie. Any questions?" He gave them a moment. "Good. I'll lead. When I cut my lights, you cut yours. Get in position as quick and quiet as you can. Three minutes after we get there, I'm going to turn on the lights and

326

bang on the door. Don't do anything until me or Henderson gives the word."

One of the deputies in the back raised his hand. "What if they start shooting?"

"Then I expect Charlie or me will give you the word."

***

Jake had driven on to Rafe's store, not because he expected it to be open, but because it seemed easier to turn around there than backing and filling to avoid the bar ditches. But when he made the first hard turn on the way back, he could see lights at the other end of the straight. Ruiz place was lit up like Times Square on New Year's Eve.

He stopped and rolled down the window. A voice carried on the chill breeze, words indistinguishable but surprisingly loud like they were being amplified. Then the unmistakable crack of a firearm, followed by a chattering volley that went on longer than Jake thought possible.

Not driving into that.

He couldn't get over far enough on the shoulder to satisfy himself that he wouldn't be rear-ended, so he backed around the turn and pulled straight ahead, picturing the adobe track that angled to the top of the mesa. Once through the fence, he drove, lights off, across the field with its thin cover of crusty snow toward the corner opposite the garage. Not too close. Didn't want to be seen. More important, didn't want to get hit.

A fence stopped him about midway. He parked, negotiated the barbed wire and climbed a slight rise where he hunkered as low as he could and tried to make out what was going on.

The firing stopped. A bulky figure rose from behind the squared-off bulk of a Bronco, bullhorn in hand. The report of a single weapon shocked the post-volley silence and the figure dropped behind the vehicle.

Got to be Blakenship.

The sheriff rose again and again an unintelligible voice wafted Jake's way.

"Who fired?" Everybody on the Ruiz property, inside and out, could hear the sheriff. "Goddammit. I told you to wait for my goddamn order. That's not too goddamn hard to goddamn understand, is it?"

"Sounded like it came from round back, C.W."

Blakenship looked at Henderson. "The back, huh. Kiernan," he swung to face the DEA agent. "Those're your men. Whose in charge?"

"Buchanan."

"Buchanan. Sweet Jesus Christ."

Kiernan shrugged. "I thought he'd be out of the way."

"Out of the way. Motherfucker won't be out of the way until he's six feet under. Get him out here."

Kiernan spoke softly into his walkie-talkie, listened to the response, then spoke sharply and with urgency. "He's coming."

The two lawmen waited in silence. Buchanan appeared out the outer edge of the lights, disappeared behind the garage then made his way to them.

"What's up?"

Kiernan started to respond but Blakenship pushed him out of the way. "Listen you little pig puke fuck. I said no shooting without my orders."

"They shot first."

"Bullshit. And even if they did, I said no shooting without my orders. I want your gun."

"I don't think that's necessary, Sheriff." Kiernan spoke soothingly, like he was trying to calm an angry child.

"But I do, Kiernan. And what I think is what counts right now." Blakenship held his hand out. "Give it."

"No."

"Daryl." Even without the bullhorn, the sheriff's voice reverberated across the yard.

"Yes, Sheriff."

"You got your riot gun?"

328

"Uh huh."

"Come here." Blakenship never took his eyes off the two DEA men, Buchanan vibrating like a tuning fork, Kiernan leaning bemused against the fender of the Bronco. At the crunch of footsteps on gravel, the sheriff spoke again. "You got a round in the chamber?"

"No sir."

"Rack it." The unmistakable grate of a shotgun's pump action echoed across the silent yard. "Point it at Buchanan's head."

"Sir?"

"You heard me. If this little sonofabitch doesn't hand me his gun by the time I count five, pull the trigger."

"Sheriff?"

"One. Two."

"Give it to him." Kiernan's voice cut across Buchanan's face like a whiplash. Slowly and carefully he reached inside his coat and placed the automatic in the sheriff's waiting hand. "Now what, Blakenship?"

"Daryl. Take agent Buchanan to his vehicle and have him sit in it. And make sure he stays there. Shit, handcuff him to the steering wheel. With his own handcuffs." Blakenship watched the two disappear beyond the light. "Now, Agent Kiernan, we'll see if we can salvage anything. And I don't mind telling you, I'm more than a little sick of the DEA fucking up in my county. Especially that little prick."

***

Dobbins had parked his truck in an arroyo about a mile and a half from the intersection, taken his hunting rifle from the gun rack and made his way along the fence until he saw the departmental Bronco. Staying low, he moved to the deputies, the three of them clustered in a knot at a high spot between road and fence.

"Riddle," he whispered, then dropped prone at the sound of pumps being racked. "Jesus. Take it easy. It's me. Harold."

"Harold. You dumb fuck. What're you doing?"

"Thought you could use an extra hand."

"There'll be hell to pay if Blakenship finds out."

"You guys keep quiet and he'll never know. " Dobbins looked around. "How're you going to deploy?"

"I figure …"

"I'm in charge here, Hooper."

"Sorry, Rob."

"Way I see it, we'll space ourselves along this fence. Close enough so's we can see each other. And if I was you, Harold, I'd go home."

"There's just three of you. How about I take the far end. That'll give you more coverage and if anything happens I can slip on to my truck and be gone before anyone knows different."

"I don't know."

"Come on, Rob."

The flash of headlights turning from the Pea Green road stopped Rob's response as he involuntarily raised his weapon to his shoulder. The approaching vehicle slowed, coming to a slow roll as it drew even with the small clot of deputies. The other three had their weapons at the ready.

The car, a pickup of some kind with dual rear wheels, was almost stopped now, and the driver rolled his window down as if to talk. Rob moved forward, riot gun waist high, when a series of flashes faster than disco lights danced along the vehicle's side. The other three were frozen for an instant as they watched Rob crumple onto the sandy snow of the shoulder. The flashing continued, accompanied by a muted coughing that claimed Hooper, then the other deputy — Ralph, it was Ralph, Dobbins thought as he squeezed off one round before the coughing flashes stitched him from one side of his abdomen to the other.

***

"What do you think, Charlie?"

330

"Near as I can tell, our side did all the shooting. I bet there's only women and children inside. We'll be lucky if none of them got hurt."

Blakenship moved to the front of the Bronco and raised the bullhorn to his mouth. "You in the house. Felipe Ruiz. This is Sheriff Blakenship. The house is surrounded. Come out with your hands up." Blakenship dropped the bullhorn to his side and replaced it with his cigar. Then he reversed the procedure. "You have two minutes to come out. Then …"

"Sheriff." A woman's voice carried across the floodlit yard. "There are no men here. Just myself and three of my children."

"Well, the four of you come on out."

A short, round woman, long hair flowing unbraided down her back and clad in a bathrobe cinched around her ample waist, shooed three children — all under ten years of age, all in pajamas — before her like she was herding ducks.

"Start checking every room — upstairs and down. And Charlie, for crissake, tell them not to tear things up." He walked back to the sedan where Buchanan sat attached to the steering wheel. "You can unlock him, Daryl. You didn't lose the key?"

"No sir."

"I'm going to have your ass for this, Blakenship."

"What do you think, Kiernan?"

"He's certainly free to file a complaint — through proper channels."

"We'll see." Blakenship looked up in time to see two men wearing DEA jackets disappear through the front door of the house. "Dammit. Charlie. Get the DEA out of there. I don't want a repeat." He turned back to Kiernan and Buchanan. "We'll see. This is still my jurisdiction. And my operation."

***

Jake backed down the rise and rose, groaning slightly from the ache in his knees. Back in the truck he turned the key and stopped his hand as it reached for the headlight switch. No. Best wait until he was on the paved road. As he slowed for the turn by the garage, he caught a glimpse of a woman and some children in nightclothes standing forlorn in the center of the floodlit circle while uniforms milled without apparent purpose on the periphery.

A flood of sympathy and remembered rage washed over the small glow of unidentified satisfaction that he'd felt earlier at the prospect that this drug business might get cleared up. The tangle of emotions lasted through Top Hat, along the county road, and into his bedroom where he lay for an unmeasured time staring at the ceiling he couldn't see.

24

March 5 — Early Morning

"I can't get it to add up, Charlie." Blakenship took a bite of donut and wiped futility at the powdered sugar that cascaded into his lap. "I'm not saying Ruiz didn't kill them, but …" He started to take another bite, thought better of it and threw the donut in the waste basket. "Never had a deputy hurt serious and now four dead." He rubbed his eyes, red-rimmed from lack of sleep or incipient tears — Henderson couldn't tell.

It was six o'clock in the morning and they were sitting in Blakenship's office.

"Who else?" Henderson yawned and wiped his own eyes. He pulled a cigarette from the pack on the desk but didn't put it in his mouth. "Only person or persons in the area we know of with weapons and attitude was Felipe Ruiz and some number of associates."

Blakenship ignored the tug from a faint memory of a vaguely familiar pickup passing the garage. "The tunnel from the hidey hole under the garage runs in that general direction, true enough."

The woman had told the truth. There was nobody left but her and the children. A search of the garage had turned up nothing, as had a search of the house. But in the basement, Daryl had tapped a section of wall that didn't sound right. Three swings of a pickax revealed a tunnel that ran to a room beneath the garage. In it was a bale of marijuana and white powder that Blakenship was willing to bet all he ever hoped to have would test out as cocaine.

That was if you turned right. If you turned left, the tunnel ran more than 200 yards to a manhole cover surrounded by chicos.

"I grant you they could have been headed toward 58.50. But it looks to me like our boys were shot from the road. Including that fuckup Dobbins," he muttered half under his breath.

"Shit, C.W. They probably had some *compadres* meeting them. Folks in that line of work got to have contingency plans. And we never did cut off the phone." Henderson finally lit the cigarette he'd been rolling between his fingers, flame flaring the paper from the end where his fidgeting had worked the tobacco out.

"Maybe. Looked like Uzis or assault rifles the way they was shot and that goes with dope dealers." Blakenship fought a yawn. "Still, the first shot fired sounded like a regular old rifle. If it was one of them inside that fired."

"Speaking of shots, what're you going to do about Buchanan?"

"I expect Kiernan and I will have an interesting discussion, by and by."

***

Jessie's black hair spread across the pillow surprised him. He hadn't expected to see her until tonight at the earliest. She raised her head at the sound of his footsteps and smiled dreamily his way. "About time. I've got your side of the bed warm."

"Can't. Just a shower and a change of clothes. What're you doing here, anyway?"

"Missed the smell of you. And I figured you'd be ready for a snuggle."

"I'm ready, all right. More than ready. But it's going to be a while."

"Problems?" She held her head up for a kiss.

"You could say that." He kissed her cheek, lined red from wrinkles in the pillowcase. "Buchanan jumped the gun. Got everybody to shooting. It's a wonder the woman and children weren't hurt."

"Woman and children?"

"Not a sign of Felipe or any other adult male. Had them an escape tunnel that ran to the middle of the field behind the house. Did find a cache of drugs under the garage." Blakenship shucked out of his shirt and sat on the side of the bed. "And I got four deputies killed. Three deputies and Dobbins," he amended.

Jessie sat straight up. "Killed?"

Blakenship pulled off his right boot. "They were on the 58.50 road, guarding the back door, so to speak. When they didn't answer the radio, I sent Daryl down to get them." Jessie traced the column of muscle that ran up the right side of his spine and then began massaging his shoulders while he worked on his left boot. "All dead as hammers. Looked like machine pistols. Or them assault rifles."

Blakenship became conscious of the tips of Jessie's nipples brushing against the middle of his back, an awareness that created a profound urge to lie down beside her. The urge became acute when she leaned her head against the top of his back, just below his neck, and her breasts flattened against him.

He stood up with a jerk and unbuckled his belt. "Charlie thinks it was Ruiz. Or help coming up the road."

"Breakfast?" she asked the broad back disappearing through the bathroom door. "If it was help, they must have been close by."

"Say what?" Blakenship's voice rose over the sound of rushing water.

"Do you want breakfast?"

"After that."

"Nothing you haven't already thought of. If it was help for Ruiz who killed your men, they must have been close by."

**

Groggy from less than two hours of fitful sleep, Jake emptied the last of the coffee into his mug and debated whether to make another pot. He was staring through the window of the kitchen door watching the nine o'clock sun melt the thin snow cover and soften the ridges of adobe by the front wheels of his pickup when the phone rang.

"You hear about the raid?" Billy's voice, pitched high with excitement.

335

"Tell me."

"Blakenship and the DEA raided that garage on the Pea Green road. Found a bunch of drugs. That going to help you?"

"Don't know. Have to talk with Fitz."

"That's not all. Four deputies got killed."

"Killed?" There'd been a lot of shooting, but he hadn't seen anything to indicate that a single person had been hurt. "Four killed?"

"Froggie says they were on 58.50. In case they run ..."

58.50? Where Dobbins had turned. Jake let Billy ramble while he tried to sort things out. When had the others got there? While he was turning around at Rafe's store?

Had they seen him? Even if they had, it wouldn't matter now.

He squelched the guilty twinge that came with the realization and interrupted Billy. "Think I'd better call Fitz."

Ten minutes later he was back at the kitchen door. Fitz agreed they needed to get all the information they could. But not today. With drugs found and four men dead, Blakenship wasn't going to have time for Jake. Have to sit tight until next week. Maybe longer.

So what do I do?

See what the newspapers have to say. Think. See Mary Margaret.

See Mary Margaret. If she's not out for a ride.

***

Five deputies clustered at the back of the Ruiz house behind Blakenship and Kiernan. A sixth came out of the back door carrying a two hundred foot tape measure. "It's a long way, Sheriff. 615 feet. From the house."

"Somebody did a lot of digging."

"And a lot of planning." Kiernan blew his nose into a handkerchief and carefully refolded it. "Ruiz has been in business for quite a while."

336

Blakenship looked at the DEA agent. "You know that or guessing? Never mind. Let's go out where Charlie is. And be careful. Don't want to go tromping everything down until we get some idea of which way they went."

The late morning sun had melted the thin snow cover, giving a slick patina to the adobe that caused a ragged chorus of low-toned curses from the men picking their way around brush and rocks. Henderson stood by the manhole smoking a cigarette and watching their progress with clear amusement.

"Laugh while you can, Charlie, because you're going to be slipping and sliding your ownself right quick." Blakenship unzipped his jacket and took his hat off to wipe his forehead with the back of his hand. "See anything?"

"Not yet." Henderson waved at where the land dropped away in a broad, shallow arroyo then climbed to clumps of brush on the other side. "Have to make like we're hunting pheasants and push through the brush until somebody spots something."

"Spots what?" Kiernan blinked his eyes against the sweat.

"We're not Indian trackers. Can't read bent twigs. Need to look for shade where there's still snow, hope we get lucky and find a footprint. Maybe a piece of clothing ripped off by a branch. If we're real lucky, we'll find a place where one of them tripped and went down, ass over teakettle.

Blakenship turned to the six men grouped behind him. "Spread out about ten feet apart along the edge of the arroyo. Henderson will be in the center. Do what he says and do it right." Blakenship turned back to the senior deputy. "Have fun."

"Where're you going?"

"Me and Kiernan are going to see how his boys are doing in the tunnel and hidey hole. Then we'll see what's been found on 58.50."

Henderson let Blakenship's head disappear through the manhole before he spoke. "Want a flashlight?"

***

337

"We had parked by the playground. The one across the street from where she grew up." Bridget Taylor twisted a handkerchief in both hands, tried looking at Jake, then concentrated on the wall behind him and fought to ignore her trembling chin. "I helped her walk to the front of the car. Where she could use the fender for support." Her voice broke and she dabbed at her nose, flicking her eyes toward the expressionless face. She blew into the handkerchief and tried to refold it but her hands shook too much. "There was a truck cab, the big kind that pull those long trailers, parked in the driveway of the first house on the other side of the playground."

"Deke Alexander's."

She gave a weak smile at Jake's words, his first since she began her story. "It didn't seem as though she noticed it. She stood by the fender, looking at her old house. She didn't say anything. It was like she was trying to bring a picture into focus. I didn't say anything, either. I wanted her to look. To give her time to remember." The psychologist sobbed again, one shoulder-racking spasm that started some place deep within her. "Then there was the sound of the truck engine starting and Mary Margaret screaming and moving away from the sound of the truck into the road screaming then a loud noise and the pickup and the driver and ..." There was no stopping the sobs this time.

A passing nurse put a comforting hand on her shoulder. "Is there anything I can do?"

"My wife ..."

"You're Mr. Grummond, aren't you?" Jake nodded. "I thought I recognized you. Mrs. Grummond is still with the doctor. Can I get you something? Coffee? Soda water?"

"No. I ..." The room started to spin and Jake's left leg buckled, throwing him against the wall. "Where's the bathroom?"

"Come with me." She took his arm and led him down the hall. "Do you want me to wait?"

"I'll be all right."

Jake let the cold water run for a handful of seconds. As he bent to splash some on his face, his stomach sprayed what was left of breakfast into the basin. He stared at the mess, uncomprehending, and another spasm set him retching uncontrollably, each throe burning the back of his throat.

When it subsided, he filled and drained the basin twice, then wiped the last traces from the white porcelain with a paper towel. He cupped water in his hand, rinsed his mouth and spat, splashed some water on his face and wiped the drops with another paper towel.

Bridget was more composed when he returned, sitting almost primly in an orange plastic chair and holding a styrofoam cup.

"Where'd you get that?"

"Someone got it for me. That way, I think." She pointed to double doors.

The bank of vending machines offered uniformly unappetizing selections. Jake settled for long slurps from the water fountain that momentarily relieved the acid burning in his throat.

Dr. Ben was with Bridget when he got back, his face sagging in sad-eyed compassion. Or relief.

"She passed." Jake steeled himself to a statement not a question.

The doctor shook his head. "No."

"She's alive?"

"Very much alive. Some scrapes and bruises but no ..."

The nose-twisting wrench of smelling salts opened his eyes to the anxious faces of Dr. Ben and the nurse who'd shown him to the bathroom. Trying to sit up brought an ache to the back of his head.

"Just lie there for a minute." Dr. Ben's hand pushed him gently to the floor. "There's a gurney coming."

"I want to see her."

"You will. But rest for a bit first."

The strong hands of a twenty-year-old orderly who'd been an all-state defensive tackle three seasons before reached under his shoulders to help him up and on the gurney's thin mattress.

"I'm all right." Jake fought to sit up.

339

"Of course you are." Dr. Ben let a practiced smile dimple his cheeks. "But do me the favor of lying there for a couple of minutes. And I'd really appreciate it if you'd drink a Coke. The sugar."

Someone handed him a glass with a straw. Surprised by how good the first sip tasted, Jake emptied the glass without stopping, slurping the last drops like a greedy child. He set the glass down. "Now."

Dr. Ben grasped him gently above his right elbow and guided him on a path of right and left turns to a room with four or five beds, empty save for the one where Mary Margaret lay on her back, closed eyes looking to the ceiling, her mouth a peaceful line despite the bandage covering the right side of her face where the pavement had ripped.

Jake touched the gauze and tape. "How bad?"

"Physically, she's hardly hurt. No broken bones. No internal injuries. Bruises and abrasions, that's about it." The doctor moved to the other side of the bed and studied the placid face. "Near as I can figure, the pickup barely touched her … if it hit her at all. The trauma is consistent with running, stumbling and falling on asphalt. Like she was getting out of the way." He checked the IV that led into her left arm. "Saline and glucose. She was just started walking, didn't she?"

"Uh huh." Jake nodded. "Then why's she unconscious?"

"I'd say shock. Of course, I'm just an old-time country doctor. It's most likely tied to what's been the problem since last summer. This is where that Taylor woman," he couldn't bring himself to call her Dr. Taylor, " where she comes in." He studied the monitor. "All I can tell you for sure is that there're no serious injuries and her vital signs are good."

Jake leaned over and kissed Mary Margaret's forehead, then kissed the forefinger of his right hand and touched it to her lips. "I love you," he whispered. Did the corners of her mouth pull into the hint of a smile? He stared at the full lips he'd kissed at least once a day for more than two decades — until last fall. He turned toward the wall to hide from Dr. Ben the pain and

340

guilt he was sure showed on his face. He turned back just as quickly and bent to kiss her full on the mouth.

Was there the pulse of a return kiss?

***

Blakenship learned of Mary Margaret's accident when he returned to the office after spending the better part of an hour watching his men search both sides of 58.50 for a full mile either side of the site where earlier he'd watched the coroner's people fill four body bags in the pre-dawn full darkness.

Dobbins' truck had been found early that morning, and the deputies were turning up brass that pointed to automatic weapons, but nothing to point to who had done it had so far surfaced.

"Hit by a pickup? What was she doing in the road?"

"I'm not sure," Luther answered. "Something about being with a psychologist."

"Who hit her?"

"Barney Shutz. Taking his wife back to work at the hardware store."

"No question about fault?"

"No. He may have been driving a little faster than the law would recommend but there's no doubt it was her fault. That's what the psychologist said."

"Jake?"

"At the hospital, far as I know."

"Shit" He dragged the expletive out into a plea for understanding. "How bad?"

"What? Oh. I don't know."

Blakenship punched in the numbers on the phone with the careful precision that warned of a fury close to breaking loose. "Page Dr. Ben ... Blakenship ... Sheriff Blakenship, goddammit." He put his hand over the mouthpiece. "Fucking ... Hello, doc... I heard ... I was calling about Mary Margaret. And Jake. Wondered what shape he's in." The sheriff chewed an unlit cigar while listened. "Unconscious but O.K.? ...."

341

Physically, yeah. And Jake?" He chewed and listened some more than replaced the receiver.

"Well?" Henderson had moved unnoticed into the office.

"Physically, she'll be fine. Mentally, who knows?"

"And Jake?"

"Calm. Concerned, but calm."

"That's a mercy."

"It is. It is indeed."

***

"What the fuck was she doing in the road?" Grandpa Grummond's voice didn't carry his usual heat when commenting on human stupidity.

"They were looking at her old house. Idea was to jog her memory." Jake stood with his back to the stove. "Seems to be working."

"This'll probably set her back like she was."

"Hard to say." Jake stared at his father's profile as the old man stared out the window, the skin on his neck and chin sagging in disconsolate folds as though bewildered by the shrinking of the man it had covered for so many years.

"It's been a tough run lately. Makes you wonder if any of it's worth it."

Jake didn't answer. He looked through the cabin's picture window to the Far Gate field where in years past the crew would be spreading fertilizer. Beyond, he could make out the roofs of some of the houses and trailers bathed a washed-out gold in the last of the afternoon light.

Almost all were empty now. How was it possible to lose so much so fast? Late August to the beginning of March. He counted on his fingers. A bare six-and-a-half months. The dairy gone after more than eighty years. All because of a lie.

But Mary Margaret had smiled. And kissed him back.

He watched the world go dark, first losing sight of the barn, then the houses and trailers, finally the field.

But she'd kissed him back.

Jake was at the hospital by seven, ten minutes before Dr. Ben came in for his morning rounds. "How is she?"

"Why don't we both find out."

Jake's stomach knotted when they entered the room. Mary Margaret was lying on her side, back to the door and knees flexed in fetal withdrawal. Dr. Ben walked to the far side of the bed and gently grasped her left wrist.

"Hurt."

Like before. Relief propelled Jake to the bedside in two strides.

"Face. Knees. Hurt."

"Of course you hurt." The doctor's voice was low and soothing. "You fell on rough asphalt. But it's just bumps and bruises. Nothing serious."

"Jake. Where's Jake?"

"He's here."

"Over here."

Mary Margaret rolled toward the light pressure of Jake's hand on her shoulder, an eager smile that widened to crease against the taped bandage on her cheek when she brought his face into view.

"You're looking better." Jake stroked her forehead and traced her mouth, making the smile broader.

Suddenly her brow furrowed and the lips pursed. "I'm sorry."

"Nothing to be sorry ..." Jake's hand patted the uninjured cheek. "She's asleep."

"What she needs most, I expect." Dr. Ben glanced toward the door. "Wouldn't you agree?"

"Of course." Bridget Taylor moved next to Jake and all three studied Mary Margaret who lay on her back, face relaxed and with what might be the trace of a smile pulling at the corners of her mouth.

"Am I imagining it, or is she losing weight?" Jake's gaze was still fixed on his wife. "Don't look like there's as much fat under her chin."

"I think so, too." The psychologist tilted her head in critical assessment. "It could just be better muscle tone from getting a little exercise, but there's no doubt her physical condition has improved."

"She talked. Like before. And she asked for me."

"Asked for you?"

"I've got to make rounds. And she should sleep." Dr. Ben ushered them toward the door. "Why don't you two talk over coffee?"

**

Jake sat on the porch in the last pool of soon-to-be-spring afternoon sun, chair tipped against the wall and feet propped on the railing, as he tried to make sense of the day.

They'd adjourned to the Chopping Block and talked for more than half an hour. Bridget Taylor hadn't had much concrete to offer, but she shared Jake's optimism that the accident wasn't going to make her disappear again. And the fact that she'd asked for him, asked for and recognized him when she saw him … that was nothing but positive. Jake hadn't told her that she'd kissed him back and he wondered why. Not sure. Too private?

He'd left with more hope than he'd had for months and a reinvigorated determination to make the bastards pay — pay for it all, but especially for Mary Margaret.

She'd been asleep during the day's two subsequent visits to the hospital. Nothing to worry about, Dr. Ben had assured him on the second.

Was he right?

The slamming of a door brought his feet down. Maria Elena waved as she got in Mary Margaret's Ranger and drove to the county road where she turned right.

Shit. Haven't talked to Dad since yesterday.

344

Maria Elena was washing dishes when he entered the cabin and hung his jacket on a peg by the door. His father grunted a greeting and continued spooning what looked to be stew or thick soup into his mouth.

"*Caldo,*" Maria Elena explained. "Would you like some?" Without waiting for an answer, she filled a bowl and handed it to him. Jake sat down across from his father and nodded his thanks at the proffered spoon. "How is *la senora?*"

"She wasn't hurt. Not bad. And she recognized me."

"*Gracias de Dios.*" She concentrated on the frying pan she was scrubbing. "It wouldn't be the same. Without …" She snuffled and blew her nose on a paper towel.

"You got that right. It wouldn't be the same." Will it ever be the same? He stood and walked to the window, trying to find a light from one of the houses across the Far Gate field. "Where's Jesus?"

"They've gone to Mexico."

"Visiting or permanent?"

"Visiting."

The picture of Mary Margaret telling him about the Montoya's immanent departure floated across his line of vision. She had, he now understood, her own relationship with the people who worked and lived at the dairy, a relationship that was not only separate from his, but deeper and more inclusive.

Jealous anger poked through optimism and the faint stirrings of remembered passion he'd had over the last two days shamed him, a shame intensified by the realization he'd been sneaking peeks down the front of Maria Elena's blouse as she bent to put the clean cooking utensils in the storage compartment under the counter.

"You look a little peaked, son." His father's voice, a faint mockery of his former rumble. "Maybe you need an early night."

"Say what? I'm all right." He looked at his watch. "It's …" He caught himself looking at Maria Elena again and took his jacket from the peg. "I'll call in the morning."

The clatter of a bowl followed hard on by Maria Elena's shriek brought him back inside before he could close the door.

Both hands over her mouth, María Elena stared in frozen horror at Grandpa Grummond slumped back in the chair, eyes vacant and jaw gaping, the last spoonful of *caldo* dribbling down his chin.

***

The hospital lobby was empty except for the girl behind the desk. "Can I help you?"

"My father …"

"His name?"

"Grummond. The ambulance just …"

"He's in emergency?"

"Dr. Ben…"

"Of course. I'll page him." She fumbled with the switchboard and sent her plea echoing along the corridors. "Won't you have a seat?"

Jake couldn't get comfortable in any of the molded plastic chairs, tried the vinyl couch and finally elected to stand against one of the plate-glass windows flanking the front door. Fourth time here today, he thought. Fucking hospitals. Wish he'd taken the CPR course with Mary Margaret. He tried to suppress the memory of his vain attempts to breathe life into the gaping mouth that tasted of chili and cumin.

He started to pace, slowly at first, then with gradually increasing tempo, beginning laterally — window to door to window — then expanding to a rough oval that brought him ever nearer to the front desk, hands clenching every step of the way. The girl watched with growing anxiety and paged again, her voice cracking in a treble climbing toward hysteria.

Dr. Ben appeared at the far end of the hall as the last echo faded.

"There he is." Relief brought a smile to the girl's face, but she immediately realized this was no time for smiles and ducked her head like she was trying to disappear behind the counter.

346

Jake didn't notice. His belly tightened and his hands went numb as the doctor walked with slow, forced precision, every step the culmination of a lifetime's controlled will.

When he got within ten feet, Jake spoke. "Dead." A statement.

Dr. Ben nodded. "Dead on arrival." He removed a handkerchief from his pocket and began polishing his glasses with the same precision that had governed his stride. "Want something to help you sleep?"

Jake shook his head. "I guess," his voice starting to crack, " I guess I better make some phone calls."

It had snowed at the cemetery, a wet, heavy snow that melted as soon as it hit the ground and put a slick finish to the clay mounded by the new grave.

All of Top Hat, it seemed, had been there — and most of the rest of the county as well. And now they seemed to be in the farmhouse leaving streaks of adobe in their wake as they offered quiet murmurs of sympathy to Jake who was sitting in one of the wingback chairs near the bay windows that looked out on the front yard Mary Margaret and her mother-in-law before her had maintained with fierce pride. A candid photo of Grandpa Grummond in front of the milking barn, waving the lead pipe cane at some out-of-frame irritant, had been blown up and mounted and held the place of honor on the end table to his right.

Many of the crowd had spent the morning at the funeral for the deputies, performed with as much military flourish as the Sheriff's Department could muster, and they eddied with barely-controlled gluttony around the tables of food and drink which were continually being replenished by Mercedes Guerrero and Ellie Stanton under Helen's direction from her command post in the kitchen.

Blakenship had taken up position in the corner of the formal dining room and was wielding a toothpick to spear Swedish meatballs with an efficiency learned through years of political fundraisers and civic club meetings. Jessie nudged him less than gently in the ribs. "Slow down, honey. Save some for the others."

"Couldn't eat this morning and now I can't stop."

"Try." Jessie bit delicately into an onion-dipped carrot stick and patted her lips with a napkin. "Who's the military man?" She bobbed her head toward a trio around Jake. "One in the middle who walks like he's reviewing troops."

Two men he didn't recognize were talking, although Jake didn't look like he was paying close attention. Johnny Davis, the prick, was standing there like they were important because they were with him. As the three turned toward the buffet table, it came to him. Last fall. At the old Sheffield place. The thin one. The other had been — where? In Helen's with Frog Bottom.

The Sheffield place was off 58.50, three, maybe four miles from where the deputies had been shot. Been well after midnight, too. Still, maybe they'd heard something.

"I recommend the meatballs," he said as they picked up paper plates. "One of Ellie's specialties, they are." He stuck out his hand at the thin one. "C. W. Blakenship. We met at your place last November but I'll be damned if I can remember your name."

"Burns, Sheriff. Bill Burns. And this is Reg Porterfield."

Blakenship offered his hand to the paunchy man. "You were talking with Froggie in Helen's. Near the end of summer." He stepped back to reveal Jessie clad in a tailored black suit, black stockinged legs balanced on high heels — an ensemble she wore twice a year, if that. "Jessie Parsons, Colonel Burns — it is Colonel? And Mr. Porterfield. You know Johnny."

The men dutifully shook her hand although, Blakenship noted, not before a flicker of distaste passed across Porterfield's face — Jessie's hair, done up in a proper bun, emphasized the cheekbones that proudly proclaimed her Ute heritage.

"Didn't realize you knew Grandpa Grummond."

"Never met him," said Burns. "But we've had some dealings with the younger Mr. Grummond. That and their situation's been all the talk. Seemed like the neighborly thing to do."

"Had some trouble out your way this week. I imagine that's been talked about some, too."

"Heard about it, of course," Porterfield volunteered. "But I … we …," his eyes slid involuntarily toward Burns, "haven't got a clear idea of what happened. Beyond the killing of the deputies. Drugs, wasn't it?"

"Looks that way. I'd like to talk with you — all of you — about that night sometime. Might be you heard or saw something that'll help us out."

A ripple in the crowd caught Blakenship's eye, giving the men an opportunity to move to the other side of the table.

The cause proved to be the arrival of Blair Stewart.

Blakenship watched the congressman make his way through the throng, head with its gray hair slicked close to the skull bobbing in somber greeting, gold-rimmed glasses fixing each face with a glint of focused recognition. Once again he felt a twinge of jealous respect at Stewart's ability to work a room. "He's good," he whispered to Jessie only to find she'd moved to talk with Helen standing in the kitchen doorway.

Stewart clasped Jake's hand in both of his and spoke with quiet earnestness. Jake's face betrayed no emotion and he answered with what appeared to be monosyllables. The congressman released the hand with a barely discernible shrug and made his way to the buffet, shaking hands with polished solemnity en route. When he saw Blakenship, he veered his way.

"Nice of you to come, Blair. Jake ought to appreciate it."

"Jake doesn't seem to be appreciating very much today."

"Hard to lose someone that way. Especially when you remember what he was like last summer." He didn't have to say before the raid.

"Nothing quite as bleak as a farm gone under. At the moment he doesn't seem to be looking with great favor on anyone in public office. I'm a bit surprised that you're here, C. W."

"I've been staying on the fringes. But Jake hasn't had a high opinion of people in public office for quite some time. I wouldn't take it personal. Besides, I thought you was helping him out."

"There's only so much I can do. Express my concern over what happened to one of my constituents to select members of the administration and to the Department of Justice. Remind them — without threatening, of course — that I chair their oversight committee."

"And?"

"Now, now sheriff. You haven't survived for five terms without keeping up with what goes on in the county. You know his claim was denied. And look around," Stewart swept his arm in an arc that encompassed the stone-faced Jake, the subdued neighbors and the emptiness outside. "Those who live in agricultural country hate to see any operation go under. Ranch, dairy, hogs, potatoes, whatever. The demise of one reminds them all of how close to the edge they live. You're only one crop away from failure in the best of times. Isn't that the saying?"

He continued without waiting for Blakenship to respond. "Failure is bad enough, but this failure wasn't caused by weather or disease. Not by impersonal market forces or heartless corporations. Not even by bankers. The Grummond Dairy is no more because of the government. And by extension, Mary Margaret is," he groped for a word, "away … and the Grandpa Grummond of legend is dead because of the government. That's what Jake believes and that is what a growing number of my — of our — constituents believe. Nobody in this room is particularly happy with any representative of government."

"Don't see anyone throwing things your way."

"Oh, they're polite. But I detect an undertone of coolness I've never felt here before. I'm the congressman who couldn't put things right for one of his constituents. If I couldn't help Jake …"

Blakenship grinned. "And this is an even-numbered year."

"Precisely. You're in better shape — in terms of time. On the other hand, you were on the raid."

"I haven't heard any talk like that. Not about me — or you, either."

"This is the first time a significant contingent of people have seen the extent of the disaster. And all at the same time. First the funeral of a community fixture. Then the drive from the cemetery here. The empty houses. The empty pens. Inside, the house shows — to the female eye — the unmistakable signs of male neglect — a vivid reminder of what happened to the woman of the house. Those images will keep alive the knowledge of why." He stared into the distance of Jake's future. Or his own.

When it looked like Stewart had said all he was going to, Blakenship started to move away. "C. W." The congressman's voice caught him in mid-stride. "I think it is in both our interests to get to the bottom of the why of the raid. Particularly in light of recent developments."

"Why the raid on the dairy? Looks like bad information from someone with a grudge."

"Maybe. Perhaps we could meet later today and you could apprise me both of what you know and of what you surmise." His tone made it an order.

Blakenship surprised himself. "Tomorrow. I've had a tough day. A tough four days."

"I return to Washington tomorrow." With the antennae that had stood him in good stead for so many years, Stewart knew better than to insist. "Perhaps a telephone conversation? Say, Monday at three. Your time."

This time Blakenship's antennae told him to agree.

***

The ground of the cemetery had frozen during the night. Jake picked his way over the ruts carved by yesterday's vehicles, shivering from the radiational cooling that made the first hour of day's light colder than the pre-dawn.

Someone had raked the naked earth of the grave, leaving narrow parallel grooves in the grayish soil — it would be months before grass grew to match that covering his mother's. And Paul's. A simple vertical slat marked the site. It looked insubstantial next to the weathered marker and the marble solidity of the newer stone.

Paul Alfred Grummond
July 27, 1971 — May 7, 1992
Beloved son of Jacob and Mary Margaret Grummond
Taken before his time

Taken before his time. Not much to say for twenty-one years of hopes and dreams and hunting trips and …

Fuck it. Jake kicked a clod of frozen adobe hard enough to break it. He looked back at the raw wound of the new grave. What to put on the stone? Was Dad taken before his time?

He shivered again. From the temperature, he told himself. A thin sliver of sun shone hazy red on the shoulder of Mt. Sanders. He squatted to his haunches and focused on the wooden marker. Grummond was all it said.

Grummond. I'm the only one in the bloodline left.

***

A sedan turned from the Sheffield's driveway onto the 58.50 road about half a mile from Blakenship's leisurely approaching Bronco. Have to stop calling it that, thought the sheriff. Although I'll be damned if I know what it should be called. The Old Soldiers Home?

The sedan had accelerated to a more-than-legally-sanctioned rate of speed by the time it passed Blakenship, although not so fast the sheriff's practiced eye wasn't able to recognize the government plates and what looked to be Buchanan hunched over the steering wheel.

Sonofabitch.

Blakenship's foot pressed to the floor, then eased back. Half a minute's not going to make any difference. It was my men were shot. And murder's still my jurisdiction, not his.

Blakenship made a looping turn onto the driveway, his right front wheel hitting a puddle as he did so, sending a muddy splash across the windshield that left him cursing and fumbling to activate the windshield washer. It took three pulls on the wiper lever to rid the glass of brown streaks that refracted the mid-afternoon sunlight. There were puddles gleaming all the way to the old house, it looked like. He drove slowly.

Tire tracks had churned the ground in front of the house to mire. Blakenship pulled up next to a blue Suburban that looked familiar. He got out, stretched, and looked around. A tire-rutted road led beyond the barn to another house a short half-mile away. The Colonel's, he remembered from his November visit. A big silver pickup with dual rear wheels and a camper top was making careful progress toward the house.

"First the DEA, then the sheriff. I didn't realize law enforcement was so busy on Sundays."

Blakenship turned toward the sound of the voice. That one's Porterfield, he remembered, taking the measure of the man standing in the open door. "Was that Buchanan I saw leaving?"

"Yes. I think so." Porterfield fumbled in his shirt pocket, withdrawing a business card. "Buchanan."

"What did he want?"

"You don't know?"

"If I knew, I wouldn't be asking."

"Don't you guys talk to each other?"

"Most of the time." Goddamn Buchanan. Have to talk to Kiernan. "Have anything to do with the raid?"

"Of course. Asked if we'd seen or heard anything. We didn't, sorry to say. It was in the middle of the night, after all."

"I guess that goes for the shooting of my men, too."

Porterfield shrugged. "If we could help at all, it would have been the sound of gun fire. But ... what? Two-and-a-half, three miles ..."

"More like one, as the crow flies."

"Whatever. We were asleep and didn't hear or see anything."

Blakenship thoughtfully poked the toe of one boot at a lump of damp earth. "Nice truck." He jerked his head toward the distant house. "The dually. The Colonel's?"

"Uh huh. He's real happy with it. Just got it. Got a good deal from a friend in LA."

"Buchanan talk to him?"

Porterfield nodded. "We were all having Sunday dinner together. We'd just finished when he got here. He's a pushy one, that Buchanan. Asked each of us the same questions. Still," Porterfield sighed, "I guess that's what investigation takes. Even had us show him around — basement, barn, the Colonel's."

"That all?"

"Oh, we shot the shit about Vietnam, too. Seems he was in country when some of us were. Or so he says."

Blakenship looked up toward the distant house where sunlight bounced off the new pickup parked by the porch. "Don't suppose Burns'd have anything to add," he mumbled, half to himself. He opened the door of the Bronco and climbed behind the wheel. "By the way, how many of you were here the night of the raid? Wednesday," he added helpfully.

"Like we told Buchanan. Six. Same as now. Four here. Colonel Burns and Petersen in the other house."

Blakenship started to back up, stopped and stuck his head out the window. "Burns go to LA for that truck?"

"Uh huh."

"And he got back when?"

"Tuesday or Wednesday, I'm not sure which."

***

"When should I tell her?" The late afternoon sun slanted across the blanket just below Mary Margaret's chin. Jake turned from the enigmatic smile that lately seemed always to be lifting the corners of her mouth when she slept to fix Bridget Taylor with a questioning look. "Or should I tell her at all?"

"That's not clear." She moved to the side of the bed and absently patted Mary Margaret's exposed right hand while she studied the relaxed face, a clean and neatly taped bandage on her right cheek the only visible sign of Wednesday's accident. "You're right. She is losing weight. Maybe we'll weigh her tomorrow." Her perfume floated to Jake with subtle warmth, causing a stir in his loins that flushed his face with guilt. "I'm sorry. I don't mean to be evasive. It's just ..." she fell silent. When she resumed speaking it was almost as though Jake wasn't there. "Another loss could ... relapse. If she understands. But doing well ... surprisingly well after ..." She looked sideways at Jake. "Tell me what happened before she fell asleep."

"I called to her from the door."

355

"What did you say?"

"Mary Margaret. It's me. Jake. Something like that."

"And?"

"She smiled. I kissed her."

"She knew who you were?"

"Absolutely. She said, 'Missed you.' I think that was it. I haven't been in since Thursday morning."

"What was your answer?"

"Said I'd been busy."

"Then?"

"She nodded. That's what I thought, anyway.   We held hands and I talked about this and that."

"Did she say any thing more?"

"Nope. We held hands. I rambled. Then she fell asleep."

Bridget thought for a bit, gave Mary Margaret's hand a squeeze and turned toward the door. "Let's see what tomorrow brings."

***

Jessie was snuggled up against one arm of the couch watching a movie on TV when he got home — something in black and white with Bette Davis. "Learn anything?" She raised her face for a kiss.

"Not a goddamn thing." Blakenship shrugged out of his jacket, hung it on the back of a chair, following it with his hat and gunbelt. "Except that that Buchanan bastard had been out there, too. Without telling me." He sat down next to her. "Man, I'm tired. Don't know why. But I've got no energy."

"Here." Jessie sat up and patted her thighs. "Lie down."

He swung his feet to the top of the couch's other arm and rested his head her lap, pleasantly aware of the breast pressing against his cheek when she bent to kiss the bridge of his nose. "We've canvassed every house on the 58.50 road within five miles of the shooting and the answer's always the same. We didn't hear nothing. We didn't see nothing. Johnny Davis didn't hear nothing — but what else is new." He burrowed his head

356

more comfortably against Jessie's stomach. "Doesn't prove Ruiz didn't have accomplices near by, like you said. But it's looking more and more like he did it."

Jessie fiddled with a lock of his hair dangling across his forehead. "But didn't you say it looked like they'd been shot from the road?"

A gentle snore told her she wasn't going to get an answer.

***

Monday morning dawned clear with the temperature hovering near freezing, a bow to the fact it was still technically winter but a promise of high forties, maybe even low fifties by afternoon.

Jake rummaged through the foil-topped dishes in the refrigerator — leftovers from Saturday — trying to find something that appealed to him for breakfast. Eggs? Too much trouble. Toast? With butter and jelly? Maybe. Later. He closed the refrigerator door and poured another cup of coffee.

The clock read 7:12 — most of two hours before Mackey Fitz would be in his office. See Mary Margaret? After Fitz.

He walked to the desk in the living room and collected the material Stewart's aide… What was his name? Eastman. That was it. …had sent him. He stacked them on the kitchen table, set his cup within easy reach and begun going through them in measured order. Then he read and reread the lists Blakenship had made and the addresses he had collected.

When he was finished, he restacked the folders and opened the top one and stared at Buchanan's face, smugly rigid in the official photograph, while the fingers of his right hand drummed a repetitive tattoo on the Formica.

***

"Line two, Sheriff."

"Better be Kiernan returning my call," he said to Henderson. "Kiernan, you've got to … Oh, hello Blair." He pushed back his shirtsleeve and squinted at his watch. "Didn't realize it was three already… Might as well. Seems like Felipe

357

and his brother Abel and who knows who else have been a stop on a drug pipeline from Mexico for some time. When Buchanan started squeezing the Sanchez brothers, it looks like Abel gave them Jake's place on account of how Jake beat the crap out of him a few years back… Say what? … No. Abel was working for him. Jake, that is… I'm not sure, but I think it was because Abel had got into it with Eusebio some way … Yeah. No sign of Felipe or Abel… We're working on it… Godammit, Blair, I lost four men. I'm doing the best I can .. and that goddamn Buchanan is still here putting his dick into … You do that."

Blakenship slammed the receiver down so hard it bounced on to the desktop and over the edge.

"It's not nice to yell at our elected officials, C. W."

"Piss on him."

"Line one this time," Luther yelled while he was reeling the receiver in by its cord. "I think it's that DEA guy."

"Kiernan?"

"That's the one."

"Listen Kiernan … all right, Tom. Listen, Tom, you've got to rein in that Buchanan. He's poking around in a murder investigation. Quadruple, at that… I know it's a drug investigation, too, but I can't have … A for instance? Like yesterday afternoon, he was leaving the Old Soldiers Home off the 58.50 road just as I was getting there… Are they suspects? No. But what if they were? I mean he'd have warned them … I know this is part of an ongoing case … I know he's been on it for a long time. Boy, do I know that."

Blakenship shifted the receiver to his other ear, glanced briefly at Henderson, then spun his chair 180 degrees and stared out the window. "I hope so," he said at last, then spun back to face the senior deputy and hung up the phone.

"Well?"

"He says he'll talk to Buchanan. Explain that he'd best let us know what he's doing before he does it. And he's calling him back to Denver in a day or two to review everything."

"Think it'll help?"

"Who knows?"

"Buchanan to the contrary notwithstanding, we still got four murders, not to mention drug trafficking which is against both state and federal law."

"Thanks for pointing that out, Charlie." Blakenship stood up and began pacing in front of the windows. "We got no more clue of who shot Duane and all than we did the night it happened. As far as drugs go, all we know is that Felipe and Abel are involved and were tied into the Sanchezes somehow. I can't believe Felipe didn't have some help in the county. Especially in light of the fact it still looks like whoever got our men did it from the road." He stopped with his hands on the chair back. "Where do we start? You tell me, Charlie?"

"Maybe when the state lab reports on the slugs and brass it'll point us someway or another."

"Maybe. But it seems like we ought to talk to Mrs. Ruiz. Shit, even if she wasn't involved, she must have seen a fair amount. Felipe's been doing it for years, for crissake."

"If that's the way you're thinking, what about trying to find some of the local clientele?'

Blakenship sat down. "Doubt they'd know much."

"They'd know who they bought from."

"True enough. You tend to that, why don't you."

"And you?"

"Me? I'm going to visit with the missus."

***

Mackey Fitz hadn't done much to clarify things. It was hard to tell whether the raid on real drug dealers would help or not. On the one hand, it could strengthen the case that the DEA had acted precipitously. On the other, it made it clear that drugs were coming through the county, that the informants were actually party to said activity, thereby making it reasonable for the authorities to act on their statements.

"So what do we do?"

"Irrespective of the propriety of the raid on your place, we still have the destruction of your property, the unwarranted removal of your employees at a critical time in the functioning of the dairy, and the indefensible physical assault on two women, one of whom was very much pregnant at the time and subsequently suffered a miscarriage."

"Meaning?"

"Meaning, keep on with finding out who instigated the same." Mackey Fitz had studied Jake over the top of his coffee cup as he spoke. Eyes somewhat bloodshot. Creases around mouth deeper. "No particular hurry. Look, Jake. We're in a marathon here. Take some time to get yourself together. Sleep. Watch TV. Whatever."

Jake sat at the kitchen table doodling in the margin of his list of Otero County deputies. Watch TV? The only thing he watched was football and the season was long over. And he hadn't managed more than two hours sleep at a stretch since the accident.

He looked at his list. Fitz was right about one thing — he wasn't ready to talk to any of those assholes. He got up and walked into the living room. Helen, Ellie and Mercedes had done a faultless job of cleaning, but they'd left things slightly out of kilter. The disruption of time-honored placements made Jake feel as though he'd stumbled into the wrong house and he walked from room to room, moving furniture a foot here, as inch there.

TV? He turned it on but the smooth overfed faces of self-satisfied experts discussing the life and death importance of Washington nuance turned his stomach. He walked to the porch. Be dark soon, but above freezing. Maybe in the forties.

Mary Margaret? Tomorrow? No. Better go today. Right now.

***

Blakenship eyed the neon Coors sign in Helen's window and decided against stopping, even though it was pushing five o'clock. He'd spent the past hour in a largely fruitless conversation with Felipe Ruiz's wife — a litany of denials

360

expressed while she made a half-hearted effort to put into some sort of order the mess left after the DEA's post-raid search of her home. "*Mira,*" she'd exclaimed, pointing to a stream of ants foraging through a mixture of laundry detergent and sugar, cornmeal and flour and Cheerios banked against the bottom of the stove like sand dunes on a windswept shore. "What kind of people do things like this?"

Blakenship held his tongue. He'd said — ordered — no destruction and as far as he knew there'd been none on Wednesday night. Must have happened later and by God that prick Buchanan was going to hear about it. Kiernan, too. "There was nobody else here?"

"How many times must I tell you? I was upstairs, in bed. So were the children — who now must sleep in the same beds with their cousins, thanks to you. Then the lights and the shooting. Felipe was downstairs. Alone, I think. But *quien sabe?*"

No matter how he'd asked the questions — Who was there? When did the drugs arrive? Who brought them? Who were frequent visitors? — The answers were the same. I don't know. The house and the children, they were my *responsabilidad.* I know nothing of the garage. Nothing of drugs.

Maybe it was true. And if it wasn't, he couldn't really blame her. Blakenship sighed from some hitherto unplumbed depths of his being as he made the turn onto the highway. But none of that was moving him any closer to the whys and wherefores and whos of either the drugs or the murders.

What had ever possessed him to go into law enforcement?

None of that. You've got a job to do. He fiddled with the cellophane of a cigar. Maybe Charlie's come up with something. Maybe Kiernan has.

Kiernan. And Buchanan. Got to reassert some authority — and find out what they know at the same time.

He sighed again. Maybe Jessie can get off work early.

26

MARCH 10 — Evening

Seeing Mary Margaret had been vaguely unsettling. Not that she was worse. Not at all. She'd recognized him and turned her face up for the kiss that was fast becoming a ritual. But the feeling that she should be told about Grandpa Grummond's death gnawed at him. She'd have to know sometime, wouldn't she? Not telling her felt like he was hiding something. Or did he feel that way because he wanted her back — and he'd never before not told her the bad with the good?

He'd called Bridget Taylor, half-resolved to insist that she be told, but as soon as she heard his voice, the psychologist launched into an account about Mary Margaret's physical condition — good, surprisingly good, considering. "And she weighed 180."

"Christ. She never weighed an ounce over 125."

"Maybe so. But I bet she's down 20 pounds since I first saw her."

"Why?"

There was a pause at the other end of the line. "I don't know. But it's got to be a good sign. In any event, now we have a benchmark. Maybe we can talk tomorrow." And with a click, she was gone.

He banged the receiver into its cradle harder than he'd meant to, sighed and rubbed his temples. A nap. Maybe that would help.

He lay down on the couch but the thought of probate jerked him upright.

Dammit. Why hadn't Mackey Fitz said anything? Where the hell was Dad's will? He did have a will, didn't he? He opened the bottom desk drawer, the one with the hanging files he avoided as much as possible, and felt his energy ebb.

He returned to the couch, but thoughts of probate got him pondering what to do about the equipment. And the trailer houses. Could sell them to those Californians. If it's not too late.

What about the land? Hate to see the Grummond fields, built up over three generations, being turned into tract housing. Once land grows houses, it'll never again be good for crops.

Maybe a dairyman?

Hadn't thought about selling land before.

But with Mary Margaret getting better — and she was, she was — and Eusebio? And Jesus? How much would it cost to build up a big enough herd?

***

"About the only good thing that's come of this is there ain't any drugs coming into Sapinero County — not at the moment, anyway." Jessie had gotten off at nine and Blakenship had once again lain on the couch with his head in her lap while he recounted the day's frustrations. "We know Rob and them were killed by an automatic weapon — or two — but we won't know what kind or how many until we get the report from the state lab, which could take a week or more." Blakenship looked up at her. "You got a cute chin, you know that?"

"If you think so, that's fine with me. You still think they were killed from the road?"

"Yeah. But that doesn't help. Shit, Felipe and whoever could have made it across the field to a vehicle they had stashed and been driving north on 58.50 when they ran into our boys."

Have you found any place where they could have hidden a car?"

"Nope. Not definite anyway. But …" The phone rang and he lifted his head so Jessie could get up.

"For you."

"Who is it?"

"Henderson."

Blakenship labored to his feet. "This better be good, Charlie."

"Good it ain't. Minnie Fletcher's boy's in the hospital. Overdose."

"Where are you?"

363

"At the emergency room."

"I'll be right there."

"Shit, C. W. I just questioned him this afternoon and ..."

"He tell you anything?"

"Nothing solid."

"Maybe now he will. If he makes it."

***

Henderson was pacing the sidewalk in front of the emergency room entrance, trying to light a cigarette from the butt of the previous one when Blakenship pulled up.

"What's the word?"

"Don't know. Dr. Ben's still working on him."

"He didn't tell you anything this afternoon?"

"Said he got the dope from a friend and he didn't want to get him in trouble. I didn't want to lean on him too hard. Not with his mother right there. Figured I could always come back."

"Speaking of, where's the mother?"

"Minnie's inside. In tears — when she isn't yelling at me about harassment and police brutality."

"Who found him?"

"She did. In the bathroom. C. W., I'm no expert ..."

"Me neither. You talk to that Munoz kid — Gabriel, ain't it?"

"He didn't have much to say, either. Seems he's lost his enthusiasm for law enforcement with Felipe Ruiz on the loose."

"C. W. Charlie." Dr. Ben beckoned from the entrance.

"When can we talk with him?" Blakenship asked.

"I lost him."

The three men eyed each other in silence while Minnie Fletcher's voice climbed the register to a piercing scream behind them.

"Something else, C. W." Dr. Ben looked into the darkness of the parking lot. "I think it was heroin. Have to run some tests to be sure, but that's what it looks like." He disappeared through the door toward the inconsolable mother who'd never been sure what was the right thing to do.

"That's what I was trying to tell you." Henderson lit another cigarette. "He had a needle and a spoon and a surgical tube wrapped around his left arm."

"Heroin." Blakenship rolled the word around on his tongue. "We just found marijuana and cocaine at Ruiz's."

"What it looked like. Of course the fucking DEA hasn't told us what their lab boys say it was."

"They will tomorrow, Charlie."

***

"Not that you know of?" Blakenship made no attempt to veil the sarcasm in his voice. "Aren't you the head of that office? Don't they tell you lab results?" He listened for as long as he could stand. "Look, I've got a dead high-school senior here, dead from what Dr. Ben thinks is an overdose of heroin. If there wasn't any heroin in what you took from the Ruiz place, then someone else is selling drugs in Sapinero County." He listened again. "I'd appreciate it. And by the way, when're you going to talk to Buchanan? ... You have? He's leaving today?" He smiled. "Best news I've heard ... shit. Oh well, three days are better than nothing."

The sheriff carefully replaced the receiver and walked to the office door. "Charlie," he yelled and returned to his seat.

"When're you going to learn how to use the intercom?" Henderson smiled over the top of his coffee cup.

"Tried and true ways are best. Look, I just talked with Kiernan. He doesn't know whether Ruiz had any heroin. If he did, it would be something new added to.. What did he call it? ... to the product line."

"What's he mean he doesn't know? Their lab's had plenty of time."

"Says this ain't the only case they're working on. But he's going to check and send us a copy of the report."

"In the meantime?"

"In the meantime, I'm going to have a talk with Mr. Munoz."

"Like I said last night, he's not real communicative any more."

"Maybe not. But since I was the one who talked with him before, he'll have a hard time going dumb on me."

***

He wasn't sure what made him stop by the metal garage. Restless in the house, he'd driven out the Pea Green road with the half-formed intention of dropping in on the Californians to see if they were still interested in the house trailers and when he got to the hard turn, the pickup, almost of its own accord, had gone straight and rolled to a stop in the yard between the garage and the house.

Jake sat behind the steering wheel for a long five minutes examining the two-story Victorian structure that had marked the S-turn on the way to Pea Green ever since he could remember. Van Shelton. That was the name of the man who'd built it and Van Sheltons had lived in there up until the time Felipe Ruiz had acquired it. When was that? He couldn't remember — been ten years, at least. Probably longer.

From where he stood, the only sign that something unusual had happened was the plywood covering the window to the right of the front door. That and the fact it was empty.

He walked up the steps and tried the door. Locked — and the curtains were drawn on the two unharmed windows that faced the porch.

The back door was also locked and the windows on either side of it boarded up. Before he turned the corner of the house on the way back to his truck, the soft purr of a well-tuned engine and the crunch of tires on gravel warned him that someone was here. A cared-for 1982 Ford 250 was parked by his Dodge and two *mexicano* men of indeterminate middle age waited between the vehicles, their postures stiff with wary tension. A somewhat younger woman, dark hair swept into a bun above worried eyes and plump cheeks, sat in the middle of the Ford's front seat.

"Didn't mean to intrude." Jake's walk was deliberately casual. "Was passing by and thought I'd take a look. Just an impulse."

"You are not with the law?" The taller of the two men took a step forward.

"No …"

"You are Mr. Grummond. Of the dairy." This from the woman who had climbed from the pickup.

"Yes. Mrs. ____?"

"Ruiz. This is my house. Although after what they did …" Her words trailed off as anger whitened a mesh of lines around her mouth.

"I know something about what they do."

She looked at Jake for a long time. "Yes," she sighed. "Why are you here?"

"Like I said, an impulse. I was headed Pea Green way and just stopped." He pulled the Copenhagen from his pocket, took a pinch and offered the tin to the two men. They both refused. "I guess if there's a reason, I wanted to see if they treated you the same as they did me."

"Come, if you want to see. I'm getting more clothes for the children. My brothers," she nodded toward the two men, "they are going to measure the windows." She led the way up the steps and inserted a key in the lock. "Perhaps by the weekend, perhaps next week we can return. But there is still work to do." She opened the door. "Come. "

It was too clean inside, a recent scrubbing and straightening unleavened by the comfortable sprawl and smells of human habitation. Even so, the signs of turmoil were clear — the windows, of course, but also a broken desk drawer, the pieces stacked neatly for repair; slashed sofa cushions piled in a corner; a odorless kitchen cupboard naked between its neighbors.

Upstairs, clothes — hanging in closets with splintered jambs where doors had been ripped from hinges — or folded on beds waiting for bureaus to be fixed or purchased. Holes punched in the walls of two bedrooms and the hall.

"You should have seen it before." Mrs. Ruiz picked through the clothes, placing the chosen in a plastic garbage sack. "Mouthwash spilled. Toothpaste squeezed out." She stood up, hands on hips. "And the kitchen. Food on the floor. Milk, sugar, even the eggs. I ask you, what can be hidden in an egg?"

Jack felt the acid burn in the back of his throat and fought the urge to retch. "Blakenship's men do this?"

"The sheriff? No. It was the others. After the …" she groped for the word, "… the trouble in the night."

"DEA?"

"Yes. The one with the funny hair …"

"Buchanan."

"If you say. I had come for things we didn't have time to take with us that night and I saw. I was so mad. I tried to stop them. Luis, my brother, he stopped me before … But that one with the hair, he was the leader. He smiled at me — an evil smile — and said I was lucky they didn't take my house." She looked directly into Jake's eyes. "How can they do that?"

"I'm not a lawyer, but I think they can claim it was bought with money earned illegally."

"That is not true." She returned to her packing. "We worked so hard to get the money for the down payment …" She put a small pair of jeans in the sack and twisted a wire fastener around the top. "If you have nothing more …"

"I'm leaving. Thank you."

Jake started his pickup and stared at the house without moving. The two brothers were on the porch where they had removed the plywood and were measuring the window, but they barely registered in his vision over the remembrance of Buchanan's narrow face shouting orders and the crack and smash of breaking possessions punctuating the cries of the children.

A tapping by his left ear. "There is something you wish?" One of the brothers peered at him.

He shook his head and rolled down the window. "Just thinking." He put the truck in gear and backed in a sharp turn, glancing back at the house and the man in the yard before shifting to drive and pulling forward to the paved road.

***

Blakenship was frustrated. An hour and a half with Gabriel Munoz had produced nothing. He'd tried the "we're in law enforcement together approach," he'd tried veiled threats and he'd finished in a towering rage, veins bulging in his neck, and still Munoz refused to budge — he knew nothing more about the Ruizes than what he'd already told him and, above all, he knew nothing about heroin.

He'd gone to the Fletcher house with the thin hope that Minnie might have something to add — who the boy's friends were, if he'd started hanging with someone new, if he'd been acting differently in anyway — but the sight of his face when she answered the door had touched off an hysterical fit that left her prostrate in the hall and him standing hat in hand at the threshold staring into the eyes of hostile relatives.

He closed the door to his office with exaggerated care, hung his jacket and hat on the coat rack, unholstered his revolver — there was a sore spot on his hipbone, the product of an unremembered bump — and was about to put it in the middle of the desk when he saw two official-looking faxes centered on the blotter.

The top one was from Kiernan saying that no heroin had been found at the Ruiz garage.

Beautiful. Just fucking beautiful. How many dope dealers did he have in the county, anyway?

The second was written in the equivocal prose of a state bureaucrat covering his ass, the gist of which being that indications pointed to two AK-47s as the weapons that had caused the untimely demise of the four deputies — one suspended, he automatically corrected — on the 58.50 road.

He sat down, removed the cellophane from a cigar and chewed the sweet tobacco while he re-read them.

AK-47s. Not your local gun-shop merchandise. But the way the gun trade was nowadays, that didn't mean anything.

He started to dial Henderson's home number, glanced at the straight up-and-down hands of the clock and changed his mind. Not like there was anything they could do tonight. And he needed a drink.

Boy, did he need a drink.

***

He pushed his way through a bigger than usual Tuesday night crowd at the Stockman, relieved to see that his regular booth was unoccupied. Jessie smiled at him as she carried a full drink tray to the big table in the back and mouthed "The usual?"

"Double," he shouted over the din.

Jessie got to his table with two shot glasses and a bottle of Bud before he got edgy enough to go to the bar himself. "Sorry." She kissed him on the forehead. "Don't know why it's so busy tonight. But the tips are good. Brought you two shots so it'd be easier to keep score."

"Thanks." Blakenship tossed one shot back in a smooth motion and followed it with a large swallow of beer. "Not been a real good day."

"Heard you caused quite a ruckus at the Fletcher household."

"Didn't mean to. I just ..."

"Jessie. Order up." The harried bartender repeated — "Jessie."

"Got to go. But I got an idea."

Blakenship watched her weave with another full tray through the crowd, marveling as he always did at the manifest unity of her mind and body. If he'd had coordination like that he'd have been an all-pro linebacker and now living a life of retired ease.

He picked up the second shot glass and sipped thoughtfully. An idea, she'd said.

370

The shot glass stood empty by a half-finished bottle of beer by the time Jessie got back. "So?"

""'So? Oh. You mean my idea." Jessie nudged him closer to the wall with her hip and slid in beside him. "I can't stay long. But I was thinking, since you're not getting anywhere talking with Minnie, maybe you'd let me try."

"You?"

"Sure. I've known her a long time. And besides, I'm a woman."

"No doubt about that." Blakenship swallowed the last mouthful of beer. "But ... Ah shit. Give it a try. You can't do any worse than me." He rolled the empty bottle between his hands. "What I need is ...."

"Who the boy hung out with. New friends. Anything that can give you a lead on where he got the heroin."

"Haven't confused you a bit, have I."

***

Jake coasted into the pullover at the top of Morris Pass and killed the engine. In the long, narrow valley below, sunlight bounced from the silvery metal roofs installed before the Town of Elwood passed an ordinance prescribing that such roofs be of muted, non-reflective colors.

It had been more than two weeks since the funeral, most of it spent tracing a triangular rut between the farmhouse, Mary Margaret, and Helen's where they counted words spoken and pounds lost with wary optimism. Burns and Porterfield had come over one day, inspected the trailers without making an offer — which was fine by Jake. But aside from that, his inactivity had been broken only by one non-productive visit to Mackey Fitz's office.

He needed to do something and trying to interview Elwood deputies had the virtue of being connected to the root cause of his problems.

He unfolded the list with the addresses and tried to place them on the map in the middle of the telephone book he'd brought along. Donaldson — no point trying there. Baker, Richard A., looked to be in the middle of town. Jones, Adam, must be in some outlying part of the county. Andrews, Kenneth R., — there, in a little cluster of streets on the edge of town.

Which edge?

He squinted to the houses below, most following the orderly checkerboard of the streets, dark lines against a background of dirty white interspersed with large irregular patches of brown — it had been unseasonably warm of late, so warm there was even talk in Sapinero County of opening the irrigation ditches by the end of the month.

There. The nearest cluster. On the other side of the river.

He found a parking space across from the sheriff's office. Good form to check in with the authorities, Mackey had said. Jake didn't care much about form, good or otherwise, but, what the hell. Wouldn't hurt anything.

"He's in a meeting, but perhaps I can help you. Mr.… Grummond, isn't it?" The startling blue eyes showed no hint of wariness or hostility. "Weren't you here last month?"

"That's right. I wonder if you could tell me where I can find …" he checked the paper in his hand, "Baker, Jones and Andrews?"

"Is this what you talked with Sheriff Mikeska about?"

"Uh huh. I'd like to talk to them."

Elvira turned to her desk, picked up a clipboard and ran her finger down the column. "Kenny, that's Andrews, is on day-shift until the end of the month. Jones is on vacation until Sunday. And Dick, that's Baker, comes on at four. You could try his house. It's only about four blocks from here. On Cascade. Do you want …."

"I've got the address."

Cascade was a street of tall shade trees and solid homes. Jake parked before a two-story brick house with white shutters and a broad porch that wrapped around both sides, avoided muddying his boots by stepping from the pickup across the verge to the sidewalk, negotiated a widening puddle, and made his way to the porch.

The door was opened before he could ring the bell by a man in his late twenties or early thirties, dressed in a uniform pants, and a T-shirt, a scrap of toilet paper or Kleenex dotted with blood stuck to his chin.

"Yes?"

"Richard Baker?"

"Yes."

"I was hoping you could answer a few questions."

"I don't know. I go on duty at …"

"Four. It's only eleven."

"So it is. Come in, Mr. _____ ?"

"Grummond. Jake Grummond."

Earnest eyes stared in surprise. "Grummond. From Top Hat?"

Jake nodded. "I'm just trying to get a handle on what happened that night, and Sheriff Mikeska said you were there."

"Mikeska knows you're here?"

Jake didn't answer.

"Come in." Baker led the way to the kitchen and sat down in front of a half-eaten bowl of cornflakes. "I don't know that I can help you that much." He pushed the bowl to the side and rubbed his eyes. "I can't say I was proud of what we did. It's made me question if I should stay in law enforcement."

"It's been better'n six months."

"Yes. Well, jobs aren't that easy to come by in Otero County. And my wife doesn't want to leave." He looked at Jake then shifted his gaze. "She teaches school — fifth grade — and she's pregnant with our first." He made a sweeping gesture with his right arm. "Besides, we're both born and raised here. My grandfather built this house …"

Jake gave him time to go on but Baker merely fiddled with the spoon in the cereal bowl. "Mikeska says you and deputies Jones and Andrews were on the raid."

"Along with Donaldson and Buck Parker. He's the senior deputy."

"Let me get to the point. Were you involved in the searches?"

Baker shook is head, "I was guarding the people. When I saw Donaldson .. ." He raised his head. "Mr. Grummond, I don't blame you for what you did. Not a bit. And I heard that you lost the dairy …" The look on Jake's face brought him to a stammering halt. "I'm sorry."

"Who was in on the searches?"

"From here?" Jake nodded. "Andrews, for sure. Not Parker. Not Donaldson — you know where he was. I can't remember about Adams."

"How'd it work?"

"That fed with the funny hair .."

"Buchanan."

"Yeah. He got the DEA guys and the deputies together and gave them instructions — it was more like a pep talk. He wanted a thorough job. 'Do it right,' he kept saying. 'Make sure these greasers know you've been there when you're done.'"

Jake leaned back in his chair and studied the deputy's solemn face.

"What we did to their homes, to the children, to them … It's been bothering me ever since." He raised his arms helplessly. "But I can't just quit."

"Would you be willing to give a statement to my lawyer? Under oath? That Buchanan ordered it?"

"I don't know if I could swear that he ordered it."

"How about repeating what you just told me?"

"Yes. Maybe. I don't know. I'll have to think about it."

Jake looked at him long and hard. "Della lost her child. I've lost my dairy. My wife's been in the hospital" he tapped the side of his head with his finger, "since the raid. And I buried my father two weeks ago. While you're thinking, think about that."

***

"I've learned a lot more about Minnie and her family, but nothing specific that could help you. Yet." Jessie hit the power button on the remote to turn off the TV, and snuggled her cheek against Blakenship's chest.

374

"Jesus, darling. It's been — what — three weeks."

"More like two. Remember, she's been upset — in shock, really. And she is my boss."

Blakenship shrugged. "Nobody else is getting anywhere. No reason why you should be different."

"I didn't say I wasn't getting anywhere. For instance, did you know that Jack — Minnie's husband — spent a lot of time at the VA hospital in Union? Came back from Vietnam with a lot of problems — mental problems."

"What they call post-Vietnam stress syndrome?"

"I guess. You do remember he committed suicide when Lonnie was two?"

Blakenship stared at the dead TV screen. "Yeah. I was at the scene. Dressed in camouflage fatigues, face painted they way they do …" He shook his head. "Sixteen, seventeen years ago."

"Yeah." Jessie raised to a sitting position and turned to face Blakenship, tucking her legs crosswise in a position that gave Blakenship the twinges of cramps in his own legs just looking at it. "But did you know Lonnie was obsessed with the Vietnam War? Read everything about it he could find. Saw every movie — you ought to see his video collection, never mind his library."

"What's your point?"

"The point is, a lot of our soldiers got into drugs over there."

"You think he got into drugs because that's what they did?"

"It's certainly possible."

Blakenship pulled Jessie back to the comfort of his shoulder. "Heroin was popular among the GIs, as I recall." He kissed the top of her head. "It's certainly possible. But I don't see that gets us any closer to where he got it."

"I'm working on it."

27

March 31 — Early Afternoon

Wednesday — the week after Deputy Baker's expressions of sympathy, disillusionment, and ambivalent willingness to be deposed — and Jake was driving him back to Elwood.

The wife had use of their personal car and he couldn't drive the department's vehicle out of the county on private business. That left either deposing him in Elwood or Jake's picking him up and bringing him to Mountain View. All parties involved thought Mountain View the preferred site, so Jake had arisen at milking time to pick Baker up. Early enough so the deputy'd be back in time for his four o'clock shift.

As near as Jake could tell, the deposition had gone well. Mackey Fitz seemed pleased, at any rate, although Jake hadn't had time to talk with him because of the deputy's schedule. Now they were climbing above the smoke from the irrigation ditches being cleansed by fire in preparation for the water set to flow at the end of the week, Baker leaning back with eyes closed in introspective thought.

Or maybe he was tired.

Jake started to ask him how to get to Adam Jone's place then remembered the county map Mackey had given him. No point in bothering Baker — or advertising what he was doing.

It lacked ten minutes to straight-up two when he dropped the deputy at his house. Jake turned the corner and pulled parallel to the curb, motor running, to match Jones' address to the map. He located the road, it looked to be two miles north of a little community labeled Baird's Settlement in the east-central portion of the county. The road itself couldn't be more than two or three miles long, ending at a lake that didn't have a name Jake could find.

The address proved to be on a dirt road marked by a bank of mailboxes at the T-intersection with the pavement, but finding the Jones place was another matter. He drove through mud puddles that turned to fast melting snow when the road started to switchback through stands of conifers that he judged marked the final climb to the lake. No hint which was the Jones place.

He turned around and thought about asking, but was loathe to leave a memory of purpose. The clock on the truck's radio said three. Time enough to locate Andrews' home and be back to see Mary Margaret.

It took longer than he thought — weaving through streets lined by small frame houses, single and double-wides and trailers of vintages that covered the full post-war spectrum before he found it at the far end of the cluster that could hardly be called a subdivision.

It was a small Airstream, aluminum dimmed by four decades of exposure, perched on cinder blocks amid a haphazard tangle of overflowing trashcans and rusting car parts. Incongruous amid the litter were a clean ATV and a neatly covered snowmobile mounted at the ready on a two-machine trailer.

There was no sign of life. Assuming he lived alone, and the premises had an air of perfunctory living unrelieved by a child's happy disorder or the decorative touch of a woman's hand, then there was no reason that there would be. Andrews, Jake remembered, worked the day shift.

The trailer was smaller and older than any his people had occupied. Was that the root of his viciousness?

A short half-mile up the grade to Morris Pass, the flashing lights of an Otero County Sheriff's Cherokee told him to pull over. He'd been within the speed limit and there was no other reason he could think of for the stop. A man of medium height wearing sunglasses that removed any hint of expression from a clean-shaven face approached. He looked to be in his thirties, although it was hard to tell. Jake rolled down the window when the deputy was five feet away and started to ask what was the matter.

But the deputy spoke first. "Understand you want to ask me some questions. There's an old logging road to the right just a little ways ahead. Pull in there and we'll talk."

Jake looked him up and down. The nametag said Andrews. "Why not talk here?"

"Look. Way I see it, I'm doing you a favor, so it's either my way or fuck you."

Jake put the truck in gear and started to edge forward.

"Pull in far enough so I can't be seen from the road," the deputy yelled.

Jake couldn't tell how long it had been since logging trucks had used it, but the road showed signs of recent travel. Why? Not hunting season and too late for snowmobilers. He looked for a place to turn around, found a gap about a quarter of a mile in and parked with enough room to make the turn. The Cherokee almost touched his bumper before it stopped.

Andrew was out of his vehicle before Jake's feet touched the ground, a 9-millimeter automatic in his hand. Jake froze, back against the open door, weighed diving for the rifle in the rack above the seat, rejected it and waited.

"You got that chicken-shit Baker to talk, but that's as far as it's going. I ain't going to have any more black marks in my personnel jacket. I ain't going to lose this job. And above all, I ain't going to jail, you spic-loving piece of dog shit."

He was a mere two feet away now and Jake felt spittle spray his cheek. "What you figure on doing, scare me or kill me?"

"Whatever it takes."

"Don't see how you can scare me off." Andrews raised the automatic as though he was going to backhand Jake. "Oh, you can hit me, all right. But if I'm alive, I'm coming after you." Jake imperceptibly shifted his weight to his left foot. "That means you're going to have to kill me. But Mikeska and Baker know what I'm doing up here. So does my lawyer. And Sheriff Blakenship."

Andrews lowered the pistol from his threatened backswing until it was pointed at Jake's gut but without the resolve of the moment before.

"Haven't thought of that, have you." Jake kept his eyes on the hand holding the gun. "What about my body? Folks travel

378

this road. Look at the tracks." As Andrew's eyes involuntary glanced down at the road, Jake stepped forward, swinging his left hand under the wrist holding the gun and driving his right knee deep and hard into the deputy's crotch.

"Arrgh." The scream of primeval pain blended with the triple-crack of shots from the automatic. Jake's right forearm was at Andrews' throat and his left hand had the wrist with the hand that held the gun. A step with his left foot. Another knee to the crotch. The gun dropped. Had him bent over the hood of the Cherokee. Another knee and the body went limp. Jake let him slide to the ground, his back against the left front wheel, an elemental moaning coming from the slack lips.

Somehow the sunglasses had stayed on.

"Don't move." Jake stepped back to lean against the side of his pickup, knees shaking and gasping for breath. He closed his eyes and fought for control. Goddamn law. When he opened his eyes, Andrews was leaning forward, trying to reach the glint of the automatic in the mud and leaves and twigs of the road.

"Cocksucker." Jake stepped with his left foot and swung his right at the head, bent by the pull of the reaching hand. The toe of his work boot caught Andrews on the point of the chin, snapping his head back to bounce off the Cherokee's bumper. Blood was welling from the deputy's chin and smearing the bumper as his upper body started to collapse when Jake's second kick drove into the chin again.

"I told you not to move," Jake gasped.

There was no answer.

Jake was bent, hands on knees, fighting for breath, when his eye caught a dark trickle seeping from Andrews' right ear. He watched in fascination as it filled the cavity, lapped over and traced a path down earlobe and neck to the ground.

"Shit." Breathing normal — but he felt cold despite the sweat stinging his eyes.

"Shit." Call Mikeska? Who the hell will believe me?

He stepped closer to look at the other ear. No blood. Maybe?

A finger on the jugular quashed the faint hope.

Can't report it. Move the body? Have to get out of here.

Where? Don't know the county. And the vehicles. How to deal with both?

Goddamn law. Ain't fair. Goddamn law.

What would Mary Margaret think?

Anger almost made him kick Andrews again.

Enough of that. She doesn't need me in jail.

He started to pick up the body, caught himself and got a pair of work gloves from the cab. He nosed his pickup into the turnaround gap. Gloves on, he grasped the uniform jacket and belt and levered the body into the passenger seat of the Cherokee, noticed the pistol glinting on the road and tossed it into the cab. A minute to drive the Cherokee past his pickup, another to back it out of the gap and pull halfway to the highway. Then he backed the Cherokee into the gap as far into the brush as it would go. He slid the body behind the wheel and put the automatic in its lap.

It took fifteen minutes of deep breathing before he felt calm enough to drive home.

***

Jake lay on the couch, alternating between fighting sleep and wishing the warmth of relaxation would spread from legs to chest and swaddle him in a comfort where no dreams dare enter.

It was ten o'clock and the morning sun lit dust motes in the living room air. Jake couldn't remember when, if ever, he'd lain down at this hour. But he was tired, tired beyond measure.

The drive home had been without incident and no calls blinked to be answered when he entered the house. On the way, he'd alternated images of Mary Margaret with reviewing everything that happened after the deputy stopped him: Had anyone driven by before they'd turned onto the logging road? What about when he pulled out? Finger prints?

Should he tell Blakenship?

Be crazy to, he kept telling himself. Law sticks together. No one would believe it was self-defense. My word against theirs. But the question kept returning.

At home, television was no relief and reading out of the question. Bed was worse. Every time he closed his eyes, the picture of the blood running from the deputy's ear played on his eyelids in a never-ending loop, the blood's flow increasing each time until by morning it was a torrent of crimson.

Exhausted, he'd risen at first light and had spent the morning brooding until the couch's horizontal allure pulled him to it.

Phone Mackey?

Have to see Mary Margaret. First thing when I get up.

And sleep came. Finally.

***

"So we don't know anymore than we did two weeks ago?"

"Pretty much."

Blakenship sighed, a long mournful exhalation that encompassed all the frustrations of his five terms. "Maybe Jessie'll turn up something." He watched the traffic in the street and on the sidewalk without registering anything — until a non-nondescript sedan with government plates angled into a slot directly in front of him. "Sonofabitch."

"Sometimes it takes time, C.W."

"Huh? No. It's not that. Buchanan just pulled up. Been so long I thought we were shut of him." Blakenship watched the fed go up the steps to the main lobby of the courthouse. "What the fuck?"

"Now what?"

"He's going into the courthouse."

"We'll see him soon enough."

"No doubt. But do me a favor, Charlie. Drift upstairs and see what he's poking into."

***

"I don't want to talk. Not now. Needed a place to rest before I drove home and this was the closest." Jake favored Mackey Fitz with a hollow-eyed stare. His nap had lasted less than an hour and the new secret — which he could never tell Mary Margaret — combined with the still unresolved question of when to tell her about Grandpa Grummond had left him unable to do more than kiss her and squeeze her hand before leaving, the questioning hurt in her eyes adding to his pain and confusion. He'd driven to Mountain View with the half-formed notion of planning strategy with the lawyer, but as soon as he walked through the door he realized that was hopeless. "You mind?"

"Of course not." He fiddled with his fountain pen and regarded the man filling the high-backed chair across from him. Jake's eyes were closed now and lines the lawyer had never noticed before etched his cheeks in vertical furrows. The face seemed relaxed but the hands resting on the chair arms twitched sporadically.

Fitz was debating offering coffee, instant soup and/or the couch in the front room when Jake spoke. "No help for it."

The lawyer waited, but Jake returned to silence. Finally he shook his long-term client by the shoulder and half-led, half-carried him to the couch.

***

Buchanan stood on the top steps of the courthouse concentrating on some document and oblivious to the exiting rush of county employees and last-minute patrons who had to veer around his unmoving figure.

Blakenship, who'd been informed by Henderson that Buchanan had been looking at property tax rolls, stood on the sidewalk below, waiting patiently for the DEA agent to descend. Finally the late afternoon sun lowered enough to glare into the fed's eyes. Jerking, he looked around, recognized where he was and made his way to the street.

"You're not fixing to bid on a plot of seized ground in my county are you?"

Buchanan folded the document so the contents couldn't be seen. "Not likely."

"Then I assume you're on official business. Am I going to have to call Kiernan to get your cooperation?"

"Just following a hunch. If it pans out, you'll be the first to know."

"Property taxes going to lead you to drug dealers — and killers?"

"Like I said, you'll be the first to know." Buchanan pushed past Blakenship to his car. "Say, isn't that Grummond? I've got ..." He started across the street in a jog to where Jake and Mackey Fitz stood beside Jake's pickup.

"I wouldn't ... Shit." The sheriff watched as the agent reached the truck, watched as he put his arm on Jake's, watched as Jake shook it off, and began his own jog across the street when Buchanan pushed Mackey Fitz, who'd stepped between the two, in the chest. By the time he got there, Jake had hit the DEA agent twice — once in the stomach and once on the chin — and had him bent backward across the hood of the car in the adjacent parking slot, left hand on the throat and right threatening to strike again.

Mackey Fitz was making a futile effort to get Jake to release his grip on Buchanan's throat when Blakenship pressed the barrel of his .357 into the small of Jake's back. "Easy, Jake. He's a prick, but that doesn't mean it's open season."

Jake looked at Blakenship without opening his hand. The sheriff increased the pressure of the gun barrel. Jake looked at Mackey Fitz.

"Let him go, Jake. We'll bring charges — and add this to our suit."

Jake thought for a moment, gave the throat a final squeeze and stepped back. "C.W., if this scum ever bothers me again I'm going to kill him."

"Can't have that, Jake. I'm sorry about your father — about everything. But we can't have that. Mackey, can you get him home? Charlie can bring you back."

"Be glad to."

Buchanan had been gasping for breath while he watched the interchange and subsequent departure with amazement. "What the fuck. He almost killed me." His voice croaked weakly but his indignation was real.

"First, you approached him, you put your hands on him and you pushed his lawyer — who happens to be over retirement age. And you heard what he said." Blakenship bent to the curb for the papers Buchanan had been studying so intently and was about to look at them when they were torn from his hand. The sheriff started to reach for them, then shrugged. Charlie'd find out tomorrow. "Second and most important from my point of view, his father died two weeks ago. He loses his dairy and his father — and his wife's a basket case — most folks around here would say all because of you."

"That's a crock."

"Maybe. Maybe not. But right now you should count yourself lucky he didn't kill you right here with most of the county cheering him on." Blakenship turned toward his office, then turned back. "Me included."

***

"Just thought you ought to know. If you can keep him under control, I'll see if I can keep Jake and Mackey Fitz from pressing charges … Say what? No, I mean locally. Ain't shit I can do about the federal suit, if they actually bring it." Blakenship looked up as Henderson came into the office. "Kiernan," he mouthed. "Well, that's what I was hoping you could tell me… Charlie just came in. Here." He handed the receiver to the deputy.

"That's right. Tax rolls. The garage, sure, and the surrounding area. Guess he's looking for accomplices. Some connection anyway. You want to talk to C.W.?" Henderson hung up. "Says he'll be in touch."

"Now that you told him, tell me."

"Xeroxed everything out in that part of the county — south, west and north of the Ruiz place, for ten miles."

Blakenship chewed abstractedly on a thumbnail. "Give the Alta a call. He could be onto something. If he is, we need to know." He worked his way from nail to nail on the fingers of his right hand while he pondered what tax rolls could show that they didn't already know. Shit. Them meskins tend to keep it in the family and they'd already investigated all the relatives they could identify.

"No answer, C.W."

"He check out?"

"Desk clerk says no."

"Ask the clerk to call us when he gets back."

***

He was able to do better with Mary Margaret the next day. Held her hand and talked, talked about trees budding, Maria Elena's upcoming graduation, irrigation water ready to flow. And she kept him going with questions. One or two-word questions that didn't make it a conversation. But close.

Afterward, he'd driven back to the farmhouse but couldn't think of anything he wanted to do there and turned toward his father's cabin. But couldn't bring himself to go inside. In Top Hat, Alma's Cafe held no more appeal. He sat at the curb undecided about what to do, where to go. The box for the Mountain View newspaper caught his eye and he bought a copy. Putting the pickup into gear, he headed out the Pea Green road with no destination in mind.

An hour later he found himself at an overlook well up the Sublette Plateau. The greening fields and pastures stretched out below and he felt the familiar surge of anticipation for the growing season only to be quashed by the memory that he had no land in cultivation.

385

Anger swept in waves building from his gut and he turned for diversion to the newspaper on the seat beside him, forcing himself to concentrate on each word of the usual stories — the city manager was under attack, the county commissioner from the westernmost precinct was charging nepotism in the letting of road contracts, both high school baseball teams were hosting their season openers. He'd finished pondering every horoscope banality when he realized there was nothing about the Otero County deputy.

Hadn't he been found? How long had it been? Two days. Just two days?

Surely he was missed by now. Why wasn't that reported? Tell Blakenship? Or Mackey Fitz?

No way. It was him or me. All there was to it.

***

"How long's it been, Rudy?"

"Since Wednesday afternoon. He radioed he was going off duty at four and nobody's seen or heard from him since. No sign of him or the department's vehicle."

"What'd he do, take the vehicle home?"

"Yeah. Andrews is one of the few we let do that. Lost everything but a shitty-ass trailer in a divorce. Without the department's Cherokee, he wouldn't have any wheels at all."

"And yesterday was his day off?"

"Uh uh."

"Your vehicle budget must be a whole let better than mine."

"Never mind that. Point is, no reports of him being seen in your county?"

"Nary a one. But I'll tell Charlie to get the word out."

"Appreciate it, C.W. I'm not saying Andrews is one of my favorite officers but I can't ignore the fact he didn't show up today. And that Otero County property is missing."

"I understand. I assume your people are combing the county."

"From river bottom to mountain top."

"Let me know what turns up." Blakenship stared at the ceiling then rummaged in his top right hand desk drawer, drew out a sheet of paper and studied the names thereon. Then he moved to the door and hollered, "Charlie."

Blakenship returned to his desk and made a list. It was short: Dobbins, Hoover, and Andrews. He'd finished doodling stars by each name when Henderson appeared. He turned the short list so the deputy could read it. "We got two dead and the other missing. Anything strike you funny about them?"

Henderson looked at the three names, then at the other sheet of paper on the desk. "They were all on the raid out to Jake's."

"That they were. And they were all in on tearing up the property."

"You're not thinking Jake ..."

"Jake?" Surprised, Blakenship drew a big star that enclosed all three names. "Not hardly." He thought for a bit. "Just looking for connections ... and the raid..." He crumpled the paper. "Maybe it's just coincidence."

"Look at the differences. Hooper and Dobbins — that clusterfuck of an operation. And the other one — Andrews? — Who knows? He's just missed a day of work, far as we know."

"We'll see."

***

"Don't worry about Thursday ..."

Blakenship voice reached Jake as he stood, hand on the doorknob, at the entrance to Helen's. "Thursday?"

"About Buchanan. We've talked turkey to him. So has his boss."

"Buchanan? Worry ain't what I'm doing about that cocksucker." Blakenship and Jake locked in a momentary stare before, as if on cue, each broke eye contact.

"C'mon. I'll by you a drink." Now why did I do that? Jake shook his head at himself. Oh well. Too late now. He held the door open for the sheriff, ushering him ahead with mock solemnity.

"What brings you ..." Helen looked past Blakenship's shoulder. "Jake," her voice carrying a rising inflection, half-question, half-surprise.

"First round's on me."

Helen shrugged and opened two Buds followed by a shot glass that she set in front of Blakenship and filled to the brim. "So. How is she? Mary Margaret," she explained to the sheriff.

"Good. Very good. I got there before she was back from her ride with ..."

"That Taylor woman taking her out again?" Doubt evident in Blakenship's tone.

"Since Tuesday. Bridget said that since she wasn't bad hurt and she hadn't gotten any worse ..."

"He means she's communicating the way she did before the accident," Helen explained.

"Better, if anything. Called me by name today. Like she did ..."

"She did?" Helen beamed. "Jake, that's wonderful."

"Anyway, Bridget figured the best thing was to keep going."

"Like getting back on a horse that threw you?"

Jake favored Blakenship with a quick smile. "You could say that. Like I said, I got there ahead of them. Mary Margaret got out of the car and walked all the way to her room without any help."

"By herself?" Helen polished an imaginary spill on the bar.

"I held her hand — so did Bridget — but she didn't lean on either of us." Jake put the beer bottle to his lips and swallowed three times. "Bridget says her weight's below 170."

"How's she losing it so fast? That's thirty pounds or more since ..." Helen caught herself before she said the fire, "... she went to Fritz's."

"No idea. No idea how she put on so much, so fast, either." Jake took a reflective swallow of beer. Blakenship looked from one to the other, waiting for the conversation to continue. Finally Jake spoke. "We're going to tell her about Dad tomorrow. You want to be there?"

***

"You getting any farther with Minnie?"

Jessie was taking advantage of a lull in the Stockman's Saturday-night crush of orders to spoon a mouthful from the bowl of green-chili stew set in front of Blakenship's beer bottle and shot glass. "Could be. Every once in a while she seems like she wants to talk, then we get interrupted."

"Be nice if we can find who the boy was hanging with these last few months."

"I know." Jessie patted his thigh. "AK-47s. Isn't that what you said Hoover and Dobbins were killed with?"

"Yeah."

"It's a military weapon, right?"

"Yeah."

"And Lonnie Fletcher was hung up on Vietnam."

"So?"

"Just a thought."

***

Buchanan tore the wrapper from a fresh roll of toilet paper, polished his burning anus and flushed.

Besides chronic diarrhea, he'd developed bleeding gums and a persistent low-grade ache in his bottom right molar. For months he'd wondered if his wife wasn't right — resign and go to work for her father running one of his tire stores in Jersey City.

But a primal refusal to admit defeat, an unthinking stubbornness that many superiors had interpreted as persistence and labeled as his best trait, kept him plugging on. Besides, he couldn't carry a gun in a tire store.

Plug on he did. Getting nowhere. Until the heroin.

That was different and it led him in a new direction. Were the Ruizes branching out? Had they formed a new partnership?

No heroin had been found during the raid, true enough.

But it was highly unlikely that new sources could move into the county without addressing the old in some way.

In his experience, it was either deal or war, and while it was true the Sanchez brothers had been killed, that didn't qualify as war. Put the possibility of new players with the disappearance of the Ruizes and that meant an alliance with someone in the area. The immediate area.

And he was getting close. He felt it.

Buchanan buckled his belt, washed his hands and returned to the county map and tax rolls spread out on the table by the window. He'd been working there all afternoon with the curtains open and the casement windows on each side of the plate glass ajar. But the sun had been down a good two hours and the night air was cooling fast.

He closed both casements and took a last look at the fast disappearing cottonwoods along the Flint River look before returning to the paperwork spread across the table. He had just bent to examine one of the documents when the bullet shattered the right window and exploded his head.

**

Luther reached Blakenship as he and Jessie were leaving the Stockman. A couple staying at the Alta enjoying a late-evening stroll had passed the room with curtains open and lights on. Looking into a lighted room, as people will, they noticed that the window seemed to be broken. Closer inspection proved that it was. And on still closer inspection, there seemed to be a body sprawled across the table.

"Buchanan shot? Dead?"

"Looks that way, C.W."

"Tell Henderson to meet me at the Alta." Blakenship spit out a chunk of the cigar he was chewing. "Looks like …"

"I heard." Jessie lifted her head to kiss his cheek. "You go on. I'll catch a ride with Jan."

"I'll drop you. Five minutes one way or the other ain't going to make a difference to Buchanan."

Both owners met him as he parked in front of the No Parking sign marking the Alta's walk to the main building. "Where the hell have you been?"

"According to Luther, you reached him about eleven-fifteen. It's now," he squinted at his watch, "it's now about quarter to twelve. What the fuck's your problem?"

"What do we tell our guests?"

"Tell them that unless they're with the DEA or are dealing drugs, they haven't got a thing to worry about."

A departmental Bronco pulled up while he was talking and Henderson got out. "Getting to be quite a little crime wave we got."

"Drugs, Charlie. Drugs is the problem. You ever do drugs?"

"Nope."

"Me neither. Wonder what there is about them."

"Money."

"I understand the money part. I just never have understood why there's so much money involved. It ain't like we're talking Canadian Club."

28

April 4 — Very Early Morning

Blakenship watched two deputies stretch yellow crime-scene tape across the windows and doors of what had been Buchanan's room. "That ought to hold things." He lit a cigar and let out the first drag in a thoughtful plume. "The body's safely tucked away in the morgue?"

"Saw if my ownself." Henderson removed his hat and wiped the sweatband with a handkerchief. "What'd Kiernan have to say?"

"Said he'd be here by noon tomorrow at the latest. He's going to notify the wife."

"Hard to imagine that sonofabitch with a wife."

"Lots of things are hard to imagine, Charlie, but that don't mean they're not so. You're the one who taught me that."

"Yeah. Well … Kiernan'll bring a bunch of his boys. State CID'll want to get in on this one, probably, high profile as it is. Which means they're likely to start poking around in the others. And it wouldn't surprise me if the FBI will stick their dicks into this, what with him being a fed and all."

"What's your point?"

"Point is, if we want to do anything before we have all them strangers tripping over each other, we better get an early start."

"True enough. Why don't you organize a little group to start combing the area at first light? I'd concentrate from along the riverbank, were I you. Looks to me like it was a long shot."

"A long shot by a marksman with a good rifle and better scope," Henderson agreed.

"And we'll need some others to check all the Ruiz relatives. The close ones, anyway."

"Right." Henderson gave Blakenship a long look. "What about Jake?" he asked softly.

"I'll see Jake. Let him know that I'm just the first of many." Blakenship dropped his cigar butt at his feet and ground it into the rectangular splotch of cement that passed as the room's patio. "Poor bastard." He bent for the extinguished cigar. "You get a look at the papers on the table?'

"Besides the part covered by blood and brains? No. But they're in evidence bags."

"Another thing I'd like to look at before the experts descend."

***

The farmhouse looked deserted. Maybe he should have called, but he'd assumed that Jake would be up. Shit, it was 7:30.

Blakenship crossed the porch with purposefully heavy footsteps and peered through the door's window before knocking. He could see Jake sitting at the table in the unlit kitchen, coffee cup between his hands. If he'd heard the steps, he gave no sign.

The sheriff knocked, three raps paced with somber authority, waited, then knocked again. Through the window he saw Jake gesture him to enter.

"Sorry to bother you …" he said to the back of Jake's head.

"Sure you are. Get to the point." Had Blakenship been able to see his face, he would have noted a flinch of worried tension.

The sheriff took a deep breath. "Buchanan was killed last night."

That got Jake to turn around. "I'm supposed to care?"

"I need to know where you were last night."

"You think I killed him? Shit. I haven't seen him since Thursday."

"When you said if he ever bothered you again, you'd kill him."

"Maybe I would have. But the fact remains I haven't seen him."

"You made a threat and I need your statement for the record. Where were you?"

393

"At Helen's. You saw me your ownself."

"I mean late. Say from nine o'clock on." Blakenship swung a chair away from the table, sat down and removed his hat. "Look Jake, I don't like doing this. But I have to. A man's been killed. A man you threatened. I want to be on your side when the others start in on you."

"Others?"

"Kiernan. State criminal investigators. Maybe even the FBI."

"After you left, Helen and I talked for ten, maybe fifteen minutes. About seeing Mary Margaret today. And … I was here all night."

"Any one who can verify that?"

"No. Not with me, if that's what you mean." Jake picked up a spoon lying on a napkin and stirred his coffee. "Eusebio and Della were home last night. Maria Elena, too, far as I know. They can tell you I didn't go anywhere. In the pickup, anyway."

"That'll help." Blakenship took a deep breath. "Next thing is, I got to look at your guns."

Jake's look was hard enough to make the sheriff's hand twitch toward the butt of his .357 but he rose and went to the closet, reappearing with a Remington twelve-gauge and both of Paul's pistols, still in their gun belts, and laid them on the table without a word. He went back to the closet, and came back with the gun case and the carbine in its saddle scabbard that he put next to the others. "All them are Paul's, except for the shotgun." He went out the door, returning momentarily with his Remington .30-.06. "Keep this in the Dodge. You should know that."

Blakenship touched the walnut handles of the Vaquero and the Blackhawk Single-Six. "He was into cowboy shooting, wasn't he?"

"Thinking about it." Jake moved quickly to the sink and busied himself washing a spoon and fork that didn't need it.

Blakenship examined each gun in turn, satisfying himself that none had been fired recently. When he was finished, he replaced Paul's carbine and hunting rifle in scabbard and case respectively. "That it?"

"Dad had a rifle and shotgun. They're down at his cabin."

"Best if I look at them, too. And talk to Eusebio or Della. That way I can tell all them others you've been checked out. Might keep them for bothering you. Might not."

"You going to tell me when that asshole bought it? Not to mention where and how?"

"Not just yet. If you don't know, be easier for you to deal with the others."

"You telling me it's not going to be on the news or in the papers?"

"That's a point. In his room at the Alta sometime in the evening. Body was discovered around eleven."

"If it was in his room, must have been someone he knew."

"He knew you." Blakenship regretted the words as soon as they left his mouth and hurried on. "But it was an ambush. Long shot, probably from the river. Right through the plate glass window."

"He must have been backlit."

"Yeah." Blakenship pushed himself to his feet. "Soon's I talk with Eusebio and them and check out the guns in the cabin I got to get to the Alta. See what Charlie's found."

***

Good as his word, Kiernan arrived shortly after noon with three other agents in tow. Blakenship and Henderson had been back from the Alta for an hour and had just returned the tax rolls and Buchanan's notes to the evidence bag and the bag to the locker when the feds trooped in.

"So … what can you tell me?" Kiernan took the chair in front of the desk while his men formed a standing arc behind him.

"Shot from ambush. We have a likely spot by the river, although we can't be sure. No brass or anything. Just what might be the print of a hiking boot. But it's where I'd have been."

395

"How far away?"

"About 250, 300 feet."

"One shot?"

Blakenship nodded. "In the middle of the forehead. Pretty good, especially when you consider it was night and the shooter had to allow for the refraction of the window glass."

"Find the slug?"

"Not yet. May have fragmented on impact, bad as Buchanan's head was tore up."

"Suspects?"

"The Ruizes're at the top of the list, of course. Assuming they aren't in Mexico by now." Blakenship favored the big man with a bland look. "Could be someone we don't know. Something he stepped into lately."

Kiernan returned the sheriff's look with equal blandness. "Go on."

"Buchanan hadn't been underfoot for — I don't know — weeks. Then he shows up Thursday afternoon. Not to bother me, but to check tax rolls. Leads me to think he was on to whoever's been adding heroin to our spectrum of problems. Or maybe he'd found some accomplices we don't know about." Blakenship handed his coffee mug to Henderson who walked to the office door and signaled someone in the main room. "If it was the Ruizes, why now? They've had plenty of time." Blakenship accepted the refilled mug with a nod of thanks. "But you're his boss. You should know what he's up to better'n anyone."

Kiernan winced. "He's — was — a hard one to control. And there's the personal issue — he was my boss until last fall, after all. I hadn't seen much more of him than you did since the raid. My fault. But life is easier if he's not under foot."

"Won't be underfoot any more."

"Yes." Kiernan interlocked his fingers and flexed, the pops of the knuckles cracking the only sound in the office. "What about Grummond? He threatened Buchanan Thursday."

"I checked him out." Blakenship gave Kiernan a level look. "Had a drink with him in Top Hat late Saturday afternoon. A place called Helen's. Talked to him this morning. Says he went home about ten minutes after I left and stayed there. His people who live across the way — Eusebio and Della Guerrero — say he never left." Blakenship's look now carried a mild challenge. "I checked every weapon on the place, including two in his father's cabin. None has been fired recently. None cleaned recently."

Kiernan rubbed his chin, apparently oblivious to the anger building in the sheriff's eyes as he ticked off each point. "Pretty good. But not ironclad. Still…" He stood up and stretched to the ceiling. "Damn. They don't build small planes with people like me in mind. Those documents … you have them?"

"That we do."

"Maybe we should take a look."

***

Monday morning dawned clear and soft, giving hope for the kind of spring day poets write about. As the sun rose higher, the promise was fulfilled, adding to Jake's sense of optimism.

Telling Mary Margaret had gone better than he had thought possible. The three of them — he, Helen and Bridget — had grouped around the bed while he had explained about the stroke. Mary Margaret's eyes never strayed from Jake's face, welling with tears as he talked. "Poor Jake," she said when he finished, loud enough for all to hear, and reached for his hand. Relief had Bridget and Helen dabbing handkerchiefs at nose and eyes.

From the porch he gazed across the greening cottonwoods and chicos to the Far Gate field and the red hint of the roof of his father's cabin. He hadn't accompanied Blakenship yesterday to examine his father's guns, sending Eusebio instead, but now, he decided, now it was time to tend to it. See what was there, at least.

It was spotless and orderly, the disarray of his final moments put right — by Maria Elena, probably — as though he'd gone away for a long weekend.

397

Jake stood in the doorway, taking in the made-up bed, the stove with kindling stacked in the box nearby, but not too near, the remote control for the TV on the table next to the leather reclining chair.

The refrigerator had been emptied — no need for perishables anymore — but neat rows of tableware and canned goods filled the cabinet shelves.

He opened one closet door. Clothes. He moved to the second, further back and larger. There they were — rifle and double-barreled shotgun. Good for C. W. to put them back where they belonged. Boots, coveralls, a battery charger and small air compressor. In the far corner, a large canvas sack he didn't remember seeing before.

He struggled with the knot in the quarter-inch manila line holding it closed, almost giving up and reaching for his knife. But it finally loosened and he spread its mouth open, reached in and felt the horn of a saddle.

Paul's. Just as he'd left it — well oiled, rope coiled on the right. Stirrup leathers a bit bent from sitting on the closet floor, but they'd straighten out. Bridle and saddle blanket were at the bottom.

He carried them to the porch, set blanket on the rail, saddle on the blanket, hung the bridle from the horn, and moved a straight-backed wooden chair to a spot in the sun.

Why did his father have them?

To keep the sight of them from upsetting him and Mary Margaret. Especially Mary Margaret.

What else had his father taken charge of out of some unsuspected depth of understanding and sensitivity? He went back to the closet.

Boots and leggings, hats and shirts. And every ribbon Paul had won. Not for nothing was he called Grandpa Grummond.

Jake sat in the warming sun, gazing across the saddle to the looming green, white, gray and dark brindle of the Presidentials. At night on their hunting trips, he and Paul would drink coffee, his laced with bourbon, and talk of summer pack trips into the Picket Stake Wilderness. A week, ten days.

But there'd never been the time.

Now he had nothing but time. Maybe Silver Dollar could give him a lead on a couple of horses.

It came as a shock when he looked at his watch. Two. He'd been daydreaming for the better part of four hours.

The news from the truck's radio gave him another shock, although one he'd been waiting for. Fishermen had found the body of an Otero County deputy.

***

Blakenship learned about the body a short hour before Jake. Mikeska was on the phone as he walked in the door from lunch and Luther handed him the receiver as he passed the front desk.

"We found Andrews. That is, a couple of fishermen did."

"Dead, I take it."

"Body was propped up in the Cherokee. Pistol in his lap. It hadn't been fired. And he hadn't been shot."

"But he's dead."

"Head injury, looks like. Autopsy's not finished. Shit, it ain't even started. But that's what it looks like."

"And he was in his vehicle?"

"Uh huh. Not likely he did it himself. You know, slipped, hit his head, got behind the wheel and then died from a delayed reaction."

"Why not?"

"The pistol, for one. And the Cherokee was in a turnaround off a logging road in the west end of the county — almost hidden. Only a mile or two from the county line. That's the Sapinero County line," he added unnecessarily.

"So? Still could have been what happened."

"The pistol?"

"In his lap, you say? Maybe he dropped it and didn't have time to holster it before his ticker give out."

"Like I said, not likely."

"Why'd it take so long to find him?"

"That logging road ain't something we check regular, not until summer anyway. Besides, it's not in a sector Andrews usually works. Took a couple of fly fishermen willing to drive to a snow bank and walk in from there. That and the radio was spitting static. What made them look that way?"

Blakenship flicked the ash off his cigar and set it in the ashtray next to the telephone. "Any ideas? He have any enemies?"

""A fair number. He wasn't your most likable sort. We'll be running them down."

"Was he working on a case?"

"Nope. Just routine patrols."

"Maybe it was somebody he pulled over."

"He didn't radio in. He was real good about doing that."

"Appreciate you keeping me posted, Rudy. I'll let you know if I think of something."

Blakenship had hardly settled behind his desk when Luther came in with a bulletin. He'd just finished reading it when Kiernan took up the chair across from him. "They found Felipe Ruiz. And three *compadres*, including brother Abel." He flipped the paper toward the DEA agent. "Shot dead in the Arizona desert. And they say there's no honor among thieves."

"Hard to tell how long they've been dead." Kiernan flipped the paper back to Blakenship. "But it's at least two weeks. Which means that they couldn't have done Buchanan."

"Not those four. Could have been another of their associates." Blakenship fiddled with a rubber band until it snapped. "On the other hand, could have been because of what he was working on lately. His papers tell you anything?"

"No. Tax rolls, which don't mean a thing to me. And his notes were so soaked with blood we can't make any sense of them."

"Can't the lab boys do something there?"

"We'll see."

"What about the tax rolls?"

"Soon as we get more manpower, we'll canvas every site. But since we don't know what we're looking for …" The big man shrugged his massive shoulders.

"Look for heroin, for one thing."

***

Three weeks passed without violent incident.

For most of that time, FBI, DEA and state criminal investigators tripped over each other and the occasional deputy as they carried out jealously guarded investigations into the murders of Buchanan and the two Sapinero deputies. A couple even went to Otero County but couldn't learn anymore than what was in the autopsy — contusions in groin and head area indicative of a struggle. They were classifying it as a homicide, but with no idea as to degree.

"Charlie," Blakenship asked one day as the waitress at the Chopping Block set their morning coffee and cinnamon rolls before them. "I been sheriff now, what, seventeen, eighteen years. And you've been with the department longer than that."

"A lot longer."

"How many murders have we had? I don't mean a Saturday-night cutting that went too far or a marital discussion that got out of hand. I mean how many cold-blooded murders?"

Henderson stared through the plate glass window until Blakenship thought he hadn't heard him and was about to ask the question again. "Five. Five since you were first elected. Three others since I joined the department."

"And that was when? Korea?"

"Close enough."

"Eight. Eight fucking murders in the whole county. And now we got three in two months. Six if you count the Sanchez brothers and Andrews up in Otero County."

"Ten — if you count the Ruizes."

***

401

The outsiders left. Finally. They may or may not have learned more about Sapinero County and the people in it, but they were no closer to solving any of the homicides than they'd been the day they arrived.

They'd tried intimidation. When that didn't work, they tried being friendly — but it was too late, so they went back to intimidation.

The Californians in the old Sheffield place had refused to let them on the property without search warrants. When issued, all that was found were a number of weapons in the form of war mementos — none of which were operational.

Searches of all the places listed on Buchanan's tax rolls revealed hardly a house without guns — a rifle, a shotgun and at least one pistol seemed to be the norm — but nothing that could be linked to the shootings. They also found a few stashes of marijuana. Some pills. Crystal meth and, in two cases, crack pipes but no crack.

And, to Blakenship's big disappointment, no heroin.

***

Jake sat on a rock in a clearing on his mountain land, a small fire in the pit with its circle of rocks at his back, some of Frog Bottom's elk sausage spitting in the frying pan. One of the two horses he'd bought from a man recommended by Silver Dollar was picketed a short distance away, saddle and bridle off.

He'd been questioned virtually ever other day for a week and a half — the DEA, the FBI, the state boys. What with the Ruizes dead, seemed like he was the only lead they had. But they didn't act like they really believed he'd killed Buchanan. More like they were going through the motions. And they never asked about the Sanchez brothers or Andrews.

He moved to the fire to turn the sausages and refill his coffee cup from the small camp pot that fit in his saddlebags. Not knowing what the snow pack was like — except that the melt had started — he hadn't brought the packhorse. He'd parked truck and horse trailer at the Hazel Lake Inn and picked his way over the ridge. Going up hadn't been bad — that was the west-facing side and the snow was mostly gone. To his surprise, it wasn't much worse on the east, except for occasional big drifts in the shade. Ground was still pretty boggy, but that wouldn't last long. Going to be a short year for water, though.

He returned to his rock and gazed out at the Picket Stake. Bet he could get in there with both horses now. Maybe try this weekend. With Mary Margaret back in Union for what Bridget Taylor called "extensive evaluation" he had the time. As long as he called in every so often. He smiled as he thought about the way she'd talk now — short sentences for the most part, but they made sense in terms of the conversation. And every once in a while she'd sound like her old self. Weight down, too. She was starting to look like Mary Margaret. Especially her face.

Last time he'd seen her — before she went to Union — he'd talked about maybe raising replacement heifers. Take a lot less help and be a lot less restricting. Shame to let some strangers have the land — especially a developer. She'd never taken her eyes off him while he talked.

He looked over at the nine-year-old gelding, a quarter horse but with thickness in shoulders and butt that bespoke some Morgan in his lineage. He'd handled the climb just fine. A small cloud of flies hovered over the metallic green pile of fresh horse apples.

Don't take them long to find shit, wherever they come from, Jake thought as he raised his cup to his lips.

What was that about flies? A fly's wings?

He let it come to him. "... see the veins in a fly's wings with that."

The fat Californian. Porterfield. Porterfield and the sniper's rifle.

He remembered how it settled into place against his shoulder. Hadn't he overheard the DEA assholes saying they had nothing but war mementos? Or was it Cecil? Non-operational.

Non-operational, bullshit. That sniper's rifle worked. That Mossberg shotgun worked.

403

Of course, they could have hidden everything except the war mementos to avoid hassles. Long shot. Cecil had said that. And what about the Sanchezes? His stomach spasmed as he remembered the head exploding. Long shot then, too. Two of them.

No reason for them to be involved. Unless they were acting as vigilantes.

If they're vigilantes, why Buchanan?

He was trying to get that to make sense when the smell of burning sausage pulled him toward the fire in a trot.

***

"A camouflage jacket? Like bow hunters wear?" Blakenship lay on a blanket with his head pillowed on his jacket, Jessie's at right angles to him, her head on his stomach.

It was the last Wednesday in April and the day had dawned so clear and bright that by mid-morning he'd been consumed by a need to get out of the office. Prompted by a romanticism he didn't know he had, he'd invited Jessie on a picnic and had astounded the counter staff at the Chopping Block by purchasing two gourmet box lunches — which he augmented with a six-pack of Budweiser.

They were high on the Sublette Plateau by a creek running strong with snowmelt. The air was clean and crisp, the sun warm in a lazy way and the breeze coming upstream was edged with a chill that would have brought shivers had they been in the shade.

Blakenship nudged Jessie's shoulder. "Like a bow hunter's?"

"More like it was military, according to the boy. Not as faded where the name tag had been."

"In the Wal-Mart parking lot, he says?"

"They met — bumped into each other was the way Craig put it — inside. Sporting goods." Jessie rolled over, crossing her arms across Blakenship's girth and resting her head on them. "Went out to the parking lot. To a dually. Silver. Dodge, he thought. With a camper top."

404

"How close was he?"

"He stayed by the door. They were a ways away. Space near the road."

And?"

"They talked for a while. Then it looked like the man gave Lonnie something and drove off. In any event, Lonnie went to his car before coming back to the store."

"What'd he tell — what's his name? Craig?"

"Craig Summers." She rolled over again, arms crossed over her eyes against the sun. "Just said it was something to do with Vietnam."

"That's all?"

"Craig didn't want to push. Says Lonnie'd been acting strange lately."

"Anything else?"

"He isn't sure. But the Dodge might have had California plates. Saw a flash of blue when it drove away."

***

Jake was coming down the post office steps when Blakenship got back from dropping Jessie off at her apartment. He pulled into the slot next to Jake's pickup, got out and leaned against the hood. Jake reached the sidewalk, nodded at the sheriff and made to walk by without speaking.

"Things ought to be quieter for you, now that everybody's left town."

"Yeah." Jake reached for the door handle.

"Tried to keep them off you, but..." he shrugged.

"They weren't too bad. Like it was something they had to do, but they didn't believe it. Not even the DEA, without that Buchanan prick."

"You still going to sue?"

"What's it to you?"

"Just asking."

"According to Mackey, we'll have a better idea in a couple to four weeks."

405

Blakenship shifted his weight to his left butt cheek. "What you going to do till then."

Jake eyed the sheriff for a long ten seconds. "Don't see as it's any of your business, but with Mary Margaret up in Union, I'm going to camp on my land. Maybe ride in the Picket Stake."

"Didn't know you had any mountain land."

"Any reason why you should?" Jake eyed him again, then turned his head away and sighed. "Ain't trying to pick a fight. It's just …" He turned back. "Got about sixty acres. Some three miles due east of the Hazel Lake Inn. Paul and I …" He masked the catch in his voice by reaching for his snuff. "Thought it would be a good time to reacquaint myself. Think a bit."

"Probably so. How long you be gone?"

"Don't know. Mary Margaret's in Union for some tests — and therapy, I guess. Told them," he jerked his head toward the post office, "to hold my mail for a couple of weeks."

Blakenship pushed away from the Bronco's hood. "Have fun."

"Say, C.W. There's is something that's been puzzling me. When you searched them Californians, all you found was non-operational guns. War mementos."

Blakenship spun on his boot toes. "How do you know that?"

"Overheard somebody say so. Can't remember who, but it was one of the folks grilling me. They were talking in the yard."

Blakenship squinted at Jake and considered. "That's right. Wasn't us. DEA, if I remember right." He pulled his hat brim down until it shadowed his eyes. "So?"

"I know for a fact they had a gun cabinet full of operational pieces." He gave operational a little extra stress. "That fat ass one — Porterfield — he showed me two. A shot gun that held fifteen rounds and a sniper's rifle with the biggest scope you ever saw."

"That a fact?"

"Held them in my very own hands."

"Does seem odd that ex-military wouldn't have at least one piece that worked."

Jake spat at the gutter just below Blakenship's shined boot toes. "Don't know what it means. But it's something to think about."

29

April 29 — Morning

"Listen." Kiernan's words came in a rush, barely giving Blakenship a chance to say hello. "I think Grummond's got a lot more to do with this than we thought. There's Donaldson and the Sanchez brothers and …"

Blakenship held the receiver away from his ear and listened to the tinny cascade of words. When they petered out, he propped it against his shoulder. "You want to slow down and run that by me again?"

"Sorry. Look at what's happened. Donaldson badly beaten."

"Say what? Oh… I remember … over in the San Marcos."

"The Sanchez brothers killed. Your deputies …"

"Rob … four killed."

"Four killed," Kiernan echoed. "Andrews — killed. And Buchanan. What's the one thing they have in common?"

"Besides the fact they're all male?"

"This isn't a joke. They all had some connection to the raid on the dairy."

Blakenship sighed and scratched his armpit. "What about Felipe and Abel and the others? You think he did them, too? All the way down in Arizona?"

"I don't know. If Abel was the one who dropped the dime on the dairy …"

"Let's see. The Sanchez brothers were killed from long distance — like Buchanan."

"Grummond's got a rifle with a telescopic sight."

"We don't know they were killed with a .30-.06. Shit, we don't know it was the same weapon. Besides, Hooper and Dobson were killed with an assault rifle — or rifles."

"There're not hard to get in this day and age. Unfortunately."

"What about Donaldson? That was on the other side of the divide. And he wasn't killed."

"True enough. But it was no more than four hours away on the road to Denver. And didn't Jake see a Denver lawyer? And he's been to Elwood recently, trying to get witnesses who'll testify in his suit."

Blakenship scratched his chin with an unopened Rum Crook. "I can see Jake getting pissed and beating the crap out of that fat fuck. Has a temper, does Jake. If you push it, really push it, I could maybe see him take on the deputy. Especially if he was being rousted or threatened. Andrews did have a gun in his lap." He peeled the cellophane from the cigar and rolled it around in his fingers. "But I can't for the life of me see him as a cold-blooded killer. Besides, why change his MO? Beating. Ambush. AK-47. Assuming he did any of them."

There was a long pause on the other end of the line. "Maybe you're right. Maybe I'm pushing too hard. This case has been like nailing jelly to a barn door. But I still think ... even if all he did was punch out Donaldson, we need to follow up."

"We?"

"I thought he might be more forthcoming if you were with me."

"Speaking of following up, word is that those Californians ..."

"The what?"

"Folks who live out past the Ruiz garage. Listed on Buchanan's tax rolls as the Sheffield place."

"I remember now. Ex-military."

"Word is they have a number of weapons, operational weapons, that they denied having to you guys."

A beat of silence. "What kind of weapons?"

"Don't know them all. But a shotgun that holds fifteen shells. And a sniper's rifle."

"Interesting. Who's your source?"

"Jake Grummond."

"That gives us another reason to talk to him."

"When you figure on getting here?"

"Be day after tomorrow — Saturday — before I can get away."

"Bring riding clothes. Jake may be up on his mountain land and we can't drive there this time of year. Can't snowmobile, either."

"Riding clothes? How long's he going to be gone?"

"Said he was having his mail held for two weeks."

"Oh." Blakenship stared out the window while Kiernan digested this information. "Well it might be fun. See you Saturday — as early as I can be."

"Another thing. Remember the kid who overdosed on heroin? Fletcher? Lonnie Fletcher?"

"Go on."

"We got a source who saw him talking with a man in the Wal-Mart parking lot the afternoon of the day he OD'd. A man wearing a military camouflage jacket and driving a silver dually with a camper top and what could have been California plates."

"So?"

"Only folks with a truck like that and California plates are them at the old Sheffield place."

"Didn't you say the boy was hung up on Vietnam?"

"That's the reason he was into drugs. As I remember, heroin was a big deal then. Something to do with the Golden Triangle," he added dryly.

He could almost hear Kiernan thinking on the other end of the line. "That's a pretty big stretch."

"Seems about the same as the stretch you're making trying to tie Jake to all the killings."

"Maybe. Tell you what." Enthusiasm replaced the doubt in Kiernan's voice. "First, we'll talk to Jake. Then we'll see what the others have to say. At the very least, Jake may give us the justification for another search warrant. See you Saturday."

"Saturday."

***

Frost rimed the ground when he pushed half-stooping through the door and netting of the cabin tent and ice skimmed the inch of water left in his coffee cup from the night before. He

410

checked the food bag strung up on a spruce branch fourteen feet off the ground. No bears had gotten to it during the night, but that doesn't mean they couldn't. Hungry when they come out of hibernation. He reached inside the tent for the .30-.30 carbine and carried it with him to the fire pit where he leaned it against the rock that served as his chair.

A quick stir of the ashes with a stick turned up no coals, and he set a square cut from a milk carton in the bottom of the pit against one side. Shavings and small dead twigs came next, laid in a grid that assured plenty of air. With dry sticks broken from spruce trees the night before — what some called squaw wood — at hand, he struck a match and held it to the piece of carton. The wax melted and flared, flames licked through the kindling. He added larger sticks until coals began to build into a bed. Larger chunks, some split the night before, brought the flames well above the top of the rocks that bounded the pit. He unfolded the legs of the grill, set it over the fire, set a three-quarter full pot of water on the grill and followed it with the coffee pot already loaded with grounds and water — the last thing he'd done before retiring to the tent.

He added two more pieces of wood to the fire and went to feed and water the horses.

Breakfast dishes washed and spaced on the rocks around the fire to dry, he saddled the gelding, put the rifle in the saddle scabbard and fitted a halter with a lead rope to the packhorse. He was about to mount when a thought struck him and he went to the tent, buckling the gun belt holding the Vaquero as he returned. You never know.

Once in the saddle, he worked the horses down the slope in long, gentle switchbacks until he reached level ground and the undulating four-wheel drive track that dead-ended at the trailhead into the Picket Stake.

He checked his watch. 8:30. Ride till 11:30, noon, then turn around. Might make the boundary of the wilderness area with its gate zigzagged to keep motor vehicles out. Might not. Either way, be a good workout for the horses.

411

"Sixteen hands was the tallest I could get on short notice. Hope your feet don't drag." Blakenship backed a second saddle horse out of the trailer. "Or mine, either, come to that."

"Hands?"

"How you measure a horse's height. At the shoulders. A hand is four inches."

Kiernan did the calculation in his head. "Almost four feet?" Blakenship, busy carrying saddles, didn't answer. "Nobody has a four-foot inseam."

"Guess we're in luck." Blakenship grinned across the saddle he'd just set on the bay mare. He lifted the left stirrup across the saddle seat and began looping the cinch through the rings, emitting soft grunts as he pulled it tight. He stepped back, the latigo hanging to the ground.

"You going to leave it like that?"

"Let her think that's all, then get the last of the slack. You'd look kind of funny, hanging off the side."

"Sheriff Mikeska's on the phone, C.W." It was the Inn's owner — Blakenship couldn't remember his name — Carter, that was it. Hiram Carter. Hi C they called him.

"Just a second, Hi." He took up the last of the slack and finished the latigo knot. "Wonder why he didn't use the radio? Oh well." He patted the mare's neck and walked to the Inn.

Inside, Hi C pointed to the phone on the bar. "Line 1."

"Yeah, Rudy. ... No. Like I said, we're just going to talk to him. If we can find him. ... About three miles due east of the Inn. That's what he told me the other day. Matches what the Otero County tax rolls have, near as I can tell. ... I parked next to his rig and trailer, so he's in the general area. ... No, we won't do nothing without your say-so. Don't worry."

Blakenship tromped back to the horses, picked up a saddle blanket in his left hand and the other saddle in his right, and flipped them in succession on the back of the remaining horse.

"What'd Mikeska want?"

412

"I think he's getting jurisdiction conscious. Wanted to make sure we wouldn't do anything but talk unless he gave the go-ahead."

"How far is Elwood from here?"

"I don't know. Fifty miles? Sixty maybe?" Blakenship finished with his cinch. "You set your stirrups?"

"No. Sorry."

"Climb aboard and I'll see to it."

Kiernan swung awkwardly into the saddle and let his feet dangle while Blakenship fiddled with straps and buckles. "Where are we going?"

"East. Up that ridge and over the other side."

"I don't see a trail."

"There isn't one. Not on this side. We should run into an old logging road once we crest the ridge, according to Hi C. Try that." Blakenship pushed his foot into the stirrup.

"I think it'll work."

He ducked under the horse's neck and began working on the right side. "But, according to Hi C, Jake went up and back Wednesday and then up again yesterday, leading a pack horse. That works out to four sets of tracks. Shit, even I ought to be able to follow that much sign, wet as it is." He finished with the other stirrup and went to his mount. "Besides, we might get lucky and see the smoke from his fire."

"I got to hit the bathroom. How long will it take to the camp?"

"Don't know. Three miles in this country could take the better part of two hours."

"Put us there around two-thirty or so?"

Blakenship shrugged and lit a cigar.

The cigar was almost finished when Kiernan reappeared. "Sorry. Maybe it's something I ate on the plane."

"Don't worry. I got toilet paper in my saddle bags."

They headed across the parking lot and gravel road and down a gentle incline toward a small creek running full and muddy from the last of the runoff. "Going to be a dry year,"

413

Blakenship flung over his shoulder. "First of May, this bottom land should have half a foot of standing water."

They rode in single file, silent for the most part, Blakenship with eyes focused on the ground twenty feet ahead concentrating on hoof prints, Kiernan shifting in his saddle, trying to get a sense of the terrain.

Midway to the crest they stopped to let the horses blow. "You sure have some beautiful country out here," said Kiernan. He reached in his saddlebags for a water bottle and offered it to Blakenship who accepted it with a nod of thanks. "It looks a lot different being in it than it does from a plane."

"Yeah. I was born about seven, ten miles from here." Blakenship gestured in the general direction of the northwest. "Father ran a small sawmill. Been a while since I've been up this way." He handed the water bottle back to Kiernan. "Been quite a while."

At the top of the ridge, they let the horses blow again, the fourth time they'd done so, only this time they dismounted. "Hope Jake's got enough sense to have a spring on his land."

"Why? I've got two more bottles, and you've got at least that many. Besides, don't you have to filter water? Some kind of parasite?"

"Giardia. Spring's not for us, it's for the horses." Blakenship looked at the DEA agent and shook his head. "If they don't drink, they'll give out. And if they do, we walk."

"It'll be easier going down, won't it?"

"Not necessarily. But even so, we've got to come back up."

Forty-five minutes later they found Jake's camp. "Halloo," Blakenship yelled. "Don't want Jake to think we're bears," he explained. "You. Jake."

They sat, listening to a silence broken only by a slight rustle in the spruce boughs. They walked the horses between the tent and fire pit.

"He isn't here." Kiernan dismounted. "Goddammit. I should have …"

"He'll be back. Left his tent. Left his food." He pointed to the canvas sack strung hanging fourteen feet off the ground. "That's the old-fashioned way to keep bears out of your groceries. Don't always work." He swung to the ground. "Let's see." He walked past the fire pit, leading his horse. "Stock was staked out over here. And by the runoff, I'd say the spring is off thataway."

"What'll we do?"

"Water the horses. And wait."

***

Jake checked his watch. 4:00. Plenty of light left, what with daylight savings time. He was in rhythm now, confident with the gelding, easy with the packhorse, comfortable in the saddle. Paul's saddle.

He'd made the gate to the Picket Stake just before noon and after going through it, he'd led the horses to the bank of the stream that ox-bowed through the broad valley, let them drink their fill and graze the young grass while he chewed on the last of the elk jerky he'd put up from his last hunting trip years before and lazily planned a two — or should it be three? — day pack trip to … where? Slide Lake, maybe.

Go all the way to Slide Lake, better bring his fishing pole. And prepare for four or five days.

He'd headed back after 1:00, soreness in his legs telling him it'd been a long time since he'd ridden this much. Long time since he'd ridden at all. But the easy walk of the gelding pushed the soreness away and he rode without conscious thought, letting the light green of budding aspens, the changing temperature from sun to shadow and the lazy swirling of the breeze lift the pressures of the year past.

He always felt better in the mountains. Why couldn't he remember that? Why let everything build? He thought about Paul. He'd liked the mountains. Seemed like that was when they were closest. When the tensions over rodeoing versus the dairy eased and they were just father and son.

415

Mary Margaret liked the mountains, too. Didn't she? She'd liked their honeymoon. Didn't come on the hunting trips — wanted that to be for the two of them, three when Grandpa Grummond would come. But she'd been happy about the land. Hadn't she? Maybe he should have come up here with her. Maybe she'll be able to come camping when she gets back.

He lifted the horses into a trot that he held for the five minutes it took to reach the start of the climb to the camp.

The horses nickered before he saw them — one — no two horses — up on the level.

He had visitors. His sense of well-being began to evaporate.

He loosened the carbine in the scabbard and removed the thong from the hammer of the .45. You never know.

Two horses, still saddled, were ground-tied near the biggest patch of just-sprouting grass. Beyond, two men sat by the fire pit, which had a fire going. Sonsabitches had helped themselves to his coffee.

Blakenship, for sure. The other was big enough to be that DEA agent.

Jake dismounted, pulled the .30-.30 from the scabbard, and walked toward the men, who had stood up at his arrival. "Hope you gathered some wood to replace what you burned."

"Just fixing to." Blakenship poured coffee into a tin cup and offered it to Jake. "Didn't think you'd mind. Getting a little chill, what with the sun starting to drop behind the ridge."

Jake propped the carbine against the rock and took a small sip, studying the two over the top of the cup. "Reason I come up here is to get away from problems. Like you. So … what the fuck are you doing here?"

"Easy, Jake. Just wanted to ask you a few questions?"

"Excuse me, Mr. Grummond, but if you don't mind my asking, why the guns?"

Jake favored Kiernan with a quick look. "Bears." Then turned to Blakenship. "What kind of questions, Cecil?"

"Oh, about what you been doing these last couple of weeks — up in Elwood and all.

416

Jake felt the pulse in his temple quicken, although he kept his face calm. "If you know I been up there, you know what I was doing."

"Like to hear it from you." Blakenship's voice was mild. "Then there's the matter of the weapons them Californians have."

"I told you, a Mossberg shotgun and what they said was a sniper's rifle."

"Any M-16's or AK-47's?"

"Could have been. The gun cabinet was full."

"What gun cabinet was this?" Kiernan's voice tone was casual.

"One in the living room. That's where it was when I was there, anyway. Had a glass case. The silver shotgun caught my eye. Porterfield got it out and let me handle it. Then he got out the rifle with the big scope."

"You'd be willing to sign an affidavit to that effect? So we can get a search warrant."

Jake reached for the snuff in his shirt pocket. "If you want me to." He took a pinch and fumbled with the lid, letting it fall. As he bent to pick it up, a bullet careened off a rock between Blakenship and Kiernan, followed by the tenor crack of a rifle's report.

The three men scattered in different directions, with Kiernan coming to rest behind the fire pit and Blakenship prone in front of the tent from where he scuffled backward on his belly until he was out of sight behind the tent's sidewall. Jake, with instincts he didn't know he possessed, had grabbed the carbine by the barrel and rolled to a stop behind some rocks on the opposite side of the tent from Blakenship. The smell of damp earth filled his nostrils and his hip ached from landing on the .45. He took the revolver out of the holster and laid it near his head.

He was closest of the three to the shooter — or at least to where the shooter had been, but he couldn't tell where. Fifty yards up the slope? One hundred? More?

Behind him, he could hear the snap and crackle of Blakenship's radio and the sheriff's voice growing louder and louder as he tried to override poor reception through sheer vocal strength.

A shot ripped the tent. Blakenship's voice paused, then picked up again, even louder. "That's what I … No, you shit-for-brains … east of the Inn. East …"

"Pete." Faint but audible, the voice sounded like it came from directly up hill, but he couldn't spot a body to go with it.

"Yes sir, Colonel." That one's off to the right. Some damn where.

A rustle of underbrush, but Jake still couldn't locate either one.

"I'll take care of it, Uncle Bill." A shot, then another, from the fire pit, cutting Blakenship's voice off in mid-curse.

Kiernan? Uncle Bill? Jake scooted around his rock until he could see the fire pit.

"Finish the job, Tommy."

"Right." Kiernan rose to a half-crouch and stepped toward the tent, right arm with the silver automatic extended and angling down. Jake snapped off a shot with the Vaquero and thumbed the hammer as Kiernan turned his way. Jake's second shot took the DEA agent in the left thigh, dropping him like he'd run full speed to the end of a rope. Jake fired another around at the foot fast disappearing behind the rock wall he'd so carefully repaired just three days before.

He was plotting a course through the brush that would bring Kiernan into sight when the rifle from uphill sent a bullet over his head, putting a second hole in the tent. He pushed himself as flat as he could, aware of the dirt in his nose, the taste of pennies on his tongue, the pounding in his ears.

Another shot. And another. Why? To destroy the tent? Trying to hit Blakenship?

But there were two — Pete, the Colonel had called. Was that Petersen?

Petersen going for Blakenship? They couldn't wait forever. Not if Blakenship had gotten through to someone.

Jake raised his head cautiously, careful to keep below the rocks, and scanned the slope above the camp with the patience of one who'd been taught to hunt by Grandpa Grummond. He followed a contour about seventy-five yards up. Nothing. He began working his way down in five-yard increments.

There. Off to his right. Something that didn't look like it quite belonged. Something too straight to be natural. As if to prove the point, the straight something moved to horizontal and a series of flashes came from the end followed by a quick pop pop popping that sounded like a short string of firecrackers.

Jake worked the lever of the carbine and aimed a round about six inches below where the flashes had been.

"Motherfucker." The flashes were aimed at him now, rocks and dirt kicking up in front of his rocks.

Jake levered the carbine and fired, levered and fired.

"Ah, shit, Colonel."

Then silence.

"Pete." The voice came up the hill, to the left. "Pete." It was sharper now. "Tommy? Tommy, what shape are you in?"

"My leg."

"Bleeding bad?"

"Not too bad."

"Can you move?"

"Maybe. I think so. I'll try."

"Crawl away from the fire pit and then see if you can reach that clump of small trees."

"Which trees?"

"Off to the right. Make that left. Your left."

"Near the horses?'

"Yes. Do it." A round over Jake's head followed the command. "As you have no doubt realized, Mr. Grummond, we can't leave either you or the sheriff alive. My recommendation is that you allow us to dispatch you quickly and painlessly. You are outnumbered, after all."

Jake couldn't resist. "Not as much as I was."

He had been scanning the hillside during the conversation between Kiernan and Uncle Bill. With the voice to help him judge distances, he'd located the Colonel — fifty yards plus up the hill, a mass against the bottom of a tree trunk darker than it should be. He nestled his cheek against the stock, took a full breath and let half out. The front sight and the rear V lined up a little above the center of the unnatural dark shape.

"As you wish, Mr. ..." The wind coming upslope carried the carbine's report into the treetops.

Jake waited. Nothing. Then, "Uncle Bill." Tempered by pain but rising in concern, nonetheless. Concern edged with fear.

Shit. Forgot about Kiernan.

Jake turned on his belly and looked at the clump of tree. Not there. Where?

A dancing and snorting by the horses. There. Mounted. How'd he done that with a bad leg? Adrenaline generated by fear.

Jake ran to the top of the slope as horse and rider angled down hill to the shelter of a thick stand of spruce. Jake focused on the valley floor, waiting for them to appear. His first shot kicked up dirt five feet short, his second hit the flat but too far in front.

There wasn't a third. Horse and rider had reversed direction. Toward the Picket Stake.

Blakenship was sitting up next to the tent fiddling with the radio. Jake dipped a dishrag in the water bucket and knelt to dab at the blood streaking the sheriff's forehead.

"That's nothing. Sonofabitch got me in the leg. Feels like the bone's broke." Jake touched near the dark hole midway up from Blakenship's left knee. "Goddamn. That hurts."

"Not bleeding too bad. May have got the bone but not the big artery."

"The ... shit. Can't remember the name."

"Me neither. You reach anybody on that thing?" He pointed at the radio.

"Rudy. He's called in the rescue guys. Helicopter." He looked at his watch. "Should be here pretty quick. Thanks," he added to Jake's lifting a water bottle to his lips. "So Colonel Burns is Kiernan's uncle. Could explain a lot. Hooper and

420

Dobbins, they were killed near the Sheffield Place. Buchanan by a sniper. Maybe the poor cocksucker was getting close." He took another swallow from the bottle. "Ain't impossible they did the Sanchez brothers, too. Going have Charlie do a thorough search of everything connected with them. Especially that damn Dodge dually."

"Why?"

"Drugs."

Jake thought for a minute. "Maybe you can explain it to me sometime." He rose. "You be all right till the copter gets here?'

"I reckon. You going someplace?"

"The Colonel and the other one are dead. But Kiernan's not."

"Rudy's boys'll be here soon."

"Be dark before long. And he's headed toward the Picket Stake. No telling where he might end up."

Blakenship watched Jake fill water bottles from a five-gallon can, lower the food bag and make some selections and store both in his saddlebags. The radio sputtered. It was the helicopter. "Yeah, pretty much east. There's a fairly level stretch … Uh huh. No trees to the north." Jake was reloading both pistol and rifle. "Keep him alive, if you can. I got more than a few questions I want to ask that smooth sonofabitch."

Jake swung up on the gelding and neck-reined around to face the sheriff. "You be all right?"

"Yeah. They should be here any minute."

"What about the law?"

"I expect they'll be a while."

"Tell them I'll bring Kiernan back here — whatever shape he's in."

"You better not be getting to like that." Jessie scowled at the button to the morphine drip Blakenship could press whenever he wanted.

"Rather have CC and a beer back."

A week after the shootout, and the pain in Blakenship's leg still came without warning in head-splitting bursts. Nerve damage, Dr. Ben said. It may get better. It may not. Hard to tell.

A knock on the half-open door followed by Henderson's creased face. "Ain't interrupting anything, am I?"

"Not yet. I was going to try a strip tease, take his mind off that damn morphine, but ..." Jessie checked her watch. "Almost noon. I got to go. Filling in for Cynthia .."

Henderson watched her depart. "She's better'n you deserve, C.W."

"If deserves what it takes, most of us would never get nothing." He closed one eye and fixed the senior deputy with the dilated pupil of the other. "Well?"

"The rest of the California bunch're trying to make bail. Got them all on weapons charges. Man, you should've seen Johnny Davis. Came over like he was going to make a grandstand play about us harassing innocent folks. Then we found the stash of weapons and ammo in the hidey-hole in the barn. He couldn't get out of there fast enough."

"What about drugs?"

"Hard to tell how many's involved. They ain't none of them the brightest lights on the porch. Drugs we found was up at the new house."

"So it's just Burns and Petersen for sure?"

"Not to forget Kiernan. At this end, anyway. DEA's trying to run down West Coast connections." Henderson started to light a cigarette, remembered the oxygen, and returned it to the pack. "They're guessing it goes back to Southeast Asia. Vietnam and all."

"Could have been a slick operation. Kiernan either getting rid of competitors or fingering them for his uncle."

422

"Raid on Jake's wasn't too slick."

"I don't know. Buchanan took the heat for that — got Kiernan in the top slot."

Henderson caught himself reaching for a cigarette again. "I got to smoke or go blind. Besides, I'm supposed to meet some DEA folks in half an hour."

"Anybody we know?"

"Nope."

"Any better than the last ones?"

Henderson shrugged. "What can I tell you? They're DEA."

Blakenship opened his right eye and watched the blurry shape move through the door, then closed both and tried to fit all the pieces together. But an electric jolt from his leg had him groping for the morphine button. He gritted his teeth until the pain dissolved into warmth and his muscles relaxed into the swaddling glow.

"Sheriff Blakenship. C. W." The voice was polite yet commanding. Blakenship forced his eyes open to the peering face of Blair Stewart. "Sorry to wake you, but I'm on a tight schedule."

"S'OK." He fought to bring into focus the face he knew was close above him by the nearness of the voice and the faint scent of bay rum.

"Congratulations."

"Say what?"

"I'd say breaking up not one but two drug rings and solving, what is it, ten murders, is worthy of congratulations."

"Don't know how many murders we solved."

"But they were related, so it's reasonable to suppose they were done by the same people."

"We'll see."

"Still, it won't hurt come election time. Drug rings, murders and unmasking a renegade federal agent. That should play well out here."

"More like he unmasked himself."

"Speaking of Kiernan, I believe that may provide the leverage Jake needs to gain compensation. I need to talk to him but he doesn't return my calls."

"No surprise there. Last I heard, he was planning to go off in the Picket Stake."

"The Picket Stake? What's he doing there?"

"Fishing."

***

Jake put the German brown on the stringer and debated whether to go for another. No. Five should get him through supper and breakfast. Besides, the mosquitoes were coming up and it was time to build up the fire.

He looked with satisfaction at the camp where he'd stayed for almost a week. Sleeping bag on a pad of balsam with a lean-to of bigger branches angled over it. Fire pit. Horses staked in the meadow between tree line and lake edge.

He added wood over the smoldering remnants against the back wall of the pit, poured the last of the coffee from the soot-streaked pot and sat back, telling himself there was no point in cleaning the fish until the fire had laid down a thick bed of new coals.

He gazed out at the shadows lengthening across Slide Lake and tried, without success, to keep from remembering the events of a week ago.

It had been dark for three hours by the time he found Kiernan. About a hundred yards off the trail and not too far from the gate to the Picket Stake. Would have ridden right by if Kiernan's mare hadn't nickered when she smelled Jake's gelding.

Kiernan had propped head and shoulder blades against a tree, the rest of him stretched horizontal. He'd been thrown, it looked like, although whether from pain, loss of blood, the horse starting, a branch, or poor horsemanship Jake couldn't tell.

Why off the trail? Disorientation in the dark? An attempt to hide?

424

Jake cocked the Vaquero he'd unholstered when the mare had announced her presence, and moved in warily.

The agent's eyes were closed and his breath came in ragged whistles. Jake felt the forehead with his left hand — moist and cool, almost cold. Shock, he guessed. No response to the water bottle pressed to his lips.

No point to going back until morning light. Jake unsaddled the horses, covered Kiernan with the yellow slicker tied behind his saddle's cantle and one of the saddle blankets, and wrapped himself in the other blanket.

Kiernan stopped breathing some time during the night.

It was mid-morning by the time Jake made it back to his land, leading the mare carrying the slicker wrapped body.

Nobody was there. But a radio was. On the wall of the fire pit, on top of a sheet of tablet paper with a handwritten scrawl of operating instructions and the information that Mikeska would wait at the Inn until after lunch.

He'd delivered the body to the Otero County sheriff, who wasn't sure how to act toward Jake, especially when Jake immediately loaded his horses in the trailer and got behind the wheel of his pickup.

"Look, you can't just drive off," Mikeska sputtered as the pickup's engine roared to life.

"Watch me."

He'd unloaded the horses at the dairy, showered and made a quick call to Union — His wife had had a tiring day and was asleep. No. No. Nothing wrong. — before falling into bed.

Bridget was in Mary Margaret's room when he got there. "With Dr. Allsup," she explained. "I expect her back any minute." She looked at Jake with what he'd come to think of as her psychologist's eye. "If you feel the need to talk. Killing two …" Her voice trailed off as she fumbled in her handbag.

If she only knew.

She found a business card and offered it to Jake.

"I know your number."

"Of course." She dropped it into her purse. "But if.. anytime."

425

"Peace and quiet's what I need. I was thinking about a week in the mountains … if you think that'll be all right with Mary Margaret."

"Why don't you ask her?" She nodded toward the door. Looking far more like the Mary Margaret of old than the passive lump of recent months, she walked toward him with something like her former grace, face turned up for her kiss.

Jake lifted the coffee pot for another cup. Empty. He sorted through the provisions bag. Only enough left for one more pot. Two if he scrimped. Hell, it was time he went back. He could always return. Maybe with Mary Margaret. She liked the mountains — at least she did on their honeymoon.

He'd milked a regular shift in those days so they didn't have long. A couple of the crew had volunteered to double up as a wedding present — giving them five days and four nights at a cabin on Rainbow Lake that belonged to one of his father's friends.

They'd made love at every conceivable time of day and on every possible part of the property. The memory called to mind the folk wisdom: Put a bean in a jar every time you make love during the first year of marriage. Then, take one out every time. You'll never empty the jar.

Could that be true? When he found himself seriously trying to make the calculation, he laughed out loud. No denying they'd been like minxes those first months. He looked across the lake, water glinting red by the far shore from the last of the day's sun.

Maybe?

***

"He needs a break and I don't blame him. Get in a firefight, kill two people and haul in a dead body — that's a hell of a capper to a tough year … He'll be back. …How far can he go, for Christ sake?" Goddamn Mikeska, Blakenship mouthed to Jessie. "How? He was smooth. Delayed to let them catch up and

I never noticed." The unintelligible voice on the other end of the line got louder. "We'll get to it. DEA's checking … They ain't my favorite people either. … Sanchezes? Andrews? Sure. … But some things we never learn. You been in this business long enough to know that."

Blakenship hung up the phone with an effort. "Wonder why Rudy's so antsy."

"Well it all did happen in his county and he was a bit player …" Blakenship was asleep. She smiled, and resumed her seat by the window.

"Goddamn." Blakenship was reaching for the morphine button.

"Slow down on that stuff, honey." Jessie came to the bed, her dark hair blotting out the light when she bent to kiss him.

"Been thinking." He smiled crookedly. "Why don't you move in with me? Even make it legal if you want. That is if you don't mind living with a man with a hitch in his git-along and may be unemployed."

"That better not be the drugs talking. And what do you mean unemployed?"

"Might not run again. Ain't made up my mind, but …"
"What'll you do?"

"Don't know." He grinned. "But shit. You got a steady job."

Jessie smiled back. "Well, my daddy always said it's a piss-poor woman who can't support at least one drunk of a husband."

Excerpt from

The Bank Job: One Thing Leads To Another

The second Western Slope Mystery

"Are you sure he's dead?"

"I'm sure. " The driver looked at the woman's profile outlined against the dense evergreens that were fast disappearing in the fading January light. Damn if she don't look like his brother's ex. Full-blooded Cherokee, she was. Hadn't that marriage turned the family upside down.

But this one wasn't an Indian. Wasn't sure what she was, come to that. "Took a .44 Magnum in the gut and another in the chest. He's dead all right."

The terrain steepened as they neared the Continental Divide, steepened and the curves became more pronounced. Besides the slope increase, the snow and ice that had been occasional patches were now the predominant road surface. He put both hands on the wheel. "Twenty-five thousand, right?"

The woman glanced at him with a quick flick of her head then returned to staring through the windshield. "That's what I asked for. I didn't have the time to count it bill by bill."

"And another twenty-five ... Goddammit." They'd cleared the summit of the pass almost without warning. The western side was far steeper than the grade rising out of the broad valley they'd left. Steeper and with more curves. No more talk. He fought to keep the big pickup between the snow banks. A quick look in the mirror. No lights. Now, just get through that wide spot in the road ... Tin Cup according to the map and...

"Motherfucker."

Lights below. Flashing lights. Bastards in Bierce must have put out an APB and the hick cops ahead had set up a roadblock,

"Hang on." A glance at the woman. Seemed calm. Eerily calm. "Get low. And get your piece out." A flick on the switches rolled both windows down. Right hand picked up the revolver from the console between the bucket seats and settled it in his lap.

He craned to assess the layout below when the highway's switchbacks permitted a clear view and looked for escape routes when the road led them back into the timber. Weren't any. Not to someone who didn't know the country.

Fuck all. Have to run it.

How ready were the cops? If he could see their lights, could they see his?

Probably. But so what?

He slowed as he neared the last curve before the descent to the flashing lights. Looked like they had a front-end loader in the middle of the road, and Broncos or Cherokees -- he couldn't tell from this distance – on either side.

He slowed like any law-abiding citizen.

"Darling," he knew how she hated him to call her that. "When we get within a hundred feet of those bastards, I'm going to put the hammer down. Go around that loader on the left where there's more room. When I floor it, you start firing at everything you can see on the right and I'll take this side. One-ton with a deer guard on the front --we'll bust through and be gone before they know what hit them."

He slowed even more as the silhouette of a figure rose from behind the hood of the vehicle on the left and raised a bullhorn.

Before the lawman could speak, the driver yelled "Now." The pickup jumped forward with a screech of tires, the heavy boom of the Magnum coming at almost the same time followed hard on by the lighter pops of the woman's automatic.

A time lag, of what? Two seconds? Five? Then volleys from both sides of the road.

The pickup hit the front of the Bronco on the left at an angle, sending it back onto the shoulder while the driver yelled in triumph as he emptied the double-action pistol. The force of the collision bounced the truck into the front-end loader, but he straightened and accelerated.

"Told you." He grinned at the woman, who had dropped to the floor in front of the bucket seat. "Oh, shit." This to a lurch and subsequent fishtailing. "Cocksuckers hit a tire." Anti-freeze and steam blurred the windshield. "Fuck. And the radiator."

At the roadblock, two deputies were braced against the front-end loader, squeezing round after round from their hand guns at the disappearing truck that was trailing a comet's tail of sparks from the rim where it's left rear tire should have been. Two other lawmen were frantically trying to turn their vehicle around when a scream from the other side of the road stopped them.

"Benny's hit. Call for an ambulance, goddammit. Sheriff's hit bad."

A short pause. "Oh fuck. Oh goddamn fuck. Larry's hit, too"